D0387682

FIRE SEASON

Also by Jon Loomis

Mating Season
High Season
Vanitas Motel
The Pleasure Principal

FIRE SEASON

Jon Loomis

Minotaur Books ✹ New York

FIRE SEASON. Copyright © 2012 by Jon Loomis. All rights reserved. Printed in the United States of America. For information address St. Martin's Press, 175 Fifth Avenue, New York, N.Y. 10010.

www.minotaurbooks.com

Library of Congress Cataloging-in-Publication Data

Loomis, Jon.
    Fire season / Jon Loomis.—1st ed.
        p. cm.
    ISBN 978-0-312-66813-6 (hardcover)
    ISBN 978-1-250-01486-3 (e-book)
    1. Police—Massachusetts—Provincetown—Fiction.   2. Arson investigation—Fiction.   3. Provincetown (Mass.)—Fiction.   I. Title.
    PS3562.O593F54 2012
    813'.54—dc23

                                                    2012010696

First Edition July 2012

10   9   8   7   6   5   4   3   2   1

For Allyson,
who will always tell you when a scene needs a monkey

RIP Miss Ellie

FIRE SEASON

Chapter 1

July 5

Gray dawn, damp and still, unseasonably cold. The police detective moved slowly, fog roiling around him. He took a photograph of one of the dead seals. Its back was dark gray, its belly mottled, lighter. Two more lay near it, their blood smeared across the broad concrete patio. Twenty feet away but barely visible, the harbor lipped at the long, lion-colored sweep of the town beach—the dark water keeping its secrets. On Long Point, an automated foghorn hooted at twelve-second intervals.

The camera flashed, then flashed again. Dozens of gulls wheeled and shrieked overhead, while others landed and tore at the seals with hooked yellow beaks. The seals had only been dead a few hours, but already the gulls had pecked out their eyes and were hungrily peeling away their spaniel faces. A litter of spent shotgun shells lay among the savaged bodies, red plastic casings glowing weirdly in the muted light. The policeman stopped taking pictures, picked up one of the casings, sniffed it, rolled it in his hand. It was a standard Winchester 12-gauge; you could buy them at any gun shop on the planet. He put the casing in his pocket.

The police detective was named Frank Coffin. He was forty-seven, dressed in khakis, black cotton sweater, leather jacket. Just under 6' 2", Coffin slouched a bit, as if apologizing for his height. He wore a mustache, once black but now closer to steel gray, not as neatly trimmed as it might have been. His partner, a young uniformed police sergeant named Lola Winters, stood a few feet away, hands on her hips.

"This pisses me off," she said, frowning.

"It's not good," Coffin said. "I like seals."

Lola scowled. "What is fucking *wrong* with people?" She stopped, gathered herself, then went on in a low, controlled voice. "Who would do this, Frank? What kind of nutcase would just walk in and shoot them?"

Coffin shook his head. "I don't know. I really don't."

Lola wiped a hand over her face. "Sorry," she said. "I just don't get cruelty to animals. It doesn't compute, you know?"

"I know," Coffin said. "You're right. It's fucked-up."

A green and yellow banner flapped glumly above their heads, a line of text between two grinning cartoon seals. YAYA'S: HOME OF THE HAPPY SEALS, it read.

Yaya's was one of the three-dozen or so tourist restaurants crammed into Provincetown's two-mile stretch of waterfront. The owner, a big Greek named Stecopoulos, gazed down into the seals' blue pool. A couple of them floated there, hectored by gulls, dark eyeholes staring, ragged streamers of blood drifting around their bodies. The other three were scattered among the plastic café tables and chairs where, during the summer season, Yaya's customers ate ten-dollar gyros or falafels. If those customers were lucky enough to arrive at feeding time, they could have watched as one of Stecopoulos's summer workers dropped live mackerel down the gullets of the sleek, sharp-toothed seals.

One of those employees was sitting at a table, staring blankly out at the harbor. His name, Stecopoulos had said, was Maurice. He was below average height, maybe 5' 8", thick through the arms and shoulders.

"What's your last name, Maurice?" Coffin said.

"It's Duval," Stecopoulos said. "It's French Canadian. He lives in Orleans, drives in every day."

Maurice nodded. "Yep," he said.

Coffin poked at one of the seals with the toe of his boot. "Any idea who might have done this, Maurice?"

Maurice shook his head slowly. His hair was dark, close-cropped. "Nope."

"You don't talk much, do you, Maurice?"

Maurice scratched at something on his arm. He wore jeans and a white T-shirt, no jacket. He did not appear to be cold. "I guess not," he said.

Stecopoulos's eyes were red. Coffin wondered if he'd been crying. Or drinking. "Maurice found them. He comes in early to feed them, scoop the seal crap out of their pool—you know. He's my seal guy."

Was, Coffin thought. "How long have you been taking care of the seals, Maurice?"

"Couple years."

"You work here year-round?"

"Off-season he just takes care of the seals," Stecopoulos said. Even though it was early in the morning, he chewed the charred, wet stub of a green cigar. "They stay right out here on the patio all winter—no problem. Summer he puts in extra hours doing this and that—handyman stuff, odd jobs."

Coffin nodded. "Got it," he said.

Maurice coughed, cleared his throat. He looked a bit like a seal himself, Coffin thought. His head was round, his hair dark and sleek. "Look, I know what you're thinking," Maurice said.

"Okay," Coffin said. "What am I thinking?"

"You're thinking I had something to do with this, 'cause I found them. That's how it works, right? The person who reports the body is the murderer, like, most of the time?"

"A lot of the time, yeah."

"But I didn't do it. I thought about setting them free sometimes, but I'd never kill them."

"Maurice is a good kid," Stecopoulos said. "I vouch for him a hundred percent. His mother used to work for me back in the day, waiting tables. We're old friends, his mom and me. I've known Maurice all his life—right, kid?"

Maurice nodded. "Yep."

"And he's not bullshitting you—he loved those seals. He told me more than once he'd come and take care of them for nothing if I couldn't afford to pay him anymore."

"Okay." Coffin nodded. "Great. You're no longer the prime suspect, Maurice."

"Cool," Maurice said.

Stecopoulos coughed, cleared his throat, spat through the fence toward the beach. "Tell me something, Officer . . ."

"Detective Coffin."

"Coffin? Really? Hell of a name for a cop."

"You should meet my cousin Tom," Coffin said.

Stecopoulos stared at him for a moment. "Why, what is he—an undertaker?"

"Bingo. In Sandwich."

Stecopoulos nodded, chewed his cigar. "Those guys fucking print money. Doesn't matter if the economy's good or bad—people still croak."

"He does all right," Coffin said, taking another picture.

Stecopoulos said nothing for a long minute. He looked at the dead seals, then out toward the fog-shrouded harbor. "I'm stuck the same place as the lady officer here," he said finally, nodding toward Lola. "What kind of sick fuck would do this? What kind of sick fuck would shoot poor, harmless seals?"

Coffin imagined the seals trying to escape, heaving frantically, slowly across the cracked concrete slab surrounding the pool, away from whomever was shooting at them. He had quit smoking again, hadn't so much as touched a cigarette in more than a month, but the sight of the dead seals made him desperate to light up. "You said the neighbors complained about them?"

"Neighbors!" Stecopoulos snorted, dismissing the looming bulk of the Crown and Anchor Hotel with a wave of his cigar butt. "Yeah, they bitched me out about the barking. Seals bark, you know. Kind of like dogs. They stay up all night—"

"The seals?"

"No, no—the fucking drag queens. They stay up all night doing whatever the hell they do, then they sleep all day. The seals wake up a little before dawn. Except when they see other seals out in the harbor, that's when they do most of their barking." Stecopoulos's eyes misted over. "Like they're happy to be alive."

Coffin walked slowly around the concrete patio. "So the drag queens complained. They do anything else?"

"They threatened to sue me," Stecopoulos said. "They called the health department, the humane society, the fish and game commission, the Coast Guard, God knows what else. They called the police a few times. You guys must have a file."

Coffin nodded. He doubted there was any such file.

"There's no law against owning harbor seals, you know," Stecopoulos said, as if he'd been accused of something. "As long as you get a permit from fish and game, which I've had since the sixties. They're not endangered or anything, and these were zoo stock, not taken from the wild. There's no law against seals barking, either, except maybe disturbing the peace. But you know what goes on over there." He waved his cigar butt again, this time a gesture of tired dismissal. "They didn't have a leg to stand on and they knew it. They were pretty pissed."

Coffin thought for a while, still yearning for a cigarette. "Do you think they did it?" he asked finally. "The drag queens?"

Stecopoulos stared at him again. "You tell me," he said, after a moment. "A guy who spends his nights lip-synching 'Don't Cry for Me Argentina' in spike heels and a feather boa? He's gonna climb my fence with a shotgun and do this? You're the cop. You tell me."

An hour later, Coffin and Lola were sitting in the Crown and Anchor's backstage dressing room, surrounded by chattering drag queens. Mostly the drag queens wore shabby bathrobes or sweatpants; a couple clutched lacy dressing gowns over their skinny chests. All of them smoked; some had cups of coffee. They sprawled on ratty couches, slouched in worn-out chairs. None had their wigs on, though a few still wore makeup from the night before, lipstick hastily reapplied, beard stubble poking through thick foundation. It was like sitting in a room full of plucked chickens, Coffin thought.

"It would really help if we could just focus for a few more minutes," Coffin said. The room quieted, slightly.

One drag queen, a slender blond, raised his hand. "Question," he said.

Coffin shifted in his chair. It was straight-backed, wooden, and squeaked whenever he moved. "Ask away," he said.

The blond took a long, slow drag from his cigarette, held between the tips of his slender middle and index fingers. He let the smoke out slowly.

Coffin waited.

"So are we *sus*pects?" the drag queen said at last. "Are we, like, not supposed to leave *town*?"

"No, you're not suspects," Coffin said. "Yes, you can leave town. Now, if we could just make sure we understand a couple of things, we'll let you-all get back to bed."

The drag queens nodded in languid agreement.

"Fine," Coffin said. "Just so we know we have it straight—none of you saw or heard anything unusual last night. Specifically gunshots, suspicious persons, unusual vehicle traffic—nothing like that?"

The drag queens shook their heads.

The blond raised his hand again. "I'll bet it happened during the fireworks," he said. "All that banging and flashing, you could set off a bomb in the middle of Commercial Street and no one would notice."

"I thought the display was kind of weak this year," a brunet said. "Must be the budget cuts. They just didn't have much oomph."

Coffin cleared his throat. "All of you were in the show as usual—nobody left early or called in sick, correct?"

The drag queens nodded.

"Now this one's important," Coffin said. "We've Xeroxed your IDs in the office, we have all of your information. Does anyone in this room own or have in their possession a twelve-gauge shotgun?"

A few of the drag queens tittered. The rest shook their heads.

"Okay, last question: Is there a twelve-gauge shotgun on the property here, that you know of?"

"No shotgun," the blond drag queen said. "Not that I've ever seen. But Rocky keeps a loaded pistol behind the bar, and Kirby carries a pistol when he makes the night deposit. A big one."

"Oh my God," one of the other drag queens said, holding his hands about a foot apart. "It's *huge*."

Coffin shrugged. "Okay. That's it for me. Lola?"

"One thing," Lola said. "Very quick."

The drag queens sighed.

"How did you-all feel about the seals?" Lola said. "They were noisy, right?"

The drag queens nodded. "Noisy," said the blond drag queen. "A pain in the ass. Even with the windows closed they'd wake you up at freaking five thirty in the morning."

"You sleep here?" Lola said.

The drag queens nodded. "Sometimes, after a show," the blond said. "After the after-party."

"And the after-after-party," the brunet said.

"We might be too tipsy to drive home," the blond said. "So we just crash here. There are a couple of guest rooms reserved for the performers."

Coffin smoothed his mustache. "So the seals were a pain in the ass?"

"But they were also really *cute*," a redheaded drag queen said. A murmur of assent went up around the room.

"*So* cute," another drag queen said. "Those soulful eyes. Like Dorothy."

"*Just* like Dorothy," another of the drag queens said, nodding fervently. "In the scene where she sings 'Over the Rainbow.'"

"So did they ever make any of you mad enough you'd want to shoot them?"

"Oh my God, no," the blond said. He made a sweeping gesture, tilting his head a bit to one side. "I mean, look at us—none of us would hurt a fly."

Coffin looked at Lola, who shrugged. "Okay," said Coffin. "We're done. You have our cards—if you think of anything you forgot to tell us, anything that might be important, give us a call."

Chapter 2

October 21, 6:36 P.M.

Coffin was slightly out of breath. He had just trotted up Town Hall's wide interior stairs to the police chief's office on the second floor, stepped over drop cloths, and pushed his way past a large plasterer's scaffold on the second floor. After decades of genteel decline, Town Hall was being restored to something like its original appearance. Built in 1886, it was a grand old hulk of a building—but the roof leaked in dozens of places, bats flew down its hallways, rats gnawed its wiring, chunks of plaster fell from its ceilings, and its plumbing backed up without warning, flooding entire floors. Finally, it had been declared structurally unsafe by a consulting engineer in 2008. Somehow the town had come up with six million dollars to perform the necessary renovation, returning Town Hall to its considerably more elegant original condition, down to the period correct Victorian paint colors. To everyone's relief, the historical purists on the board of selectmen had granted a few grudging concessions to the twenty-first century: broadband Internet would be installed, along with high-efficiency air-conditioning and unisex bathrooms.

The building had been seething with contractors since June: roofers, plasterers, painters, HVAC guys, electricians, plumbers, floor men, carpenters, IT specialists, you name it—they were in and out of offices and hallways, up and down the stairs, inside and out, drilling, sawing, sanding, grinding, and banging, all at tremendous expense to the town. No work of any note would be done to Coffin's permanent office space in the basement, though—the town couldn't afford it. The workmen would come and go, and the fat sewer pipe that spanned the office ceiling would still drip ominously onto Coffin's desk.

Coffin sat down in the leather desk chair and inhaled deeply once or twice through his nose, then made a sour face. Chief Preston Boyle had resigned back in May amid considerable uproar—all that remained of him was the slight, rank smell of his farts, which Coffin believed were still embedded in the desk chair's leather-covered seat. Now Coffin was acting as interim chief until a replacement could be hired—just as he had when his uncle Rudy had finally been forced to resign as chief of the Provincetown police department three years before. At the request of the new town manager, Coffin had moved the contents of his filing cabinets and desk upstairs, though most of it was still stacked on the floor in banker's boxes. There was no point in unpacking the nonessentials, Coffin thought—the résumés were piling up on the town manager's desk, and the interview process would start in a matter of weeks. He'd be back in the basement by February at the latest.

Still, for now the upstairs space was a big improvement over Coffin's windowless office in the basement, with its Di-Gel green cinder block and rumbling, dripping sewer pipe. Boyle's office had blue-gray institutional carpeting, a broad mahogany desk, and in daylight a nice view of the harbor.

Coffin stood, looked out the window. In mid-October the days were mostly bright and warm, the evenings often chilly and damp. Commercial Street was busy, for the off-season. It was the week of Provincetown's annual transgendered/cross-dresser's festival and small clusters of men, mostly in their fifties and sixties, strode up and down the sidewalks of Commercial Street dressed in various stages of drag—everything from evening gowns, feather boas, and tiaras to ratty wigs worn with jeans and tennis shoes. They shopped, had dinner and drinks in Provincetown's upscale restaurants, went on whale watches and moonlight sailboat cruises, sometimes with their wives and even their children in tow—but they also attended workshops on gender reassignment, how-to sessions on wig buying and makeup, group counseling for self-esteem, and mentored discussions of transgendered spirituality. There was an awards banquet, a talent show, a formal ball, and, at the end of the week, a culminating fashion show, to be followed this year by a special drag show featuring performers from New York and San Francisco. The event's official title was Fantasia Fair, but the locals called it Tall Ships Week, and the men in their drag finery were known as Tall Ships. It was mostly an affectionate term, Coffin thought: a not exactly reverent description of those tall men in their wigs and makeup, muumuus flapping in the harbor breeze.

Coffin heard a siren—a fire engine, he knew, heading east from the station on Shank Painter Road. A few seconds later the intercom buzzed, and Coffin punched the button. "Yeah, Jeff," he said.

"Dumpster fire, Frank. Behind Rossi's Package Store. I guess it's goin' pretty good—lots of cardboard." It was Jeff Skillings, that day's desk officer: his Cape Cod accent was even thicker than Coffin's—"cardboard" came out something like "cahdbowed."

"Another one?" Coffin said. "That's two in two weeks. Not good."

"Probably kids," Skillings said. "Like the one at the high school."

"Probably. Anybody called Pete Wells?" Pete Wells was an investigator with the state fire marshal's office in Stow, assigned to the Cape and Islands.

"Think we need him?"

Coffin thought for a second. "Let's hold off," he said. "You're right. It's probably just kids." He punched the glowing intercom button again, breaking the connection. Then he stood up and put his coat on.

Chapter 3

Rossi's Package Store was the first structure you came to if you entered Provincetown by Conwell Street off Route 6. It was a small, full-range liquor mart, selling everything from thirty-six-packs of Old Milwaukee Light to high-end single malt scotch, premium cognacs, and $250 magnums of Dom Pérignon. It was perfectly normal to see down-and-out fishermen standing next to Porsche-driving real estate lawyers at Rossi's checkout counter; the former with maybe a case of Pabst Blue Ribbon, the latter with a fifth or two of Grey Goose, both on their way to very different kinds of parties, both with very distinct notions of what constituted a good time.

By the time Coffin pulled into Rossi's crushed oyster-shell parking lot, the Dumpster fire was already out. A loose half-circle of volunteer fire and rescue guys stood smoking and telling jokes near the front end of the idling pumper, a shiny new-to-them four-door Ferrara that had been bought used with money the volunteer firefighters had raised at raffles, bingo games, and pancake breakfasts. Wisps of foul-smelling smoke still rose from the Dumpster.

Coffin shook hands with the fire chief, a short, barrel-chested man in his fifties named Walt Macy. "What've we got here, Walt?" Coffin said.

Macy took off his PFD ball cap, scratched his bald head and put the cap back on. "Nasty little fire," he said, crossing his arms over his big chest. "Must have used some kind of propellant—probably gasoline or lighter fluid. Pretty much the whole contents of the Dumpster were involved by the time we got here. Flames maybe ten feet high. Once we put the hose on her, she went out just fine, but it was pretty impressive when we first drove up."

Coffin wrinkled his nose. "What's that smell? Plastic?"

"Yep, plastic juice jugs, the clerk says. Nasty shit in those things—that what d'ya call it—PBA or BPA or whatever."

"So why so much cardboard and plastic in the Dumpster—don't these guys recycle?"

"Clerk says they do, big-time. Evidently whoever set the fire pulled a lot of cardboard and other stuff that was waiting to go to the recycling center out of the bins there—" Macy pointed a thick index finger at a row of waist-high, chicken wire, and two-by-four bins with hinged lids that ranged along the side of the building. "Then they threw it in the Dumpster, poured in their gas or whatever, tossed in a match and up it went."

"Nice of them to put it all in the Dumpster, and not just torch the bins," Coffin said.

Macy nodded, pursing his lips. "Hadn't thought of that. Yeah, I guess it was kind of nice of them. Relatively speaking."

"Who called it in?" Coffin said.

"First call was the clerk. Then a few others from drivers passing by." Macy tugged at the suspenders of his big, rubberized firemen's pants. Bunkers, they called them. "Pretty bold, tossing all that stuff in the Dumpster, pouring in the gas and torching it before it's even fully dark," he said. "Could've been spotted pretty easy from the street."

"Maybe he was," Coffin said. "We'll get in touch with the folks who called it in, see if they saw anyone."

Macy nodded. "They're on caller ID. I'll phone the numbers over to your office."

"What's the clerk's name?" Coffin said.

Macy pulled a notebook out of his pocket, flipped it open. "Szabo," he said. "With a S-Z. From Hungary, he says."

Coffin shook Macy's hand. "Good to see you, Walt. Wife and kids all right?"

"Doin' fine. How's your ma?"

"God," Coffin said. "Don't ask."

There were no customers in the store, but the chemical smell of roasted plastic was strong. The clerk, Szabo, stood by the window, looking out at the parking lot. He was tall and slender, with pale eyes and dark hair. His fingers were long, his nose hawkish.

"Pretty exciting out there, for a while," Coffin said, pulling his shield out of his jacket pocket, flipping it open.

"Yeah," Szabo said. "Exciting. I guess you could say that. Scared the living shit out of me." Coffin had a hard time telling one Eastern European accent from another. They all sounded like Boris and Natasha from the old *Rocky and Bullwinkle* cartoons to him.

"Big fire?" Coffin said.

"Fucking huge." Szabo shook his head. "Flames five, six meters high. Burning cardboard flying around. I thought the shop was going to go up. Lucky those firemen come so fast."

Coffin looked out the window, too. The fire and rescue boys were climbing back into their shiny new truck. It had hot rod flames painted on the sides. "So, what happened—you looked out the window and there's the fire?"

Szabo frowned, shook his long head again. "Was customer," he said. "Guy comes in, gets a couple forties out of the cooler. I'm reading my book." He held up a weathered paperback: *Flying Saucers* by Carl Jung. "Guy's walking up to the register, past window. He says, 'Holy shit, fucking Dumpster's on fire,' so then I look."

"So you called it in right away?"

"Right away. Picked up the phone and called 911."

"What happened to the guy—the customer?"

"He pays up and pffft—takes off. Doesn't even wait for change. His car was in the lot, so maybe he worries."

"What kind of car?"

Szabo thought for a second, looking away. Then his pale blue eyes focused on Coffin's face. "I don't know," he said. "Didn't see. Guess I was watching fire."

"What did he look like, this customer?"

"American. White guy."

"Tall? Short? Heavy?"

"I don't know—medium."

"How old?"

"Late twenties."

"Did you card him?"

Szabo shook his head. "He looks over twenty-one."

"Dressed how?"

"Jeans, hoodie, ball cap. You know—like everybody."

"What color hoodie?"

"Gray."

"What about the ball cap? Did it have a logo or anything?"

Szabo thought for a few seconds, then shook his head. "I didn't notice. It was dark. Black or navy blue."

"Facial hair, tattoos you could see?"

"I don't think so. No."

"Didn't wait for change, so he paid with cash."

"Right."

"You didn't see anybody outside, hanging around the Dumpster?"

Szabo held up the book again. "No."

"See or hear anything unusual—anything we should know about?"

Szabo frowned and shook his head again. "Sorry," he said. "Not much help, right?"

Coffin tapped the cover of Szabo's book. "I didn't know Jung wrote about UFOs," he said. "He was the archetypes guy, right?"

"Archetypes, collective unconscious, complexes—all Jung. He was one of the fathers of modern psychiatry."

"So why UFOs?"

"Jung wrote the book during the big UFO craze in 1950s," Szabo said. "Thousands of UFO sightings all over the world. Front page stories in newspapers, everything. People freaking the fuck out. Jung said there's two possibilities."

Coffin raised an eyebrow. "Weather balloons? Swamp gas?"

"First possibility is they're real—there's hundreds of flying saucers buzzing around and people are seeing exactly what they think they see. Second possibility is people *want* them to be real, and so anything they see in the sky that seems strange is alien spacecraft."

Coffin grinned. "So that second thing, then."

"Probably." Szabo shrugged. "But interesting question is why? Why, all of a sudden after the end of World War II, thousands of people want flying saucers to come to Earth from outer space?"

Coffin rubbed his chin. "Because God was dead. After World War II, with all the carnage, people couldn't believe in a merciful God. So they believed in little green men instead."

"That's what Jung thinks," Szabo said. "Me, I don't know. Ever seen the Herring Cove lights?"

The Herring Cove lights were an occasional local phenomenon. On clear nights, maybe two or three times a year, strange clusters of white lights seemed to float above Herring Cove beach, moving slowly, apparently at random. "Sure," Coffin said. "We get calls about them sometimes, so I finally drove out there to see for myself."

"And?"

"We tell people it's commercial air traffic, backed up from Logan. The lights are the planes' headlights."

"That's what you tell people. But what do you *think?*"

Coffin shrugged. "Didn't look like planes to me," he said. He paused. "But that's what I *wanted* it to be."

Chapter 4

Coffin parked the big, unmarked Crown Victoria in front of his house and climbed out. The Crown Vic was another perk of the acting police chief's job: in his usual role as Provincetown's only police detective he mostly drove his own car, a cantankerous 1984 Ford Fiesta. Coffin hated the Fiesta: its floorboards were rusting out, its steering wandered, its clutch slipped, its wipers didn't wipe, and its engine gagged and farted on even the slightest incline. He would have enjoyed shooting it, or setting it on fire, or driving it into the ocean—but between the taxes on the house, technically his mother's, and the cost of her nursing home care, it was the best car he could afford.

The house was a small, two-story Cape Cod–style, in Provincetown's old working-class neighborhood, down the hill from the inland side of Bradford Street, at the edge of the town cemetery. In Coffin's neighborhood the streets were narrow, the houses packed close together. His house had no water view; it looked out on the weathered cedar shingles of the houses next door, their tiny gardens and postage-stamp yards. If you leaned a bit as you looked out of his bedroom window, you could see Valley View Nursing Home, where his mother lived.

The waterfront homes along Commercial Street still sold in the millions, although they no longer sold as quickly as they had five or six years ago, and prices were down by half, maybe, from their peak during the height of the Bush-era real estate madness. Coffin knew he'd never be able to afford his own private water view unless he won the lottery: and if he did win the lottery, he thought, he'd be gone—quit his job, move someplace warm. Jamie, his girlfriend, had been talking about Tuscany, maybe going to cooking school. He shook his head. He didn't play the lottery—it was, as his uncle Rudy liked to say, a tax on stupid people—and Tuscany was a long way away from the damp fog of an October night in Provincetown.

Meanwhile, if he wanted to look at the water he could walk down to the town beach and stand at the high tide line, small waves sloshing, gulls giving him the stink eye. Meanwhile, it had started to rain.

Coffin stepped on to his screened porch, pushed open the front door. The house was full of light and music—Queen Latifah singing "I Put a Spell on You," slow and soulful. The savory smell of roasting chicken drifted from the kitchen. Jamie lay curled on her side on the uncomfortable Victorian sofa, shoes kicked off, eyes closed. She was five months pregnant and very pretty. She was also very pale.

"Uh-oh," Coffin said. "You okay?"

"Thought I was gonna barf," Jamie said.

"What did it this time?"

"Ginger. I was slicing ginger, and the smell made me feel like I was about to hurl. Or pass out. Or both. I love ginger—it's so unfair."

"Last time it was shrimp."

"No, last time it was rhubarb. Time before that was shrimp. All things I love. What's next—ice cream?"

"That would be weird." Coffin sat in one of his mother's strict straight-backed chairs. It still felt like his mother's house. The low ceilings and narrow doorways, the punitive antique furniture upholstered in wool and stuffed with horsehair, the unexpected taxidermy, including the big stuffed goat's head that leered down from above the mantel, yellow-eyed, dust in its long beard—it all seemed like a metaphor for her Alzheimer's, which was a disease of disorder and anachronism, of closed doors, blocked corridors. "Ice cream's in the cravings column," Coffin said. "It would be a first if something went from the cravings column to the aversions column. Unprecedented."

"Whatever," Jamie said. She sat up. The color had returned to her face. "It's my sense of smell. It's turned up to eleven suddenly. You smell like cop car, for instance—like pine air freshener with piquant undertones of vinyl and adrenaline sweat." She yawned. "Now I'm hungry again. Freaky."

Coffin went to the kitchen, poured a glass of water from the Brita pitcher on the counter, and brought it back for Jamie. "Great. Me, too."

"You're a nice man," she said, sipping the water. "I never see you anymore, but you're a nice man."

Coffin made a face. "Paperwork. Budgets. Requisitions. Payroll. Blah. Being police chief sucks."

"Except for the office," Jamie said. "And the car."

"And the paycheck. It's gone up since last time I was chief."

"That's my man," Jamie said, patting her belly. "Bringing home the bacon for little fatso here. Mmm, bacon."

Back in the kitchen, Coffin opened the liquor cabinet and took down the bottle of Famous Grouse. "Time for a predinner beverage," he said. He dropped a couple of ice cubes into a high-ball glass and poured a big double.

"Wow," Jamie said.

Coffin sipped. "I'm drinking for two," he said. "Actually not the most boring day ever, paperwork notwithstanding."

"No?"

"Dumpster fire over at Rossi's. Apparently it was exciting for a little while. The fire and rescue boys put it out before I got there, though."

"Another one? Was it a prank, like last week?"

"Skillings thinks so. Whoever did it was pretty bold. Or maybe just dumb. Could have easily been spotted from the road, or inside the store."

"Bold and dumb—sounds like kids."

Coffin shrugged. "Probably."

Jamie opened the oven to check on the roasting chicken. From the back she looked the same as ever—a view Coffin had always enjoyed—but from the side she was definitely showing. " 'Notwithstanding' isn't a word, you know," she said.

"How can it not be a word if we both just used it?"

Jamie poked the chicken with a long fork, then picked off a bit of white meat and ate it. "It just isn't. Look it up—it won't be there."

"If it's not a word, what is it?"

"A nonword." Jamie grinned at Coffin. "Don't argue with the pregnant lady."

"Should I kiss her instead?"

"Yes, but I'm warning you—I have zero apparent sex drive. My need for you in that department is evidently over. Sorry!"

Coffin kissed her anyway. She responded with brief enthusiasm, but it was true—the old zero-to-sixty acceleration wasn't there.

Jamie took a step back, picked another bit of breast meat and chewed it, eyes narrowed.

Coffin sipped his drink. "So what's for dinner besides chicken?"

"You want something besides chicken, you're on your own."

Coffin looked at the cutting board. Jamie had chopped a clove of garlic, and started to slice a small chunk of ginger. A bag of raw spinach sat on the counter, and a slick of olive oil was beginning to smoke in a wok on the stove. "Looks like you were doing something with spinach, garlic, and ginger."

"Sautéing. About to. Prenausea. Not so much anymore. I don't even want to look at that damn ginger right now—I have my suspicions about the spinach, too."

"Okay," Coffin said. "How about some rice? Should I make some rice?"

"Feel free, but I'm not interested. I will, however, wrestle you for a chicken thigh."

"Sounds good to me," Coffin said.

Jamie kissed him on the cheek. "Hope springs eternal," she said.

Later, Coffin lay asleep in the big four-poster his parents had slept in. Jamie lay beside him. The night was quiet—there was no sound except for a low wind outside, the slight patter of drizzle on the windowpanes.

"Fire," Jamie said.

Coffin opened one eye, then closed it and went back to sleep.

Jamie reached out with a slender arm and whacked him loosely in the chest. *"Fire,"* she said, eyes closed. "The house is on fire."

Coffin sat up and sniffed. "I don't think so." He got out of bed, walked to the top of the stairs. He smelled nothing. The smoke alarm in the hall ceiling displayed its little "ready" light. Coffin padded back into the bedroom. "There's no fire. You must have dreamed it," he said, but Jamie was sound asleep. Coffin climbed into bed, stretched out, and closed his eyes. He could feel his mother's stuffed owl staring at him from the top of the wardrobe, outrage in its glass eyes, ear tufts awry. Then, coming from the east, he heard the sound of sirens.

Chapter 5

The fire seemed larger than it was, but in Coffin's experience that was the way of fire. Leave the frying pan on the burner while you answer the phone, Coffin thought, come back to foot-high flames and feel the adrenaline rush that skydivers and mountain climbers risked their goofy necks for. Clap a lid down on the skillet and the fire's out, nothing to it—but still your heart's pounding and the hair on your arms is standing up like you've just been chased by a bear. And this was no skillet fire: the flames would have been visible from Truro, most likely, roaring twenty or thirty feet into the night sky, completely engulfing a garage-sized shed by the time Coffin got there. The shed was down a dirt track—just a path, really—on the east end, up the hill from Bradford Street, jumbled in among a clutter of summer cottages and artist's studios built back in the 1950s, where the western fork of Atkins Mayo Road petered out, maybe thirty yards from the nearest house. The fire crackled and popped like a small-caliber gun battle. Burning shingles and sheets of flaming tar paper rose in the column of flame and smoke, then wheeled off on the breeze, sailing toward town center like demonic kites. *Lucky it's raining*, Coffin thought, *or the whole town could go up*.

Walt Macy was there, and the fire and rescue boys with their shiny new truck. They were struggling with the big hose; the Italian pumper was acting up, revving and slowing, and every time the engine raced the hose bucked out of control—the fat stream of water firing over the shed and into the neighbor's garden, knocking over bird feeders and Adirondack chairs. The grass had been torn up by tires and boots, and the path was turning into a shallow river of cold, soupy mud. The rain fell, a morose drizzle.

Lola was there, too, and Coffin's cousin Tony—trying to keep a small knot of onlookers out of the way. Tony had surprised Coffin by staying on the force, despite all the money he'd made during the real estate boom, despite having inherited another small fortune— almost two million dollars—from his mother-in-law back in July.

"Not 'til my twenty years," he'd said, when Coffin had asked him whether he planned to retire. "I've earned the full pension—I want every cent that's coming to me. Besides, what would I do all day?"

"What do you do all day now?" Coffin had said.

Tony had laughed. "Always the kidder, Frankie," he'd said. "Just like your old man."

Coffin stood beside Lola, who was watching the fire with arms crossed, uniform hat planted squarely on her head. "This isn't good," she said. "Two in one day."

Coffin nodded. "I don't think it's a prank anymore. Kids or not."

"Whoever it is," Lola said, "they're getting more ambitious." She was 5' 10", 155 pounds or so of solid muscle, slim and fit beneath the bulky Kevlar vest she always wore under her uniform shirt. She could outlift, outrun, outfight and outshoot any man in the department, Coffin knew. She could also kill a man, if it came to that. Her blond ponytail was beaded with raindrops. Coffin made himself look at the fire.

"Got a camcorder in your squad?"

"Of course," Lola said. "It's on the checklist, isn't it? Charged and ready to go."

"I want film of any onlookers, just in case."

Lola walked back to the road to fetch her camcorder. The fire and rescue boys had sorted out their fancy Italian pumper, and were having better luck putting water on the fire. There was a long, loud hiss, and steam rose with the flames and smoke. What was left of the shed's roof collapsed in a shower of sparks.

A tall, thin man walked up to Coffin and shook his hand. "You're with the police, yes?" the man said.

"Yes," Coffin said. "Detective Coffin."

"My name's Hallowell—Mark Hallowell. I'm the owner."

Hallowell had a beak of a nose and small, quizzical eyes surrounded by wrinkled lids. He looked like a friendly ostrich. He was around seventy years old, Coffin guessed.

"Any idea how it caught fire?" Coffin said.

Hallowell pointed to a house just up the hill. "We live right there, me and my wife Khaki."

"Khaki?" Coffin said. "Like the pants?"

"Right," Hallowell said, pointing a long, curved finger at Coffin's chest. "Like the pants. Her family's from Connecticut—they gave all the kids funny names. Her brother's named Skipper, if you can believe that."

"About the fire," Coffin said.

"Right. When I saw the fire out the window I said, 'Khaki, call 911,' and I ran down here. First thing I noticed was it smelled like gas."

"Gasoline? That kind of gas?"

"Yep, real strong smell of gasoline. You know that smell—there's no mistaking it for anything else."

"Did you keep a gas can in the shed? A lawn mower, maybe, or a chain saw? Anything that might have gas inside it?"

Hallowell looked at Coffin with his bright little eyes. "Well, no," he said. "That's the funny part, isn't it? We keep all that stuff up at the house, in the garage. This is Khaki's studio. Was, I should say."

"Studio?" Coffin said. "What kind of studio?"

"Wood sculpture. Khaki makes erotic wood sculpture—driftwood, mostly. It's pretty hot stuff, I don't mind telling you."

"So what's inside there is mostly driftwood, tools, that kind of stuff?"

"Yup, that's about right. Tools, driftwood. She had a nice lathe and some power saws and that."

"So, Mr. Hallowell," Coffin said, scratching his neck. "Can you think of any reason someone would want to burn down your shed? Any feuds with the neighbors? Any ex-wives mad at you?"

Hallowell snorted through his long nose. "Ha," he said. "Nope. We get along with everybody, far as I can tell. We're Unitarians, you know—live and let live."

Tony sidled up, shirttail sticking out on one side, big gut hanging over his belt. "What's Lola doing?"

"She's filming the onlookers," Coffin said, pulling him out of Hallowell's earshot. "Tuck in your shirt, for God's sake."

"What, those rubbernecks?" Tony said, tucking in his shirt with one hand, scratching his belly with the other. "How come?"

"SOP in arson cases," Coffin said. "Firebugs like to watch it burn—it's part of the thrill. There've been a few famous cases where they've come back and mingled with the spectators, and been caught on camera. I'll bring it up in tomorrow's squad meeting."

"So, what?" Tony said. "You get two or three more fires, you keep seeing the same guy, he's your guy?"

"Maybe," Coffin said. "It's a lead, anyway."

"Know what I wish I had right now?" Tony said, gazing at the dwindling fire.

"No idea."

"Some beers and a pack of hot dogs. Those coals are gonna be awesome."

The man in the gray hoodie stayed as far back in the shadows as he could, up the hill a bit, next to an empty rental cottage, half-hidden in the deep shadows cast by a couple of good-sized scrub pines. It had been an ugly surprise when the lady cop had started filming—he hadn't expected that—but he was pretty sure the camera wouldn't pick him up from that distance in such low light. He wore his usual outfit: jeans, hooded sweatshirt, ball cap. A guy in a guy suit. He could see at least three other men in the crowd down by the fire dressed almost exactly the same way.

He thought about leaving—walking casually away, staying in the shadows as much as he could without being obvious about it—but decided instead to stay put. No need to draw unnecessary attention to himself, he thought. If you wear what everybody else is wearing, stay in the shadows and keep still, you're practically invisible.

Chapter 6

Coffin sat at Boyle's desk, drumming his fingers on the polished mahogany. He was wearing his uniform, even though the pants were a bit tight in the hips, and the shirt felt snug across his chest. He was not a fan of the Provincetown Police Department uniform—the pants were navy blue with a red stripe down the leg, and the shirt was pale blue with navy epaulets. Coffin did not like epaulets, and he did not like pale blue. He did not like neckties, but he wore the standard navy tie with his uniform shirt, the collar of which seemed to have shrunk in the six or seven months since he'd last worn it.

Lola sat across from him in one of the leather guest chairs. The new town manager, Monica Gault, stood by the window, fiddling with Boyle's Venetian blinds. "This *is* rather worrisome," she said, flipping the blinds open, then closed, as if she were sending a coded signal to someone across the street. "I don't like it at all."

She was a tall, pale woman who'd been hired away from the town of Washington, Connecticut, where she was held in high regard as an honest and effective public servant—exactly the opposite of the previous town manager, Coffin's cousin Louie. After nearly a year, Coffin was still having trouble getting past her vaguely British accent, tweed skirts, and short strands of freshwater pearls—she looked a bit like a young Margaret Thatcher.

"Well," she said. "What is there to *do*, exactly?"

"Unfortunately, at the moment, not a whole lot," Coffin said. "We know that the two Dumpster fires were arson, and probably the shed, but we don't know who set them, or if they were set by the same person. We've contacted the state police and the state fire marshal—the fire marshal's sending an investigator later today, but the state police can't spare any detectives right now— apparently they're working on some big meth factory in Fall River. And we have a witness that Sergeant Winters spoke to."

"Oh, really?" Gault said. "That sounds promising, no?"

"Not so much," Lola said. "One of the call-ins on the Dumpster at Rossi's said she saw a white male, age uncertain, wearing jeans, a gray hooded sweatshirt, and a ball cap fleeing the scene—or at least walking very quickly toward a car parked along the road. She wasn't sure what kind of car it was, but thinks it was black. Or blue. And it might have been an SUV. She was distracted by the fire."

"That's *not* very useful, is it?"

It was a clear, sunny day, with a brisk wind blowing off the harbor. Bands of sunlight appeared on Boyle's desk, vanished, then reappeared as Gault fiddled with the blinds.

"It corresponds roughly with the store clerk's description of the guy who first noticed the fire—a customer. He could be our firebug, or he could just be a guy who was in the store to pick up a couple of forties."

"Then there's nothing else to be done at the moment," said Gault. "Is that what you're saying?"

"Right," Coffin said. "Except to add on extra patrols, if you'll okay the overtime. We could also request help from the public—ask people to keep their eyes open, and to secure their homes, sheds, garages and so forth. I'll call the *Banner* this afternoon, if you'll okay it."

"Call away," Gault said. "The overtime might be a problem, but I'll see what I can do. We're strapped for cash, you know. Strapped!"

Later, Coffin and Lola stood outside the charred remains of the shed with Pete Wells, the state fire marshal's lead investigator for the Cape and Islands. Wells had a mop of dark curls and wore a down vest, a flannel cowboy shirt with mother-of-pearl snaps, jeans with a pair of old work gloves stuffed into the back pocket, and tall rubber boots.

"Sure looks like arson," Wells said, sipping coffee from a tall paperboard cup. The rain had started again, a slow, raw drizzle. It was cold, just above freezing, and everything smelled like smoke. "You break in, slosh some gas around, light it, and run. If you're not a complete moron, you try real hard not to get it on your clothes—your really dumb arsonists have a tendency to set themselves on fire by mistake." Wells pointed to a scorched line in the grass leading up to where the shed's door used to be—the back wall was the only part of the shed that was still standing. "Pour a little trail out the door, hit it with a lighter, and you're off to the races. Easy—just like you'd imagine doing it yourself, probably."

Coffin nodded. The rain dripped from the trees onto on his uniform hat. A few dispirited sparrows flickered back and forth in the bushes. "How much gas would it take, do you think?"

"A shed this size, full of dry wood, sawdust, and such, you could probably torch with less than a pint. But if the owner said he smelled gas real strong, probably your guy used more than that. An amateur would go heavy, just to be on the safe side."

"And this is definitely amateur stuff?" Lola asked. She wore a big, black rain slicker over her uniform; her hat was pulled down a bit to keep the drizzle out of her eyes, which were gray in the muted light.

"Sure. No professional arsonist is going to mess with Dumpsters and sheds. Your working torch man is in it for the cash: they do commercial and industrial work."

"Like what—warehouses? Factories?" Lola said.

"Yep," Wells said. "Smaller stuff, too. We get called in on lots of bars and restaurants."

"So maybe you've got a business that's failing," Lola said. "You're in debt up to your ears, the bank's coming for your house, your car—you've got no cash, but the business is fully insured."

Wells nodded. "You call your cousin's wife's brother Vinnie out in Providence, who calls a buddy of his, and a few nights later the place is destroyed by fire. Nobody's hurt, thank God. Local police and fire authorities determine the burn's electrical in origin—maybe it spread from the grease fan; probably a short. Insurance pays up, Vinnie and his buddy get their cut, you're good to go."

"We had a couple of big arson fires when I was working homicide in Baltimore," Coffin said. "One time, this guy comes home from work unexpectedly, finds his wife in the sack with the UPS man, shoots them both with a shotgun—boom, boom. Decides he's going to try to make it look like a burglary homicide gone wrong and sets the place on fire to destroy the evidence. It's a freaking row house—he burns down most of the block. An old lady two houses down dies in the fire, and he barely gets out alive himself—he's spotted by several witnesses running out the door with his pants literally on fire. Tries to do a getaway in the UPS truck, but crashes head-on into an ambulance arriving at the scene, injuring both EMTs." Coffin shook his head. "Ronnie James," he said. "Real polite guy—confessed right away. Middle school teacher. Killed in a riot at Jessup about a year before they closed it."

Wells raised an eyebrow, took a pack of Camel nonfilters from the pocket of his cowboy shirt and lit one. Coffin tried not to watch. He was still chewing Nicorette from time to time. He patted his pockets, but found none.

"That's the other category," Wells said. "The nonserial amateur. Sometimes motivated by revenge, or trying to conceal evidence of a crime. You said one of the Dumpsters was lit in daylight, right?"

"Twilight," Coffin said. "In a very visible spot."

Wells shook his curly head. "Very dumb or very bold. And obviously escalating."

"But this fire wasn't completely dumb—it's in an isolated spot, at least," Lola said. "This dark little street."

"So maybe he's learning," Wells said. He waggled his empty coffee cup. "Mocha," he said. "Five bucks for coffee, milk, and a squirt of chocolate syrup. Stupid, but I'm hooked." He took a long drag from his cigarette, blew twin streams of smoke from his nose. "What can I do? I have an addictive personality."

"If he's learning," Lola said, "does that mean he's going to keep lighting fires—keep escalating?"

Wells shrugged. "Maybe this one was enough for him. That's best case—he's a kid who's dicking around a little bit with trash cans and Dumpsters, then he sets a real fire, something burns down, and it scares him enough that he gets it out of his system."

"What's worst case?" Coffin said.

"Worst case is bad. Worst case, you've got a real live pyromaniac. This is a guy—and they're almost one hundred percent men—who may be a tad smarter than the average bear, and who's got a fire fetish that escalates as he negotiates the learning curve."

"So the better he gets at burning stuff," Lola said, "the more he gets off on it?"

"Bingo. And the bigger the fires have to be. That's obviously not what you want in a place where most of the structures are frame and cedar shingles, and, like, two feet apart. You guys get a major fire in town center, it could all go up—no joke."

"So what's the good news?" Coffin said.

Wells gestured with his cigarette. Coffin watched. "The good news," Wells said, "is that real-deal pyros are rare, so probably what you've got here is just some jerk-off kid who's setting fires because he's mad at his father and bored with playing shooter games on Xbox. The bad news—"

"The other bad news," Coffin said.

"Do you *want* a cigarette, Frank?" Wells said, offering the pack from his shirt pocket. "Or are you happy just staring at mine?"

Coffin waved the cigarettes away. "No thanks. Finally quit. Jamie's pregnant, so I'm trying to get healthy."

" 'Healthy,' " Lola said, making finger quotes.

Wells smiled. "Good luck with that," he said. "And congratulations, you old dog, you."

"With any luck the kid will look like Jamie," Coffin said.

Lola cleared her throat. "You were giving us the other bad news."

"The other bad news is that only about fifteen percent of arson cases are resolved in arrest. Fire destroys evidence, so even if your arsonist is sloppy as hell he's likely to be hard to catch. He could drop his wallet in the middle of the crime scene, but if it's a hot fire you'd never find a trace of it."

"What about a profile?" Lola said. "Any help there?"

Wells shook his head. "The profile's pretty broad: typically you're talking about a white male between seventeen and twenty-six, probably unemployed, probably grew up in a dysfunctional or abusive family, socially awkward, bad at relationships with women— maybe even lives with his parents. Probably resides within a mile or less of most of the fires he sets."

"Sounds like half the townie kids between here and Orleans," Coffin said.

"Told you it was broad," Wells said, grinning. "Your typical excitement arsonist sets fires because it makes him feel powerful: the damage, the chaos, the fear. But there's a catch."

"A catch?"

"These profiles are compiled from interviews with the fifteen percent—the dumb-asses that get caught. We don't know anything about the eighty-five percent that get away."

Lola squinted. "So they're all straight? The fifteen percent?"

"Pretty much," Wells said. "Or at least they think they are. Back in the day most serial arsonists would've been classified as latent homosexuals, which is another way of saying a kid that hates his dad and jerks off a lot, which is pretty much everybody. If you look at the national stats on arson, gay men don't even show up on the graph. They've got other ways of getting attention, maybe. Of course, your guy could be the exception."

"Perfect," Coffin said. His head had begun to throb. The craving for a cigarette was powerful; it was all he could do not to snatch the pack of Camels from Wells's shirt pocket.

"You want the *other* other bad news?" Wells said.

Coffin looked at Lola. "The *other* other bad news."

Wells picked a tobacco flake from his tongue, flicked it into the bushes. "Serial arson is all about rage. You look at the files on these guys, the needle on the rage meter is pegged every time—arson is a way of acting out, getting revenge. Which means your guy may not be all that concerned about hurting people. The real pyros usually aren't. That's the part that would keep me up at night."

"Yep," Coffin said, rubbing his temples. "That would do it."

In the Crown Vic, heading back toward Town Hall, Coffin asked, "Okay, what was that crack about me getting 'healthy'?" He mimicked Lola's finger quotes.

Lola grinned, glanced at Coffin, then back at the road. Compared to the summer crush of tourists, Commercial Street was calm. A few stout retirees ambled past the library, now housed in a deconsecrated church and home to a sixty-six-foot, half-scale wooden schooner, the building of which had been overseen by a distant cousin of Coffin's in the late 1980s. The harbor rumpled in the sudden breeze. The sun was going down, invisible behind a thick ceiling of pink-tinged clouds. A cluster of Tall Ships wobbled across the street in front of them, muumuus billowing like spinnakers. "Well," Lola said, "it's just that maybe you've put on a few pounds. Either that or your uniform shrank."

"It's made of freaking petrochemicals," Coffin said. "It can't shrink. Hell, it can't biodegrade."

"Okay, then," Lola said.

"Look," Coffin said. "I quit smoking, okay? Do you know how hard that is? I should never have to give up anything else, ever. Besides, food tastes really good now. And I'm *hungry*. *Feed* me, Seymour."

"I was really proud of you back there," Lola said, "when Wells offered you that cigarette. But, Frank, it's not enough to just quit smoking. You're going to be a dad—you've got to take care of yourself. I mean, how's your cholesterol? Aren't you almost fifty? Shouldn't you have a colonoscopy?"

"So, what—you're saying I look fat?"

"Oh my God," Lola said. "You're such a girl."

Coffin laughed. "So what's the plan for tonight? Got a hot date?"

Lola gave him a sideways glance. "Dinner and Netflix at Kate's. If it's any of your business."

"Excuse me—were you not just expressing an interest in the state of my colon?"

"Okay, okay. I'm just a private person. Comes from growing up a lesbian in Eau Claire, Wisconsin."

"Fine," Coffin said. "Two can play at that game. From now on, my personal life is a closed book. We'll keep it strictly professional from here on out."

"How's Jamie?"

"Incredibly sexy. Her boobs are *huge.* It's like they're everywhere, suddenly—I can't take my eyes off them, and I'm not even a boob man, really. But."

"But?"

"She's not interested. Nada. Zip. Zilch."

"Uh-oh."

"Doctor says it's totally normal. Basically her body just wants food and sleep—the desire hormones are turned off. Could reverse itself in a week, or could go on like this for a year or so, depending on how long she breast-feeds. A year!"

Lola laughed. "Poor Frank," she said, pulling into the chief's reserved parking space behind Town Hall. "Boobs everywhere you look, but they're not for you."

Coffin climbed out of the Crown Vic and stretched. He looked up at the looming stone phallus of the Pilgrim Monument, imagined it toppling over, destroying Town Hall as it went down. "Well," he said, "that's Provincetown. You'd think I'd be used to it by now."

After Coffin had spent an excruciating hour or so at his desk reviewing reports and working on the duty roster for the coming week, he decided to call it quits and drove the Crown Vic over to Billy's for a drink. As he pulled into the potholed parking lot—*his* potholed parking lot—across from the Stop & Shop, he wondered if Kotowski would be there. Coffin had hired him to manage Billy's when he realized he could no longer run the place himself—it was that or sell it off to some developer who'd turn it into a condo complex, or some godawful minimall selling T-shirts and cheap, Chinese snow globes with lighthouses or fishing boats inside them.

Inside, Billy's was surprisingly busy. All of the bar stools were taken, and several of the booths were full. A young Eastern European woman was feeding quarters into the jukebox. It was thumping out a blues song by Albert King, "Born Under a Bad Sign." Coffin felt a tingle of dread: customers were good, but why so many? He had learned not to trust apparent good news where Billy's was concerned. On Kotowski's first day as manager, he'd hand-lettered a large sign that said FREE BEER, and propped it up in the parking lot. It was a hot Saturday afternoon in July, and the place filled almost immediately—Kotowski giving out tickets for one free beer per customer at the door.

"What in the hell are you doing?" Coffin had said, driving over in the rattling, backfiring Fiesta after a patrol officer had called him about the sign.

"Business!" Kotowski had crowed. "When was the last time you saw this many people in here?"

Kotowski had him there, Coffin had to admit. "Never. Not even close. There's just one problem."

"Problem? This isn't a problem—it's a brilliant promotional scheme. Look at them—they've had their free beers and now they're buying drinks and ordering food. I don't know why every bar in town isn't doing this."

"Because it's illegal," Coffin said. "I could lose my liquor license. You can't advertise free drinks. Ever. Period."

"Fucking fascists," Kotowski had grumbled, bringing in the sign. "Whatever happened to free enterprise? Whatever happened to getting the government off our backs?"

But now there was no sign in the parking lot—just a decent happy hour crowd of mostly young, attractive people. But then

Coffin remembered: they'd hired Yelena, the pretty Croatian barmaid Coffin had met back in May. She said she'd try a few shifts, see how it went. Coffin caught a flash of her dark hair between standing room customers at the bar. That was it—she must have just started. And apparently she'd told a few friends.

Coffin squeezed between two tall, Eastern European men and found Kotowski sitting at the bar. Kotowski was wearing patched corduroys, a paint-splattered T-shirt, and flip-flops, even though the temperature outside had dropped into the midforties. His two-day beard was shot through with gray, his hair stringy and uncombed. He looked the way he always looked.

"Wow," Coffin said.

"Not bad, right?" Kotowski said. He was sipping a Newcastle ale and smoking a cigarette, despite Provincetown's nonsmoking ordinance.

Coffin waved to Yelena, who was busy pouring pints of Guinness.

"Hello, Frank!" she called out.

Billy's regular bartender, Squid, was busy shucking oysters and arranging them on paper plates in their half-shells, with lemon wedges and little paper cups of cocktail sauce. "Hey, Frank," Squid said, looking up from his work. He was hunched over a large tub full of ice and very fresh oysters. His long, spatulate fingers worked the oyster knife with surprising dexterity. "Some crowd, right?"

"No joke," Coffin said. "It's like a real bar, almost."

Squid laughed. "Yelena showed up with, like, five of her girlfriends. I gave them a round on the house—hope that's okay. They sat around looking bored for about fifteen minutes. You know, the way a hot girl would in a dump like this."

"I've seen it myself," Coffin said. "Every time I bring Jamie here."

"Yep," Squid said. "That's the look. Their eyes kind of glaze over, and they start fiddling with their cell phones. But then Cap'n Nickerson spoke up."

Captain Nickerson was a moldering green Amazon parrot that Coffin had inherited, indirectly, from his father. No one knew how old he was, but he'd acquired a large and salty vocabulary in his years aboard the *Nora Jean*, the old man's fishing boat. Captain Nickerson's cage hung behind the bar; he bobbed his head in time with the music and swung manically on its little swing.

"Uh-oh," Coffin said. "What'd he say?"

"What he always says when he sees a pretty girl."

"Show us your tits?"

"Bingo."

"So?"

"So they all cracked up. And then they did."

Coffin shook his head. "I'm not following."

"They all showed their tits. Then they got out their cell phones and took pictures of each other showing their tits. Then about ten minutes later, like, fifty people showed up. Me and Yelena can hardly keep up."

Coffin turned to Kotowski. "He's making this up, right?"

"Nope." Kotowski held up three fingers—Scout's honor. "It's the gospel truth. Cap'n Nickerson to the rescue."

"Holy crap," Coffin said. "What'll they do if he says 'eat me'?"

Squid grinned. "Hadn't thought of that. Things could get ugly. We're dealing with a highly literal crowd here, evidently."

Yelena handed three pints of Guinness across the bar, took the money, made change. When she was done, she poured a short Newcastle for herself and sauntered down to Squid's station at the end of the bar.

"What's up, boss?" she said.

"I'm impressed," Coffin said. "These are all your friends?"

"Some," Yelena said, sipping her beer. "Not all. Some friends of friends. Some just people who come in." She was small and a bit angular, with high cheekbones and a strong nose. She wore her black hair in a long ponytail. Her eyes were blue, but so pale in the dim light they seemed almost silver. She was, Coffin thought, one of the most strikingly beautiful women he'd ever met.

Captain Nickerson emitted a loud wolf whistle, and much of the crowd wolf whistled back.

"You know," Coffin said, "we might actually be making money."

"There's just one problem," Kotowski said.

"Don't tell me," Coffin said. "Yelena doesn't have a work visa?"

Yelena frowned. "Of course I have," she said. "All papers in order. Good to go." She brushed her hands together twice, first the left on top, then the right—*that's that.*

"Then what?" Coffin said. "I don't get it."

"I can't hang out here anymore," Kotowski said. "It's too fucking crowded."

Kate Hanlon lived on Alden Lane, a cross-street between Bradford and Commercial in what the travel Web sites liked to call Provincetown's "quiet east end." The sun had set, the clouded sky was half-dark. The rain had started again.

Lola climbed out of her Camaro and stretched, arms overhead. She'd gone to the gym after her shift, had a good workout, showered and dressed in jeans, loose cotton sweater, engineer boots, and a black leather jacket. She retrieved a bottle of wine from the passenger seat—a nice pinot noir. Then, out of habit, she took her personal use .38 from the glove compartment and put it, in its clip-on holster, into her jacket pocket.

As usual, Kate was waiting for her in the open door. A shaft of buttery lamplight fell out onto the front steps. Kate was lanky and dark-eyed. A full-time pilot for Cape Air, the commuter airline that flew ten-passenger Cessnas between Boston and the Cape and islands, she barely made enough money to afford her year-round rental. She was barefoot, dressed in jeans, a snug white T-shirt, no bra. The house was warm. Lola stepped inside, rain dripping from her jacket onto the braided entry rug. They kissed.

"You're wet," Kate said.

"Getting there," Lola said, kissing her again.

Kate smiled. Her teeth were very straight and white. "Me, too. But maybe we should have dinner first. Seared tuna—your favorite. Shame to let it go to waste."

"I brought wine," Lola said, offering the bottle. "It's red, though."

"Perfect," Kate said. She held the bottle at eye level, looked at the label, did a wide-eyed little double take. "Wow," she said. "Sea Smoke. Where'd you get this?"

"My sister lives in Santa Barbara. We went in on a few bottles a couple of years ago."

Kate smiled again. "A special evening, then. Let me hang up your jacket."

Lola shrugged it off, handed it over.

"Whoa," Kate said. "Heavy. Are you packin' heat, Sergeant?"

"Sorry," Lola said. "It's kind of a reflex these days. I can leave it in the car from now on."

Kate shook her head, put a slim hand on Lola's cheek. "After what you went through last spring," she said, "you can bring it to bed if you want to."

Chapter 7

The big man squirted a generous squiggle of charcoal starter onto the pile of paper and cardboard he'd gathered, and the plywood subfloor around it. He hit the walls, too—there was no hurry, and the damage had to be extensive or the insurance might not pay. He knew that if he got the ground floor cooking, the fire would take care of the rest. Heat rises—the physics were simple. He'd gone through the building and opened a few windows, figuring they'd act like the vent holes in a charcoal grill. He'd been careful not to let anyone spot him. He was dressed in jeans, ball cap, sweatshirt—even if someone did see him, what would they see? Anyone. No one.

Open some windows, squirt the lighter fluid, do a thorough job. It didn't matter if they knew it was arson—as long as they didn't know who set it.

He kept low, squirting a trail of charcoal starter out the back door and onto a concrete patio, hidden from the street. There was no one around. No cars moved on Brewster and most of the windows in the neighborhood were dark. He found the lighter in the pocket of his sweatshirt: one of those long ones people use for grilling out. He pressed the child safety button, clicked the trigger, and a long tongue of flame squirted out, curling upward at the end—*heat rises.* He lit the trail of starter fluid and watched for a second as it burned blue and orange, the fire chasing itself into the half-finished building like the famished animal it was. He turned quickly, walked away through the muddy backyard, and then made a quick right onto Brewster. He heard a kind of roaring whoosh as the charcoal starter on the ground floor caught and the fumes ignited but he didn't look back—he just kept walking at normal speed toward the little junction Brewster made with Pearl Street before dipping downward sharply for thirty yards and butting into Harry Kemp Way, where his car was parked, out of sight of the burning building.

Something whacked Coffin's ear—once, then again. Softly at first, then hard enough to wake him up from the dream he'd been having—a blurred image of naked breasts, the dream still hovering in the room like a whiff of perfume. But whose? Jamie's, he hoped, although part of him thought the dream might have been about Lola, or maybe Gemma, his uncle Rudy's girlfriend. The thing whacked him on the ear a third time: the back of Jamie's hand, the edge of her ring scraping the cartilage a bit.

"Fire," Jamie said, her back to him—her voice hollow, as though it came from the bottom of a well.

"Ow," Coffin said, sitting up, rubbing his ear.

"Fire," Jamie said. "The house is on fire." She waved a slender arm, went back to sleep.

Coffin sniffed the air and smelled nothing—just the damp of October, the faint scent of dust, maybe, a whiff of decay from the taxidermied owl glaring down from the big walnut wardrobe. Coffin stood, walked to the window. More rain. In his neighbor's garden the black skeletons of three sunflowers leaned, left over from summer, their big heads long ago picked clean by the birds. He noticed a strange orange glow on the eastern horizon: it seemed to rise and expand as he watched. The digital clock by the bed said 2:43. Then he heard sirens.

The shed fire had seemed impressive at the time, Coffin thought, but this one was enormous in comparison. The entire two-story structure on Brewster Street appeared to be engulfed—flames roared from the upper windows and danced in the night sky, throwing a lurid orange glow against the low cloud cover. Sparks and bits of roofing rose above the building on a powerful thermal, then drifted out toward the waterfront, carried by the offshore breeze. The fire and rescue boys were struggling again with the idle speed on their new pumper: Walt Macy had a control panel open and was fiddling with knobs and buttons while a tall, bony firefighter held a flashlight on what appeared to be the owner's manual. To Coffin, it looked like the building was already a total loss.

"Well," Lola said, yawning. "This is exciting." She was in her off-duty clothes—jeans, boots, leather jacket. Her hair hung loose around her shoulders—Coffin couldn't remember ever having seen it down before—dark blond and a bit tousled.

"Wonder who owns it," Coffin said. "Seems like it's been under construction off and on for months and months. Mostly off, lately."

Lola yawned again, rubbed her eyes. "God," she said. "I'd just gotten to sleep when I heard the sirens."

"Total hot date," Coffin said.

"Is there any other kind?"

Coffin grinned, said nothing. The rain had stopped, finally. The breeze was picking up, though the sky showed no sign of clearing.

"Wait a minute," Lola said, peering at Coffin. "I know your 'what if' tone when I hear it."

"It's just a thought," Coffin said.

"You have a dark view of human nature, Frank Coffin," Lola said.

Coffin shrugged. "It's possible, that's all I'm saying."

"So, okay: What if you've got a building under construction but you've burned through your loan and it's still unfinished."

"The market's tanking, even prime, waterfront condos aren't turning over . . ."

Lola held up a finger. "But *your* building's fully insured!"

"Coincidentally, somebody's been setting things on fire."

"That somebody might even be the owner of a half-finished building."

"Might be, or maybe it's a different somebody," Coffin said. "Either way, the other smaller fires appear to be the work of a serial arsonist."

"Which could represent an opportunity," Lola said, thumbing a strand of hair behind her ear. "If you happened to own a building you wanted to get rid of."

"That happened to be fully insured," Coffin said.

Lola took a deep breath, let it out. The fire was growing more intense. The pumper was working, finally, and the firefighters were aiming a heavy stream of water into one of the downstairs windows. "I don't know how you look at yourself in the mirror," she said. "Thinking the way you do."

"It's not easy, living on the dark side."

A crowd of forty or fifty sleepy-looking spectators had gathered in a loose, L-shaped cluster at the corner of Brewster and Bradford streets, well below the muddy rise on which the burning building stood. Lola held up a camcorder and started to film them.

"It's not going to be easy making an ID with this," Lola said. "Lots of hats and hoods."

"Chilly out," Coffin said, and it was—the damp October wind was picking up, and Coffin felt himself gritting his teeth. He'd worn only an old suede jacket over his jeans and flannel shirt: time to get out the winter coat. "Nothing you can do."

Lola nodded, peering into the camcorder's view screen. "It also occurs to me that we're likely to keep seeing the same people over and over, it being the off-season and all."

She had a point—even in October, Coffin began to feel that he was seeing the same faces over and over, day in and day out: Jamie, Lola, Tony, and the rest of his co-workers, the new town manager Monica Gault, the beautiful Haitian girl behind the counter at the Yankee Mart, where Coffin usually stopped for coffee on the way to work. Kotowski, maybe. Squid. Captain Nickerson. The stuffed goat in his mother's house. By the time the winter nor'easters began to blow, half the town seemed to be in hibernation: it was as though the locals—year-rounders, they called themselves—stayed in their burrows as much as possible, emerging only to forage now and then at the Stop & Shop.

"Maybe we're looking for the guy who only shows up once," Coffin said. "The guy who looks uncomfortable being filmed."

"So don't be subtle about it," Lola said.

"Right."

Lola paused the camcorder, walked up to within ten feet of the crowd of onlookers, pushed the record button again and slowly panned the camera across their faces.

Coffin watched. No one walked away. No one pulled their hat brim over their eyes. A pair of Tall Ships in faux mink primped their wigs for the camera.

"Okay," Coffin said when Lola was done. "It was worth a shot."

"I hate this," Lola said. "I want some freaking evidence to think about."

Coffin's cousin Tony came bounding toward them from behind the burning building, struggling a bit in the mud. He'd probably been taking a leak, Coffin thought.

"Yo, Frankie," Tony said. He was in uniform, holding a big policeman's Maglite. "I think I got something." He pointed to the backyard. "Looks like fresh boot prints back there."

Coffin had scheduled him for the graveyard shift at Tony's own request. Things hadn't been going so well at home, Tony had said. Doris, his small, frowning wife, wanted to leave the Cape, move closer to Boston, send the kids to private school. Tony would only leave the Cape in a box, Coffin thought—he was local to the core. What would big, sloppy Tony do with himself in some upscale Boston suburb? What would Tony's kids—five little versions of Tony in graduating sizes, like Russian matryoshka dolls—do in a private school?

"Tony?" Coffin said.

"Dude."

"Are you sure they're not *your* footprints?" Coffin was looking down at Tony's muddy boots.

"Frankie—for fuck's sake," Tony said. "Do you really think I'm that dumb?"

Coffin raised his eyebrows, said nothing.

"Okay," Tony said, waving his hands. "I admit it—I fuck up sometimes. But here's how I know: I got kind of small feet for my size—just an eleven. This guy's feet are bigger. Plus, his boots have a different tread."

Coffin and Lola exchanged glances. Coffin inclined his head a bit and Lola nodded. "Okay," Coffin said. "Let's see the boot prints."

Incredibly, Tony seemed to be right. A trail of boot prints led from the back of the burning building, through the hedge and out to Brewster Street, which was a narrow one-way for most of the block. Coffin also wore a size eleven—not that big for a man his height (*you know what they say*, he thought)—the boot prints leading out to the hedge appeared to be at least a size or two larger than his own.

"What would you guess?" he said. "Thirteen?"

"Sounds about right," Lola said. "You're a what? Ten?"

"Eleven," Coffin said, trying not to sound defensive.

"Eleven?" Tony said. "That's it? What are you, six-two?"

"For Christ's sake," Coffin said.

"So we're looking for a fairly big guy," Lola said, kneeling down, pointing Tony's flashlight at the scorched trail across the patio. The fire leaped from the second-storey windows into the night sky. It was much too hot to get close, but the scorch marks were unmistakable. "Long stride, too—not a small guy with big feet, or a small guy wearing big boots."

"Definitely not a woman," Coffin said. The prints were reasonably clear, and bore a distinctive tread design—the interlocking chain that, as far as Coffin knew, was unique to L.L. Bean duck boots.

"A really big woman, maybe," Lola said. "But yeah, probably not."

"Well, there you go," Coffin said. He patted Tony on the back. "Good find. You're a regular Sherlock Holmes." The fire seemed to be gathering strength, burning hotter and faster—the flames shooting from the windows maybe thirty feet into the night sky. If you watch a fire long enough, Coffin thought, it becomes beautiful:

malevolent but lovely, a dancing, many-armed Shiva, bent on destruction.

"I always hated that guy," Tony said. "You know, as a kid? What a freakin' know-it-all. I kept hoping Dr. Watson would get fed up and punch him out."

Coffin said nothing. A section of the roof collapsed, throwing a shower of bright cinders into the air. Big sheets of burning tar paper rose on a column of smoke and sparks, and wheeled toward town center on the breeze. *Like something out of Dante*, Coffin thought. *Like the souls of the damned.*

Chapter 8

The next morning all of Provincetown smelled like a doused campfire, smoky and damp. Kotowski sat with Coffin's mother in her room at Valley View Nursing Home, watching the big, flat-screen TV Coffin had bought for her at Best Buy in Hyannis. Kotowski often stopped in to see her before the "art for seniors" class he'd been teaching at Valley View for the past eight years.

Film of the condo fire played over and over on the Boston FOX affiliate. A banner scrolled across the screen that said, *P 'TOWN FIREBUG STRIKES AGAIN.* A blond news model was interviewing a TV minister from South Carolina, who seemed to think that God's judgment was finally being visited on Provincetown.

"Look at that fat dickwad," Coffin's mother said, black eyes glittering, bright and empty as a doll's. "What's he grinning about?"

"He sure seems happy," Kotowski said. "What's up with his hair? It looks like molded fiberglass."

"Somebody ought to set fire to this place," Coffin's mother said. "Put the drooling idiots out of their fucking misery."

She looked at Kotowski. She wore a blue housecoat. Her hair

was brushed and her teeth were in. She smiled with them, her face a bit lopsided. Kotowski wondered if she'd had a small stroke.

"It's nice of you to come visit. You're a good son."

"We've been through this, Sarah. I'm not your son. Frank's your son."

Coffin's mother scowled. "Frank? Who the hell is Frank?"

"Jesus," Jamie said, sitting up in bed, scowling at her copy of *What to Eat When You're Expecting.* "These people are Nazis. Brown rice and broccoli, my ass. Do you know what I want right now?"

Coffin shook his head, retying his tie for the third time. "No idea. Banana split? Fried calamari?"

"Fried calamari at"—Jamie glanced at the clock on the bedside table—"seven twenty-three in the morning? Don't be a goofball. I was thinking pork chops with onion rings. That banana split sounds pretty good, though." She Frisbeed the fat book across the room; it flapped into the corner like a dying grouse.

"Excellent choice," Coffin said, frowning into the mirror as he untied the tie again. "Crap."

"Trouble?"

"Can't get the knot right. Too loose, too tight, too crooked." Coffin slid a finger into his shirt collar and tugged. "Plus, this fucking collar is strangling me. Must've shrunk in the wash."

Jamie was sitting cross-legged in bed, chin resting on her elbows. "You know, Frank," she said.

"You know, Frank," Coffin said, after a long beat.

"Never mind."

Coffin turned for a moment. She seemed stunningly beautiful—hazel eyes set wide, bed-tousled hair. Her face a bit rounder now, the cheekbones less pronounced. "No fair with the never minds," he said. "Say what you think."

"Well . . ." Jamie paused.

"Oh, for Christ's sake."

"I'm a little worried about your health. You're going to be a dad, you know."

Coffin grimaced into the mirror. "You're saying I'm getting fat."

"Not fat. Stout, maybe. Husky. It's cute."

"Husky," Coffin said, finally getting the knot right. He looked down: The inside end of the tie was three inches longer than the outside end. "Great."

Jamie stood, put her arms around him from behind. "See, now your feelings are hurt."

"No," Coffin said. "You're right. I'm a little out of shape. I need more exercise."

"And a checkup," Jamie said. "Cholesterol, the works. I'll even make the appointment for you."

"Have you and Lola been conspiring?"

Jamie kissed his ear, and Coffin felt goose bumps rise on the back of his neck.

"I want you around for the long haul," Jamie said. "You have to live to be eighty, at least."

Coffin caught one of her wrists, tasted the fine, pale skin where her pulse beat. "Good luck with that," he said. "No Coffin man has ever lived past seventy, as far as I know. We have a genetic disposition to drowning."

"Be the first." Jamie slid a hand down to Coffin's groin, gave his stiffening penis a squeeze through his uniform pants, then another. Then she stopped. "Uh-oh," she said.

Coffin caught her reflection in the mirror. She was wide-eyed, pale. "Uh-oh," he said. "You okay?"

Jamie bolted for the bathroom, slammed the door. Coffin could hear her retching, spitting. The toilet flushed. Water ran. She emerged a minute later, wiping her mouth on a hand towel. "It's not you," she said, meeting Coffin's eyes. "You know that, right?"

The property tax assessor's office was on the first floor of Town Hall; it had two narrow windows looking out toward Bradford Street and the Pilgrim Monument. The assessor was a tall, heavy black man named Marvin Jones. He wore a maroon sweater vest, pale blue Oxford shirt, khaki pants, and bifocals with tortoiseshell rims. He looked much too big for the small task chair parked in front of his desk.

"It's 376 Bradford Street?" he said.

"That's what it says on the mailbox," Coffin said.

"Which unit?"

"How many are there?"

"Two."

"Different owners?"

"No."

"Both, then."

"Ha," Jones said, clicking with his mouse. "You're going to like this."

"Whenever you say I'm going to like something," Coffin said, "I don't."

"It's not my fault you're so hard to please."

"Marv?"

"Marvin." Marvin's pale blue eyes flickered up from the screen, met Coffin's. "Not Marv."

"Marvin. What am I going to like?"

"Maybe 'like' is too strong a word."

"Marvin!"

"The building belongs to a company—R. S. Investments. Title

transferred two years ago from another company, Outer Cape Properties, which I happen to know is now defunct." Marvin looked up from his screen and smiled brightly. "R. S. Investments is owned outright by an individual whose initials also happen to be—*so* original—R. S. Care to take a guess?"

Coffin closed his eyes. "Oh, Christ. Uncle Rudy."

"Ding, ding, ding!" Marvin grinned. "Former chief of police and man of mystery, Rodolfo Santos. Give the detective a Kewpie doll."

Twenty minutes later, Coffin sat in one of Monica Gault's leather guest chairs. Somehow a spot of grease had appeared on his tie. *Christ*, he thought. *I'm turning into Tony.* Vincent Mancini, the Cape and Islands district attorney, sat with one haunch propped on Gault's broad desk. A pair of state police detectives lurked near the door—Pilchard in his brown suit, and a new one whose name Coffin hadn't caught. Pete Wells sat in the other guest chair, and Monica Gault, the new town manager, stood by the window, gazing out at the harbor.

"Well, it's very bad news," Gault said. "*Very* bad news."

"Which part?" Mancini asked. "The escalation, or the possibility there's a copycat?"

Gault frowned. "I just don't *believe* there's a copycat," she said. "Not in Provincetown. *Two* psychopaths setting fires? *Here?*"

"You haven't lived here very long," Coffin said.

"Probably just one psychopath," Wells said, "and an outside chance there's also an opportunist trying to get out from under some debt."

"You need to talk to your uncle, Coffin," Mancini said. "Stat."

"I'm not sure he's in town. He doesn't keep a residence here, I don't think. I haven't seen him since May."

"What about his son? He's one of your patrol officers, right?"

"Tony, yeah. He might know. Rudy has a girlfriend in town, too. Or had. I think I can probably locate her."

"This uncle of yours," Gault said, still peering out at the harbor. The clouds had lifted, finally, and the day was bright. A herring gull sailed past the window, a small green crab in its beak. "He used to be police chief, right? Left under a bit of a cloud?"

"Right," Coffin said.

"A *bit* of a cloud?" Mancini said. "Ha. You could call it that. The guy had a finger in every drug deal and rent-boy operation in town. And that was just for starters."

Mancini had his trying-not-to-look-too-out-of-place-in-Provincetown outfit on: pressed jeans, tassel loafers, pastel polo shirt. His hair gelled into an artful rumple. A pair of blue-mirrored sunglasses parked on top of his head.

"You could have prosecuted," Coffin said, "but you passed."

Mancini narrowed his eyes. "What are you implying, Coffin?"

"Gentlemen," Gault said. "If you must mark your territory, you must. But please don't do it in my office."

Pete Wells snapped his fingers. "You just reminded me."

Everyone turned to look at Wells.

"In forensic terms, most serial arsonists have signatures—a very specific way of going about things. Sometimes even down to the pour patterns for accelerants, or the ways they try to disguise—or not disguise—the fact that it's a set fire, even down to using specific kinds of batteries in electronic timing devices. Darker stuff, too, speaking of marking your territory. Thrill arsonists sometimes leave DNA at fire scenes—"

"DNA?" Gault said. "I don't understand."

"They masturbate," Mancini said. "Or they take a crap."

"Or both," Wells said. "If they're having a *really* good time. The point is that if you know what to look for, you can read an arsonist's signature, even if his methods evolve somewhat over time."

Gault ran a bony finger under her nose. "And?" she said.

"And—the shed fire and the condo fire have very similar signatures. Use of liquid accelerant, line of accelerant out the door, no matches or containers left on the scene, all pretty deliberate and organized, no apparent DNA, nothing too weird or pathological, beyond the fires themselves. Simple—arson 101—but very similar. The probability that the two fires are set by the same person is pretty high. Unless."

"Oh, for Christ's sake," Mancini said. "Unless *what*?"

"Unless," Coffin said, "the person who set the second fire knew how to read the signature of the first fire."

"Right," Wells said, "and you'd probably have to have at least a little training in forensic fire investigation to be able to do that."

"And who gets this kind of training?" Gault said.

"Firefighters," Coffin said. "Professional and certified volunteer. Some law-enforcement people. Academics in the field."

"Ah," Gault said, swallowing. "I see."

"But like I say, the odds are very good that we have a single firebug, and not a copycat," Wells said.

"I'd feel better about those odds if Rudy fucking Santos wasn't involved," Mancini said.

You and me both, Coffin wanted to say, but he kept his mouth shut.

Chapter 9

Coffin leaned back in his office chair, loosened his tie and unbuttoned his collar. His neck felt sore and constricted, as though a noose had been cinched around it. He rubbed it, cradling the phone in his other hand. "Dr. Sengupta," he said. "Four forty-five. Right."

"Labs anytime before noon. You're supposed to fast for twelve hours. Have you eaten anything yet?"

"Nope," Coffin said. "Just coffee."

"They're squeezing you in. Don't be late." Jamie's voice sounded distant, thin. The phone made a faint whooshing sound that seemed to get louder whenever the wind blew particularly hard against the windows.

"What happened to Dr. Frankel? I liked her."

"She left," Jamie said. "Five years ago."

"I hope it wasn't something I said."

Jamie laughed. "It's good that we're doing this. You need to be in tip-top shape if you're going to chase a toddler around, you know."

"Right," Coffin said. "Tip-top."

"Listen, it's getting late. If you're going to get your blood drawn in time, you'd better go now."

"Right-o," Coffin said. "I'll run right over."

"Love you, Frank."

"Love you, too."

Coffin hung up, punched the intercom button. "Arlene?" he said.

Arlene was the secretary Boyle had brought in. She was very skinny and very tan, and smelled of menthol cigarettes. She looked slightly scorched, as though she'd been overroasted in a big oven; Coffin guessed that she spent a lot of time in tanning salons.

"Yes, Chief," she said.

"My cousin Tony's the desk officer today. Ask him to come up, would you?"

"Will do."

Ten seconds later the intercom beeped. "He's on his way," Arlene said.

"I ain't seen him, Frankie," Tony said, standing just inside Coffin's office door. "Like I said."

"He hasn't been in touch with you? No phone calls? Nothing?"

"Nope. Nada."

Tony seemed nervous. Frightened, even. He was wide-eyed, sweatier than usual.

"What's up, Tony?"

"What's up with what?"

"You look like someone's been chasing you."

Tony turned, opened the door a crack, peeked out, then shut the door again as silently as he could. He looked like a frightened bear. He shambled across the rug, lowered himself carefully into a leather guest chair. Outside, in the hallway, workmen started banging on something metal. There was a brief barrage of drilling.

"Frankie," Tony said, when the noise subsided for a moment. "They're back."

"Who's back? You mean Rudy?"

Tony shook his head so hard that his jowls flapped like a basset hound's. "Not Rudy. I told you I ain't seen him."

"Who, then?"

"You're gonna think I'm crazy."

Coffin raised an eyebrow.

"The saucers, Frankie. I saw 'em again this morning as I was driving in. Over Pilgrim Lake."

Tony lived in Eastham, about a half-hour drive from Province-town on Route 6.

"Saucers," Coffin said.

"Three of 'em, Frankie. Big silver ones. Hovering in formation over Pilgrim Lake as I'm coming down the hill there. Then when I get almost underneath 'em, they zoom off, like *that*." He snapped his fingers. "Out toward the Atlantic. Gone. Just like the last time."

"What last time?" Coffin said.

Tony rubbed a hand over his face. His forehead was sheened with sweat. "I shouldn'a said nothing. Forget it."

"Tony. What last time?"

Tony looked over his shoulder again, then leaned forward, meeting Coffin's eyes. "Back in '95. October—right around this time of year. I'd only been on the force about six months. I saw 'em then, too. Right before."

Coffin's eyes itched. He rubbed the lids with the thumb and index finger of his right hand. "Oh, for Christ's sake," he said.

"Ask me, Frankie," Tony said, eyes suddenly fierce.

"Tony."

" 'Right before what?' " Tony said, poking at Coffin's desktop with a thick forefinger. "You're my first cousin. My best friend since we were kids. Go on, *ask* me."

"Look," Coffin said. "This isn't helping me. Somebody's setting fires." He looked at his watch. "I'm supposed to be getting my blood drawn."

"They took me, Frankie. They came in the night and took me."

"Tony."

"They *did* things to me."

"They," Coffin said, "did things to you."

Tony stared out the window—past Coffin's shoulder, over the harbor toward Pilgrim Lake. "And now they're back."

Coffin took a deep breath, smoothed his mustache. "Look," he said. "Why don't you take a few personal days? I'll get one of the temps to fill in. Take Doris and the kids up to Boston. It'd make her happy, right?"

Tony nodded. "Okay," he said. "It's worth a shot. Maybe they'll take somebody else, instead. Some tourist, maybe."

"They can have 'em all," Coffin said. "As long as they leave their wallets behind."

At the clinic, Coffin waited to have his blood drawn. The waiting room was pleasant enough: it had a high, cathedral ceiling with skylights and no TV. Coffin picked up a copy of *Entertainment Weekly*: Someone named Lady Gaga was on the cover. She looked, he thought, like a well put-together drag queen.

There was only one other patient: a young man, reading a rumpled copy of *Newsweek*. He looked familiar: not tall, deep chest, close-cropped hair. He had a bandage wrapped around his right hand. Coffin fished in his memory for a name, but couldn't come up with it.

The young man looked up from his magazine, squinted at Coffin. "You're Coffin, right?" he said.

Coffin nodded. He remembered now. "Yep. And you're Maurice. From Yaya's."

"That's right. Only I don't work there now, since the seals got killed."

"Sorry to hear that." Coffin pointed. "What happened to your wing?"

Maurice held up his bandaged hand. "Dog bit me. Schnauzer."

"Ouch," Coffin said.

"It's no big deal," Maurice said. "I'd still rather hang out with dogs than people, any day." There was a minute-long silence before Maurice stirred in his seat. "So, any progress?" he said.

"On the fires? Not much."

Maurice nodded, picked at something on his pants leg.

Coffin set his magazine down on an end table. "But you're talking about the seals, right?"

"Yeah—that's right. I meant the seals."

Coffin shook his head. "Not so far, no." He shrugged. "The trail's pretty cold at this point. Sorry."

Coffin jumped a bit when his cell phone buzzed in his pocket, then started to play a boisterous electronic version of "La Cucaracha." He wasn't used to having a cell phone and didn't like having to carry one, but Monica Gault insisted he be "reachable" at all times. He did not like the fact that his cell phone played "La Cucaracha" whenever someone called him, either, but despite numerous attempts, he could not get it to play anything else, or make any other sort of sound. He had been tempted on numerous occasions to throw it into the harbor, and had he been close to the water he might have done so then.

Coffin pressed the glowing button, put the phone to his ear.

"Coffin," he said.

"Detective, it's Dr. Branstool from Valley View. Sorry to bother you in the middle of what must be a busy day."

"What's she done now?" Coffin said. "Bitten Mr. Hastings again? Staged another jailbreak?"

"I'm afraid it's more serious than that," Dr. Branstool said. If his voice had had a color, Coffin thought, it would have been beige. "She set Mrs. Pickerel's room on fire. I'm afraid she's caused quite a bit of damage."

"Mrs. Pickerel? Is that the lady that thinks she's on a cruise?"

"We need to have a conversation about your mother's options at this point," Branstool said. "Can you come in this afternoon?"

"You're kicking her out?" Coffin said, sitting across from Dr. Branstool in Valley View's cramped conference room—table, chairs with little wheels, mouse-colored carpet, broad window overlooking the cemetery. "Just like that?"

"Just like that, Detective?" Branstool leaned forward in his chair.

A young woman who'd been introduced as a patient's advocate sat next to him. She appeared to be about twenty-five and wore a neat navy blue suit, her highlighted hair in a loose bun. She handed Branstool a green folder.

"This is your mother's behavioral file." Branstool opened the folder on the conference table, leafed through several pages of forms and handwritten notes. "October 2006, only a week after she became a resident here, she struck a nurse's aide with a baked potato."

"The nurse's aide kept calling her 'hon,'" Coffin said. "She hates that."

Branstool looked up, pale eyes behind round horn-rimmed glasses. "April of 2007, she bit Mr. Hastings."

"He cheats at Monopoly," Coffin said. "Not that that would justify biting, of course."

"June of 2007, she refused to speak for almost an entire month."

"She was upset about the food."

"August of 2008 she repeatedly ran naked through the main hall."

"She was hot."

"May of 2009, she left the facility without permission on nine occasions."

"She had a boyfriend. They wanted some privacy."

"She routinely uses abusive language toward our caregivers. She was barred by the other patients from our weekly game of charades for making obscene gestures. She refuses all medication—"

"Look," Coffin said. "She's difficult. I get it. She has Alzheimer's. That's why she's here."

"But none of it rises to this level of seriousness, Detective. None of it seriously endangered our residents and staff—not until today."

"So you're kicking her out," Coffin said. He flexed his arm. The nurse who'd drawn his blood had done a good job—he'd hardly felt the needle going in, but now the square of gauze she'd pasted over the wound with a Band-Aid was beginning to itch.

"Relocating," the patient's advocate said. "To a facility in Sandwich that's better equipped to care for someone with her degree of dementia. We've already been in touch with them, and they have a bed available."

"So, what," Coffin said, "they'll shoot her full of Thorazine and strap her to a wheelchair all day?"

"I'm sorry, Detective," Branstool said. His suit was muted beige, his tie a pale, watery green strip of raw silk. "As Ms. Haskell says, we're just not equipped to care for her here. She's crossed the line from being difficult, as you say, to being a real danger to herself and others. The rules are very clear—there's nothing I can do."

Coffin looked at Ms. Haskell. She was plump, but her face was quite pretty. She seemed very young. "Could I have a word alone with Dr. Branstool?"

Ms. Haskell's eyebrows went up. "Well . . ."

"It's all right, Ms. Haskell," Dr. Branstool said. "Detective Coffin and I are old friends." He laughed a weak, dry laugh. Outside, dark clouds herded slowly in from the west. A line of starlings pecked among the gravestones, the cemetery grass was silver green and shaggy in the slanted light.

When the door had closed behind Ms. Haskell, Coffin leaned forward and propped his elbows on the conference table. "Where did my mother get the matches?"

Dr. Branstool's eyes widened behind his horn-rimmed glasses. Something about the way their lenses caught the light made Coffin wonder, not for the first time, whether they were flat glass—worn purely for effect. "We're looking into that," he said. "We think one of the orderlies may have mislaid his lighter."

"If a patient has dementia," Coffin said, "and a nursing home operator leaves lighters lying around, who's liable if the patient sets the place on fire? I'm just curious."

Dr. Branstool smiled weakly. "Detective," he said. "Really now. If we're going to be legalistic about this, I think Valley View wins that battle hands-down. It states clearly in our residential contract that any action by the patient that endangers or injures staff or residents will result in his or her immediate removal from the premises. We've been more than tolerant, Detective—mainly out of deference to you. But now, as I say, she has crossed the line into genuinely dangerous behavior. She *has* to go."

Coffin frowned. "How soon?"

"The facility in Sandwich will accept her tomorrow."

Coffin met Dr. Branstool's eyes. They were watery and blue behind their fake lenses. "Out of deference to me," Coffin said, "could you hold off for a few days? Give me a chance to look into the alternatives?"

"No one will take her, Detective. We've tried. But all right—I'm not unsympathetic to your plight, whatever my feelings are about your mother. Three days—then out she goes."

Coffin sat in his mother's room. His mother lay on the bed, watching the big TV, hands folded neatly across her chest. Her eyes were bright and fierce.

"I hate that little cocksucker," she said. "What's his name."

"Branstool."

"No, not that cocksucker"—she waved at the TV's bright screen—"*that* one." The TV was tuned to FOX News. A chubby little man with wet lips and a blond crew cut was standing in front of a chalkboard, writing feverishly. The sound was off.

"Oh, *that* cocksucker," Coffin said. "Everybody hates *him*."

"I shouldn't have set that crazy bitch's nightstand on fire," his mother said after a silence.

"No," Coffin said. "That wasn't good."

"It was supposed to be a joke. She thinks she's on a cruise, you know."

"I know."

"Well, it isn't fair," his mother said. "She gets to be on a cruise to freaking Puerto Rico and the rest of us are stuck in this craphole. It pisses me off."

"So it was a joke, Ma? You weren't trying to hurt her?"

"Oh, hell no—if I'd wanted to hurt her she'd damn well be hurt. I was just trying to screw with her. I waited 'til she was taking her nap and snuck in and set her box of Kleenex on fire. Once it got going pretty good I started yelling, 'Abandon ship! Abandon ship!' You should've seen her scamper out of there. I pissed my diaper, I laughed so hard. But then the damn lamp shade caught on fire and next thing you know the alarm's going off and the sprinkler's trying to kick on."

"Trying? It didn't work?"

"Nope. Kind of made a grinding noise but nothing came out. So fatso-the-nurse had to put it out with a fire extinguisher. Whoosh! Took about three seconds."

Coffin took a deep breath, let it out. They sat for another minute or two, not saying anything.

"So they're kicking me out," his mother said finally. "Good. I can't stand this dump. I don't know what I'm doing here, anyway—these people are all daffy."

"We'll see about that, Ma," Coffin said. "We will see about that."

"You're a good boy, Eddie," his mother said, reaching over to pat his hand. "You were always my favorite."

Eddie was Coffin's older brother, MIA in the jungles of Vietnam, almost certainly long dead. "Thanks, Ma," Coffin said. "I love you, too."

Coffin sat in the Crown Vic for a minute or two outside Gemma Skolnick's house, heater on and engine running. Wind again, the sun already low above the shingled rooftops on Brewster Street. Coffin turned on the radio—nothing but static except for WOMR, the local all-volunteer FM station. They were playing Irish music, something lively with fiddle and bagpipes, lots of fast little notes. It made Coffin's jaw clench; he turned it off.

"I am *so* going to regret this," he said, shutting off the Crown Vic's purring V8 and climbing out.

Gemma answered the door after the third knock, just as Coffin was about to give up and check her studio on Commercial Street, above the post office. She wore a short black kimono, a towel wrapped around her head like a turban. She held the kimono together with one hand; a pink cigarette burned in the other.

"*This* is a pleasant surprise," she said, throwing her arms around Coffin's neck and kissing him on the mouth. On her tiptoes, she was almost as tall as Coffin. "What's with the uniform?"

"I'm acting chief," Coffin said. "I'm supposed to wear it."

Gemma's bare legs were slick with lotion, her nipples stiffening against the black silk of her kimono. "You've put on weight," she said, giving his belly a pat. "I like a man with a little substance."

"That makes one of you," Coffin said.

"You'd better come in," she said. "It's freezing out here."

She lived in a converted barn that had, until a few years ago, housed a number of small artist's studios, but was now a big, open-floor-plan dwelling with a spacious loft upstairs. It had all been done in polished wood and stainless steel, and must have cost a bundle. Gemma was an artist, but didn't have a job that Coffin knew of. She was the kind of young woman who attracted wealthy gentlemen friends.

"I'm looking for Rudy," Coffin said, once Gemma had led him upstairs to the master suite, seated him on a stainless-steel chaise longue covered in spotted cowhide, and put a glass of bourbon in his hand. "He around?"

"Depends," Gemma said. Soul music drifted from speakers mounted in the rafters—a woman singing over a driving beat, horn section in the background. "What's he done now?"

"Probably nothing," Coffin said.

Gemma grinned. "Don't try to bullshit a bullshitter." She took the towel off her head and shook out her hair. Last spring's blond dreadlocks were gone—it was cut short, dyed a light pink.

She looked up, caught Coffin's eye, and dropped the kimono. She was naked underneath (*of course*, Coffin thought), firm, but with rounded hips and big breasts.

"See," she said, arms raised, back arched: ta-dah! "The carpet matches the drapes." Her pubic hair was topiaried into a neat heart shape, and dyed the same cotton-candy pink as her hair. "I figured what the hell, for once."

"You're incorrigible," Coffin said, as Gemma rummaged through a dresser and stepped into a black thong.

"You love it," Gemma said. She pulled on a shiny green bra, then stood regarding him for a moment, head tilted, arms crossed. "At least I think you do. Figured maybe I'd be seeing a bit more of you around here."

"Don't think I wasn't tempted," Coffin said. "Seriously."

"I know, I know," she said, wiggling into a pair of skinny jeans. "You've got a nice girlfriend."

"Who's pregnant."

"Holy shit, she's pregnant?" Gemma said, stopping mid-wiggle, looking at Coffin over her shoulder.

Her ass was spectacular, Coffin thought, framed for a moment between the black thong and the waistband of her jeans.

"The minute you quit trying," he said.

"Badda bing," Gemma said.

"Exactly. Plus, you're dating my uncle."

"Ha. You could call it that," she said. She zipped the jeans, pulled on a T-shirt. "Color me disenchanted."

Coffin sipped his bourbon, smoky and a little sweet, warm in his throat. "He's a busy guy."

Gemma smiled a slow half-smile. She sat down on the edge of the big, rumpled bed and crossed her legs. Her toenails were painted sparkly chartreuse, like a Stratocaster. "Busy in more ways than one," she said. She refilled her glass from the bottle of Rare Breed on the nightstand, stubbed out her cigarette and lit another.

"Sorry," Coffin said.

"After a while a girl wants to know what's what," Gemma said, swirling the ice in her glass. "God, slap me. I sound like I'm waiting to be asked to the fucking prom."

Coffin glanced at his watch. It was 4:52. He levered himself off the cowhide chaise. "Thanks for the drink," he said, setting his empty glass on the dresser. "And the excellent floor show."

"What," Gemma said, "that's it? No third degree? You're not even going to ask me where he is?"

"He's in town, but he's not staying with you. Now you see him, now you don't."

"You're practically psychic. And your uncle's a son of a bitch."

"I've known that son of a bitch all my life." Coffin put on his hat. "Nice to see you, Gemma," he said.

"Leaving so soon?" Gemma said. She sat back against the headboard, drew her knees up. "What's your hurry? You scared or something?"

"Terrified," Coffin said, trotting down the stairs.

"Sissy!" Gemma yelled after him.

Except for the narrow window that looked out over a landscape of sand and scrub pine, the exam rooms at Outer Cape Health could have been in almost any clinic anywhere. There was a white enamel exam table with a black, padded cushion, retractable chrome stirrups and a little pull-out step. There were two color diagrams on the wall: one of a human spine, the other of a human heart, and a wooden rack stocked with informational pamphlets with titles like

"Help With Smoking Cessation," and "Seasonal Depression: Treatment Can Help." A computer monitor and keyboard crouched on a built-in desk; beside them, a small swivel chair on which the nurse sat to take his blood pressure, the cuff tightening at his elbow, the air hissing out when the nurse released the valve. "Up a little bit since last time," the nurse said, making a note on Coffin's chart. "You been drinking coffee today?" She left, and after a short wait, there was a quick knock on the door and Dr. Sengupta stepped into the room.

Dr. Sengupta was a short, smiling man with a full beard. He shook Coffin's hand—up, down, release—in the little exam room and sat down. "Well," he said, "your cholesterol's elevated. Two twenty-six. What are you going to do about that?"

"Well, I—"

Sengupta crossed his legs at the knee. He wore purple socks. "Your good cholesterol's okay but not that great. Your bad cholesterol's much too high. What are you eating—cheeseburgers every day?"

"Well—"

"What about exercise? You've put on quite a bit of weight."

"My job's pretty demanding right now," Coffin said. "I don't have a lot of time."

"You must *make* time," Sengupta said, meeting Coffin's eyes. "Do you want a heart attack at fifty?"

"No," Coffin said.

"Fifty-one?"

"No."

"Fifty-two?"

"Ah—"

"Well," Sengupta said. "What are you going to do about that?"

Coffin waited a beat. "Watch my diet? Go to the gym?"

"Bingo!" said Sengupta. "I want to see you again in six months.

If there's no improvement, I'm going to put you on a medication to lower your cholesterol. We don't want to mess around here, okay?"

"Okay," Coffin said.

Sengupta jumped to his feet and stuck out a small, delicate hand. "Six months," he said.

"You know," Coffin said, "I'm sure you're very good at what you do, but your manner's kind of confrontational."

Sengupta smiled broadly. "Oh, yes," he said. "Patients say so all the time."

"Well," Coffin said, "what are you going to do about that?"

Coffin decided to stop at the Oyster Shack on his way home. It had been a long day, and he needed a drink. The place was quiet, Squid tending bar, Kotowski perched on his corner bar stool, poring over a slim, paperback volume. A couple of down-and-out fishermen sat a few stools down, watching ESPN on the wavery Zenith that squatted behind the bar. They were the only customers except for Pat—an old woman with steel gray hair, drinking Blue Ribbon draft, her dentures on the bar at her elbow, a lit cigarette clenched between the upper and lower plates.

Captain Nickerson stopped climbing the bars of his cage. "How's Frankie?" he called. "How's Frankie?"

"It's like déjà vu all over again," Coffin said, sitting next to Kotowski. "Where's Yelena and all her good-looking friends?"

"It's her day off. She's probably home, reading up on international finance."

"Really?"

"Yep," Kotowski said, sipping his bottled Newcastle. "She wants to go to Wharton and get an MBA, then work on Wall Street."

"Smart girl. If you can't fight the plutocracy, be the plutocracy."

Kotowski grunted. "Like you'd ever fight the plutocracy. You're one of their hired lackeys."

"Aren't lackeys supposed to make money?" Coffin said.

Squid sidled over. "Stooges make money," he said. "Lackeys and lickspittles not so much. What can I get you, boss?"

"Macallan. A little ice."

Squid poured a fat double and set it on a small, white paper napkin in front of Coffin. The scotch seemed to glow from within: *Like a jar of honey*, Coffin thought, *held in front of a candle flame.* Coffin sipped it, savoring the slow burn as it went down.

Kotowski waggled his book. It was about the size of a volume of poetry. "Seen this?" he said.

It was the annual town report, published every year by the board of selectmen, as required by statute. It listed every town official, whether elected or appointed, descriptions of their departments and duties, their budgets, their salaries, and telephone numbers. It contained transcripts of every town meeting, and a complete accounting of tax receipts and expenditures. It was a kind of official snapshot of the town government, in all of its various functions. It also contained a section called "Vital Statistics," which Kotowski was holding open under Coffin's nose. Page after page of marriages were listed, almost all of them same sex, almost all from out of town. Two pages of deaths. And, after the deaths, a notation of the number of births (names withheld out of respect for the parents' privacy): six boys and three girls—a grand total of nine.

"That's going to be some graduating class," Kotowski said. "Go, Fishermen!"

"Fisherpersons," Coffin said. "What's your point?"

"My point is that your kid is going to be lonely and weird. Who's he going to play with? You? Captain Cholesterol?"

Coffin shrugged. "A hideous fate."

"Exactly. It's practically child abuse!" Kotowski took a rumpled

pack of Camels from his T-shirt pocket, shook out a bent cigarette, and lit it. "You should get out of here, Coffin, you and your
girl," he said, smoke streaming from his nose. "She can teach yoga
anywhere. You can pretend to be a cop anywhere, more or less. Go
to some nice suburb. Some little *Leave It to Beaver* neighborhood
in the Midwest—'Mr. Coffin, can Billy come out to play?' Besides
your mother, what's keeping you here?"

"Besides my mother? My job. My pension. This place. Which is
allegedly smoke-free, by the way."

Kotowski took a deep drag, blew it out. "Ah," he said. "Tastes
like—freedom. So basically, nothing."

"Pretty much." Coffin sipped his scotch. "They're throwing her
out, you know. Sending her down to Sandwich where they can
manage her."

"I heard. So what are you going to do about that?"

Coffin stared at Kotowski for a second. "Not sure there's much
I *can* do."

"What about that little prick, what's his name?"

"Branstool."

"He looks like a guy with something to hide. Why don't you get
a search warrant and ransack his house, just to fuck with him?"

"With no probable cause? Good luck with that."

Kotowski spat out a fleck of tobacco. "Pussy. It's what your uncle would've done. With or without the warrant."

Coffin laughed. "You sound like my mother."

Chapter 10

In the parking lot, Coffin checked his watch: 6:45 and almost dark. There was just one vehicle on Shank Painter Road: an incongruous black Town Car, lights on high beam, gliding silently into town from the highway. The breeze was damp and raw. Coffin shivered, and wondered if it might not be an early winter, one of those years of howling winds and heavy snow. Provincetown would turn into a ghost town, all but cut off from the rest of the world, deserted except for people like him, the few hardy souls who had to stick around to keep the place from shutting down. Most years he liked the off-season, but now the thought of Provincetown's midwinter isolation filled him with dread: the same faces, day after day. The narrow streets filled with snow.

To Coffin's surprise, the Town Car turned into the Oyster Shack's parking lot and pulled up next to the Crown Vic, the front tire stopping about four inches from his toes. A dark-tinted rear window powered down, and a cloud of marijuana smoke rolled from the car's interior into the stiffening breeze, along with a blast of rock music—George Thorogood's raunchy version of "Who Do You Love?"

The passenger was a big man in his early sixties, gray-haired, thick through the neck and shoulders. "What it is, Frankie," he said. It was Coffin's Uncle Rudy.

The driver—Coffin could only see a bulky outline through the tinted window—switched off the Town Car's stereo.

"Always the dramatic entrance," Coffin said. "You got a chauffer, now?"

"My business manager," Rudy said. He turned to the driver. "Loverboy, shake hands with my nephew, Frankie."

The driver's door swung open, and a man climbed out. It seemed to Coffin that he took a long time to do it. He was about the size of two normal human beings—six foot ten, Coffin guessed, and at least three-sixty. He was brown-skinned, and had thick, black hair that hung in curls down to his shoulders. *Polynesian*, Coffin thought. *Samoan, maybe.*

"Loverboy?" Coffin said.

"My real name's Tāufa 'āhau Niutupu 'ivaha Topuo," the big man said, sticking out a hand. It was like shaking a piece of furniture. "But haole people never get it right."

"Why Loverboy?" Coffin said.

Loverboy shrugged. "They say I have a way with the ladies," he said. He spoke slowly, a nearly subsonic rumble. *The way a tree would talk*, Coffin thought.

"He's got a schlong the size of a freaking python," Rudy said. "Back home in Tonga he's a god king or a chief or something."

"My dad was the king's first cousin," Loverboy said. "I'm an MBA."

"Listen," Rudy said. "Don't worry about your ma. I'm on that prick Branstool like a cheap suit."

"Rudy—"

Rudy held up a hand, a fat joint between the tips of his thumb and forefinger. "You don't have to thank me. We're blood, Frankie. Am I right?"

"We're not blood. You're my father's sister's ex-husband."

"Whatever. It's taken care of."

"What did you do, Rudy?"

Coffin's uncle took a long toke, held the smoke a few seconds, then released it slowly. "Don't worry your pretty little head. Let's just say I'd be real surprised if Dr. Fuckface continues to be a problem." He held the smoldering spliff out to Coffin. "Want a hit? It's excellent stuff—Humboldt County, one hundred percent organic."

"No thanks," Coffin said. "Weed makes me paranoid."

"Just 'cause you're paranoid," Rudy said, "doesn't mean they ain't out to get you."

"There's another thing," Coffin said.

"How's your girlfriend?" Rudy said. "Something sexy about 'em when they're knocked up—they get so *female*, you can almost smell the estrogen. You're not sticking around here, are you, once the baby's born?"

"Of course I'm sticking around," Coffin said. "Where would I go?"

"You could go anywhere." Rudy waved the joint, then puffed at it to keep it lit. "Sell the house, take the money and run. Even with the market down the place is still worth a few hundred grand. This is no place to raise a kid, Frankie. Trust me—I know."

"Tell me about 376 Bradford Street, Rudy."

Rudy shrugged. "I owned it. Some fucknut burned it down. What do you want me to say? I didn't do it?"

"Sure. Humor me."

"Look, Frankie," Rudy said, black eyes gazing up at Coffin from the Town Car's dark leather interior. "I'm a businessman. And the first rule of business is, shit happens. Second rule is, when shit happens, money always changes hands. Know what the third rule is?"

"Rudy—"

"The third rule of business, Frankie, is that when money changes hands, make damn sure you get your share." Rudy pinched out what was left of the joint between his thumb and forefinger and flicked it out the window. "You know the weirdest thing about pregnant chicks?"

"Rudy, for Christ's sake—"

"Their asses get square. One day their asses are nice and round like always, next day"—Rudy snapped his fingers—"square. It's one of the great mysteries."

"Oh my God."

"Nice meeting you," Loverboy said. He levered himself back into the purring Town Car, shifted into reverse and let it roll in a slow, backward arc onto Shank Painter Road.

"Don't let your meat loaf, Frankie," Rudy called, the window gliding silently shut, the big car surging forward and disappearing around the bend, going much too fast.

Jamie was fresh from the shower, a big white towel still wrapped around her head. Coffin stood behind her, kissing her neck, both hands on her belly's taut bulge.

"You know the weirdest thing about being pregnant?" Jamie said, standing naked in the bedroom.

She was gorgeous, Coffin thought. He cupped her breasts: They were heavy and full, the nipples big, suddenly brown.

"Tell me," Coffin said.

"I haven't seen my pubic hair in three weeks—and I guess I won't see it again 'til after the baby's born. Freaky, right?"

The whole day had been full of these odd echoes, Coffin

thought—now a little replay of his encounter with Gemma, but without the complicated agenda. He brushed Jamie's dark pubic ruff with his fingertips. It had grown luxuriant in the last month or so, longer and thicker, spreading nearly from hip bone to hip bone. "Still there," Coffin said, "and then some."

"I kind of gave up on the hedge-trimming," Jamie said squirming her hips a little against his hand. "Out of sight, out of mind."

Coffin rolled her clitoris gently under the tip of his middle finger. "Works for me," he said. "Variety is good."

Jamie sighed, squirmed her backside against him. "What you're doing right there? *That's* good," she said.

Coffin changed directions.

"That, too," Jamie said, taking a sharp little breath.

"See?" Coffin said. "Variety."

"Well," Coffin said later. "No Frank aversion this time."

"That's the good news," Jamie said.

"There's bad news?"

Jamie yawned. She was lying on her side, covers pulled up to her chin, Coffin spooning behind her. "You know that nesting thing women are supposed to do when they're pregnant?"

"Yeah?"

"I think it's kicking in."

"Uh-oh."

"How are you with paint?"

"Choosing or applying?"

"I choose. You apply."

"It's not my best thing, but I'll get the hang of it." Coffin yawned, tried not to doze off.

"Frank?"

"Hmm?"

"I know this is your mom's place and everything."

"But."

"But how would you feel about, you know, making some changes?"

"Great."

"I mean, it's kind of *dark* in here, all this mahogany and oak—and all these chairs are crazy uncomfortable. I'm thinking sell some of the antiques. Get some new furniture that human beings can actually sit on."

The stuffed owl on top of the wardrobe stared down at them, ear tufts awry, something like outrage in its yellow glass eyes.

"Can we get rid of the taxidermy, too?" Coffin said.

"Everything but the goat."

"Did you not tell me two weeks ago you got the feeling the goat was looking at your ass?"

"*You* told *me* that your dead father was haunting that thing. I'm not selling your father's ghost on eBay."

"Can I ask a practical question?"

"How are we going to pay for all this great new stuff?"

"Bingo," Coffin said.

"Did I ever tell you about my trust fund?"

"You said it was small—no big deal."

"It was. Ten years ago."

"And now?"

"Well, my grandfather wasn't really a good investor. He just bought stock in companies that made cool stuff. And he thought Apple was kind of cool."

"Holy crap."

"So he bought a couple thousand shares of Apple for, like, twenty dollars a share."

"Can we get a car? I hate my car. Nothing fancy—just a nice Lexus, like Mancini's, but bigger."

"Frank. The money's for the baby."

"Babies need cars."

"I was thinking minivan."

"Oh my God," Coffin said. "I'm going to be a guy who drives a minivan."

It was late, almost 2:30 A.M., and Officer Pete Pinsky was lonely, cold, and bored. He sat in his squad car at the corner of Standish and Commercial streets, trying to keep warm. He'd thrown on a lightweight uniform jacket as he was leaving Town Hall—it had been warmer then—but the temperature had dropped in the last hour or so, and the wet fog had rolled in. Worse, the squad car's heater wasn't working again, and *that* wouldn't have been so bad if it wasn't for the no-smoking rule, which, Pinsky knew, actually meant "no smoking unless you roll the window down." Late, dark, lonely, too cold for October, no traffic, nobody walking or riding a bike—just the fog blowing around like wet laundry on a clothesline. Pinsky took a drag from his cigarette and tried to keep his teeth from chattering. What he wanted to do was start the car and drive home to his fiancée, LaWonda, who would cook him up a shrimp étouffée, give him one of her patented massages, and then love him long and strong until he begged her to let him sleep.

Love, he thought, was the biggest mystery of all. He'd grown up the one half-Jewish kid in his school in Pomeroy, Ohio—never even knew any black people, straight as an arrow, always had the hots for the cute, blond cheerleader types who never gave him the time of day. And now he was engaged to a drop-dead gorgeous, black, six foot four inch, preoperative transsexual who was hung like a mule and cooked like a Creole angel. Only love could do that to a man, Pinsky thought. Only love. His tenth high school reunion was coming up—he couldn't wait to take LaWonda back to Meigs High School in Pomeroy and show her off.

There was no sound except the slight crackle of static from his police radio, the slop of the harbor waves on the town beach—somewhere a faint clinking sound, rhythmic, the wind talking in one of its thousand voices. Then someone rapped on the passenger window, and Officer Pinsky nearly crapped his drawers.

"Hey, cop," a man said. It was Ticky, one of the local homeless men. He was a brain-rotted alcoholic, a gluehead, skinny, scruffy, and stinky. His face always looked to Pinsky like it had been stuck on to someone else's head and didn't fit right—it twitched and rippled uncontrollably, with no connection to whatever it was that Ticky might be saying or thinking.

"Jesus, Ticky," Pinsky said. "Try not to sneak up on a man like that."

Ticky laughed a high, warbling laugh. "Did I scare ya, cop? Ha?" He held up two fingers—the universal gesture. "Hey, you ain't got a spare smoke by any chance?"

"You're starting to annoy me, Ticky," Pinsky said. "Go pass out somewhere, why don't you."

Ticky put his face close to the half-open window. "I'm just messin' with ya, cop," he said. "But listen—somebody left the door to the Fish Palace open a couple inches. Thought I'd better tell somebody, else I'd prob'ly get blamed for it."

"I'm moved," Pinsky said, "by your dedication to public safety."

"Gotta take a piss," Ticky said. He staggered off into the fog, heading for town beach.

"Try not to freeze to death," Pinsky called after him.

He climbed out of the car, straightened his hat, took his baton from the rack inside the squad and slipped it into its holster. "'Cause I'm the guy has to frickin' clean it up if you do," he said to himself.

The Fish Palace's glass front door was, indeed, open a couple of inches as Ticky had said. Pinsky ran a finger over the door frame; it was bent outward under the latch—somebody'd sprung it with a pry bar. Despite the ADT sticker in the front window, no alarm had sounded.

It was very dark inside; a dim wash of ambient streetlight filtered in through the big rear windows, and Pinsky could just make out the silhouettes of a few chairs that had been turned upside down and placed on top of the tables. *So's they can vacuum*, Pinsky thought. The shadows were very deep, and the long, windowless kitchen, which stretched to his left between the front door and the dining room, was pitch-black. The hair on the back of his neck prickled. He crouched down, listening. There was almost no sound—just the burbling of the water filters in the big lobster tank, a few feet ahead and to his left.

Pinsky slid his big Maglite out of its loop. "Police!" he said, with as much authority as he could muster. "Anybody in here?" There was no reply, no sound except for the lobster tank's faint gurgle, no movement anywhere in the dark restaurant. He clicked the Maglite on, panning its beam in a slow arc across the dining room. The Maglite flickered, dimmed, died.

"Oh, shit," Pinsky said. "Not *now*, for Christ's sake." It was one of those moments, he thought, where you feel like you've got an extra sense, like a shark: sharks could "see" electromagnetic fields, he knew, he'd seen it on the Discovery Channel. The magnetic field in the Fish Palace was seriously screwed up—the pried-open door, the dying Maglite—and just now the feeling that somebody was definitely *looking* at him. He stood, felt for a light switch, but couldn't find one.

"Fuck, man," he said. He gave the Maglite a shake and the beam came back, weak and intermittent. He keyed his shoulder radio. "Marge?" he said, half whispering.

The dispatcher's voice crackled into his earpiece. "Pinsky? That you?"

"Yeah, listen—I'm down at the Fish Palace. Somebody pried the door open and I'm inside. I don't think there's anybody in here, but the lights ain't working and the whole deal just don't feel right. Send over a backup unit, would you?"

"That's a ten-four. Sergeant Winters is on. She's checking an alarm call up at the Heights. I'll have her run right over."

Pinsky took a deep breath. It was in the kitchen, he thought. Whatever it was that was watching him. The big open kitchen that customers passed on their way to the dining room; the kitchen with its big commercial ranges and refrigerators, everything in stainless steel, oversized copper-bottomed pots and pans hanging from metal racks overhead. The workspace was separated from customer traffic by a wide counter, where the cooks plunked down the finished orders—steamed lobster, watery corn, microwaved potato—hefted on big trays by the waitstaff and delivered to tourists wearing plastic bibs. Pinsky stood on his tiptoes, trained the Maglite behind the counter as well as he could, aiming it down toward floor level—nobody back there, he was pretty sure. The Maglite dimmed to almost nothing, came back.

"Come on, baby," Pinsky said. "Don't die on me now—you've got a fucking lifetime guarantee!"

Nobody back there, he thought, but still, he could feel it—*somebody's looking at me.* The lobster tank burbled. The lobsters. Pinsky laughed. "The fucking *lobsters*," he said, training his flickering light on the tank.

It was a big tank, maybe four feet long by three feet wide and two feet deep, standing behind and slightly above the counter, about halfway between the front door and the dining room. It was full of murky water; the filtering system bubbled fervently.

Dozens of lobsters strode around in its depths, climbing over one another or staring with bright bead-eyes out at the red-haired police officer with his flashlight. They varied in size from little pound and a quarter chix to a few venerable giants of five pounds or more. They seemed excited: waving their antennae, bonking each other with their banded claws. Three or four swarmed slowly over a melon-sized object that rested on the tank's slimy bottom. In the split second before Pinsky dropped his sputtering Maglite, killing it once and for all, he realized that the thing in the lobster tank was a human head. It wore glasses. Its expression, he would remember even years later as he told the story yet again to his fellow officers, seemed remarkably bland.

Chapter 11

T he house was on fire. Coffin ran to the stairs, but they were awash
in flame—a storm of smoke and sparks roared up from the living
room, hot little embers showered onto the rugs, Coffin's arms, his bare
feet.

"Jamie!" he called, but she was gone. For a brief moment he wondered if she'd set the fire; and then he thought that he might have, just
a small fire in the living room, never intending the whole house to burn
down. Then he remembered the baby—the baby! He ran to the baby's
room, which was filling with smoke. Huge stuffed animals leaned
against the walls, baring their sharp teeth—a lion, a monkey, a dragon.
He had to save the baby—he could hear it crying out in its crib, catlike,
alarmed. Somewhere a phone was ringing—it sounded very far away.

"I've got you," Coffin said, reaching for the baby, which had turned
into a sleek and glistening harbor seal. "I've got you . . ."

Coffin sat up with a start. The phone was ringing. "Jesus fuck," he
said. His T-shirt was damp with sweat.

"Phone," Jamie said, still asleep.

There was no smoke, no fire. Coffin answered the phone.

"Frank?" It was Lola. "Sorry to call so late."

"What's up?"

"We've got a homicide. And you're really, really not going to like it."

Twenty minutes later, Coffin was standing in front of the big glass lobster tank at the Fish Palace. "Son of a bitch," he said, vision blurring. "It's Dr. Branstool."

Branstool's hair floated like kelp. A lobster appeared to be nibbling his ear. Coffin put a hand out, steadied himself on the varnished oak countertop.

"You all right, Frank?" Lola said. "Maybe you'd better sit down."

"Yeah," said one of the EMT's, a stout, mustached man in his forties named Johnny Sousa. "You ain't lookin' so good, Frankie." He turned to Lola. "Is this his dead body phobia? I heard about that—thought it was a joke. Funny thing, a cop with a fear of dead bodies."

"They got a name for that," said another EMT. He was Sousa's physical opposite—slim and clean-shaven—Coffin didn't know his name. "Necrophobia—fear of death and dead bodies. There's, like, hundreds of different phobias you could have. Know what homichlophobia is?"

Sousa shook his head. "No freakin' idea."

"Fear of fog," the slender EMT said. "How about bufonophobia?"

Coffin waved a hand to get their attention. "Guys?"

Sousa winced. "Sorry, Frankie."

For a long minute no one said anything. They stood, gazing

into the tank. A big two-pounder crouched on Branstool's head, delicately waggling its mandibles.

"You know," Sousa said finally, "it puts a whole new spin on the idea of a lobster dinner."

Coffin and Lola stuck around, along with the two EMTs, waiting for the coroner to arrive from Chatham. Jeff Skillings was there, too, and Pinsky—the former summer cop that Coffin had decided to hire permanently—looking pale but resolute. It was late, almost 3:00 A.M., but a small crowd of onlookers huddled in the cold across the street, in front of the Captain Alden.

While they waited, a couple of state police detectives Coffin didn't know pulled up in a red, unmarked Mustang. They were big, burly men with close-cropped hair, all business in nearly identical jeans and leather car coats. They flashed their badges for the local cops, then went about the task of documenting the crime scene, each with a silver Flip Cam.

"Where's Tony?" Lola said. "He usually comes out for these kinds of things."

"Yeah," Pinsky said. "I'm surprised he'd want to miss a deal like this." Pinsky was small and skinny, with brick red hair. Coffin hadn't thought much of him at first. Pinsky had had trouble coming to terms with Provincetown's LGBT population—now the majority in Provincetown, even in the off-season—his first summer on the job, and Coffin had been certain that it wouldn't work out. But then Pinsky met LaWonda, a very tall and very beautiful African American transgendered woman, and his attitude had changed markedly for the better. He and LaWonda moved in together, and Pinsky quickly evolved into a kind of unofficial liaison between the PPD and the transgendered community. He didn't look like much, Coffin thought, but he was turning out to be a pretty good cop.

"Tony's in Boston," Coffin said. "Or should be. I gave him some leave time. He's under some stress."

"Is it about them flyin' saucers of his?" Pinsky said. "Seems kind of crazy to me."

"Flying saucers?" Lola said. "The ones over Pilgrim Lake?"

Coffin's head was beginning to hurt. "Not you, too," he said.

Lola shrugged. "I haven't seen them, but Kate has. She said the Cape Air pilots see stuff out here all the time. She thinks it's probably experimental military aircraft from the Air National Guard base."

"That ain't what Tony thinks," Pinsky said. "He thinks it's aliens, and they're coming for him."

Lola laughed. "Poor Tony."

Pinsky took a pack of Camel Lights out of his shirt pocket and lit one. "What do you think, Chief?" he said. "Ever seen a UFO?"

"Those things'll kill you," Coffin said.

Pinsky grinned, offered the pack. "Want one?"

Coffin took a cigarette, puffing it to life while Pinsky lit it with a plastic Bic.

"I'm telling," Lola said.

"You wouldn't."

"I most certainly would."

Coffin dropped the cigarette, crushed it out with the toe of his boot. "You women are relentless," he said.

"Seriously," Pinsky said. "Ever seen anything like that out here, Chief?"

"Just some lights in the sky over Herring Cove," Coffin said. "They say it's jet traffic, backed up from Logan."

"It's a funny business." Pinsky took a meditative drag on his cigarette. "On the one hand, you got stuff that looks like flying saucers all the way back in prehistoric cave paintings. On the other hand, everybody you see that's a big UFO buff is either a scam artist or crazy as a shit-house mouse. Kinda hard to sort it all out."

"If they're really here," Sousa said, "it's the biggest government cover-up in history. By far."

"If they're really here," Lola said, "what's with the cat-and-mouse game? Show your little green selves already."

The two state police detectives put their cameras back in their coat pockets and stepped out onto the sidewalk.

"You're Coffin, right?" the taller one said.

The shorter one lit a cigarette. "You're like a freakin' living legend."

"This is my partner, Sergeant Winters," Coffin said. "And this is Officer Pinsky."

"Bitters," the tall one said. He stuck out a big, bony hand, and Coffin shook it.

"Hump," said the short one.

"Hump?" Lola said.

"His real name's Humphrey," Bitters said. "He goes by Hump."

"Anybody know the guy in the tank?" Hump asked.

"His name's Branstool," Coffin said. "He ran the nursing home."

"Where's the rest of him?"

Coffin shrugged. "Hasn't turned up yet. Where's Mancini?"

"Home fuckin' his new missus." Bitters snickered. "If he's got any sense."

"Wouldn't count on him having any sense," Hump said.

Coffin rubbed his chin. He needed sleep. Failing that: coffee, a cigarette. "He remarried?"

"Yeah. Trophy blonde. Maybe five years older than his daughter. He'll come out tomorrow, probably, along with the CSS boys."

"I thought all the Crime Scene Services guys got laid off," Pinsky said.

"There's still a couple of teams," Bitters said. "Part-timers." He made a gesture: a loose fist bobbing up and down over his groin. "Mancini'll probably put in a request, since it's high profile." He turned to Hump. "We're done, right?"

Hump pursed his lips. "Yep," he said. "Unless we're forgetting something."

"I'm hungry," Bitters said, climbing into the Mustang. "Let's put the flashers on and see how fast we can get to Denny's in Hyannis."

"There's no Denny's in Hyannis," Hump said, squeezing his broad bulk into the passenger seat. "You're thinking Friendly's. There's a Friendly's in Hyannis, but it ain't open now."

"The hell there isn't a Denny's in Hyannis," Bitters said.

"Bet you twenty bucks," Hump said. They shut the doors. The Mustang's engine rumbled to life, and they disappeared around the corner on Standish Street.

The coroner pulled up in a gleaming white van with SHERMAN FUNERAL HOME painted on the side in gold script. The coroner, Sherman, was an undertaker in Chatham. He and his assistant climbed out of the van. Sherman was sixty or so, thin and saggy-faced. Coffin had never seen him without a Pall Mall stuck in the corner of his mouth.

Sherman whistled softly, peering at the head submerged in the lobster tank. The lobsters had nibbled away some of Branstool's lower lip. "My oh my," he said. "Someone's had a *very* bad day."

Coffin's vision swam, refocused. "This doesn't get to you?" he said. "Even a little?"

"Sure it gets to me." Sherman lit a fresh cigarette from the smoldering butt of his old one, then flipped the butt out the door and into the gutter. "Just 'cause I'm a funeral director don't mean I'm not human." He pulled on one long, black rubber glove, then the other. "Where's the giblets?"

"Haven't turned up yet," Coffin said.

Sherman sent his assistant to the van for a large Ziploc bag and a folding stepstool. When the assistant returned Sherman climbed up onto the stepstool and reached into the tank with a gloved hand.

Lola winced. "Oh shit," she said. "Here we go."

"I ain't got nobody," Sherman sang, slapping a couple of hungry lobsters aside. "Nobody, nobody cares for meeeee!" He grabbed a fistful of Branstool's hair and hauled the dripping head out of the tank. "Who does this remind you of?" he said, holding the head aloft, something like triumph on his baggy face.

Coffin and the assistant stared blankly. "Perseus, you ignoramuses," Sherman said. "Brandishing the head of Medusa! Jesus Christ—don't you people read?"

As Sherman and his assistant climbed into their van and drove off, Roz O'Malley oozed up to the curb in her green Cadillac. She was small, olive-skinned, Coffin's age. She wore rubber duck boots, a fur coat thrown over a flannel nightgown. She was Coffin's distant cousin on his mother's side; they'd gone to school together, even dated briefly as high school juniors. Roz had gone on to marry Johnny O'Malley, owner of the Fish Palace. He handled the money and she worked the hostess podium—the last line of defense against the lowing herds of summer tourists, waiting in long lines for their early bird specials. Then Johnny died and left the place to her. She popped out of the Cadillac like a cork out of a bottle.

"What the fuck," she said, looking up at the Fish Palace's peeling façade, the neon lobsters hanging dark in its front windows. "It's not on fire."

"It's not quite as bad as that," Coffin said.

Roz turned on him. The top of her head came up to his sternum. "*Bad*? You think a fire would be *bad*? Do you have any idea how much work it is, running this dump?"

"Well—"

"I've got a heart condition, Frankie—an arrhythmia. On account of the stress—that's what my cardiologist says. You ever had an arrhythmia?"

"I don't think so."

"Well, it sucks. You think you're gonna freakin' die, but you don't—you just feel like crap. But do I get a day off from the work and the worry? No, I do not."

"Why not sell the place?" Coffin said.

Roz laughed, a sharp little bark. "Don't think I haven't tried. Know what the profit margin is in the restaurant business?"

Coffin shook his head.

"Two percent, Frankie—two percent! And you make it all on liquor—you give the food away at break-even. You'd have to be a freaking masochist to get into it, especially now with all the taxes and regulation. No smoking! No trans fats!" She paused, shook her head. "Then you got your hepatitis outbreaks, your health inspectors with their hand in your pocket, your food poisoning lawsuits, holy shit! One bad clam could put me out of business, Frankie—one bad clam! The place is eating me alive with repairs—the roof leaks, the plumbing's shot—*and* I suddenly got freakin' immigration agents crawlin' up my ass, and now I gotta pay *them* off. If I thought I could get away with it, I'd burn the fucker down myself." Roz spread her arms—an elaborate shrug. "So if it's not on fire, what the *fuck* am I doing here at three in the freakin' A.M.? I get a call says there's a situation. What's up?"

Coffin pointed at Pinsky. "The officer here was checking on a possible break-in. The front door was pried open."

"That's right, ma'am," Pinsky said, lightly pinching the brim of his hat. "When I entered the premises"—he hesitated, searching for words—"I found a . . . body part."

"I'm sorry," Roz said. "You found a *body part*? What the fuck does that mean?"

"A human body part, ma'am," Pinsky said.

"He found a guy's head in the lobster tank," Coffin said.

Roz's eyes widened. "Holy shit," she said. "Who was it? Anybody I know?"

"Dr. Branstool—the guy that runs Valley View."

"That little weasel? Why was his head in *my* lobster tank?"

Coffin shrugged, hands in his jacket pockets. "Good question."

Roz scratched her earlobe. "Lobsters are carnivores," she said. "Did you know that?"

Coffin nodded. "Yep."

"They mostly eat crabs and stuff, whatever they can catch on the seafloor."

"If you say so," Coffin said. A faint, reddish glow had risen just above the horizon to the southeast. Not dawn, Coffin thought, checking his watch—it was too small, too close, and too early.

"What's-his-name's head," Roz said. "Was it—intact?"

"Mostly," Coffin said, after a beat.

Roz closed her eyes. "Aw, shit, Frankie," she said. "Do you have any idea what those fucking crustaceans cost me? What am I supposed do with a tankful of lobsters that ate some guy's head?"

"Maybe you could sell 'em as souvenirs," Pinsky said.

"Do you smell smoke?" Coffin said. Just then the wail of a siren pierced the wind and the darkness—a fire truck roaring east on Bradford.

Pinsky's shoulder radio crackled. He thumbed the button. "Yeah, Marge."

"You done at the Fish Palace?" the dispatcher said. "Big fire at St. Mary's."

Roz threw up her hands. "St. Mary's? *St. Mary's*? What kind of God would burn his own house down and leave this place standing?"

Pinsky looked at Coffin.

"Why don't you tape off the door here and then head home," Coffin said. "Ask Marge to call Tony and tell him to get his ass in to work—leave's canceled. Lola and I are heading for St. Mary's right now."

Chapter 12

St. Mary's of the Harbor was a pretty, 1970s-era Episcopal church that sat on the harbor side of Commercial Street in Provincetown's east end, commanding a broad view of the water, from Wood End to the long sweep of beach at North Truro. Coffin had never been inside. He'd been raised nominally Catholic; his parents had dragged him off to mass at St. Peter's at Christmas and Easter, but neither his mother nor his father had been particularly interested in religion.

Like most of the buildings in town, St. Mary's was a wood-frame structure finished in cedar shingles—a satisfying meal for the fire that roared like a hungry animal in its sanctuary, gnawed its windowsills, and licked the edges of its roof. The church was not yet fully engulfed, but Coffin knew there was little hope of saving it, even with outside help. Both of Provincetown's working pumpers were in the parking lot, delivering their measly spritzes to the flames with little effect, aside from a lot of hissing and steam.

Walt Macy was there, along with Provincetown's full contingent of volunteer firefighters. The crew of EMTs Coffin had just seen at the Fish Palace rolled up behind the Crown Vic, lights flashing.

"Busy night," Macy said. He stood in the parking lot, thumbs in the suspenders of his big fireman's pants.

"No joke," Coffin said. "What are the odds here?"

"Lousy." Macy shook his head. "We've got a pumper inbound from Truro, and another on the way from Eastham, but these frame buildings go up like torches—especially when you pour gas on 'em."

"Another one, then? You sure?"

Macy shrugged. "I'm no expert in this stuff—I mean, I'm a pharmacist, right? But just judging from how much of the building was involved by the time we got here, and how fast the fire's grown since then, you gotta figure there's an accelerant involved."

"He's escalating," Lola said. "Jesus, what's next?"

"What's bigger than the Episcopal church?" Coffin said.

A crowd of about fifty onlookers had gathered—neighbors, insomniacs, and police-scanner junkies, Coffin thought. They looked cold—the night was damp and unseasonably chilly—and, for the first time, afraid. It was one thing to watch a shed or an empty developer's folly burn to the ground, another thing entirely when a structure as central to the community as St. Mary's was on fire.

A lime yellow, 1960s-vintage pumper sirened to a rattling halt less than a foot from the parked Crown Vic, and a team of yellow-coated volunteers from Truro jumped out. There was a shouted conversation between Truro's chief and Walt Macy about where the next closest hydrant was—the pumpers from Provincetown were hooked up to a hydrant across the street—the two chiefs pointing this way and that before coming to a decision and sending a couple of firemen scurrying off with a hydrant wrench and a thick black hose.

A small, slender man dressed in a raincoat and pajamas rode

into the parking lot on a bicycle. A stocky woman firefighter tried to wave him away, but he let the bike fall with a clatter and elbowed past her. "Oh my God," he said, pushing his hands through his hair—it was sandy, thinning. "What in the *hell* have you done?"

"Father Brian?" Macy said. "I almost didn't recognize you."

The man turned, smiled a weak smile. "Yes, it's me." He looked down at the pajama legs sticking out from under his raincoat. "Out of uniform, I suppose. How bad is it?"

"Honestly?" Macy said. "I don't know. We're going to try to get a hose inside, see if we can put some water on the base of the fire. If it's not too far along already, we may be able to save the structure."

Father Brian nodded glumly. "Please tell your men to be careful. And women."

"Well," Macy said, "if it's too hot, we won't go in. We're talking volunteers here."

"What in the hell has *who* done?" Coffin said.

The priest jumped a little bit. "I'm sorry, what?"

Coffin took his shield out of his pocket, held it up. "You said 'Oh my God, what in the *hell* have you done?' I'm curious who you were referring to."

"I said that? Out loud?"

Coffin nodded.

Father Brian turned pink. "I was referring to God. We haven't been getting along lately."

A couple of firemen in full breathing apparatus had dragged a canvas hose toward St. Mary's front door. They threw the door open, knelt down, and pointed the hose at the base of the fire. At their signal, the tall, skinny fireman standing next to the pumper opened a gleaming brass valve. Water gushed from the pumper, thoroughly dousing Walt Macy before the skinny fireman could turn it off and connect the canvas hose to the proper valve.

Coffin shook his head—he half expected it to rattle. "*Who* hasn't been getting along?"

"God and I. I've been very angry at him."

"You've been angry at God?" Lola said. "Are you allowed to do that?"

"I'm thirty-eight years old and I've got a prostate the size of a softball," Father Brian said, eyes magnified behind thick glasses. "My wife left me for a bass player in Chatham. My fourteen-year-old daughter just got her boyfriend's name tattooed on her neck. Know what his name is?"

Coffin and Lola shook their heads.

"Jeremy. Want to guess how the genius tattoo artist spelled it?"

"J-E-R-M-Y?" Coffin said.

"Bingo!" Father Brian cried.

"Ouch," Lola said.

Father Brian spread his arms. "So I *think* I'm *allowed* to be mad at God, thank you very much." He waved loosely toward the flames billowing from St. Mary's belfry. "I mean, *look* at this. Just look at it!"

Coffin looked. The fire was strange and beautiful, roaring from the windows, speaking in rough tongues. It was as primal and fierce as anything he could imagine, a lovely animal, alive and hungry. He felt an odd almost-memory beginning to surface—something like déjà vu: the burning church, bare trees, harbor gleam in low moonlight. He tried to imagine himself inside the dark sanctuary—gas gurgling from the can, the fumes, the soft scritch of the lighter—but the image wouldn't solidify. It hung in the air for a moment like an interrupted dream and then vanished. Coffin shivered. From the cold, he wondered, or from teetering just on the edge of some kind of discovery?

"You know what's going on at Saint Peter's right now?" Father Brian said.

Lola raised her eyebrows, shook her head.

Father Brian's lip curled into a sneer. "Nothing, that's what. Not a godda—" He stopped himself, took a deep breath. "Gosh darned thing. Saint-freaking *Peter's* isn't burning to the ground while a bunch of guys in big rubber pants trip all over themselves trying to squirt water at it." He pointed an accusing finger at the sky. "Play favorites much?"

Lola shrugged. "I'm one of those people that thinks God is kind of a universal energy. You know—nature. I don't think I could get mad at nature."

Father Brian laughed—a couple of loud barks. "*Nature,*" he said. "Must be nice."

The two firefighters at the church door managed to get their hose working and were advancing slowly into the building, one heavy step at a time. A loud hissing and a cloud of steam escaped from the open door just before the big, east-facing stained-glass window shattered and fell in bright, glinting shards into the parking lot. A thick tongue of flame shot from the window's empty socket, blackening the eaves.

"Nice move, God," Father Brian said, under his breath.

"Excuse us, Father," Coffin said. "Sounds like you and God have some things to work out."

"You're telling *me,*" Father Brian said.

There was a great clanging crash from inside the church, an eruption of sparks from the blown-out window. The two firemen came stumbling out, dragging the bucking, squirting hose behind them.

"What the hell was that?" Macy shouted.

The shorter of the two firefighters took off his breathing apparatus—he was red-faced and sweaty. "Pipe organ down," he said. "Frickin' thing just missed us."

"Oh *thanks*, God," Father Brian muttered. "Thanks a *lot.*"

Coffin tilted his head toward the street and started walking.

Lola followed. When they were out of earshot, Coffin said, "Listen, can you handle things here? Let's call in Skillings to help secure the area. I've got to follow up on Branstool—find out if there's family to notify, run over to his place and, you know—"

"Find the rest of him?"

"Bingo."

"No problem. Jeff can handle the traffic, I'll fire up the video camera." She paused. "You sure you're okay? I mean, if you find the body and all?"

Coffin grinned, not sure at all. "Yes, dear," he said. He glanced at his watch: 3:45. "Where the hell is Tony?"

When the two cops went back to their car—the pretty girl cop rummaging in the trunk, the tall one with the mustache talking on the radio—the man in the gray hoodie decided he'd seen enough. He knew what was next: they'd videotape the crowd like they had at the condo fire, and he didn't want any part of that. He turned and walked away from the cops, casual, hands in his pockets, heading east on Commercial Street. Just another guy in a guy suit, walking home after a night at the bars.

He concentrated on walking slowly, keeping to the inland side of the street where a tall hedge threw a shadow over the sidewalk. He must have been nearly invisible, he thought. Another fire engine roared past—a big red and white one from Eastham—siren howling, lights a dizzying whirl of color. *All good,* he thought, *the more noise and commotion, the less chance anyone will notice me.* But a few seconds later, when the fire truck had pulled up at the church and killed its siren, he heard a voice behind him.

"Excuse me," it said.

A woman's voice. He kept walking, hood up, head down. Footsteps coming up behind him.

"Sir? Excuse me!"

The lady cop! The lady cop was following him! He didn't turn around. He tried not to speed up. He was almost at the corner of Atkins Lane, a dark, block-long private way that connected to Bradford Street. Footsteps quick behind him—closer. He turned into Atkins Lane and broke into a run, sneakers crunch-crunching on the pale road surface—crushed oyster shell, gleaming faintly in the dim trickle of streetlight. He ducked left again between a couple of darkened houses, staying low, hidden in deep shadow. He stopped, flattened himself behind a shed, then crouched down, watching the road, listening.

Coffin yawned. It was very late—and more than anything, he wanted to go home, crawl into bed next to Jamie and go to sleep, untroubled by dreams of fire. Instead he was driving out to Pilgrim Heights in North Truro, to the house where Dr. Branstool had lived until sometime that evening.

The good news, if you could call it that, was that Truro's police chief would be waiting at the house when Coffin got there. The thought of going in alone had made the hair on the back of Coffin's neck prickle, though he couldn't have admitted it to Lola. The bad news was that while Chief Willoughby had a great depth of experience in handing out traffic citations, settling domestic disputes, and responding to off-season burglar alarms (99 percent of which were false, Coffin knew), he was unlikely to be much use in the event that Branstool's murderer had chosen to stick around. The chances were slim, Coffin thought, but still—he would have been happier if Lola had come along.

The wind had died, and the fog hung in low patches over the highway. It was still dark, the horizon just gray to Coffin's left, above the long march of dunes between Route 6 and the Atlantic.

He passed Pilgrim Lake, flat and still as a sheet of glass, and the sad, romantic summer cottages at Beach Point, along the parallel stretch of 6A—Shore Road, to the locals—just before the highway started to rise toward High Head. The cottages had been there since 1931, somehow surviving the postwar onslaught of tourist motels, standing in a precise, compact row—tiny, identical, white with green trim, each one named after a different flower: Zinnia, Dahlia, Lilac, Wisteria—like the daughters of an obsessive gardener. Coffin had never stayed in one—why would he?—but still, they filled him with a bleak nostalgia: they were relics of a lost time, a time of modest expectations.

Something moved in the fog, just at the edge of Coffin's peripheral vision, close to the car—a *man*, appearing out of nowhere, suddenly *in* the roadway—Coffin swerved, stomped on the brake, expecting to hear a hard thud as the Crown Vic's black plastic grille crushed the man's pelvis and sent him flying down the embankment, into the cold, wet tangle of weeds in the ditch. The antilock brakes juddered under Coffin's foot—the Crown Vic yawed wildly but didn't lock up or spin—two wheels went off the edge of the pavement and Coffin feared for a moment that the car would roll, but he managed to nudge it back onto the highway and bring it to a safe stop. He unbuckled and climbed out—smell of hot tires, a cloud of dust and sand. A man stood on the pavement, fifty yards behind the idling cruiser. A fat man. Coffin squinted, walked toward him.

"Tony?" he said. "Is that *you?*"

When the man in the gray hoodie turned the corner onto Atkins Lane, Lola started to run—she didn't want him to get too far ahead, too far out of sight. Then she heard him running, too, footsteps crunching in the oyster shell lane, and a surge of adrenaline swept through her—the cop's houndlike impulse when a suspect runs away: chase them, catch them, throw them to the ground. But just as Lola reached the corner the running footsteps stopped, and she stopped, too—listening, thinking. She stayed in the shadows, reached into her pocket for her keys. Took them out. Shook them. "Sir? Are you there? You dropped your keys!"

"Don't come near me!" Tony said, backing away. His eyes looked like they were about to pop out of his head on long springs.

"Tony," Coffin said. "It's me, Frankie."

Tony stopped, stared at Coffin. His feet were bare, and his pants appeared to be backward—the seat blousing awkwardly above his crotch. "Frankie? What are *you* doing out here?"

"Looking for a body," Coffin said. "You?"

Tony thought for a minute. "I'm not sure," he said. He pointed toward the dunes. "I woke up over there. I feel like I've been walkin' around out here for hours."

"You woke up out in the dunes?"

Tony nodded. His hair was wild. "What *day* is it, Frankie?"

"Tuesday."

"*Tuesday*. You sure?"

"Yep."

"Holy shit." Tony looked down at his bare feet. "What happened to my shoes, Frankie?"

"Want a ride?" Coffin said. "You can stay in the car while I check out this guy's house. Warm up. Listen to the radio."

"Sure, Frankie. That sounds nice."

He was sure it was the lady cop, even though he couldn't really see her face in the dark—the woman with the keys was the right height, the right build. Besides, what woman who wasn't a cop would follow a man down a dark alley to give him back his keys, even in Provincetown?

The lady cop was staying in the shadows, moving slowly on the grass at the edge of the lane, almost silent. She was listening, he thought—trying to pick up any slight sound he might make. She'd put the keys back in her pocket. She had to be carrying a gun, though the man in the gray hoodie couldn't see it.

He'd picked a bad place to hide, he realized—he was cut off by fences on three sides—unless he wanted to climb, the only way out was toward the street. He'd sit tight, let her go by, and then double back, cut between the waterfront houses to the beach. Except she wasn't going by. She'd stopped maybe ten feet from where he was crouched and seemed to be almost sniffing the air, which made him wonder if he smelled. The gas fumes in the church had ignited unexpectedly, the fireball blowing him out the door and into the parking lot, singeing his eyebrows. Did he smell like smoke? Like burned hair?

She took a step toward him—slowly, quietly—then another. Not looking at him, though: she was peering into the gap between the shed and the house instead, the deep shadows at the back of the lot. His heart was pounding. If she caught him back there, it wouldn't be so easy to explain. Why had he run? Why was he hiding? He needed something—a weapon. He reached out blindly in the darkness, feeling on the ground—a rock, a big stick, anything—and found (perfect!) a few bricks stacked beside the shed, solid and gritty to the touch. He picked up the top brick as quietly as he could, trying to move just one muscle at a time, holding his breath. The cop had her back to him now, just a few feet away. He stayed low, took a half-step forward, the brick in his raised hand.

———

Branstool's house stood in a wooded patch at the end of Kestrel Lane, overlooking the bay. Coffin pulled into the driveway and put the Crown Vic in park. Chief Willoughby was already there—his old Chevy police cruiser idling next to the garage.

"You stay put," Coffin said to Tony. "When I'm done here I'll take you home. Doris must be worried about you."

"Oh, crap," Tony said, rubbing a hand over his face. "Doris. What am I gonna tell her, Frankie?"

Coffin pursed his lips. "Tell her you were out getting laid."

"Yeah, right." Tony snorted. "Like she'd believe *that*."

Coffin dug in his jacket pocket, handed Tony his cell phone. "Here, give her a call. Let her know you're okay."

Coffin grabbed a big Maglite from the Crown Vic. He was not carrying a sidearm. He thought about pulling the shotgun from its overhead mount behind the front seats but decided against it—too cumbersome, and almost certainly unnecessary—only a fool or a madman would go back to the victim's house after cutting off his head and placing it in a tank full of lobsters ten miles away.

There was no one in Chief Willoughby's car. The front door of Branstool's house was standing halfway open, and the lights in the entryway were out.

Coffin reached inside the door, felt for the light switch, flipped it up, then down—nothing. He wavered for a second, then went back to the car, pressed the hidden button, and unclipped the shotgun from its rack.

"You need me, Frankie?" Tony said.

"The shape you're in?" Coffin said. "No thanks—you just sit tight. Don't come in the house behind me or I might shoot you by mistake. If you hear anything funky, call for backup."

"Maybe you ought to call for backup now," Tony said. "Just in case."

"Not yet. We're stretched pretty thin. I just want to make sure Willoughby's okay."

He cradled the shotgun in his left arm, aimed the flashlight with his right hand, and stepped inside the dark house.

I can almost smell him, Lola thought—he was that close. She stopped a few feet from the shed, listening intently while she searched the gloom behind the house for any sign of movement, any shape that didn't belong. Her right hand went silently into her jacket pocket, touched the Glock 9 mm she carried when she was off duty.

Lola felt the movement before she heard it, saw a quick blur in her extreme peripheral vision and tried to duck away as the brick came down, hard, on the side of her head. It was like a small bomb going off inside her skull—a loud clack, an explosion of red light behind her eyes. Stunned, she fell to all fours, ears rushing, vision narrowed to a fizzy gray pinhole before it widened again. She heard running footsteps heading out toward Bradford Street. She staggered to her feet, tried to run, but she was too dizzy and had to stop, hands on her knees.

"*Fuck*," she said. "Fucking motherfucker." She touched her head, two inches behind the right ear: a lump already rising—some blood, but not rivers of it. She felt a wave of nausea, took a few deep breaths. Had she lost consciousness for a second? She wasn't sure.

"Lola? You back here?"

It was Jeff Skillings. Lola had never been more glad to see him.

"Yeah," she said. "I'm over here. He got away."

"He?"

"Sweatshirt guy. Hit me and took off." She waved toward Bradford Street. "Long gone by now."

Skillings was already on his shoulder radio, talking to Marge.

"Yep, backup and ambulance to Atkins Way and Commercial. Lola's injured."

"I'm not *injured*," Lola said. She straightened up, got dizzy again but shook it off. "It's just a bump on the head."

Skillings put a hand on her shoulder, peered into her face. "Easy there, tough guy," he said. "You don't look so great."

Lola touched the bump behind her ear again, winced a little, then grinned. "Hell, Jeff—I used to ride motocross. I've been beat up *lots* worse than this."

Coffin passed through a high-ceilinged foyer and into a large living room, sweeping the area with his flashlight. He held the big Maglite the way he'd been trained: up by his ear, gripping it just where the lens housing met the shaft. *The better to crack you over the head with,* he thought. He felt a bit silly carrying the twelve gauge, but at the same time was glad for its solid lethality—around seven pounds of badass, fully loaded. The only trouble, he thought, was that the shotgun didn't have a flashlight mount—that would have made things easier.

The house was quiet—no sign of Chief Willoughby. *Your basic McMansion,* Coffin thought, probably four times the size of Coffin's place, perched on the bluff overlooking the beach. Looking across the bay through the big back windows he could see St. Mary's burning quite clearly. The fire had gotten very large: it lit up the low cloud cover over Provincetown, and a pillar of smoke and sparks rose high into the sky. Coffin could see the flashing lights of the fire trucks, too, and what looked like an ambulance heading up the east end of Commercial Street.

He swept the Maglite slowly back across the room, into the corners, into the hallway that led off to his left—probably to the bedrooms—down the three broad steps into the open kitchen. The furniture was as bland as Branstool himself: it was hard to make out much color in the flashlight beam, but it appeared that everything had been done in varying degrees of beige: beige chairs, beige couch, beige carpet. The only things that gave the room any character at all, Coffin thought, were the ducks.

There were at least a hundred of them in the living room alone: wooden decoys, realistically carved and painted. Some appeared to be antiques, some were new. There were mallards, scoters, buffleheads, wood ducks, hooded ducks, teal, loons, grebes, mergansers, geese, and swans—and those were just the ones Coffin could identify. There were ducks on shelves from floor to ceiling, ducks on tables, ducks on the mantel, ducks on the floor under the baby grand piano. Evidently, Coffin thought, Branstool liked ducks.

Coffin turned and slowly made his way down the dark corridor that led away from the living room—pausing to try a bank of light switches, still with no luck. One after another he checked the two smallish bedrooms facing the street, then the home office with its blond desk, beige executive chair, and glass cases full of life-sized wooden ducks. The master suite was on the bay side of the house, naturally—Coffin pushed the door open with his elbow, swept with the Maglite—bed, dresser, fifty or sixty ducks—and stepped quietly into the room. The hair on the back of his neck prickled—he heard movement to his right, from what, the bathroom? The bathroom door was closed; a pale strip of light leaked out from under it.

Coffin doused the Maglite and crossed the room in five silent steps. He set the big flashlight on the carpet, then braced his shoulder against the wall beside the bathroom door. His heart stuttered, then beat fast—big adrenaline surge, live wire deep in his veins. *Too old for this,* he thought. He took a deep breath, swung away from the wall, and delivered a solid kick to the bathroom door, just below the latch. There was a splintering of wood and the door flew open as Coffin racked and mounted the shotgun, aiming it directly into the round, startled face of Clarence Willoughby, chief of the Truro Police Department.

"Jesus Christ—don't shoot!" Willoughby shouted, dropping his flashlight and covering his face with the magazine he'd been reading—the October issue of *Fine Woodworking*.

"Willoughby?" Coffin said, lowering the twelve gauge.

"Coffin?" Willoughby lowered the magazine slowly. "For fuck's sake—are you out of your mind?"

"What are you *doing* in here?"

Willoughby pointed at the toilet he was sitting on with both index fingers. "I'm taking a crap, Coffin. What does it look like?"

"Here? You're taking a crap *here?*"

"You were late. I had to go." Willoughby shrugged. "Anyway, there's nothing here. I checked the whole place. No body, no blood, no struggle. They must have done it someplace else."

"You checked the whole place," Coffin said.

"Yep."

"Every room."

"Yep."

"Did you check the garage?"

"The garage?" Willoughby paused. "Well, no—not yet. I was gonna hit the garage on my way out."

Branstool's garage was a detached, three-car affair with a large upstairs coach house that could have been rented out for a great deal of money during the summer. The garage itself was unlocked, the interior large and clean—the concrete floor looked scrubbed—no oil stains, no mud or sand. There were two cars: a recent and unremarkable Lexus sedan, and a sleek, beautiful Ferrari convertible.

"Holy smokes, Bullwinkle," Willoughby said. "Would you look at this baby. What do you think it cost—a couple hundred grand?"

"No idea," Coffin said. "More, maybe."

Willoughby scratched at his beard stubble. "You know, I've been thinking—you said this guy runs a nursing home, right?"

"Right," Coffin said.

"So how much does a guy like that make, would you say?"

Coffin shrugged. "Maybe a hundred—hundred fifty, tops."

"A hundred fifty grand a year, but he's got a trophy house on the bay and a Ferrari convertible. How does a guy pay for all that?"

"Powerball?" Coffin said. "Inheritance?"

"Sure, Powerball. Good one, Coffin."

"Did you see any car keys in the house?"

Willoughby raised his eyebrows. "You thinkin' about taking a spin?"

"I was wondering what's in the Lexus's trunk," Coffin said. He tried the door, aimed his flashlight in the window. "But it's locked up."

"Shouldn't be too hard to find the keys, if we had some light."

"It can wait. Whatever's in there isn't going anywhere."

"Ha." Willoughby grunted. "That's for damn sure."

A set of broad wooden steps led up to the garage's second floor. In recent years, as the housing bubble swelled and it seemed that the supply of well-heeled renters was limitless, the typical garage apartment had evolved from a small, modestly appointed living space into a miniature luxury vacation home, complete with gourmet kitchen, master suite, and a Jacuzzi overlooking Cape Cod Bay. That's what Coffin was expecting as he climbed the stairs—something gleaming, with a marble-tiled master bath and a view to die for.

The door at the top of the stairs was slightly ajar. Willoughby and Coffin exchanged looks—Coffin touching a finger to his lips.

Willoughby took a deep breath, then pushed the door open and swept the room with his flashlight, while Coffin stepped forward with the shotgun mounted, its barrel following the spot of light around the room.

"Whaddya know," said Willoughby. "It's a wood shop. Must be where the ducks came from."

He was right—instead of a lucrative summer rental property, Branstool had built himself a deluxe wood shop. It was equipped with woodworking tools of all sorts: there was a lathe, a drill press, a jigsaw, a table saw, a radial arm saw, racks of chisels, screwdrivers, mallets, a belt sander, what might have been a computer-controlled carving machine (Coffin's knowledge of woodworking began and ended with his eighth grade wood shop class), routers, drills, planers—it all looked like top-of-the-line stuff, Coffin thought, new or practically new.

Coffin pointed. "Put the light back on the radial arm saw," he said. "I saw something over there."

Willoughby panned the light slowly back to the big, table-mounted saw. "Oh, shit," he said. "I thought it was just shadows. Son of a bitch."

It was true, Coffin thought. In the pale beam of Willoughby's flashlight, all that blood did look like shadows—but of course there was too much of it. Dried or drying blood was everywhere: pooled on the floor, spattered in a dark, indefinite strip across the ceiling. Blood on the saw—the blade, the steel legs, the saw bed. Blood on the lathe and the drill press, six feet away. Blood on the walls, the cabinetry, the pegboard loaded with hand tools, the workbench. More blood, Coffin thought, than you'd think a person could possibly contain.

Willoughby cleared his throat softly. "You said they cut off his head, right?"

"Yep."

"So they brought him in here and did it with the radial arm."

"Looks that way."

Willoughby whistled a low note. "Holy *shit*," he said. "These are some bad boys we're talkin' about."

For a moment neither of them said anything. The flashlight quivered slightly in Willoughby's hand. "You think he was still alive," he said, "when they, uh—"

"I think so," Coffin said.

Willoughby nodded. "I guess you wouldn't get spurting blood on the ceiling if he was already dead. Although that could be mostly tissue up there. Probably the Crime Scene Services boys can tell us."

Coffin was sweating. His head felt light, inflated—like a balloon that might float away. He looked at Willoughby. "I need some air. Better get hold of your dispatcher, have her give Mancini a call."

"Mancini," Willoughby said. He was still staring at the radial arm saw.

"Come on," Coffin said. "Let's go find the breaker box and then see if we can't dig up Branstool's car keys."

"Son of a bitch," Willoughby said. "This is *my* homicide, isn't it?"

"Yep. Unless all that blood came out of something other than a person."

"Son of a bitch," Willoughby said. "Son. Of. A. *Bitch*."

Chapter 13

It took ten minutes to find the breaker box—it was in the furnace room, which was behind the laundry room, which was off the exercise room, which was equipped with a treadmill, Nautilus machines, and a big flat-screen TV. Coffin had retrieved two pairs of latex gloves from the box in the Crown Vic: one for him, one for Willoughby.

The breaker box's metal door was standing open: Coffin flipped the main switch and the house seemed to come to life—the furnace kicked on, the chest freezer and basement fridge hummed into action.

"Why do you think they shut off the juice?" Willoughby said.

"Don't know," Coffin said. "They did it after they killed Branstool, though."

Willoughby snapped his gloved fingers; they made a soft, rubbery pop. "Right—the saw. Weird."

"They flipped a breaker where we found his head, too, but not the main—just one circuit."

"Go figure," Willoughby said. "Just fuckin' with the cops, maybe."

"Could be," Coffin said. "Could be they wanted to disable the alarm system or any surveillance cameras that might be around. Just a guess."

They found the car keys dangling from the beak of a meticulously painted, life-sized wooden Canada goose that crouched on a stand in the foyer. Coffin wondered how he'd missed them earlier—he'd passed through the foyer three times in the dark. Funny what you saw and didn't see when the only light was a flashlight's narrow beam.

When Coffin and Willoughby emerged from Branstool's house for the second time, they found Tony's blue Chevy pickup truck idling in the driveway. Tony sat in the passenger seat, smoking a cigarette. Doris, Tony's wife, waited beside the truck, arms crossed over her breasts. She had always seemed unhappy to Coffin: a small, sour, cylindrical woman who managed to walk without any apparent movement of her hips. Coffin had wondered more than once how she put up with Tony's goofiness—she was a woman with no apparent sense of humor. *And now this,* he thought.

"Oh, Frankie," she said. "Thank God. Thank freaking God *you* found him, and not some criminal."

"Criminal? I'd be more worried about the cops picking him up," Coffin said. "How's he doing?"

Doris lowered her voice. "Not good, Frankie. I don't know what to do here. I mean, he's crazy, right? *Completely* crazy. He thinks he was abducted, Frankie. By aliens."

"Uh-oh."

"I know, right? I mean, what do you say to a man who says he was abducted by *aliens*, Frankie? I feel like I'm married to a stranger all of a sudden."

The St. Mary's fire wasn't visible from Branstool's driveway, but

Coffin could see its deep orange glow reflected on the cloud cover. He imagined the flames rising a hundred feet into the sky, and for a moment wanted very much to go back and watch St. Mary's burn. The gathering fog smelled like smoke.

"Well," he said, "I guess the first thing I'd do would be to have him see a doctor—try to rule out anything physical. You know— seizure, stroke, early Alzheimer's. Then get a referral."

"To a shrink, you mean?"

Coffin nodded.

Doris looked down at the ground. "Well, I guess that makes sense." She paused. "Frankie?"

"Doris, I've got to get back to work here."

"Frankie, can you talk to him? He loves you. You're his oldest friend."

"Doris—"

"Frankie, please? He's not going to go see some doctor, you know that."

Coffin pursed is lips. "Yeah," he said. "You're probably right. But talking to me isn't going to help him, either."

"Just try, Frankie."

"Okay." Coffin took a deep breath, let it out. "I've got to finish up out here. Then I'm going home and get some sleep. How's tomorrow? I'll come out for breakfast."

"You're a good man, Frankie," Doris said, climbing into Tony's truck. "No matter what people say."

To Coffin's considerable relief, the trunks and interiors of both cars were empty. No decapitated bodies, not so much as a lost shoe or stray button to indicate that the cars had been involved in any way. Still, Coffin knew, the state police would impound the Ferrari as evidence.

Outside, the paling sky smelled like wood ash. The glow over Provincetown had dimmed: It was possible that the firefighters had gotten the upper hand, Coffin thought, though it seemed more likely that the church had simply burned to the ground and now the fire was running out of fuel. The firefighters would be watching the neighboring structures now, keeping an eye on the drift of burning embers in the wind. More than anything, Coffin wanted to go home and sleep for a day, or a week, or however long it would take until all the fires finally stopped burning.

When Coffin pulled up outside his house it was almost 5:00 A.M. Thick fog had settled over Coffin's neighborhood—you could hardly make out the gravestones in the cemetery a hundred yards away. It was still mostly dark, though the few birds brave enough to stick around for the New England fall were waking up, making their small sounds from the red cedars that separated Coffin's house from Mrs. Prothero's place next door.

Coffin climbed out of the Crown Vic, stepped into his scruffy, postage-stamp yard, and stopped in his tracks. Someone was sitting on his screen porch. The cat funk of marijuana smoke hung in the air.

"Isn't it a little early in the day for that?" Coffin said.

"Early, late—it's all in how you look at it," his uncle Rudy said.

Coffin stepped onto the screen porch. His uncle was parked in one of the decomposing wicker chairs. Loverboy was swinging slowly back and forth in the porch glider. Its chains creaked ominously.

"Why is it," Coffin said, "that you always show up at the worst possible times, but when I want you I can never find you?"

"Kind of like a cop," Loverboy said.

"You should always fuck with people's expectations," Rudy said. "It's how you build a mythology, Frankie." He took a long hit from the joint he was holding, then pinched it out between his thumb and forefinger and pocketed the roach. "I figured I'd save you the trouble of looking for me. Figured you'd have some questions."

Coffin leaned his back against the wall. He was utterly exhausted—if he sat down, he wouldn't be able to get back up. He felt a tight little ache behind his eyes; his ears were ringing faintly. "Okay," Coffin said. "Tell me about Branstool. Who did him?"

"That's the thing," Rudy said. "I don't know. When I said I'd take care of him, I didn't mean I was gonna have him whacked. That was just a crazy coincidence."

"Unbelievable," Loverboy said, shaking his lion-sized head.

"Okay," Coffin said. "Let's go with that for now. So what *did* you mean?"

"You dig into any life, Frankie, you're gonna find some dirt. Sometimes it's hidden, sometimes it's real close to the surface. Branstool's was lying around in plain view, pretty much."

"Like what?"

"Well, when you suspect somebody's making money illegally, where do you look first?"

"Bank records."

Rudy nodded. "Bingo."

"How'd you get his bank records?"

Rudy waved a hand. "It's a long story. Boring. You look tired—let's just cut to the chase. Loverboy?"

The big Tongan stopped swinging for a moment. "He had an interesting deposit history. Eight thousand here, nine thousand there. Sometimes once or twice a month, sometimes more than that. Never quite ten thousand, though. It was a dead giveaway."

"Over ten K, the bank has to report it," Rudy said.

"Of course," Coffin said. "So where was the money coming from?"

"More than one place, probably," Rudy said. "Did you know there's a big-time audit underway at Valley View?"

Coffin shook his head. "He was skimming? What a weasel."

"Mostly laundering," Loverboy said. "There were no cash deposits to his account. It was all checks from the nursing home for 'expenses.'"

"So what will the nursing home auditors find?"

"They'll find a history of lots and lots of cash deposits to some side account—some little slush fund started by Branstool. It'll be called something like the 'bingo account,' or the 'cash donations' account. And lots of checks in that eight or nine K range written by Branstool to Branstool. So the books would always balance, more or less, and the main accounts would be untouched. Not a bad system, but it assumes nobody's paying attention."

"Who was paying attention?" Coffin said.

"I've been watching that little weasel for years," Rudy said, pointing a thumb at his chest. "In the business world, Frankie, nothing's more valuable than information."

"So you tipped the auditors?"

Rudy stood. "You should see Loverboy in a suit. He's very daunting."

"Oh my God," Coffin said. "You've been posing as state auditors?"

"You're not asking the big question," Rudy said. "You're getting a little slow in your old age."

Coffin yawned, closed his eyes. "Okay, the big question: Whose money was Branstool laundering?"

Rudy pushed open the screen door, and the two men stepped

off the porch. Coffin half expected the house to rise a few inches, freed from their weight.

"Next time you're out at his place," Rudy said, scratching his beard stubble, "take a good look at the ducks."

"The ducks? What about the ducks?"

"*Vaya con queso,* Frankie," Rudy said, waving to Coffin with his back turned.

"Rudy!" Coffin yelled, but the two big men had already disappeared into the fog.

Chapter 14

He reached into the crib and picked up the baby, its mottled fur cold and wet to the touch. Everything smelled like smoke. The big stuffed animals bared their savage teeth.

"It's okay," Coffin said. "I've got you. It's okay."

The baby stared at him with its dark, liquid eyes. He thought of his father, drowned in the ocean, seaweed in his hair. What would his father say about the seal baby, he wondered?

"I've got you," Coffin said. "I've got you."

Flames licked the curtains, flowed up the walls. Coffin wrapped the slick, squirming seal baby in a blanket, ran with it down the hallway. Sparks and smoke were everywhere—he could hardly breathe . . .

"Frank."

The stairs were a cauldron of fire. He had to get out—had to save the seal baby. He retreated into the bedroom, opened the window. The smoke was choking him. He was drowning in smoke . . .

"Frank!"

Something poked him in the ribs.

"Frank, wake up!"

"What?" Coffin said. His eyelids felt as though they'd been glued together. "Wake up? Why?"

Jamie was jabbing him with her finger. "You stopped breathing. It freaks me out when you do that. Turn over on your side, okay?"

"Sorry," Coffin said, rolling onto his side. "Sorry."

Jamie grunted and went back to sleep. Coffin looked at the clock—7:23—closed his eyes, opened them again. He was exhausted, but wide-awake.

"Shit," he said.

"Hmph," Jamie said, pulling the covers up around her chin.

Coffin got out of bed, pulled on a T-shirt and pair of sweatpants, and went downstairs to the kitchen. He put a filter in the coffeemaker, half-filled the carafe at the sink, dumped the water into the reservoir, then spooned four scoops of ground decaf into the filter—Jamie wasn't drinking regular coffee now, on her OB-GYN's advice.

It was raining outside—a gray drizzle, occasionally driven by an easterly gust of wind. He turned on the radio, hunted around for NPR. Sometimes it came in, sometimes it didn't, depending on which way the wind was blowing, Coffin thought, or sunspot activity, or variations in the Earth's magnetic field. The whole FM band was static except for WOMR, the local all-volunteer station. They were replaying an old episode of *Ptown 02657*, a homemade radio drama: a gay character and a transsexual character were having a breathless conversation about a lesbian character who'd given her straight married lover chlamydia.

Coffin switched the radio off, poured a cup of decaf, added half-and-half and sugar. He sipped it, made a face. "Decaf," he said to the rain on the window, to the starlings pecking in the yard. "Why bother?" The phone bleeped. He picked it up.

"Frank?" It was Arlene, his secretary. "Listen, Dr. Gault wanted me to ask you to come in ASAP. You and she have an eight thirty meeting with Mancini and a federal agent—guy from ATF."

"Miles Kendrick? Boston office?"

"Yep, that's the gent."

"Great," Coffin said. "See you in a half hour."

On his way to Town Hall, Coffin stopped at the Yankee Mart for a cup of real coffee. The girl working the cash register was a slender Belarusian named Ioana: she'd been a brunette when she first arrived in Provincetown, but lately she'd been dying her hair a tawny, reddish blond. She was small-breasted, her features slightly Asian. The Mongols had made it as far as Poland, Coffin knew— had they passed through Belarus on their way?

"Did you find everything you were looking for?" she said.

Her accent was wonderful, Coffin thought—the dark vowels, all that lingering on the terminal *g*'s. She was probably twenty.

"Yes," Coffin said, holding up his paperboard cup of convenience-store coffee. "The coffee machine is well marked."

"Another satisfied customer," Ioana said. "This is what I live for."

"No doubt your corporate masters have taken note."

"One can only hope. How is Yelena?"

"Fine, I think. I didn't know you were friends."

"It's the Eastern European mafia," Ioana said. "Haven't you heard? We're taking over this dump."

Taking gover, Coffin thought. "Be my guest," he said. "It's all yours."

At Town Hall a half-dozen painters were working on scaffolds in the main stairway. Drop cloths covered the floor, and a heavy metal song roared from a boom box—Metallica or Megadeath, Coffin thought, but he'd never been able to tell them apart. Coffin's head began to throb: the smell of latex paint was thick, the music was loud, he hadn't gotten nearly enough sleep. He trotted up the stairs with his coffee cup and ducked into his office, shutting the door behind him.

Lola was waiting in one of his leather guest chairs. She was in uniform, legs crossed, hat balanced on her knee.

"Holy crap," she said. "Look what the cat dragged in."

"That bad?" Coffin said. He sat in his desk chair, a fancy executive model, and put his feet up on the desk.

"I probably don't look so good myself," Lola said.

Coffin peered at her. "You look fine," he said. "Why, what happened?"

Lola's cheeks reddened. "It's embarrassing," she said. "I screwed up. But I got a look at our firebug. Sort of."

She told Coffin about the man in the gray hoodie—how'd he'd drifted away from the crowd of onlookers the minute she'd gone to retrieve the camcorder, how she'd followed him into Atkins Lane.

"He stopped running too soon," she said. "I would have heard his footsteps if he'd kept running all the way out to Bradford. So I knew he'd ducked into one of the yards. The first one on the left was real dark—it's got a tall hedge on the Commercial Street side, and the streetlight's funky, so the whole thing was in deep shadow. I figured he might be back there, but I couldn't see anything, and I didn't have a flashlight. Couldn't call for backup, either."

"Doesn't sound like you screwed up," Coffin said. "You were dealing with some limiting factors."

"Yeah, like my brain. You know how when you're trying real hard to see in the dark, the rest of your brain kind of shuts down?"

"Yeah, when I get lost in the car I have to turn the radio off. Can't navigate and listen to music at the same time."

Lola nodded. "Same thing. So I'm trying like a son of a bitch to see what's behind this little saltbox house, and I forget about the shed. I'm just not thinking about it, because I can't see behind the house. And that's where he was hiding—behind the shed."

"Okay. So?"

"He's quick. And stealthy." Lola touched the spot behind her ear.

"What'd he hit you with?"

"A brick, I think."

"You okay?"

"Yeah. There was a pretty good lump. But I iced it down last night and it's not too bad now."

"You're going to see a doctor, right?"

"I'm fine. The EMT said it was no big deal. Didn't even need stitches."

"You're going to see a doctor, right?"

"Yes, dear. Whatever you say."

"Ha," Coffin said. "If only."

Monica Gault's office was crowded. Gault sat behind her desk, while Mancini and Miles Kendrick, the ATF agent, sat in the two leather guest chairs. Other chairs had been brought in: orange plastic with slim metal legs, like the one in Coffin's old office in the basement. Coffin sat in one of these; so did Pete Wells. Lola and the state police detective in the brown suit, Pilchard, stood against the wall. Outside, in the hallway, workmen were banging on pipes with hammers. It was hard to hear what anyone was saying.

"Fun town you've got here," Kendrick said, voice raised. He was around Coffin's height, but in better shape. His hair was cropped close, silver gray. He had a narrow face with pale eyes, a large chin, and a long upper lip.

"You should catch the drag show sometime," Coffin said. "Talk about fun."

"I'm sorry, what?" Kendrick said, cupping a hand at his ear.

"Coffin's a little defensive," Mancini said. "You can't blame him, really."

"*What?*" Gault said, leaning forward. "I didn't hear any of that, I'm afraid."

Kendrick consulted his notebook. "So . . ." he began, pausing for an especially energetic burst of hammering from the hallway. "You've had multiple fires, including three recent structure fires, correct?"

"Correct," said Mancini.

"All of the recent fires appear to be arson, correct?"

"That's my judgment, yes," said Pete Wells, practically shouting over the din. "They appear to be the work of an amateur thrill arsonist."

Gault put her hands over her ears. "Good Christ—I can't stand it!" she said. "Gentlemen, I propose we find a quieter space in which to discuss this."

"My old office in the basement is probably okay," Coffin said.

"I'd rather hold a meeting in purgatory." Gault stood. "Come on, gents, I know just the place."

Gault led them down the back stairs to the main floor, where there was no pounding. They followed her into the police department's squad room: Gault shut the door behind them with a sigh.

"Oh, hell's bells," she said. Heavy metal music from the front stairway vibrated the squadroom's south wall. For a moment Gault seemed nonplussed.

"How about the men's room?" Mancini said. "It's on the other side of the hallway—should be quieter."

"Not on your life," Gault said. "The ladies', on the other hand, will do just fine." She strode from the squadroom, crossed the hall, opened the door of the ladies' room, and disappeared inside.

Coffin looked at Kendrick. Kendrick looked at Mancini. The three of them looked at Wells. They all shrugged.

"Works for me," Coffin said.

"Good times," Wells said.

"I love this town," Kendrick said.

"What a freak show," Mancini said. And then they all went inside.

The ladies' room had last been refurbished in the 1950s. It was done in kelp green tile, floor to ceiling, with a long, pale green counter and two pink porcelain sinks. There were two stalls, and a large metal sanitary napkin dispenser. It was blissfully quiet, but crowded: Gault propped her backside against the counter; Coffin, Mancini, Wells, and Kendrick stood with their backs against the wall; Lola leaned against the door; and Pilchard sat in one of the stalls, the only space left.

"All right, gentlemen," Gault said, her voice echoing slightly in the tiled room. "Where were we?"

"God, the acoustics in here are fabulous," Kendrick said, smiling broadly. "All that natural reverb! Couldn't you just burst into song?"

Mancini glowered. "Only in Provincetown," he said.

"This is a first for me, I can tell you that," Pilchard said, from his seat in the stall.

"Is it that different from the men's room?" Gault said, eyebrows raised.

"It's not *that* different," Lola said. For a moment everyone looked at her.

"Pinch me," Kendrick said finally. "I must be dreaming."

"Could we get back to business?" Mancini said, looking at his Rolex. "There's a decapitated nursing home director that also requires my attention."

Kendrick sighed. "Killjoy," he said. "Fine. How about DNA? Any left at the sites?"

"Not that we've found," Wells said.

"Thank God," Gault said, crossing her arms over her chest.

"Ah, well," Kendrick said. "And what about commercial motives?"

"Only one of the fires has a potential commercial motive," Coffin said. "We're working on that."

Mancini made finger quotes. "Working on that," he said. "Right."

"The fires so far appear to have been set by the same individual," Coffin said. "Could be the guy that Sergeant Winters had an encounter with last night. It's possible he may have set multiple fires to cover up a commercial arson, but it seems unlikely at this point."

Kendrick gazed at Coffin, pale eyes hooded. *Sizing me up,* Coffin thought.

"How so?" Kendrick said.

Wells tilted his head a bit. "The fires appear to be amateur work, like I said. Very simple execution. No timing devices. What seems like randomly selected targets. The fact that the firebug may be showing up in the crowds of onlookers also points to a thrill arsonist. A smart professional wouldn't stick around."

"A *smart* professional wouldn't," Mancini said. "Nobody's suggesting this guy is particularly smart."

Coffin cleared his throat, ran a finger around the inside of his collar. He was in uniform, and his tie was strangling him. "He's smarter than we are, so far."

"You've heard of John Orr?" Kendrick said.

"Of course," Wells said.

"Help me out," Mancini said.

"John Orr was a fire captain and arson investigator in Glendale, California," Kendrick said. "He was convicted of arson after setting something like two thousand fires through the 1980s and early '90s in the Los Angeles area, including a fire in a busy hardware store that killed four people. Right before we arrested him he was spotted in the crowd watching a warehouse fire he'd started."

"Orr knew a lot of tricks," Wells said, "but he wasn't motivated by money. He just liked to watch it burn. He liked to hurt people, too."

"Are you suggesting we're dealing with someone like this Orr fellow?" Gault said.

"You'd better hope not," Mancini said.

Coffin felt a bit woozy. The ladies' room was starting to feel very small with all of those people in it. A cool sheen of sweat had formed on his forehead.

There was a soft knock at the door, and Lola pulled it open.

Arlene, Coffin's secretary, stood in the hallway. "Oh, look," she said. "A party."

"Arlene," Coffin said, after a second. "Were you looking for someone?"

"I'm looking to see a man about a horse," Arlene said. "There's a fellow with a very large drill in the upstairs ladies' room. Call me old-fashioned, but I didn't feel comfortable going in there."

They all filed out of the ladies' room, waited for Arlene, and then filed back in. When Lola had shut the door and leaned her back against it, Gault cleared her throat. "All right, tell me, gentlemen, who are we looking for?"

"White male," Wells said. "Early twenties. Probably unemployed. Probably doesn't have a girlfriend—"

"Or boyfriend," Mancini said.

"Most likely not in the market for a boyfriend, if he fits the profile," Wells said, "and so far he does. Pyros almost always identify as straight, although in the old days they were generally typed as latent homosexuals."

"Who wasn't?" Kendrick said.

Wells looked up from his notes for a second, then went on. "He certainly fits in terms of the types of fires he's setting and the order he's setting them in," Wells said. "There's clear escalation. Although the church is a weird touch."

"How so?" Kendrick said. "If you're going to set fires, you might as well set fire to a church as anything else, no?"

"But why St. Mary's?" Coffin said. "Why the Episcopal church? He didn't burn down the Unitarian Meeting House—there you'd have an obvious antigay hate crime. And he didn't burn down St. Peter's, so it's not about lapsed Catholic rage. Why would anybody hate Episcopalians? It's like he's trying to make it *look* random."

"Which could be cover for a commercial arson," Wells said.

Mancini rolled his eyes. "Could this get any more circular?"

"A hate crime against the whole town," Gault said. "That's what it seems like to me." She sighed. "I used to love sitting in that church on Sunday, looking out at the harbor."

Coffin nodded. "He's certainly trying to get our attention." He paused for a second. "There's another thing that separates him from this Orr guy."

Mancini rolled his eyes. "Really, Coffin? You're an expert on John Orr now?"

"He's right," Wells said. "There's a big difference, for now at least."

Mancini held out his hands, palms up. *Well?*

"Our guy hasn't set fire to an occupied structure," Wells said.

"Yet," said Coffin.

"Yet?" Gault said. "*Yet?* Is that supposed to be the *good* news?"

Coffin's heart skipped a beat, then another. He wondered for a second if he was going to have a heart attack—not a good thing in Provincetown, the closest emergency room was an hour away by car. He took a deep breath and his heart started beating normally again. "The good news is that we may have him on videotape," he said. "We've been shooting video of the onlookers—if he fits the profile, he might be in the crowd. Since Sergeant Winters saw him from the back last night, we might be able to pick him out based on his height and build."

"So then all you need is an ID and you've got your guy," Mancini said, waving both hands in the air—*hallelujah!* "Easy, right?"

Lola raised her chin a bit. "Two problems with that," she said. "First, our guy was wearing a hooded sweatshirt last night. Hood up. I didn't get a look at his face. He's a white guy—I saw his hands—a little less than medium height, maybe a little heavier than medium build."

"Like half the Cape," Coffin said.

"I couldn't pick him out of a lineup at this point," Lola said. "And what I've seen of the video is pretty low resolution."

"Lighting is always such a problem," Kendrick said.

Coffin nodded. "We'll take a good look at the video this morning and see if anybody in the crowd matches up."

"And the second problem?" Gault said.

"There are plenty of people in town who might not want to be videotaped by the cops for reasons that have nothing to do with arson."

"Seriously, Coffin?" Mancini said. "You're gonna hit a cop with a brick because you've got an unpaid parking ticket?"

"Maybe you've got warrants that'll get you sent back to Framingham or Walpole. Maybe you're on parole and you've got a gun or a bag of weed in your pocket."

"Okay, Coffin," Mancini said, "you've got a lot of maybes. I get it. But just to humor me—get an ID on the fucking sweatshirt guy, okay?"

Kendrick raised an index finger. "About your headless body— or bodyless head, or whatever it is."

"That second thing," Coffin said.

"What are the odds it's connected to the fires?"

Coffin thought for a minute. "For now I'm operating on the theory that they're not connected. But obviously we don't know anything for sure."

Kendrick looked at his watch—a big Casio G-Shock. "Well," he said, "this was fun. I'm starved—anybody want to get a bite?"

"Careful what you wish for in this town," Mancini said.

"That's right," Gault said. "Watch out!" She bared her teeth and growled.

"She's a little defensive," Coffin said. "You can't blame her, really."

"Are you okay, Frank?" Lola said, once they were back in his office. "You were starting to look pretty green back there."

"Did I mention I'm a little bit claustrophobic?" Coffin said.

Lola shook her head. "It's been a tough twenty-four hours. For you and me both."

"I wish this guy would set fires in the daytime," Coffin said. "This up-all-night stuff is killing me."

A figure swam into view on the other side of the frosted glass panel in Coffin's office door. The glass still had the former police chief's name painted on the outside:

PRESTON BOYLE
CHIEF OF POLICE

The door opened and Mancini stuck his head in. "Got a minute, Coffin?"

"For you? Anytime."

Mancini stepped into the office, closed the door, and flopped into one of the leather guest chairs. For the time being, the banging out in the hallway had stopped—instead there was the sound of energetic drilling, coming from somewhere under the floor.

"Jesus Christ," Mancini said, rubbing his temples. "What is it with this fucking town?"

"It's all the gay," Coffin said. "It makes people crazy."

Lola stifled a laugh.

"Very funny, Coffin," Mancini said.

"How's Mrs. Mancini?"

"Current, or ex?"

Coffin shrugged. "You pick."

"Ex is pissed off. Current is expensive. Are we done now? Can we talk about your head?"

"It's not *my* head," Coffin said. "It's Willoughby's head."

"It's your head," Mancini said. "Until we get the DNA results back from Branstool's woodshop, anyway. Which could take a while."

Coffin closed his eyes. "How long?"

"Since the last round of budget cuts they're down to two DNA technicians. They're saying the backlog is six months to two years."

"Wonderful," Coffin said.

"I'll try to get them to expedite, but you know how it is."

"You realize we're sort of busy out here."

Mancini held up a hand, like a traffic cop stopping traffic. "Talk to the hand, Coffin. Look, based on my experience of this place I'm gonna go way out on a limb here and guess that Branstool was mixed up in some kind of creepy love triangle. Somebody got jealous and the rest is history."

"How many people do you think it would take to hold you still while I cut off your head with a table saw?" Coffin said.

"So they drugged him. Or held a gun on him."

"Any chance it was a robbery?" Lola said.

"The house was immaculate. No indication of robbery—but I'll go back out in daylight and take another look. You never know."

Coffin's phone bleeped. It was Arlene.

"Doris Santos on line one, Frank," she said. "Says it's urgent. I told her you were in a meeting, but she sounds pretty upset."

"I'll take it. Thanks, Arlene." Coffin held up the phone, looked at Mancini. "Was there anything else?"

"Nah," Mancini said. "I was thinking about asking the two of you to please try not to get beat up, drowned, stabbed, shot, or hit in the head with a brick for a change, because of the considerable expense to the taxpayer. But then I thought, since when do they listen to me?" Mancini pushed himself out of the leather chair, nodded at Lola, and stepped out into the hallway just as a furious barrage of drilling broke out.

Coffin punched line one. "Hi, Doris," he said. "Sorry, I know we had plans—"

"Oh, Frankie, thank God. You've got to come talk to him. He's gone crazy."

"Crazy how?" Coffin said. "Are you safe—you and the kids?"

"Oh, God, Tony wouldn't hurt us. Not ever, Frankie. No, but he's acting really weird. Thank Christ the kids are in school."

Coffin looked at Lola, slowly rotated an index finger beside his temple. "Weird like what?"

Doris took a ragged breath. Coffin guessed she was crying. "Well, he's talking about getting rid of all the screens."

"Screens? You mean window screens—for bugs?"

"No, the other kind. TV screens—computer screens. He thinks that's how the aliens keep tabs on him—through all the screens."

Coffin closed his eyes. "Okay, that doesn't sound good. I'll be there in about a half hour, Doris. Try to keep him calm."

"Easier said than done, Frankie," Doris said. "You'll see."

Chapter 15

Tony lived in a big refurbished '70s ranch house in Eastham, a town that most visitors to the Outer Cape experienced as a congested commercial strip of gas stations, clam shacks, and motels with cheesy nautical names like the Captain's Quarters or the Blue Dolphin, strung like beads on a thrift-store necklace along Route 6, between Orleans and Wellfleet. Coffin liked Eastham because it wasn't trying to *be* anything—not upscale Republican cute, like Chatham, not artsy-woodsy like Truro, and certainly not whatever Provincetown was trying to be. *Something with sequins*, Coffin thought. *Something that makes money.*

Tony lived just off Herring Brook Road, at the top of a bluff. His house overlooked the gray chop of Cape Cod Bay to the west, and Great Pond—a blue-green jewel in the woods—to the southeast.

"Wow," Lola said, stepping out of the Crown Vic. "Nice spot."

It *was* a nice spot, Coffin thought—it had a sense of openness that Provincetown lacked, with its cramped neighborhoods and narrow sidewalks. He'd thought more than once about selling his mother's place and moving out to Truro, maybe (artsy-woodsy!), which at least had a bit of space between the houses.

Coffin unfolded his long frame from the passenger seat, put on his hat. "You haven't been out here before?"

"Nope," Lola said. "I guess I was out of town for the housewarming."

The sound of a woman yelling came faintly from inside, followed by the sound of a glass door sliding open. Tony appeared on the side deck, wearing only green camouflage boxer shorts and hiking boots, and staggering under the weight of an enormous flatscreen TV. Doris followed him outside, hands held out in a gesture of supplication.

"Tony, for God's sake," she cried. "Not the new Samsung!"

Tony lurched to the railing, pressed the huge TV high overhead, and flung it over the edge with all the strength in his flab-upholstered, two hundred and forty pound frame. The bluff was steep—the house with its panoramic water view perched maybe sixty feet above Bowline Lane, a narrow strip of packed sand that wound through the scruffy mix of pine, juniper, and scrub oak on its way to the bay-side beach. It was strangely exhilarating, Coffin thought, when the glistening black TV sailed over a stand of scrub pines like some failed stealth bomber, bounced off the rocky cliff and struck the road edge-first, exploding into a thousand shards of plastic.

"Oh my fucking God," Doris wailed. "The kids are going to *freak!*" She collapsed into a heaving puddle on the deck and started to weep.

Tony paused for a moment, looking down at Coffin and Lola. "Hi, guys," he said. "What's the occasion?" He galumphed back into the house in his big boots, then returned a moment later with a large computer monitor, which also went over the side.

"Tony!" Coffin said. "Why don't you take a break and come talk to us."

Tony wiped his hands on his boxer shorts. "Oh, sure, Frankie," he said. "Be right down."

A few seconds later, Tony opened the front door and stepped out onto the lawn. He was sweating—the hair on his big belly was damp—but otherwise he seemed perfectly calm. "So what's up?" he said. He glanced over his shoulder, into the house. "Kind of busy here. Not a lot of time to chitchat, if you know what I mean."

"Can I ask you a question?" Coffin said.

"Fire away."

"Why did you just throw a four-thousand-dollar TV off your deck?"

Tony put the his hand loosely over his mouth. "Aliens," he said, in a conspirator's whisper.

"Are you worried they're watching you through the screens?" Lola said.

Tony nodded. "Talking to me, too. Telling me to do stuff."

"What kind of stuff?" Coffin said.

"Last night they told me to go outside in the yard. That's when they got me."

"They got you?"

Tony stared at Coffin for a moment, his eyes dark and intense. "They took me, Frankie. In their ship. I was gone for, like, hours. They must've hypnotized me or something, 'cause I don't remember much until they dumped me out in the dunes."

Coffin hesitated. "Oh," he said finally.

Tony looked away. "I know. It sounds crazy."

Coffin wanted to climb back into the Crown Vic and drive to the Bookstore Café in Wellfleet for a beer and a big plate of fried oysters. Instead he said, "Is that it? The TV's not telling you to do anything else?"

"Well, there's a guy on FOX that keeps telling me to buy gold," Tony said.

Coffin took his hat off, scratched his head, put his hat back on. "This isn't good, Tony," he said. "This worries me."

"I'm fine, Frankie. I know it sounds crazy, but I'm fine."

"It's Doris I'm worried about," Coffin said. "Look at her. She seems pretty unhappy."

Tony turned, his big belly slopping over the waistband of his boxers. Doris was crouched on all fours, looking down at them from the deck, her face mascara-streaked.

Tony nodded. "She looks like a raccoon," he said. "A sad one."

"You don't want that, right? I mean, you love her, don't you?"

Tony's eyebrows went up. "Sure I do, Frankie. 'Til death do us part. I take that shit seriously."

"I know you do," Coffin said, "but here's the thing. She wants you to see a doctor. She's a little worried."

Tony frowned. "What kind of doctor?"

"A doctor doctor. You know—a regular doctor. She just wants to make sure you're okay. If everything checks out, you can come right back and throw the rest of the screens off the deck, no problem."

"You swear? I can come right back?"

Coffin crossed his heart. "I wouldn't bullshit you, Tony. We're family, right?"

"That's right, Frankie. Like brothers."

"Why don't you get dressed. We'll run you over to Outer Cape Health in Wellfleet. If everything checks out okay, you'll be back in two shakes."

"Awesome," Tony said. "While I'm over there I think I'll have the doc take a look at my bunghole. I think the aliens musta probed me. I got a wicked bad hemorrhoid all of a sudden."

————

Coffin drove Tony to Outer Cape Health, while Doris and Lola followed in Tony's truck. As Tony slid out of the Crown Vic, Coffin said, "Listen, I want you to do whatever the doc says, okay?"

Tony shrugged. "Sure. Like what?"

"If he wants to send you down to Hyannis to the hospital, say."

"Just to have a look, though, right?"

"Right—just to have a look."

"Okay. Sure, Frankie. We got good insurance, right?"

"Right. And you listen to Doris—she's the boss for now, okay?"

"Ha," Tony said. "When the fuck isn't she?"

Coffin slumped down in the passenger seat with his hat over his eyes while Lola drove. It had started to rain again—the fat drops blowing slant against the windshield. The windshield wipers' rhythmic thwonking should have been relaxing, but it only made Coffin more tense.

"Well," Lola said, after a long silence. "That was weird."

"Yes," Coffin said. "Yes, it was."

"So, what do you think—psychotic break?"

"Sure looks like one," Coffin said. "Delusions, paranoia. That thing about the aliens talking to him through the TV is classic stuff."

"Didn't Son of Sam have that?" Lola said. "The TV telling him to kill people?"

Coffin pushed his hat back, sat up. "I'm having a hard time processing this. I think of Tony as being goofy—not crazy. Mentally ill. Whatever."

"Well, there's another possibility, maybe."

"Don't even go there."

"Come on—thousands of people claim they've been abducted by UFOs. You think they're all having the same hallucination?"

"Yep."

Lola smiled a wry half-smile. "Yeah. Me, too. Want to stop in Wellfleet for a bite? I'll buy."

"Seriously?"

"Of course, seriously. How about the Bookstore Café?"

Coffin grinned. "It's like you're reading my mind," he said.

The Bookstore Café was on Kendrick Avenue, just past the Wellfleet town pier. Coffin liked to eat in the bar: it had big windows that looked almost due south over Mayo beach—a strip of coarse, lion-colored sand—and the broad expanse of Wellfleet Harbor, beneath the calm, gray surface of which lay the Cape's most exquisitely productive oyster beds. If you wanted a fresher oyster than those served at the Bookstore Café, you'd have to cross the street, wade out into the harbor, and harvest them yourself. If you wanted a better oyster, Coffin thought, well, good luck with that—the cold, clean saltwater and strong tides of Wellfleet Harbor produced a small, firm, and briny oyster that was plump and flavorful but not overpowering or swampy-tasting. Coffin had eaten them for almost fifty years, and believed them to be the best in the world—far better than the Co-tuits, Blue Points, or Chesapeakes, which, he knew, were genetically identical, and a superior experience entirely to the funky-smelling, pancake-sized Gulf oysters he'd eaten in New Orleans and on the Florida panhandle. Coffin barely glanced at the menu, focusing mostly on the beer list. He knew what he wanted.

"What are you getting?" Lola said.

"I think I'll try the fried. Maybe a Newcastle—looks like they've got it on draft now."

"Good plan. I'd get a lobster roll, but after last night I'm not sure I could look it in the eye."

Coffin shuddered. "When we get back to the office I'll give

Shelley Block a call, see if she's had a chance to take a gander yet."
Shelley Block was the state medical examiner for Cape Cod; her
office was in Sandwich, at the far west end of the Cape, about
three miles from the canal. Coffin had dated her briefly before he
met Jamie—she was a pale, angular woman who always smelled
faintly of menthol. Coffin liked her and thought her very attractive, but had found himself unable to stop thinking about what
she did for a living—with embarrassing results.

She'd been ironic, good-humored. "It happens," she'd said. "To
me. A lot."

They'd parted on good terms, and remained friends. Branstool's
head would have been transported to her domain at the morgue by
now most likely. Coffin guessed that it would have been an object
of considerable interest to her. He shuddered again.

"Toxicology?" Lola said.

"Yep, and whether there are any other wounds we didn't see last
night."

The bartender took their order: fried oysters and a Newcastle
for Coffin, fish and chips and a Diet Coke for Lola.

"Let's stop at Branstool's for a bit on the way back," Coffin said,
when the bartender was gone. "One or two things I want to check
out."

"Like?"

Coffin told her about the ducks, and his conversation with Rudy.
"He must have also had a place to keep lots of cash; he was too
meticulous to just shove it under the mattress."

"So you're thinking what—a safe, somewhere?"

"Maybe a safe—some kind of stash box. He almost had to have
one."

Lola nodded. The bartender brought their drinks.

"Dude, should you be drinking this?" he said, setting Coffin's
beer down on a white napkin. He looked barely twenty-one, and

wore his hair in blond dreadlocks. "I mean, you're, like, in uniform."

Coffin met the bartender's eyes. "You stay out of my business, I'll stay out of yours."

"Ha! Right on, dude," the bartender said. "Good one."

"I should've gotten a Bloody Mary," Lola said.

"It's not too late," Coffin said.

Lola grinned. "I guess one of us should probably keep a clear head."

"That would be you," Coffin said. Outside, the wind had picked up. Small whitecaps raced across the harbor; a dull gray rain pelted the window.

The bartender brought their food. "Beer's on the house," he said, pointing a ringed index finger at Coffin. "You stay out of my business, I'll stay out of yours, right? Awesome, dude!"

The oysters were perfectly fried: the breading was light, crispy, and golden brown, the oysters sweet and piping hot. They were not greasy or overbreaded, not skimpy, either—the helping was generous. The fries were okay, Coffin thought, the coleslaw disposable, the beer cold and rich. He wanted to go home and take a nap— maybe after Branstool's, he thought. Maybe.

"So how's Jamie doing? Everything okay?"

Coffin knocked on the table. "So far so good," he said. "Sleeping, eating. Sexy as hell. She wants me to go car shopping with her. And furniture shopping. Also, I'm supposed to paint."

"Paint? You mean the baby's room?"

"Yep."

"Do you know *how* to paint?"

"Am I a man? I know how to paint. It's the car shopping that worries me."

"Don't like negotiating?"

"I don't like anything about it," Coffin said. "The creepy salesmen, the fake friendliness, the weird little test-drive. And don't get me started on all the hidden fees. You negotiate a deal, they make you wait around while they 'talk to the manager' "—he held up finger quotes—"then when they come back with the contract it's got a $500 advertising charge, a $250 transportation fee—next thing you know you're $1500 over the price you thought you'd agreed on."

"Huh," Lola said, dipping a piece of cod into a plastic cup of tartar sauce. "I've never had that problem."

"You haven't?" Coffin said.

"Nope." There was a faint smudge of tartar sauce on Lola's upper lip. She licked it off with the tip of her tongue.

"Okay," Coffin said. "So what's your secret?"

"I tell them I'm a cop," Lola said.

"That's it? You just tell them you're a cop and they don't screw you over?"

"Well, kind of. I tell them I'm a cop and they ask me where. And I say Provincetown, and they get all jokey and say, oh, P'town—that must be *interesting*. And I say yep, I love it. And you know what? My brother's a cop, too. And they say really? Two P'town cops in one family? And I say no—he's with the FBI. And they say oh, *really?* They're a little more serious now. What does he do in the FBI? And I smile very sweetly and I say he's in the fraud division. They've been investigating a bunch of auto dealerships, although I probably shouldn't be telling you that. They couldn't get me out of there fast enough. I got my new Camaro below dealer cost, zero percent APR."

"Wow," Coffin said. "I'll have to try that. You don't have a brother, right?"

"Nope."

Coffin pointed a finger at her. "Awesome, dude."

———

Branstool's driveway had been sealed off with yellow crime scene tape by the Truro PD. Coffin and Lola parked the Crown Vic by the road and walked to the house—beige clapboard, beige trim. No one was around except a Truro police officer Coffin didn't recognize. He was young, crew cut under a blue uniform ball cap. He stood on the porch, smoking a cigarette and trying to look tough.

"Well, who have we got here?" he said, squinting at Coffin's uniform. "P'town cops? Are you lost or something?"

Coffin stuck out his hand. "Coffin. You must be new."

"You're Detective Coffin?" the young officer said, all smiles now, shaking hands emphatically "Wow. You're practically famous."

"Hear that, Frank?" Lola said, patting Coffin on the back. "Next thing you know, you'll have your own reality TV show."

"America's Most Stunted?" Coffin said. *"Clam Shack Investigations?"*

The young cop turned to Lola. "So you must be Sergeant Winters, then. I guess I should've put two and two together. I'm Adams. I'm just a part-timer. I'm studying criminal justice at CCCC—hoping to go full time when I'm done."

"There's no money in it," Coffin said.

"No benefits, either, once the legislature's done with us," Lola said.

Adams squared his chin. "It's all about catching the bad guys, right?"

"In Truro?" Coffin said.

"You've got to start somewhere," Lola said.

"Hey," Adams said. "Two murders in ten years. That's not nothing."

"Maybe I should apply," Coffin said.

———

Inside, Branstool's house was just as Coffin remembered it from the night before—neat, beige, crowded with wooden ducks—except that during the day the sun streamed in through the big, west-facing windows, filling the living room with yellow light, motes drifting in the still air. There was a large print on the living-room wall—a solid field of dark blue, fading into turquoise at the edges, with a pale green stripe across the top. It looked, Coffin thought, like one of Branstool's silk ties—the ones he'd worn to offset the beige suits he always wore to work. Except for the ducks, it was the only splash of color in the room.

Lola stood near the fireplace. "Wow," she said. "The man liked his waterfowl."

A life-sized merganser swam in place on the glass coffee table. Coffin picked it up, turned it over, tapped on it. It appeared to be solid.

"You said he made these in his woodshop?" Lola said.

"There's a hell of a lot of woodworking gear up there, and a hell of a lot of ducks down here. Two plus two."

"You'd think after making so many of them, he'd eventually get good at it."

Coffin looked at the merganser more closely. Its beak was slightly off-center, its feathers were lumpy, its eyes out of whack.

"Look at the paint job," Lola said. "It's like a kid did it."

She was right—the paint was messy, thick and gloppy in some spots, scant and spotty in others. "Huh," Coffin said. "Maybe this is an early one."

Lola retrieved an eider from the mantel. It was as poorly made as the merganser, as were the wood duck, the teal, and the mallard Coffin took from the shelves.

"Okay," Lola said, after they'd examined another dozen of the decoys. "This is something I clearly don't get about men."

"You mean, how we can spend thousands of dollars on a hobby and still suck at it?"

"Well, yeah. It just seems like such a waste of money and time. It's like the more inherently pointless it is, the more obsessed you-all get. I'm not upsetting you, am I? I mean, you're not secretly into model trains or anything, right?"

Coffin laughed. "I tried playing golf for a while," he said. "I did pretty well at first—kind of got sucked in. There's nothing like the feeling of hitting a good drive—no matter how frustrating the rest of the game was, one or two good shots in a round were enough to keep me coming back."

"Were you, like, incredibly bored with your life then?"

"Totally," Coffin said. "It was a long time ago. Thank God I stopped getting better. After a few months I developed a wicked slice—if there was water or a sand trap, I was in it. I'd hit the ball into the parking lot, into the club swimming pool if they had one, onto the practice green, you name it. Finally it occurred to me that life is humiliating enough without golf. I haven't played since."

Lola picked up a wooden grebe and looked into its off-kilter eyes. "But life was not humiliating enough without this duck, apparently. Not for Branstool."

"Maybe the passion just hadn't worn off yet," Coffin said. "I bought a whole new set of clubs before I realized the problem wasn't the clubs."

Lola turned the grebe over. "Huh," she said. She held it up, showed it to Coffin. "Look what I found."

Coffin took the grebe; it was faintly tacky to the touch. There was a neat seam running around its underside, a fine indentation visible through the paint. "Well now," he said. "This is interesting." He tapped the grebe with his fingernail; it emitted a hollow *thwonk*.

Lola picked up another duck, but it appeared to be solid. After checking six more, they found another that had been hollowed out. Then after eight more, another.

"Are you thinking what I'm thinking?" Lola said, after they'd found five hollow ducks.

"I'm thinking I wish we had a drug dog," Coffin said.

"So, smuggling?"

Coffin nodded. "Not a lot of volume, so something pricey—high-quality heroin or coke, maybe."

"Could be some other smuggling thing," Lola said. "Diamonds. Krugerrands."

"And any minute now Cary Grant could jump in through the window," Coffin said.

Lola punched him in the shoulder.

"Ow," Coffin said, arm tingling. He shook his head. "It's weird. He's making the ducks in the wood shop—loading them with God-knows-what that probably comes in on a fishing boat or a yacht, and shipping them off, where?"

"What are the odds he kept meticulous records in an easy-to-decipher spreadsheet program on his desktop computer?"

"Ha. A girl can dream."

"It doesn't make sense," Lola said. "Who smuggles coke inside a wooden duck? Plain old FedEx isn't good enough? It's so . . . elaborate."

Coffin held the grebe up in front of Lola's face. "What looks less suspicious than a duck?" he said. "Seriously, look at his little face. The sincerity!"

"Don't make me hit you again," Lola said.

The search for Branstool's stash box didn't go well. Coffin combed the ground floor, while Lola took the upstairs bedrooms. They looked in closets, bathroom and kitchen cabinetry, dressers, behind the bookshelves full of ducks, behind the watery, blue-green pictures on the walls—checking especially for hidden panels and false bottoms, any concealed space big enough to contain a quantity of cash, drugs, or weapons. When they were done, they were careful to put everything back in its place. After an hour and a half, they met downstairs in the living room. Coffin flopped onto the big, beige sectional couch.

"Nada," he said. "You?"

"Zip," Lola said. "That drug dog might come in handy—you're right."

"I'll call Mancini. The state police have a few. Assuming their budget hasn't been cut."

"There's still the garage. And the wood shop."

"I'm not entirely sure I can go back into the wood shop," Coffin said. "It's pretty bad up there."

Lola shrugged. "Fine. You do the garage, I'll take the wood shop."

There was a commotion in the front foyer, and then two big men dressed in jeans and leather car coats strode into the living room.

"Be still, my heart," Bitters said. "It's *him.*"

"Oh, to touch the hem of his blues," Hump said.

"So you met Adams," Coffin said.

"Nice kid," Hump said. "He wants you to autograph his chest." Bitters unbuttoned his coat. "He wants to have your baby."

"So what brings you gentlemen out this way?" Coffin said.

"Oh, you know," Hump said. "Investigating and shit. You?"

Coffin told them about the ducks, but not about the search for Branstool's stash box.

"That's interesting," Hump said, stroking his chin. "Hollow ducks." He looked at Bitters.

"Maybe they float better," Bitters said, looking at Hump.

"Right," Hump said. "That's probably it."

"Why don't you two go get a bite?" Bitters said. "We'll take it from here."

"Absolutely," Hump said, tapping on one of the hollow ducks. "You two look exhausted. Go get a tasty beverage. We'll make sure nothing gets overlooked."

Coffin nodded. "Sure. You guys help yourselves. We're pretty much done here."

"Yep," Lola said. "Knock yourselves out."

Outside, the wind had grown chill and sharp, and the sun was already going down. Long shadows stretched from the house and garage. Coffin's shadow looked monstrous—long legs and torso, tiny little pinhead. He waved. His shadow waved back, freakish, demented.

"If I didn't know better," Lola said, "I'd think those mutts were trying to get rid of us."

Coffin grinned. "Ya think?" He wanted a cigarette. He thought about bumming one from Adams, but resisted the urge. Instead he asked Adams for the keys to the garage.

"Those two state police detectives," Adams said, keys jingling as he handed them over. "They weren't too happy when I told them you were here."

"No," Coffin said. "I don't imagine they were."

Coffin's search of the garage yielded nothing new. He thought again that it was probably the cleanest garage he'd ever seen—not a drop of oil on the floor, nothing out of place. The cars were immaculate, too—as though Branstool had had them polished every day, but didn't actually drive them. Coffin was about to go bum a cigarette from Adams when Lola came pounding down the stairs from the wood shop in her engineer boots.

"Frank!" she said. "I've got something."

"Great," Coffin said. "It had to be in the wood shop."

Climbing the stairs, he felt dizzy—his legs suddenly too long, the wooden steps slanted and far away. He stopped, took a deep breath, then kept climbing.

"It might not be anything," Lola said when they'd stepped into the wood shop, "but it sure looks like a hidey-hole." She'd pulled aside a wheeled metal shelving unit full of small power tools: behind it, a section had been cut out of the drywall just above the wood shop's floor and then replaced with drywall screws. It looked innocent enough—it could have given access to the plumbing, or hidden the wiring necessary to install a flat-screen TV. It was about two feet square—plenty big enough for a good-sized lockbox, Coffin thought.

"We've got about five minutes," Coffin said, trying not to look at the blood-splattered corner where the radial arm saw crouched. "Find me a cordless drill and a Phillips bit, would you?"

"Ask and you shall receive," Lola said, handing Coffin a Makita drill with a bit already in the chuck. "I was going to take the panel off myself and surprise you," she said, when Coffin shot her a look, "but I figured that being a man you'd want to do the part that involved tools."

"Thank God somebody's watching out for my ego," Coffin said, backing out the first of the four drywall screws holding the panel in place.

"See?" Lola said. "Look at you go."

The last three screws came out just as easily, and Coffin lifted the panel carefully from its rough frame.

"Well, now," Lola said. "What have we got here?"

"Come to Papa," Coffin said.

Chapter 16

Okay," Lola said. "Now what?"

They were in the Crown Vic, heading back toward Provincetown. To the right, Pilgrim Lake was silver gray in the lowering light; to the left, behind Beach Point's neat row of cottages, the bay spread out toward the horizon. Coffin felt himself yearning toward them, their strange romantic tug.

"I could use a drink," Coffin said. "How about you?"

"Sure—but what about the you-know-what?"

A black leather gym bag bulged on the backseat. It was packed with bricks of light brown heroin, tightly wrapped in plastic bags.

"We could sell it," Coffin said.

"Yep," Lola said. "We could."

"Fun to think about."

"Mm-hm."

"I could totally use a new car."

"I thought you said Jamie was getting a minivan."

"Right."

There was a minute or two of silence, broken only by the low growl of the Crown Vic's big V8 and the rushing of the wind.

"How much do you think it's worth?" Lola said finally.

"Depends how much it weighs," Coffin said. "A million? Two? Who knows."

"Think it's real? Not just brown sugar or something?"

"It's real."

There was another silence. Lola reached into the glove box, found a pack of gum, opened it, and folded a stick into her mouth. A faint whiff of artificial mint drifted through the Crown Vic's interior.

"I'm going to hand it over to Gault," Coffin said.

"You trust her?"

"Even if I don't," Coffin said, "it establishes a clear chain of custody, with witnesses. She'll hand it over to Mancini, maybe, or the FBI."

"Bitters and Hump aren't going to be happy."

Coffin laughed—a sharp bark. "They might still end up with it, is the funny part. Where it goes after Mancini or the Feds get it is anybody's guess. But at least we made it a little more complicated for them."

"Frank?"

"Mm?"

"You ever think about cashing in—seriously?"

"Who hasn't?" Coffin said.

"You had opportunities, though. Back in Baltimore."

"Me? Not so much, in homicide. The guys in narcotics—that's a different story. You'd hear all kinds of stuff. Bribes, shakedowns, robberies. Big sacks of cash or drugs lying around—if you find it first, nobody knows how much is in there but you, right? Stuff disappearing out of the evidence cage. You name it, it happens—and if you play it smart . . ."

"Frank?"

"You're asking?" Coffin leaned back in his seat. "Really?"

Lola kept her eyes on the road. "No. Not really."

"I had a partner in homicide—great guy. Rashid Johnson. Before I worked with him he was a narcotics detective for awhile, and one night when we were out for drinks after a rough shift he told me this story. You ready?"

"Sure. Ready."

"Okay. So Rashid's a young detective, and he's got this older partner named Rizzuto. Rizzuto's a decent guy, a little on the take but not a big-time crook the way a lot of the guys in narcotics are. He pays a call on a distributor he's been after—guy they called Woodrow—stops by his apartment. Rizzuto's undercover, doing his very convincing mob guy routine—the full Tony Soprano, right? He's almost ready to make the big buy he's been setting up for weeks, that's his story."

"Got it."

"Woodrow's place is a penthouse—zebra rugs, gold chandeliers, full view of the harbor, the whole bit—Woodrow's big-time. He's not home—but his girlfriend is. She wants to have a drink, so they have a drink. Then she wants to do a few lines, so they do a few lines. *Then* she tells Rizzuto she's pissed at Woodrow because he's been fooling around with the other strippers at her club."

"So she's a stripper?"

"Right—and she's gorgeous. Big, tall redhead—and Rizzuto's got a thing for redheads, right?"

"Where's Rashid?"

"He's home sick. Can I tell the story now?"

"Sorry."

"So Rizzuto's there by himself—Rashid's home sick. Okay? And the pissed off stripper girlfriend practically jumps out of her panties and does Rizzuto right there on the couch. He's loving it—

he's thinking it's his lucky day. Then, when they're done, she leads him to the hall closet and hands him a suitcase and says, 'Take it! I don't want this shit in my house no more.' He looks inside and it's full of coke and hundred-dollar bills. Rizzuto's thrilled—his ship's come in, right? But he's a little nervous—something doesn't feel quite right. So the girlfriend—get this—does him *again,* down on her knees in the front hall."

"Uh-oh."

"Right? So when she's done she zips him up, puts his hat back on his head and out the door he goes with the suitcase—he's so goofy on fancy vodka, coke, and endorphins he can't think straight."

"This is not going to end well, is it?"

"Gold star for Sergeant Winters. Rizzuto rides down in the elevator figuring he's got it made. The doors open up and there's six agents from the FBI corruption task force, shields out and guns drawn. They've got the whole thing on tape."

"Bye-bye, Rizzuto."

"Bye-bye is right. He's *still* in prison—they sent him out to Hazelton in West Virginia and he's been there ever since."

"So that's it? That's why you stayed clean? You were worried about the FBI?"

Coffin made a sour face. "The FBI? Of course not," he said. "Rizzuto was an idiot. And it's not like I was some kind of avenging angel out there. I turned a blind eye to a lot of stuff I probably should have reported. But I was never on the take—I have a hard enough time sleeping at night."

"What a great and ultimately pointless story."

"I know, right?"

Monica Gault peered into the black gym bag sitting on her desk. "Good God," she said. "Is that what I think it is?"

Kirby Flint, the town attorney, stood next to her. He was trim and muscular. His shaved head gleamed in the fluorescent light. "I believe it's heroin," he said. He was, Coffin knew, very active in Provincetown's leather scene.

"We haven't tested it," Coffin said, "but that'd be my guess."

Each of the plastic-wrapped bricks was sealed with a red stamp that bore a faint image of a mosque surrounded by a wreath, with a squiggle of Arabic script at the top. Flint reached into the bag, hefted one of the bricks. "Roughly a pound, I'd say. So, a half kilo?"

"About that," Coffin said.

"If this were a film," Gault said, "this gym bag would be the MacGuffin."

"The ma-what?" Lola said.

Gault looked at Lola over the tops of her glasses. "MacGuffin. It was Hitchcock's word for the otherwise meaningless object around which the plot of a thriller revolves. You know—the diamond necklace, or the stolen microfilm."

Flint unpacked the gym bag onto Gault's desk. "Twelve pounds," he said. "Any idea of the value?"

"A lot," Coffin said. "Over a million, if it's any good. Maybe two. Maybe more."

"You'll want a receipt, I suppose," Flint said.

"I will," Coffin said.

"Mr. Flint," Gault said. "May I trouble you for a moment?"

"Certainly," Flint said, brushing a speck of lint from the lapel of his suit jacket.

"Can you explain to me why Acting Chief Coffin has brought this large quantity of heroin to my office?"

Flint pushed his black, rectangular glasses onto the bridge of his nose with his index finger. "He wants to establish a clear chain of custody, but he doesn't trust the state police. That would be my guess, at least."

"Bingo," Coffin said.

"But you're not going to leave it here, surely?" Gault said, her voice rising, almost plaintive.

"I suggest we place it in the safe until such time as a representative of the appropriate state or federal agency can pick it up," Flint said.

"We have a safe?" Gault said.

The Tax Assessor's office on Town Hall's second floor was equipped with a 1,200-pound safe, manufactured in 1915 by the Diebold Safe and Lock Company, of Canton, Ohio. The safe had been acquired originally to protect tax receipts and vital town records in case of fire or attempted theft; no one had ever thought it necessary to replace it with a newer model. Without the combination, Coffin guessed, you'd need a direct hit from an artillery shell to get it open.

"I'd suggest calling the FBI in Boston," Coffin said. "The less we have to deal with DEA the happier we'll all be. I was going to request FBI assistance with the fires tomorrow anyway. It'll be a twofer."

"A twofer," Gault said. "How wonderful."

After Gault and Flint had finally locked the gym bag away in the big safe—with Lola, Coffin, and Filson, the town clerk, as witnesses—and handed Coffin a notarized receipt, Lola practically dragged Coffin back upstairs to his office.

"Sit," she said, pointing to his desk chair.

"Yes, ma'am," Coffin said.

Lola pulled an Apple laptop from her briefcase and opened it on Coffin's desk. "I've uploaded the video files from the fires, but I haven't had a chance to really look at them, things have been so crazy. Do you mind? I need your eyes."

"I need a drink," Coffin said.

"Soon—there's only about fifteen minutes of video altogether." Lola opened a video editing program, which showed six video clip icons arranged in a neat grid. "Okay, here's clip one of the shed fire." She clicked on the first icon, and the clip began to play in a window about half the size of the laptop's screen.

"Hard to make out much detail," Coffin said. "The faces are all pretty blurry."

"Well, duh," Lola said. "It was dark. But you can see body size and shape, posture, clothes, attitude. That's something."

"It's something, but it's not much," Coffin said, staring at the smeared faces of the gawkers as the camera panned slowly to the left, then back to the right again. The lens bounced upward a bit, pausing for a second on a grainy figure on the hillside, deep in shadow, before returning to the crowd closer to the fire. "Wait a minute—" Coffin said, pointing at the top of the screen. "Who's that guy? Up there on the hill. Go back."

Lola rewound the clip until she found the figure on the hill, then paused it. "Huh," she said. "I don't remember seeing this guy, but I must have, right?"

"You sure it's a guy?"

Lola squinted. "Nope, too blurry. Could be kind of a bulky woman, I guess."

"Sure doesn't want to be seen, whoever he is. Or she."

"Jeans and a hoodie," Lola said.

Coffin pushed a hand through his hair. "Jeans and a hoodie. Could be your guy."

"Yep. But there's what," Lola said, rewinding the video again, "three guys in jeans and hoodies in the crowd? It's like it's frickin' jeans and hoodie season. What about them?"

Coffin touched a fingertip to the dime-sized bald spot on the top of his head. Was it getting bigger? "There's definitely something going on with the guy on the hill. What's he even doing up there?"

"Could be somebody that's staying in one of the cottages," Lola said. "Or maybe somebody that wants to watch but doesn't want to get too close."

"It's his body language," Coffin said. "Go back again. See how he reacts when the camera turns his way? He hides himself behind that tree a little bit more."

"Huh," Lola said. "Good eye." She clicked on the second clip of the shed fire, but the camera did not return to the figure on the hill.

"Let's see if he shows up at the condo fire," Coffin said.

"Way ahead of you," Lola said, clicking on the first of three clips of the condo crowd. The camera panned from right to left—maybe thirty people, Coffin thought, hands in their pockets, little puffs of breath vapor visible in the cold night. The fire's glow was much brighter than in the clips of the shed; its roar and crackle clearly audible.

"Two guys in jeans and hoodies," Coffin said.

"That one's a girl," Lola said, touching the screen with a fingertip.

"Right. Sorry. So what about the guy—same one?"

Lola squinted again. "The light's better," she said. "I can see his face, sort of—narrow features, looks like. Skinny."

"The first guy was stocky, though, right?"

Lola clicked on the clip of the shed fire again, still paused at the ghostly figure on the hill. "Yeah," she said. "I think you're right. Could be a thinner guy in big, floppy clothes, maybe. Or he might look bigger because of the blur. But I don't think it's the same person."

"What about the girl?"

"Skinny jeans. The character on the hill's wearing baggies."

Coffin rested his chin in his hands. "What about the guy that hit you over the head? Any video of him?"

Lola shook her head. "I don't think so—not unless Jeff took some. I handed him the camera as soon as I saw sweatshirt guy walking away." She clicked on the single, short clip from the church fire.

Maybe twenty people, Coffin thought. It was late, so not much of a crowd. "There's skinny jeans girl again," he said. "What's her deal?"

"Are there fire groupies?" Lola said.

The camera turned suddenly to the left, and for a moment it focused on a man's back as he walked away from the lens. He was bulky, but not tall. Hands in his pockets, hood up. The picture wobbled, swung to the right and turned on its side, blurring as the camera tried to focus on the front of Jeff Skillings's uniform jacket. Then the clip ended.

"Wow," Lola said.

"Got him," Coffin said.

"Yeah, but is it hill guy?" She clicked on the shed fire clip again.

"Same build. Same posture. Hands in his pockets the same way. Could be . . ."

Lola closed her eyes, rubbed her temples. "I just want a look at his face. Is that too much to ask?"

"Go back to the condo fire," Coffin said. They looked at all three clips of the condo fire, which together produced a kind of evolutionary timeline of the crowd as people came and went. "Wait," Coffin said, when they'd gone back to the first clip again. "Back up a little."

Lola rewound the clip a few seconds, then hit PLAY.

"Pause it," Coffin said, pointing at the screen. "Check him out."

The same bulky man was caught in freeze-frame, standing just behind another, taller spectator in the crowd—a man wearing a billowy chiffon gown and a fur stole, who stood well over six feet in spiked heels. Coffin squinted: one of Hill Guy's eyes and part of his cheek and forehead were visible on the grainy video. The rest of his face was either obscured by the hood of his sweatshirt or hidden behind the shoulder of the tall cross-dresser. When Lola backed the video up, Hill Guy's head was turned, his face entirely obscured by his hood. When she hit the forward button, he disappeared completely behind Chiffon Man. He was not present in the second clip, or the third.

"Shit," Lola said. "One eye? That's all I get? One frickin' eye?"

"It's kind of an interesting eye," Coffin said, face close to the laptop screen. Hill Guy's one, visible eye was wide, bright in the firelight, fierce. Only part of the eyebrow was visible—it was dark, arched. "Probably got dark hair," Coffin said. "Not old, I don't think."

"He doesn't hit like an old guy," Lola said. "Wait a sec . . ." She increased the film clip's window-size to full screen.

"That just makes it grainier," Coffin said.

"I'm going to remember that eye," Lola said, feeling the back of her head. "Guy hits me with a brick, he'd better hope I don't spot him on the street."

Coffin nodded. "Yep," he said. "Still sore?"

Lola winced, then grinned. "Nah," she said. "Sore is for wussies." She paused. "What about one of those drawings? You know, an artist's composite."

"Like a pencil drawing of the suspect? Who'd do it?"

"What about your friend, what's-his-name? He can draw, right?"

"Kotowski?" Coffin thought for a second. "So he draws a picture of sweatshirt guy, then what? We put up posters? Put it in the *Banner*?"

"Sure. Isn't that what cops would do in a situation like this?"

"It's going to take some extrapolation," Coffin said, pointing at the laptop screen. "We've got one eye and a sweatshirt."

"He's an artist. He can't extrapolate?"

"If you were a serial arsonist," Coffin said, smoothing his mustache, "and you saw a sketch of yourself on a poster or in the newspaper, what would you do?"

"Change the way I look," Lola said. "Cut my hair, wear different clothes. If I was a guy maybe I'd grow a mustache, or shave one off."

Coffin nodded. "To fool the cops," he said. "But it wouldn't fool your friends, or your family."

"They'd say, dude, what's up with the mustache?"

"It's worth a shot," Coffin said. "I have to run over to Valley View. I'll stop by Kotowski's place before I go home."

"Jamie doing okay?"

"She says she's nesting," Coffin said. "Why don't you come by for a drink in a bit? With any luck, I'll have a sketch to show you."

Coffin sat beside his mother's bed, the volume turned down on her big TV. His mother stared straight ahead at the bright but silent screen, her features feral and sharp, hair the color of galvanized steel.

"They tell me somebody killed what's-his-name," she said, gesturing loosely at the nurse's station down the hall. "They're acting all upset about it."

"They probably *are* upset, Ma. I'm sure it was a shock to everyone."

She turned and stared at him for a moment with her bright crow's eyes. "Not to me," she said.

"No? How come?"

Her lip curled—a tight half-smile. "'Cause I had him whacked." She drew a slow finger across her neck. "Ha! The dirty little prick had it coming."

"Ma. You didn't have him whacked. Don't say that in front of people, okay?"

The remote lay on the coverlet. She picked it up, flipped through a few channels, settling on a home shopping show. "You don't believe me? Ask your uncle."

"Uncle Rudy?"

"Who? No—the one who's a crook."

Coffin shook his head. He knew it was pointless arguing with her. The deeper the Alzheimer's dug its tentacles into her brain, the less she resembled the woman he remembered—warm, but with a deep ironic streak, ferociously loyal, beautiful, *like a movie star*, his father had always said. She hardly recognized him now, but the feeling was mutual—Coffin's mother was all but gone, and this strange old woman had taken her place.

"He didn't do it himself, of course," she said, touching a finger to her temple. "Too smart for that."

"Right," Coffin said. "Way too smart."

"It was that accountant he's running around with. Huggybear."

"Loverboy?"

"Who?"

After he'd left his mother's room—patting her hand, kissing her temple—Coffin paused outside the director's office. The door was open. Ms. Haskell, the patient's advocate, was sitting at Branstool's desk. She waved Coffin in.

"Detective Coffin," she said. "Have you got a minute?"

"Just," Coffin said.

"Thanks, I know it's a busy time for you. But I wanted to let you know we've decided to consider your mother's appeal of the relocation decision."

"Her appeal?"

"We were contacted by her attorney this morning. She pointed out that under Massachusetts law, there's a ten-day window during which an appeal must be heard, if requested."

"Her attorney? She has an attorney?"

"She's retained an attorney, yes. A Ms. Sarah Baldritch of Baldritch, Torkel, Nash. Of Boston."

Coffin touched his mustache. It was spiky, needed trimming. He thought again about shaving it off. "Has my uncle been to see her? Rudy Santos?"

"Not to my knowledge, no, sir," Ms. Haskell said. "But feel free to check the visitor log."

On his way out, Coffin glanced through the log—a yellow pad on the day-nurse's desk, next to a small printed placard that said "Please Sign In." Rudy's name wasn't on it—but Coffin already knew it wouldn't be.

Kotowski lived in a ramshackle old house near the breakwater, at the far west end of Commercial Street. The house had a small insignia above the door—a blue rectangle with a white house floating on white waves—which meant that it had, in its earlier form, been one of the houses floated across the harbor from the old Long Point salt works, an abandoned settlement of fishermen and salt workers once known as Hell Town. He'd bought it for almost nothing in the seventies, had weatherized it himself, built crazy additions without permit or license, almost lost it to unpaid taxes and greedy developers multiple times. Somehow he was still there, still making his strange paintings—the dusty living room crammed with poorly mended furniture he'd picked up at the dump: the armchairs repaired with duct tape, the three-legged coffee table supported by a cinder block. A large outboard motor lay in pieces on the living-room floor, in a state of greasy and perpetual disrepair.

"You want me to do a *what?*" Kotowski said. They were sitting at Kotowski's warped and tippy kitchen table, peering at the screen of Lola's laptop.

"I want you to do an artist's rendering of the guy standing behind the guy in the big poofy dress."

"An artist's *rendering?* That's what you get when you melt down an abstract expressionist, right? Or when Thomas Kinkade takes a crap."

"He'll be here all week," Coffin said.

"*I* thought it was funny," Kotowski said. "Hell, I can't even *see* the guy. Can you make him any bigger?"

"Nope."

"Any clearer?"

"Sorry."

"Does he ever come out from behind the guy in the dress?"

"That's as good as it gets."

Kotowski closed the laptop with a definitive snap. "Forget it," he said. "It's not dignified. I'm an artist—not some police technician working with composites on a computer. I went to RISD, for Christ's sake."

"Fine. I thought it might be kind of a challenge—putting together a whole face from the fragment. Plus, you were doing the crime theme for awhile."

"Doing the *crime theme?*" Kotowski said, making finger quotes. "Are you talking about the Frog Marches? Those were deeply subversive paintings, Coffin. If you think they had anything to do with your conventional little arsonist, you've entirely missed the point."

The Frog Marches were a series of life-sized, photo-realist paintings Kotowski had done in 2008 and 2009. *Frog March 1,* depicting a weeping George W. Bush being led away in handcuffs by FBI agents, had sold immediately for a price that even Kotowski thought ridiculously high. He'd done several more: *Frog March 2* showed Dick Cheney being dragged into a courtroom in an orange jumpsuit; in *Frog March 3* Donald Rumsfeld was tarred and feathered; *Frog March 4* imagined the prison strip-search of Condoleeza Rice, complete with latex-gloved matron; and *Frog March 5* showed Alberto Gonzalez, strapped to a table, cloth wadded into his mouth, eyes wide behind his glasses as a large man in camouflage poured water over his face. All had been sold to the same anonymous collector.

"Good series," Coffin said. "Very lifelike."

"Very lifelike?" Kotowski said. "Is that all you can say? What about the content, Coffin?"

Coffin shrugged. "They were terrible people. I'm glad they're gone. I'm pretty sure I wouldn't want their pictures in my living room."

Kotowski poked Coffin in the chest with a long, bony forefinger. "But they're *not* gone," he said. "That's the point. You can drive out the Devil with a pitchfork, Coffin, but he always comes roaring back again. Just look at Cheney—he was in the fucking *Nixon* administration, for Christ's sake."

"Whatever," Coffin said, rubbing his chest. "Will you do it, or not?"

Kotowski tapped a filterless Camel from the pack and lit it. "I told you—no. N-O. I don't work for the cops, even if they're my best friend."

"I'm touched, Kotowski. Sort of."

"Well, don't be. It's all relative. You're just the person in this town I dislike the least. Want a beer? I stole some Newcastles from the Oyster Shack."

"Sorry," Coffin said. "I can't. I have to get home."

"All right, all right, twist my arm. I'll do your fucking rendering. It'll take a few minutes. The beer's in the fridge."

Coffin opened a Newcastle for Kotowski, and one for himself. They were very cold. Kotowski fetched a large sketch pad and a stick of charcoal, opened the laptop and started to draw.

"So," he said. "Are you going to take my advice and leave town?"

"Jamie doesn't want to," Coffin said. "She likes it here."

"What about you? What do *you* want?"

"Does it matter?"

"Nope," Kotowski said, sketching. "Not in the least."

Coffin sipped his beer. "I like it here. I like the seasonal change. It's too crowded in the summer and too cold and deserted in the winter, but maybe that's better than living someplace that never changes. Sometimes the streets seem too narrow. I don't know—you'd leave?"

Kotowski curled his lip. "Provincetown isn't the same anymore. It's too *cute*. It's like a fucking theme park. Welcome to Queerland! Come and gawk at the quaint and lovable locals in their fanciful homosexual garb!" He made a loud retching sound. "I was getting drunk at the Vault a few nights ago and a guy walks in with his wife and a couple of bored teenagers. Teenagers, Coffin! The guy said he wanted them to get a look at a real alternative lifestyle." Kotowski made finger quotes again, rolled his eyes. "He said, 'It's all about recognizing each other as human beings, right?' I had to stop myself from caving his head in with a bar stool. What the fuck is the point of having a leather bar if you can't shock the yokels with it?"

"The whole gay thing is so twentieth century," Coffin said.

"Exactly! We'll have to come up with something new— something completely *vile*. Then, in a few years, they'll accept that, too, and we'll have to come up with something *else*—it's like a freaking arms race. I'm telling you, Coffin, all this accepting you breeders are doing—it's taking the fun out of being homosexual."

"Maybe you should move to Texas, or Uganda," Coffin said.

"I like a challenge," Kotowski said. "But get serious—Texas?"

Coffin drained his beer. "Okay," he said. "Nice chatting, but I've got to get going."

"Don't you want your rendering?" Kotowski said. "All done— free of charge." He turned the sketch pad around. It was the man in the gray hoodie, stocky, hands in his pockets—except that all of his features had been squashed together in the upper-right corner of his face: eyes, nose, mouth, ears.

"What the hell is *that*?" Coffin said.

"It's cubism, you philistine," Kotowski said. "Jesus, don't you know *anything*?"

Lola pulled up in front of Coffin's house in her new Camaro just as Coffin was climbing out of the Fiesta. The two cars were a study in contrasts, Coffin thought: the Camaro was shiny, black, and powerful—a decent contemporary take on a classic muscle car. The Fiesta was salt-faded, rusty, and sagging. *Kind of like me,* Coffin thought.

"Jamie will be happy to see you," he said, when Lola had eased herself out of the driver's seat.

She glanced at her watch. "It's mutual," she said. "I haven't seen Jamie in, like, a month."

"You'll be amazed. She's out to here." Coffin held his hand a few inches in front of his belly.

"Can't wait," Lola said. "Did you get the sketch?"

Coffin shook his head. "No dice," he said. "He wasn't in the mood."

The sound of R&B music filtered through the front door as

they stepped onto the screen porch. It was a CD Jamie had just bought: Sharon Jones and the Dap Kings, the horn section chugging through the minor-chord progression of "100 Days, 100 Nights."

Coffin pushed the door open.

"Dude," Lola said.

"Whoa," Coffin said. The living room was empty. There were no strict Victorian chairs, no lumpy Victorian sofas stuffed with horsehair. There were no glass-fronted cabinets full of his mother's knickknacks, no clutter of end tables, no doilies, no threadbare Persian rugs. Except for the Bose CD player thumping away on the floor and the taxidermied goat's head leering down from above the fireplace, the living room had been cleared out.

"Jamie?" Coffin said. "Anybody home?"

Jamie appeared at the top of the stairs. She was wearing yoga pants and a skimpy green camisole, tight across her belly. Her breasts, Coffin thought, were spectacular.

"What do you think?" Jamie said, spreading her arms.

"I think you look amazing," Coffin said.

"I'll second that emotion," Lola said.

Jamie rolled her eyes. "You guys are goofballs. Not me, the living room. Isn't it awesome?"

"It has a certain *je ne sais quoi,*" Coffin said.

"Minimalist," Lola said. "Very hip."

Jamie trotted down the stairs, a careful hand on the rail. "Seriously," she said. "Look how much lighter it is without all that dark *stuff.*"

She had a point, Coffin thought. "It looks a lot bigger, too," he said.

Jamie kissed his cheek. "Well, duh," she said. "It's empty, right? Goofball."

"You kept the goat," Lola said.

"Frank thinks it's haunted by his father. How could I get rid of it?"

Lola tilted her head, looked at Coffin, then the goat, then back at Coffin again. "Total resemblance," she said.

"Hey!" Coffin said.

"Who's up for a cocktail?" Jamie said. "I'm pouring."

"But not drinking," Coffin said, watching Jamie's backside as she strode into the kitchen. *Still not square,* he thought. Then he shook his head. *You don't want to start channeling Rudy.*

"Only vicariously," Jamie said, taking a big plastic jug from the fridge, holding it up by its neck. "I'll stick with Clamato."

"Clamato?" Lola said. "Seriously?"

Jamie tossed a few ice cubes into a tall glass, filled it with the viscous clam-and-tomato-juice cocktail. "I know," she said. "It sounds like a sexually transmitted disease. I sort of hate it—but the baby wants, wants, *wants* it." She drank it halfway down, refilled the glass.

"Freaky," Lola said.

"Told you," Coffin said. He retrieved a bottle of Famous Grouse from the cabinet over the stove, waved it at Lola. "Scotch, or scotch?"

"I think I'll have scotch."

"Doris called," Jamie said.

"How's Tony?" Lola said.

"In the psych ward, down in Hyannis. They're keeping him for observation."

"Good," Coffin said.

Jamie put a hand on Lola's arm. "Can you stay for dinner?"

"What are we having?" Coffin asked. "Pig's knuckles and Cheez-Whiz?"

"Mmm," Jamie said. "Cheez-Whiz."

Lola glanced at her watch again. "Sorry," she said. "I'd love to, but I've got a date."

"Another date?" Coffin said, pouring scotch into a pair of high-ball glasses. "Getting kind of serious, aren't we?"

"Well, yeah," Lola said. Coffin handed her a glass and she took a sip. "I've got a date with a Realtor. I'm thinking about buying a house." She propped her hip on the kitchen counter, next to a pile of mail: a few bills, a catalog from Pottery Barn.

"Really?" Jamie said. "In P'town?"

"I'm looking at half of a duplex, yeah," Lola said. "Prices have come down, but rents are higher than ever, seems like. It's cheaper to buy, if you can get a loan."

Coffin grinned. "Our little girl is finally settling down."

Lola cocked a fist, and Coffin ducked away. "Never hit a man who's holding scotch," he said.

"How exciting!" Jamie said. "When's the housewarming?"

"Oh, God—not anytime soon, probably. We're still trying to figure out if we can afford it," Lola said.

"We?" Coffin said. "*We?*"

Jamie gave Lola a hug. "Well, this *is* cause for celebration," she said.

Coffin raised his glass. "Mazel tov," he said.

"So," Coffin said, when Lola had finished her drink and driven off. "Two questions."

"Is this an enhanced interrogation, or just your basic?" Jamie said, opening her eyes very wide.

"Your basic."

"Too bad. What's question number one?"

"What should we eat?"

"I was thinking popcorn."

"Popcorn? That's it?"

"And Clamato."

Coffin laughed.

"And question two?"

"What happened to our furniture?"

"Your mother's furniture. It's on a truck, heading to an auction house in Sandwich."

"And will we be getting new furniture, eventually?"

"That's three questions. I wasn't expecting the Spanish Inquisition."

Coffin pulled her close, kissed her neck. "No one expects the Spanish Inquisition."

"Frank . . ."

"It's fine—we'll get lawn chairs. Do we still have a bed?"

"Frank." Jamie pushed him away. She was suddenly pale. She fanned herself with the Pottery Barn catalog. It had a picture of white wicker deck furniture on the cover.

"Ah. The Frank aversion is back."

"It's not me," Jamie said. "It's the baby. He doesn't want us to fuck. Very Oedipal."

"It starts early," Coffin said, smoothing his mustache.

Jamie shrugged. "Sorry."

"Let's go out for dinner," Coffin said.

"Great," Jamie said, color already coming back. "I'm starved."

"How about the Oyster Shack? On me."

"How about the Mews?" Jamie said. "On Grandpa Bill."

A black Lincoln Town Car was parked in the official lot across from Town Hall on Ryder Street, next to the Center for Coastal Studies. Rudy Santos and his accountant, Loverboy, did their best to scrunch down in their seats—not an easy thing, especially for Loverboy—listening to the rain as it pattered on the roof.

"He's late," Loverboy said, his voice rumbling inside the Town Car like a bass guitar through a subwoofer.

Rudy yawned enormously. "Patience, grasshopper," he said. He took a drag from his cigarette, blew smoke out the half-open window. "Let's go get a bite after this."

"Sure," Loverboy said.

"I want a steak."

"Terrible for you. All that cholesterol."

"I've got the cholesterol of a six-year-old vegetarian," Rudy said. "I could eat the whole cow, if I wanted to."

"Bad karma," Loverboy said. "What'd a cow ever do to you?"

"Cow farts contribute to global warming. It's our duty to rid the planet of them."

Loverboy frowned. "I don't eat anything with a face."

"Yeah, yeah," Rudy said. "Come on—not even fish?"

"Do fish have faces?"

"What about shrimp?"

Loverboy sighed. "Shrimp have eyes." He held his fingers up in front of his mouth and waggled them at Rudy. "And mandibles. That's a face."

"What about clams or oysters?"

"Too slimy."

"But they don't have faces," Rudy said. "So you can eat them, right?"

"Nothing with a face, and nothing slimy."

"Don't you know that salad screams when you pull it out of the ground? That's a scientific fact all you leaf-eaters choose to ignore."

"Check it out," Loverboy said, pointing a bratwurst-sized finger. A red Mustang GT pulled into the far end of the lot and sat idling, slow plumes of exhaust rising from its dual tailpipes. "It's those two state cops. What do you think they're up to?"

"Same thing as us," Rudy said. "More or less."

Located on the water-side of Commercial Street, not far from the charred shell of St. Mary's, the Mews was one of a handful of Provincetown restaurants that stayed open year-round. The dining room was broad and inviting, with big windows that looked out on the harbor. The bar was handsome, if a bit claustrophobic—a clutch of small, two-person tables crowded close to the bar stools—it was hard to sit there without feeling surrounded, Coffin thought. Even though Yelena was working behind the bar (she waved, Coffin waved back), Coffin was glad when the host showed them to a table near the window.

"Just so you know," the host said, "tonight's piano bar. Miss Dawn Vermilion will be performing, starting in about ten minutes."

"Oh, good," Jamie said. "I'm in the mood for Cole Porter."

"Great," Coffin said, opening the menu. "I'm in the mood for another scotch."

"Grouch."

"Tired grouch."

Jamie reached across the table, ran her fingertips through the hair at his temple. "Poor man," she said. "It's all so awful—the fires, now this business with Dr. Branstool."

"Kotowski thinks we should move. Get out of P'town."

Jamie's eyes widened. "Really? That's what Corinne said."

"She's the one with the fake boobs, right?"

"Mine are bigger now. She's incredibly jealous." Jamie stuck her chest out. She was wearing a low-cut, off-the-shoulder dress with an empire waist. Two women sitting at the table across from them looked up from their drinks.

"Who wouldn't be?" Coffin said.

"You'd really move?"

Coffin shrugged. "Maybe," he said. "You know how many babies were born in this town last year?"

Jamie sipped her water, shook her head.

"Nine. You know that little playground on Bradford Street, across from the Walker gallery?"

"I think so—sure."

"Every time I drive by, it's empty. I've never seen a single kid there in the off-season. Not once. It's sad, those empty swings."

"But it's beautiful here," Jamie said. "That's worth something, right? And there's a good charter school in Orleans. I've been doing some research."

The waiter came, a trim, forty-something man that Coffin recognized. He told them about the specials—swordfish, rack of lamb—and took their drink orders: a Shirley Temple for Jamie, Walker Red for Coffin.

"You're Detective Coffin, right?" the waiter said, pen poised above his order pad.

"That's me," Coffin said, "and your name's Mel?"

"That's right!" Mel turned his face in profile, gazed up toward the ceiling. "Good memory—I'm flattered." Then he bent down, touched Coffin's shoulder. "So come on, tell me—who's setting all these fires? It's got me so scared—I feel like I can't trust anybody!"

"I wish we knew," Coffin said. "We need the public's help, so if you hear anything, you give me a call, okay?" Coffin gave Mel his card.

Mel clutched it to his chest. "Oh, *hell* yes," he said. "I mean it's all so crazy, right? I can hardly sleep at night. I just keep thinking to myself, what's next?"

"Flirt," Jamie said, when Mel was gone.

Coffin grinned. "Worried?"

"Not about Mel, no."

"I don't know—he's pretty handsome."

"What waiter in Provincetown isn't handsome?"

"Good point."

"I'm worried about the bartender. She's the one you hired, right?"

"Right," Coffin said. "We only get her when she's not working here."

"You have a little crush on her."

Coffin shook his head. "Yelena? No. I like her, though—is that the same thing?"

"Your face lit up when you saw her." Jamie pursed her lips, which made Coffin want to kiss her.

"No worries. I'm not her type."

"You'd better not be," Jamie said, looking at the menu.

"If we moved," Jamie said, after Mel had brought their drinks, "where would we go?"

"Someplace inland," Coffin said, sipping his scotch. "No boats. Eau Claire, Wisconsin."

Jamie's eyebrows went up. "Where?"

"Eau Claire, Wisconsin," Coffin said. "Lola grew up there. She says it's very *Leave It to Beaver*—nice neighborhoods, not much crime. Hardly any homicides."

"That's what you thought when you moved back here from Baltimore."

"You're saying I'm a homicide magnet? They're following me?"

Jamie patted his hand. "I love you, but I'm not moving to Eau Claire, Wisconsin. Too cold. Plus, I'll bet there's no Trader Joe's."

"There's no Trader Joe's here."

"I know, but if I'm moving inland to someplace really cold, I want Trader Joe's."

Coffin's cell phone buzzed in his pocket, then burst into "La Cucaracha." He stood, dug it out. The caller ID showed an Eastham number. "Sorry," Coffin said. "It's Doris."

Coffin touched the TALK button and started walking toward the front door. "Coffin," he said.

"Frankie? Thank God you picked up."

"What's up, Doris?" Coffin said, looking up at the night sky—thick clouds, no moon. *Thanks a lot, God.*

There was a brief fusillade of static. ". . . Tony again. He's escaped."

"What? Escaped?"

"From the hospital. They had him on the second floor—you know, the psych ward. But sometime after they brought him his dinner he disappeared. They think he must've found a pair of scrubs to put on and just walked out."

"Walked out of a locked ward? Has the hospital called the police?"

"Yeah—the Hyannis cops are lookin' for him. State cops, too. They think he'll try to get home somehow. Maybe hitchhiking, or he'll panhandle for a bus ticket. If he can get to a phone, he might call you, Frankie."

"We'll put out a watch for him," Coffin said. "I'll have Margie give the Dennis, Orleans, and Eastham PDs a call, too. We'll find him."

"God, Frankie—I'm so scared. I never dealt with anything like this before. I mean, what do I tell the kids, for Christ's sake?"

"Tell them not to worry," Coffin said. "Tell them their dad's going to be just fine."

There was a pause. "Thanks, Frankie. You're a good guy."

"Take care, Doris."

It was starting to rain. Coffin shivered and walked back inside.

Bitters and Hump sat in their red Mustang GT in the lot across from Town Hall, the big engine idling, heater blowing warm air. Hump lit a cigarette. "What we need," he said, "is a diversion."

"Too many cops in there, for sure," Bitters said.

"Yep." Rain pattered on the Mustang's roof. The Pilgrim monument loomed above them.

"We could just walk in, wave our shields, and call jurisdiction," Bitters said. "Tell them to hand it over 'cause it's our case. I mean, it *is* our fucking case, after all."

Hump shook his head. "We'd have to sign for it. Does us no good at all."

"We could start a fire. Just a small one, but way across town. All the cops would run over there, we'd let ourselves into Coffin's office . . ."

"He's not completely stupid. He's not gonna leave it in his office."

"Okay, the evidence cage, then."

"We could do both, maybe. You start a fire, and I'll do the evidence grab while everybody's running around, confused. Walk in, wave my shield, walk out with the shit before they even think about making me sign."

Bitters frowned. "Fucking Coffin," he said. "He could have cut us a deal, right? We'd have been amenable to that. But no—he's gotta go all fucking Serpico on us. Hell, I'd have settled for half of whatever's in that bag."

"And I'd have settled for the other half," Hump said.

A light went out on the second floor of Town Hall. A second later it flicked on again, then off.

"See that?" Bitters said. "Looks like some kind of signal."

A minute later, a little man emerged from Town Hall through a side door. He wore a bowtie and round horn-rimmed glasses, and carried a black leather gym bag. When he crossed the street, Bitters and Hump nearly jumped from their car.

Coffin was glad they'd gotten there early: The Mews was filling up, tables and booths all busy, the bar packed, the sound of conversation swelling, boisterous. Jamie had ordered for him while he was on the phone: his favorite appetizer (ahi sushi tempura, sliced and well presented with wasabi, ginger, and soy sauce), and a lobster and scallop risotto, accompanied by a glass of pinot grigio. She'd ordered the rack of lamb for herself. "The baby wants meat," she said. "I thought we'd share the appetizer."

"Good," Coffin said, glancing down at his belly. "It's huge."

Dawn Vermillion was sitting at the piano—resplendent in a large crimson wig, turquoise-sequined gown and long white gloves. She waggled her ringed fingers over the keyboard, cracked her knuckles loudly, and then launched into a slow, bluesy version of "Love for Sale." Her voice was smoky, a bit rough around the edges. The usual Absolut Citron on the rocks sat on the little ledge above the keyboard. Dawn's trademark cigarette—smoldering in its long, ebony holder—had been banished, a victim of the town's nonsmoking ordinance. Coffin felt a momentary surge of nostalgia for the old Provincetown, the way it was before the fishing economy had collapsed, before the town had sold its soul entirely to the tourist economy, before, as Kotowski said, it had been upscaled and cutesified to death.

He looked up. Miles Kendrick, the ATF agent, was standing just inside the door while the host checked his seating chart.

"That's Kendrick," Coffin said, waving. "He's the ATF guy."

"Why don't you ask him to join us?" Jamie said.

"You sure?"

"Why not?" Jamie said. "You like him, right?"

"I'm not sure yet. I liked that he made fun of Mancini, anyway." Coffin waved Kendrick over. "Join us," he said.

"Nice of you," Kendrick said. He offered Jamie his hand. "I'm Miles," he said.

Jamie shook it. "Jamie," she said. "Please, sit down."

"I hope you don't think me too forward," Kendrick said, spreading his napkin across his lap, "but are you—"

"Pregnant?" Jamie smiled. "Yes. Lucky for you."

"I deduced it. You don't seem the sort of woman to drink a Shirley Temple, otherwise."

"Good save," Coffin said.

Kendrick smiled. "There were other clues," he said. "Anyway, congratulations. To both of you."

"I've been meaning to get in touch with you," Coffin said. "Busy day, it turns out."

"I knew where to find you if I needed you. I spent the afternoon poking around in your fire scenes. The church was very impressive."

"In terms of scale?" Jamie said.

"There's that, yes," Kendrick said, "but I was thinking more in terms of the sheer recklessness and stupidity of the arsonist."

"Let me guess," Coffin said. "Lots of accelerant."

Kendrick nodded. "Gallons of it, looked like. A good bit poured far from any exit, with no apparent timing device—the fire appears to have started in the *back* of the church. Hard to say for sure; lots of debris to wade through, but that's where the heaviest damage is. If that's the case, then your guy is either a complete moron or he has a serious death wish. If not both."

"They're not exactly mutually exclusive," Coffin said.

"You know the redneck's last words?" Kendrick said, to Jamie.

She grinned. "Hey y'all! Watch this!"

"You sound like home," Kendrick said.

"South Carolina," Jamie said. "I grew up in Charleston. I can still do the accent when I want to."

"Heaven," Kendrick said. "I grew up in Knoxville. I miss it every day."

Mel brought Kendrick's drink—a Bombay Gibson. Kendrick sipped it, closed his eyes, smiled. "God is good," he said. He looked at Jamie. "Gasoline is the accelerant of choice for your basic large-structure arson. It's not the only choice—you can start a fire with anything that burns, obviously—but gas is cheap and easily obtainable, and totally unincriminating. Who doesn't buy gas? If you know what you're doing it doesn't take much. Pour it on something combustible, use a simple delayed ignition device and you're good to go. A burning couch can put a house in flashover within minutes."

Jamie frowned. "Flashover."

"It's basically the point at which everything combustible in a room ignites at once," Kendrick said. "The heat and smoke from the burning couch or TV set or recliner, say, gathers below the ceiling, then begins to spread down the walls. Every surface in the room becomes superheated; then the furniture—carpet, appliances, you name it—releases flammable gases as they begin to thermally decompose. When it all gets hot enough—"

"Boom," Coffin said.

Kendrick smiled. "That's the technical term for it, yes." He fished the onion out of his cocktail and ate it.

"Flashover's the killer," Coffin said. "Once the couch or mattress or whatever really starts cooking, you've got very little time to get out."

"It depends on the size and contents of the room," Kendrick said. "But yes. It can happen very quickly."

Jamie stirred her Shirley Temple with the little pink umbrella. "So if you're the arsonist, and you're going heavy on the gas—"

"Way heavy."

"Then you're putting yourself at risk. So, not smart."

"Exactly. If the fumes become concentrated enough, any stray spark—from a heater, a lamp, a string of Christmas lights, you name it—could ignite them while you're still in the building. And, of course, that's unpredictable. The environment might be fine, and it might not." Kendrick leveled an index finger at Jamie. "So not smart at all, our boy. I doubt he knows how much danger he's putting himself in."

"He's doing a good job," Coffin said.

"Sorry?" Kendrick said.

"He really wants them to burn, and he's making damn sure they do. He's not thinking about the risk to himself—he wants to do a good job."

"I like it," Kendrick said. "On the one hand he's a careless amateur with a very limited understanding of the forces he's dealing with. On the other hand he's committed to completing the task, risks be damned. I don't suppose those attributes are mutually exclusive, either."

"No," said Coffin. "I don't suppose they are."

Coffin was glad when Mel brought the appetizer: a large tuna roll dipped in tempura batter and deep-fried, then cut into slices and arranged artfully on a white plate, along with a soy dipping sauce and a small, green ball of wasabi. Coffin pushed the plate into the middle of the table, between himself and Jamie. Jamie offered Kendrick a piece.

"It looks delicious," Kendrick said, "but I wouldn't want to deprive you, since you're eating for two. And your husband has the lean and hungry look of a man who hasn't eaten since lunch."

"We're not married," Jamie said, with her mouth full.

"No?" Kendrick said. He raised his glass in a mock toast. "Mazel tov," he said.

"I keep asking, she keeps turning me down," Coffin said.

"Not true," Jamie said, helping herself to another piece of sushi. "It's been months since you asked me. Months!"

"Will you marry me?" Coffin said.

"Nope," Jamie said. "Sorry."

"See what she does to me?" Coffin said.

Jamie pointed her fork at Coffin's nose. "More than half of all straight marriages end in divorce, Frank. More than half! Straight people suck at marriage. And we think *gay* people are going to wreck it?"

"I'm of the more-the-merrier school myself," Kendrick said, "but then, my father was a divorce lawyer."

Coffin grinned, sipped his wine.

"So," Kendrick said, after a brief silence. "What would someone like me do around here for fun?"

"That depends," Jamie said, "on what someone like you enjoys doing."

"Oh, you know—drinking. Men."

"Try the A-House," Coffin said, chewing. "It's Thursday, right?"

Kendrick nodded.

"Oh!" Jamie said. "Tighty whitey night!"

"You've said the magic words," Kendrick said. "God, I love this town."

When the two big men in leather coats climbed out of their car, Filson felt his heart stutter in his chest. He was certain they were cops: they had the square jaws, the cropped hair—and cops were the last thing he wished to encounter at that moment, especially big, tough-looking, smiling cops from out of town. He fingered the leather strap of his gym bag and kept walking.

"'Scuse me," the taller one said, blocking his path, "but do you work in there?" He indicated Town Hall's mint green bulk with a tilt of his head.

"Yes," Filson said. "I do."

"What's the matter?" the shorter one said. "You seem a little nervous. You okay?"

"I'm fine," Filson said, knees practically quaking. (*Ridiculous,* he thought. *You've done nothing wrong.*) "Now if you'll excuse me, there's a meeting at which my presence is required."

"What do you do in there, exactly?" asked the shorter one.

"I am the town clerk," Filson said, drawing himself up to his full 5'7". "My name is Filson. To whom am I speaking?"

The taller cop pulled a badge out of his pocket. "State police," he said. "That's whom."

"So you know Detective Coffin," the shorter cop said.

"Yes—I've known acting Chief Coffin since I began as town clerk."

The taller cop smacked himself lightly on the forehead. "Of course!" he said. "I got it!" He gave the shorter cop a slight shove. "Who does he remind you of, Hump?"

Hump scratched his head.

"I got nothin,'" he said.

"Oh come *on*—it's Mr. Peabody! He's a dead ringer!"

"Mr. who?"

"Mr. Peabody," Filson said. "He's a cartoon. A talking dog— from the old *Rocky and Bullwinkle* show. I always thought Wally Cox did the voice, but he didn't."

Hump shrugged. "Before my time, Bitters," he said.

"It's uncanny," Bitters said. "The bow tie, the little round glasses.

He even talks like him. I'll show you on YouTube. You won't believe it."

Hump cleared his throat. "Did you notice if Coffin was carrying anything when he came in tonight? Any kind of briefcase or bag? Maybe like the bag you've got?"

Filson blanched. He hoped it didn't show. "No," he said, trying to keep his voice from quavering. "No, I didn't see anything like that."

"So you wouldn't know what was in it, or where he might have put it," Bitters said.

"No. Sorry."

"We're worried, you see," Hump said. "Detective Coffin may have committed a crime."

Bitters pooched his lips out, nodded. "He may have removed evidence from a crime scene without proper authorization," he said. "A felony."

"That is a nice bag you've got there," Hump said. "You mind telling me what's in it?"

"That would be none of your business, I'm sure," Filson said, voice rising a half octave.

"Would you mind getting in the car, Mr. Filson?" Bitters said, a hand on Filson's elbow. "I think we need to have a little talk."

"Well," Rudy said. "This is awkward." He reached into the glove box, pulled out his Glock 21, a chunky .45 caliber semiautomatic, and put it in his coat pocket.

"For real," Loverboy said, opening his door and emerging gradually into the slow rain. "These situations just make me cringe."

"Jesus Christ," Hump said, as Loverboy extruded himself from the Town Car. "What the fuck is *that*?"

"That's one big-ass Negro," Bitters said.

"African American," Hump said.

"Melanesian," Rudy said.

"That's our clerk," Loverboy said. He spoke quietly, just above a whisper. In the still night his voice sounded like the rumbling of distant thunder.

"*Your* clerk?" Hump said. "Who the fuck are *you?*"

"You don't want to piss him off," Rudy said.

"State police," Bitters said, reaching for his gun. "Back off, Sasquatch."

Loverboy grabbed Bitters by the crotch with one hand, caught a fistful of his shirtfront with the other and snatched him off the ground, pressing him effortlessly overhead like a power lifter warming up with an unloaded barbell.

"Ack!" Bitters said, dropping his pistol, badge and keys falling out of his coat pocket. "My balls!"

"Have a shrubbery," Loverboy said, throwing Bitters six or seven feet into a clump of bushes.

"Oops—too late," Rudy said, leveling his Glock at Hump's face. "Are these men bothering you, Filson?"

"Are you in*sane?*" Filson said. "They're state police!"

"You're in pretty big trouble, then," Rudy said, reaching under Hump's jacket and lifting his service weapon out of its belt clip.

"Me?" Filson squawked. "*I'm* in trouble?"

Rudy pocketed Hump's pistol. "Well, you are *now*," he said, pushing Filson toward the Town Car, Glock still pointed at Hump's nose.

"Hey," Hump said. "I remember you!"

"You do?" Rudy scratched his temple meditatively with the Glock's barrel. "Sorry, I meet a lot of people."

"It was last spring—you robbed us. Fuckin' A—I knew you looked familiar. Hey, Bitters!"

Bitters groaned from the bushes.

"It's that guy that robbed us. Remember? We tossed that girl cop's apartment, and when we came out some guy pointed a big-ass gun at your balls?"

Loverboy had popped the hood of Hump's red Mustang and was rummaging around in the engine compartment. "Uh-oh," he said, pulling out a length of hose and tossing it aside. "That can't be good. You gents should have this thing serviced." The Mustang strained forward a few inches as Loverboy tugged at something under the hood. There was a loud snap, and the Mustang settled back on its springs. "Wow," Loverboy said, throwing a thick length of rubber belt over his shoulder. "What a mess you've got under here."

Bitters crawled out of the shrubbery on all fours. "Son of a bitch," he said. "There's a fire hydrant in those bushes."

"You shouldn't have used the 's' word," Rudy said. "He hates that."

"Here's your problem," Loverboy said, emerging from the Mustang's innards with a fistful of multicolored wiring. "Someone left these in your car." He held the long tangle of wires aloft like a snake handler brandishing a copperhead in a backwoods church, then turned and threw it in a high, home-run arc onto the roof of the Center for Coastal Studies. "You're lucky I was here to fix that."

Rudy pushed Filson into the Town Car's backseat and slammed the door. "This was fun," he said, waving the Glock at Hump. "Let's do it again sometime."

"We'll look you up, for sure," Hump said.

Bitters was curled up in a ball on the narrow sidewalk. "Motherfucker," he said. "I think I ruptured my spleen."

"That must be painful," Loverboy said, squeezing himself into the idling Town Car, dropping the shifter into reverse. "You should see a physician."

After the entrées had arrived and been consumed (Coffin's risotto had been perfect—big chunks of steamed lobster, perfectly grilled scallops, and spinach over a bed of rich, seafood stock–infused rice), Dawn Vermilion finished her set and sat down at their table in a gust of vodka fumes, and with a considerable rustling of sequins.

"I was hoping you'd join us," Coffin said.

"Always happy to see an old friend," Dawn said. "Especially when he's in the mood to dish some dirt."

"If you can't say anything nice about anyone," Coffin said, "Dawn will come sit by you."

Coffin introduced Kendrick. Dawn and Jamie exchanged air-kisses.

"My," Dawn said, "what enormous knockers you have."

"Aren't they something?" Jamie said. "The boob fairy giveth, baby."

"Did you say 'baby,' baby? I knew it!" Dawn turned to Coffin. "All right, Detective. Give! What's the latest? Who's this loon that's setting all the fires? Who put the nursing home guy's head in the lobster tank? What the hell is going *on* in this town?"

"The latest is that there's a special agent from the Bureau of Alcohol, Tobacco, Firearms, and Explosives in town," Coffin said.

"Well, that's something," Dawn said, leaning a bit closer. "Is he undercover?"

Kendrick smiled, waved. "Not unless posing as a federal agent counts," he said. "Strictly advisory."

Dawn looked Kendrick up and down. "Well, at least he's handsome," she said. "What is it with all the good-looking cops these days?" She put a gloved hand on Kendrick's arm. "Not that I'm complaining."

She turned to Coffin. "What else?" Dawn said. "I mean, that

can't be all you've got." She turned back to Kendrick. "No offense, darling."

"None taken."

Coffin shrugged. "It looks as though Branstool's head was cut off with a radial arm saw."

Dawn inhaled sharply. "Well," she said, fanning herself with a gloved hand. "*Now* we're talking." She put an arm around Coffin's shoulders and looked at Jamie. "This man of yours," she said. "He understands what a girl *wants*."

Jamie patted her belly. "You can say that again."

"Your turn," Coffin said.

Dawn shrugged elaborately. "Well," she said, "it's not much, but here's what I've got." She peered around the room, checking for eavesdroppers. "The nursing home director, what's his name?"

"Branstool."

"Right, Branstool. Well, he used to be married, you probably knew that."

Coffin shook his head. "Nope. News to me."

Dawn smiled. Up close, Coffin could see a faint five o'clock shadow poking through her pancake makeup. "Well, that's not even the good part. His wife was a big spender—she's the one who wanted the trophy house overlooking the bay. Cars, clothes, you name it—especially jewelry. She maxed out a dozen credit cards, took out a big home equity loan, and ran up a tab like Newt freaking Gingrich at Tiffany's. This was at the height of the real estate market, when everybody thought they were getting rich." She looked at Kendrick. "You had to be here, honey—it was *nuts*."

"So what happened to the wife?" Jamie said.

"Well, that's the thing," Dawn said, lowering her voice to a raspy stage-whisper. "Nobody knows, do they? She's just *gone*. Here one day, *whoosh*—vanished the next. I hate to deal in *rumor*, but the word is that Branstool knew *exactly* where she ended up." Dawn raised her painted eyebrows. "The beech forest, most likely. Or out in the dunes, pushing up poison ivy."

"Jesus," Rudy said, turning around to face the little clerk from the Lincoln's front seat. "Have you lost your mind? What the fuck is up with the gym bag?"

"It's just my workout clothes," Filson said, unzipping the bag and showing Rudy the contents. "It's step aerobics night at Muscle Beach."

"Step aerobics," Loverboy said, "great workout."

"You've got the combination?" Rudy said.

"Of course," Filson said. He reached into his coat pocket, pulled out a folded slip of paper, and handed it to Rudy.

Rudy unfolded the paper. "For Christ's sake," he said, "it's the same as it was six years ago."

Filson shrugged. "Why would we change it?"

"Good man. You're in for ten percent. You trust me?"

"I trust your associate," Filson said.

Rudy pursed his lips, nodded. "Good call," he said.

Later, at home, Coffin and Jamie lay on a mattress in their otherwise empty bedroom, the only light flickering from a big pillar candle on the floor. "I kind of miss that pissed off stuffed owl, staring at me from the dresser," Coffin said, cool glass of scotch resting on his belly.

Jamie opened one eye and patted his chest. "Poor Frank. I can call the auction house if you really want him back."

"Nah," Coffin said. "That thing would definitely scare the baby. We should get rid of that moth-eaten goat, too. Seriously."

"The goat stays," Jamie said, yawning. "It's bad luck to sell your father."

"I wonder what I could get for my mother."

"Uh-oh. What now?"

Coffin shook his head. "Who knows? It's some new disaster every week now. Next she'll be running a geriatric prostitution ring, or sneaking Ex-Lax into Mrs. Pickerel's scrambled eggs. I'm going to see her tomorrow. The acting director wants me to drop by."

Jamie propped herself on an elbow. "Sorry," she said, "it's funny but it's also really not funny."

"And then there's Tony."

"I can't believe he just walked out of the psych ward."

"He may be losing his mind, but he's not as dumb as he looks." Coffin sipped his scotch. "Not quite."

Jamie kissed Coffin's neck, slid a hand down his belly. "Frank," she said.

He caught her wrist, gently, and set his drink on the floor.

"No?" she said.

"You," he said, rolling over, lifting her nightgown—a short, hot pink item with black lace at the hem. She wore nothing underneath.

"No, Frank—I feel bad."

Coffin stopped. "You do?"

"Not *bad* bad, just bad for you." She stroked his hair. "I haven't been that much fun lately, I don't think."

Coffin kissed her thigh, her hip, the slight crease where they met. "You've been fine," he said. "I'm fine."

"Really? Because fine isn't exactly fantastic. Fine isn't great. Fine is just *okay*."

Jamie's pubic hair was dark and lush below the curve of her belly. Coffin kissed around its border, nuzzled into the soft nest of it, breathed its salt musk. He found her clitoris with his tongue, felt her thighs open, her hips lift.

"Frank," she sighed. "What about *you?*"

"I'm fine," Coffin said.

"Not me," Jamie said, groaning a little.

"No?"

"I'm great," Jamie said. "I'm *fantastic*."

"Great. Fantastic."

"Frank?"

"Yeah."

"That thing you're doing with your finger?"

"Yeah."

"Do it with *two* fingers."

Later, Jamie pulled the covers over her breasts and looked at Coffin with hooded eyes. "Frank?"

"Yes."

"That was sublime."

"Good. I was going for sublime."

"But now I'm hungry."

"Ah."

"Starving."

"What can I get you?"

"A malted."

"A malted?"

"Chocolate. From Arnold's."

"Arnold's? In Eastham? What time is it?"

Coffin checked his watch—almost nine thirty. Arnold's closed at ten. He could make it if he hurried. He swung his legs out of bed, found his pants.

"God," Jamie said. "You're so *nice*."

Coffin yawned. "Yeah," he said. "I know."

Chapter 17

Thick cloud cover; no stars, no moon. A wet fog crouched across Route 6. Coffin cranked the Fiesta's wipers and defogger, but they failed to keep the windshield clear. The Fiesta chugged tentatively past the dunes and Pilgrim Lake, struggled up the hill at Mayflower Heights, past Branstool's house, Truro center, and Head of the Meadow beach, past the exit for the Highland Light and the sandy little nine-hole golf course that more or less surrounded the old lighthouse, which had been moved away from the crumbling Cliffside a few years before—a delicate operation that had taken months.

Coffin had driven the stretch of highway between Provincetown and Eastham two or three times a week for most of his adult life, and he always felt the same tug of nostalgia as he passed North Truro, the same surge of elation on the way back, cresting the ridge at Pilgrim Heights and looking northeast at the long curve of Provincetown, the sweep of tawny beach, the waterfront with its crowd of white buildings, the Pilgrim Monument looming over everything, casting its long shadow.

Like a sentry, Coffin thought. *Like a sundial. Like one of those big stone heads on Easter Island.*

The Fiesta backfired weakly and the front end shuddered as Coffin steered down the long hill past Gull Pond Road and Truro's Fire and Rescue headquarters. Coffin was concentrating on keeping the Fiesta on the road—the steering wheel felt loose in his hands, and when he pumped the brakes they barely responded, the pedal going almost all the way to the floorboards—when he passed a hitchhiker going the other way. Coffin didn't see the man's face, but from the back he appeared to be heavyset and was dressed in hospital scrubs.

"Tony," Coffin said, the Fiesta's front end shimmying wildly as it rattled down the hill in near free-fall. "Fucking Tony!" He pumped the brakes again, downshifted after a struggle with the clutch, brought the Fiesta to a gradual stop at the bottom of the hill, and turned around in the parking lot of a little roadside liquor store. It seemed very dark, and Coffin wondered if his one functioning headlight had gone out. He pulled onto Route 6, heading the other way—back toward Provincetown. Tony seemed oblivious—he was sure now that it was Tony—standing in the same spot, thumb out, smoking a cigarette.

"Yo, Frankie," Tony said, when Coffin had pulled up beside him and reached across to roll the passenger window down.

"Tony," Coffin said, "for Christ's sake, what are you doing out here?"

"I gotta get to Highland Light." Tony climbed into the Fiesta, which sagged noticeably under his weight. "Jesus, what a piece of shit this car is."

"What's at Highland Light?" Coffin said.

"You'll see."

Coffin shifted the Fiesta into first, stepped on the gas. The little car picked up speed so listlessly on the hill that Coffin felt the urge to pedal. "I've got to go to Arnold's," he said. "I'm turning around."

"Arnold's? For what?"

"Jamie wants a malted."

"Don't turn around, Frankie," Tony said, looking intently at Coffin's face. The Fiesta's interior was very dark, but Tony's eyes seemed to gleam for a moment. *Jesus,* Coffin thought. *He really is crazy.*

"You have to tell me why you need to get to Highland Light, Tony," Coffin said. "Tell me why, and I'll take you."

Tony shook his head. "I can't."

Coffin swung the Fiesta hard left, into the Truro Fire and Rescue lot. The tires squealed dramatically and the brakes seemed even softer than before—he had to pump them again to keep from running into the bright yellow fire truck that was parked outside one of the bays. The station looked deserted, though he knew it wasn't—the dispatcher would be sitting at her desk, playing computer solitaire, listening to the scanner.

"Can't, or don't want to?" Coffin said, both feet on the brake, engine idling, out of synch—missing on at least one cylinder.

"It'll sound too crazy," Tony said.

"Everything you've said to me in the last week has sounded crazy. Just tell me."

"I'm supposed to meet them there."

"Them."

"Yep. Them." Tony rubbed his hands over his big, rubbery face. He needed a shave. His hair was wild—he looked like he'd stuck his head in a blender. "Frankie, I swear—this is the last thing. They promised. Just drive me out to the lighthouse and then we're done. Tell Jamie you found me and had to take me home. She'll understand."

"She's pregnant, Tony. She wants a malted. If I come home without one, she will not understand."

"Frankie, come on. Seriously. You'll see—it'll blow your mind. There's more to heaven and earth than you ever dreamed of, Horace."

"Horatio," Coffin said.

"Who?"

"All right, I'll take you," Coffin said, pulling back onto the highway. "But if they're not out there we're leaving, and I'm taking you home. If Doris has to call me again after I drop you off, I will personally drive out to your place, cuff you, and drive you back to the psych ward in Hyannis, where they will have every reason to keep you sedated and in restraints. Got it?"

"Got it. You're aces, Frankie," Tony said, punching Coffin in the shoulder.

"Jesus fuck, Tony," Coffin said, swerving the Fiesta half onto the narrow shoulder, a hot stinger shooting down his forearm. "Don't *do* that."

Town Hall was mostly dark—only the police department was lit up; three windows on the west side of the main floor. It had stopped raining, but the clouds were thick. Only a slight silvering at the edges showed the moon's position behind them—high in the sky over the harbor.

Loverboy had parked the Lincoln in the official lot behind Town Hall, in the space reserved for the chief of police. He and Rudy slipped in through the same side door that Filson had used, to which Rudy happened to have a key; it opened directly onto a dank stairwell that hardly anyone used. Until the renovations had begun, the stairwell's exterior wall had been inhabited by a large colony of bats, and the smell of hamster cage was still powerful months after the flying rodents had been driven out.

On the second floor, Rudy checked his watch: 10:07. They'd

have maybe three or four minutes to get into the assessor's office, open the safe, grab the bag, and get the hell out. Plenty of time. No one was around; all the lights were out.

"You know the great part about this?" Rudy said, using another key to open the door to the assessor's office.

"Aside from what it's going to do for my portfolio?" Loverboy said.

"The great part is that once they get over being surprised, they'll all be relieved it's gone. I'm doing them a favor, really. I just love helping people out like that."

"You're a humanitarian. A liberator of the human spirit."

"Exactly," Rudy said, slipping into the dark office, finding the safe's square bulk in the corner. "Now let's liberate some smack and get the fuck out of here."

The current Highland Light was built in 1857. It consisted of a modest light keeper's cottage—now a museum and gift shop— attached to a sixty-six-foot tower, which was in turn outfitted with a two-way beacon that emitted a very bright pulse of white light every five seconds. In 1996 the lighthouse had been moved a hundred and fifty yards to the southwest, away from the edge of a cliff that had been considered remarkable for its tendency to erode since Thoreau made note of it in his nineteenth-century tourist memoir, *Cape Cod*. Had the light not been moved, it would have eventually tumbled into the surging Atlantic, a hundred feet below. From its new, safer location, the Highland Light kept watch over a long, treacherous stretch of the Atlantic coast, aquatic grave-yard to dozens of ships, still notorious for its shifting sandbars and unpredictable currents.

At night the lighthouse stood in black silhouette against the horizon—like a big middle finger, Coffin thought, raised to the dark and rumpled sea as it ground away at the cliff base. The clouds were beginning to break up, passing slowly overhead like rush-hour traffic on a celestial freeway. Coffin parked the Fiesta in the gravel lot just on the cliff side of the lighthouse, nose pointed east, toward the ocean. There was a slight downward incline, so he gave the emergency brake an extra-firm yank after double-clutching the gearshift into reverse.

"Okay," Coffin said, climbing out. "Where are they?"

"What time is it?" Tony said, rummaging in the Fiesta's glove box. "The hospital took my watch."

"Five 'til ten. What are you looking for?"

"Cigarettes. I'm out."

"Good luck. I'm still not smoking."

"I've been smoking like a freaking chimney," Tony said, ducking down to check under the seats.

"When was the last time you ate?"

"I don't know. Yesterday? I haven't been very hungry. Plus, I'm pretty sure the hospital tried to drug my food."

"Of course you are."

"Eureka!" Tony said, emerging from the Fiesta's grungy interior. "Look what I found." He held up a single, badly bent cigarette. "It was stuck behind the gas pedal. I always say, if you keep trying, good things happen. Got a light?"

"Nope." Coffin patted his pockets. "Sorry. I don't carry a lighter anymore."

Tony stuck his upper body back into the Fiesta, pushed the lighter into its socket. "Man—I'm fuckin' dying here. This thing work?"

"I don't think so," Coffin said.

"What time is it now?"

"Straight up ten, give or take. Which is when Arnold's closes, by the way."

"Here we go," Tony said, holding up the glowing lighter. "My lucky day." He puffed the rumpled cigarette to life.

"I'm giving this maybe one more minute, then I'm taking you home. I've had a hell of a long day."

"They'll be here, Frankie," Tony said, puffing happily. "They always show up. Very reliable."

Coffin shook his head. With any luck, Jamie would be asleep when he got home. He shoved his hands into his pockets, walked down the sloping gravel path that led from the lighthouse to a small, circular observation area near the cliff—the golf course's elevated eighth green to his right, the ninth tee and fairway to his left, five or six good-sized boulders straight ahead, arranged in a neat line maybe three feet apart, to prevent potential suicides from driving over the edge.

Coffin stood for a moment gazing out at the dark water, the slow whitecaps rolling in to the beach below, endlessly, one after another. He wanted a cigarette. He wanted to go home, crawl into bed, and go to sleep.

A minute passed. Coffin turned, started to walk back. Tony was leaning on the Fiesta's trunk, smoking. Coffin could guess what it would be like now, for Tony and his family—month upon month of hope and disappointment, slow improvement and crushing setback. He'd be on his meds, then off them, then back on again. *Tough on everybody,* Coffin thought. *Tough all around.*

"Come on, Tony," Coffin said, walking up the gravel path, the ocean at his back. "Time to go home." He had to raise his voice to be heard above the dull roar of the surf, and something else—in the background at first—a rushing, thwonking sound, coming from behind him, growing louder. There was a sudden wind, leaves and sand blowing, then white and orange lights flashing overhead.

"Holy shit," Tony shouted, pointing at the sky. "They're here!"

For a moment Coffin could see only flashing lights amid the swirl of sand and debris. There was a great, hectic roaring overhead, then a single blinding spotlight sizzled out of the night sky. It probed the Fiesta for a moment or two, then found Tony, who stood with his arms raised, exulted, like a TV preacher about to speak in tongues. He shouted something. I'm here, maybe. Take me!

Coffin visored his eyes with one hand, still nearly blinded by sand and light, hair on the back of his neck prickling. *Jesus Christ,* he thought. *Seriously?* But then, as his eyes adjusted to the glare, he could make out the dim silhouette of a helicopter, hovering overhead like a huge metallic dragonfly. He squinted—*Coast Guard*—white with red markings, one of the big MH-60 Jayhawks the Coasties used for search and rescue.

A woman's voice boomed out of the chopper—probably the co-pilot, Coffin guessed, speaking over the PA system—"*Get back in your vehicle. The park is closed. Repeat: the park is closed. Get back in your vehicle and leave at once.*"

Coffin held up his shield, tried to wave the chopper off, but the Coasties kept the searchlight on Tony, who was waving his arms and yelling something Coffin couldn't quite make out. It sounded like, "It's me, it's me!"

"This is your last warning," the voice from the chopper said. "The park is closed. We will contact law enforcement in two minutes."

"Oh, for Christ's sake," Coffin said. "Tony! Get in the car!"

The spotlight went dark, and Tony stood blinking next to the Fiesta. The helicopter gained altitude, then swiveled and headed out to sea.

"Wait!" Tony yelled, waving his arms wildly, the red coal of his cigarette weaving bright, frantic trails. "Come back!"

"Tony, it's a fucking *helicopter!*" Coffin yelled, as the chopper took a hard right and roared along the coastline heading south, toward Chatham, taking its noise and rotor-wash with it.

"Oh, shit," Tony said, arms limp at his sides. "It's a fuckin' helicopter." He sat down heavily on the Fiesta's blunt rear-end, which produced a sharp crumpling sound. And then the Fiesta started to roll.

"Tony—" Coffin said.

"Whoa, fuck!" Tony said, losing his balance as the little car rolled away from him, tires crunching slowly across the gravel lot, nose pointed straight for the footpath. Tony staggered a few steps after the wayward Fiesta, stepped in a pothole, and fell hard on his side.

Coffin stood for a moment, the Fiesta's blunt snout slowly bearing down on him. The little car had picked up a bit of speed on the footpath's downhill slope: It was rolling at six or seven miles an hour, Coffin guessed—too fast to simply jump into its path and stop its momentum. He could open the driver's side door, jump in, and pull the handbrake (but hadn't he pulled the handbrake when he parked it?)—easy in the movies, maybe, easy for James Bond.

He took three quick steps to his right, out of the Fiesta's path, and started to jog, matching the little car's pace as it rolled toward the barricade of boulders at the path's end. He reached for the door handle, caught it, pressed the latch button.

"Come on, you rotten little piece of shit," he hissed. "Open!" The door was locked or stuck—he couldn't budge it. He tried digging his boot heels in, leaning his weight up the hill, hanging onto the handle with both hands, but the Fiesta dragged him down the path, closer now to the boulders than he cared to be. He let go, jumped clear, landing without much grace on all fours, scraping his palms on the gravel. *At least,* he thought, *it won't go over the edge—the boulders will stop it.*

The Fiesta was rolling faster, jouncing down the footpath, heading straight for the boulder at the far left of the row. Coffin felt a little surge of excitement—a part of him had been wanting to do this to the Fiesta for a long time—but he knew, too, that all sorts of questions would be raised if the Fiesta met its end out at the Highland Light on a damp October night when, as the Coasties had reminded them, the park was closed. So he clenched his teeth and half-closed his eyes as the Fiesta struck the leftmost boulder headlight-high—crunch of metal, tinkle of broken glass—crumpling the right fender and popping the hood latch, the impact bouncing the little car sideways, spinning it ninety degrees so that it rolled backward slowly down the slight embankment toward the golf course, following the contour of the fairway, picking up speed again in the cropped grass.

"Oh, shit," Coffin said, as the Fiesta rolled backward over the slightly elevated ninth tee and then disappeared down the bank toward the cliff's edge. He ran. He could hear the Fiesta's tires and undercarriage ripping through the grass and weeds a few feet from the cliff. He got there just in time to watch it tumble backward over the edge, bumping still on its wheels at first down the soft limestone face before gravity took it once and for all, flipping it end over end before it finally struck with a loud, grinding *whomp* on the beach below. Coffin waited a moment, half hoping the Fiesta would burst into flames the way cars always did in the movies when they went dramatically over a cliff, but nothing happened. There was the smell of gas, to be sure, but the engine was cold—no heat or spark to ignite it. Coffin took a deep breath as Tony appeared at his side.

"Well," Tony said. "Scratch one Fiesta." He took a last hit from his cigarette, and before Coffin could say anything, flipped the glowing butt over the cliff.

Chapter 18

For a long moment, nothing happened. Coffin drew a deep breath, let it out. He could just make out the dark, crumpled corpse of the Fiesta, lying on its roof at the bottom of the cliff. The tide was up, waves sloshing maybe twenty feet down the beach, just below the dark line of dead seaweed that had been regurgitated by the last big storm. Then a small, bright bloom of flame appeared, below the Fiesta's trunk. It spread quickly, backlighting the ruined Fiesta—Coffin could see the shattered windshield hanging from its frame, its thousand broken facets sparked by fire.

"Uh-oh," Tony said.

"No shit, uh-oh," Coffin said.

"You're gonna have some splainin' to do, boss."

"Yeah. Thanks."

The Fiesta was burning merrily, flames sprouting from the undercarriage—all of the hundred little leaks of flammable fluids catching at once.

"We'd better go, Frankie," Tony said.

"Suit yourself," Coffin said. "I'm waiting for the gas tank to—"

Coffin paused for a moment as the Fiesta's gas tank produced a hard *whomp* and then erupted in flame. The blast wave traveled up the cliff face and pushed him in the chest like a big, hot hand.

"—go."

"Whoa," Tony said. "That was frickin' awesome."

"All right, let's get the fuck out of here." Coffin turned and, walking back toward the footpath, fished in his jacket pocket for his cell phone. To his mild surprise, it was still halfway charged, and two signal bars appeared in the upper-left corner.

"Who you calling?" Tony said, breathing heavily as he followed Coffin up the slight incline.

"Lola. Even though I hate to bother her with something this stupid."

"I hear she's got a girlfriend now," Tony said, snickering.

"Great girl," Coffin said. "She's a pilot with Cape Air. Apparently she's seen these UFOs of yours. She thinks they're experimental military aircraft."

Tony snorted. "Yeah, right," he said. "Some people will believe anything."

Coffin touched the speed dial for Lola's cell phone. There was a rush of static, then a loud busy signal. He hung up.

"Great," he said.

"Why don't you call my pops," Tony said. "He'll come get us."

Coffin stopped walking. "You know his phone number?" he said. "Holy shit."

Tony shrugged. "Sure. I mean, I think so. He changes phones a lot."

Coffin handed Tony the phone. "Call him," he said, "but keep walking. I don't want to be around when that chopper comes back."

Twenty minutes later, Rudy and Loverboy picked them up at the entrance to the deserted Adventure Bound campground just off Highland Road, where they'd crouched in the shadows as the Truro police, a Truro fire truck, and a Truro ambulance had raced by, sirens howling. The Coast Guard helicopter was back, too, rotors churning the sky like a big Mixmaster, searchlight working the cliff base below Highland Light.

"Jesus, boys," Rudy said, turned half around in the passenger seat. "You sure know how to draw attention to yourselves."

"You shoulda left it in gear, Frankie," Tony said.

"I *did* leave it in gear," Coffin said.

"So, what's your story?" Rudy said.

"Stolen vehicle," Coffin said.

Rudy pursed his lips. "Sure. Sounds good. What kind of car was it?"

"Eighty-four Fiesta."

"Jesus. Really? Who'd steal a piece of shit like that?"

"The key's been stuck in the ignition for almost a year. It was a crime of opportunity."

"Then what? The guy got disgusted and ran it off a cliff?"

"Works for me. I'll call it in first thing in the morning."

They dropped Tony off at his Orleans ranch house—Doris frowning and worried in her bathrobe, a couple of late-season bugs lazily circling the porch light. Coffin reminded Tony of their deal: any more trouble, and back to the psych ward.

"But, Frankie," Tony said.

"What now?"

"They said they'd come, but they didn't. They *always* come when they say they're going to."

"I don't know what to tell you, Tony."

"Maybe the helicopter scared them off," Tony said.

Coffin steered him toward the front door, gave him a push. "Maybe so," he said. "Get some rest. No more of this now."

"Sure, Frankie," Tony said, yawning, shuffling into the house like a bear into its cave. "No worries."

"Frankie," Doris said, when Tony had disappeared inside. "What am I supposed to *do?*"

"I don't know," Coffin said. "I really don't."

"He's crazy, right? I mean really *crazy.*"

Coffin nodded. "Seems that way, yeah. Maybe wait 'til morning and talk to his doc down in Hyannis? If he gives you any trouble tonight just call me and I'll send an officer out to pick him up."

"You can't come?"

Coffin took a deep breath. "Okay. If you need me, call and I'll come out. But I think he'll sleep. He's had a big day."

Doris put a hand on Coffin's arm for an awkward moment, then put both hands in the pockets of her bathrobe. "Thanks, Frankie."

Coffin shrugged. "We take care of the family," he said. "It's what we do."

"So," Rudy said, on the drive back to Provincetown. "How bad is he?"

"How bad does he look?" Coffin said.

"He looks completely fucking crazy. But how bad *is* he?"

"He seems pretty manic," Coffin said. "He's delusional, a little paranoid. He's not making a lot of sense. Either that or he's been serially abducted by aliens."

"You speak from experience," Loverboy said. A statement, not a question. His shoulders blocked out most of the view of the road ahead.

"My ex-wife was bipolar," Coffin said. "She had occasional psychotic breaks—every few years, things would get bad. She'd get very manic, not sleep for days. She'd go on crazy spending binges, get into all kinds of risk-taking. If you talked about medication she'd accuse you of wanting to poison her, or control her. She thought Bill Clinton was calling her on the phone—this was during the whole Lewinsky thing. She thought her father had implanted an electronic device in her abdomen—a bomb, maybe, or some kind of transmitter. She thought Baltimore was going to be destroyed by race riots. It was . . . freaky. She was like a different person."

"It's not that uncommon," Loverboy said, "something like two percent of the population is psychotic."

"How is she now?" Rudy asked.

"We're not in touch, really. I send the alimony checks and she cashes them. That's the extent of our correspondence. But before we split, she was fine as long as she took her meds. Really, totally fine. But one of the symptoms of the disease is resistance to taking the meds."

Rudy shook his head. "Jesus. I hate to see him like this. I mean, he was always a fucking goofball, but this alien shit is just way over the top."

"That's what's hard about mental illness," Loverboy said. "You can't reason with it, and you can't kick its ass."

"Sounds like you're talking from experience, too," Coffin said.

Loverboy nodded. "My brother is schizophrenic. Like you said—if he takes his meds, he functions fairly well. If he doesn't, he doesn't."

"Jesus fucking Christ," Rudy said. "I need a drink. Got any booze at your place, Frankie?"

"Booze I got," Coffin said. "No furniture, but plenty of booze." Coffin yawned and slouched down in the backseat, with its mingled smells of marijuana smoke and cheap leather.

"Something I've got to ask you," Coffin said, after a minute or two, as they passed the turnoff to Wellfleet town center and then Moby Dick's, an old-school tourist restaurant decorated in fishing nets, lobster pots, and rusting anchors. It was closed for the off-season.

"Ask away," Rudy said.

"I had a weird conversation with Mom today. Your name came up."

"Okay."

"She said she had Branstool whacked. She said you did it."

Rudy half turned in his seat. "She *is* delusional, you know. She also thinks they're slipping saltpeter into her oatmeal."

"You mean they're not?"

"Look, I told you I didn't have anything to do with what happened to Branstool."

"Any idea who did?"

"I wish I knew, Frankie."

Coffin closed his eyes. "Figured you'd say that."

"No, seriously—I wish I knew. There are a couple of options. Maybe three."

"Okay. Like?"

"Like MS 13. You know about them."

"Duh. Very serious gang—started by Salvadoran immigrants to L.A., spread into Mexico and Central America. Extremely violent. Lots of facial tattoos. Active in the East Coast heroin biz. Zero presence on the Cape. What else?"

"Chechens."

"Chechens?"

"Well, they call themselves Chechens but they're mostly Ukrainian converts to Islam. Chechen just sounds a lot more badass. They're not very organized but they've been moving some heroin in the region, is what I hear, selling mostly at street level to all the

little Eastern European waitresses and retail workers—ten bucks
a bag for new customers."

"Would they be in for a couple million? Would they cut off a
guy's head with a radial arm saw?"

"Don't know," Rudy said. "Maybe, if they're trying to make a
name for themselves."

"What's the third choice?"

"You're gonna hate it."

"I hate the whole conversation."

"DEA."

"Oh, come on. I understand that you think it's fun to bullshit
your nephew, but that's just ridiculous."

Rudy turned around in his seat, pointed a thick finger at Coffin's face. "Ridiculous? Why do you think there's high-quality
smack flooding the eastern U.S., Frankie? Where's it all coming
from?"

"Afghanistan."

"Right. And who runs Afghanistan?"

"Pakistan."

Rudy rolled his eyes. "Okay, smart-ass, who besides Pakistan?"

"Us?"

"Right! Us. As in the CIA. The CIA runs heroin distribution
out of Afghanistan, Frankie. They have to in order to fund their secret wars in Pakistan and Somalia and wherever the fuck—that
way it's off the books, right? No inconvenient questions from
Congress."

"Sure, Rudy. If you say so."

"Damn right I say so. The DEA is the conduit at this end. You
think with all the money we've spent on the war on drugs since the
eighties, and all the power we've put into the hands of law enforcement, we couldn't keep drugs out of the country if we wanted to?"

Loverboy laughed, a low, slow rumble. "DEA is a law unto itself," he said. "They want your house, your cash, your car—they just take it. No due process for you, motherfucker."

"Exactly," Rudy said. "There's two ways to get rich working for the government. You can get elected to congress, or you can sign up with the DEA. The drug wars in Mexico? That wouldn't happen unless the DEA made it happen. They make money on every piece of it: guns, coke, ganja, human trafficking, protection, the whole deal."

"Come on, Rudy. Now who's paranoid?"

"Fine—laugh it up. But don't act all surprised if they show up here, looking for their missing bag of smack. It's not like the old days, Frankie, when it was a few cowboy smugglers against the law. If it's big, and it moves, it's because DEA wants it to move."

"What missing bag of smack, Rudy?"

Rudy grinned. "Just a lucky guess, Frankie. Just a lucky guess."

"Man," Loverboy said, as the Lincoln crested the hill at High Head, and the long curve of the shoreline from North Truro to Wood End opened up before them, the lights of Provincetown reflecting off the black water, the moon bright among broken clouds. "What a vista."

Coffin's phone sputtered to life in his pocket, playing a muffled "La Cucaracha."

"Uh-oh," Rudy said, pointing. "Check it out."

Coffin dug for his phone and craned his neck at the same time, trying to see past Loverboy's pumpkin-sized head. A crimson halo of fire was erupting from a structure on the West End, on what appeared to be the harbor side of Commercial Street. "Son of a bitch," Coffin said. "This guy's fucking relentless." He checked the caller ID—Lola—then touched the TALK button.

"Yeah," he said.

"Frank? We've got another fire."

"I'm looking at it right now. I'm on Route 6, on my way in."

There was a blast of static as they passed the dunes on their right. Then Lola said something that sounded like "Kotowski's house."

"What?" Coffin said. "What about Kotowski's house? Hello?"

His phone was dead—no service bars, no dial tone. He felt a powerful urge to lower the window and throw the phone out into darkness, but put it in his pocket instead.

Loverboy got them to the West End in record time, taking the length of Bradford Street at a smooth eighty miles an hour, swerving adeptly around two bicyclists, a Winnebago, and a cluster of stout, ruddy men in their sixties crossing the street in front of one of the more upscale guesthouses, all dressed in variations on the Dolly Parton theme—big blond wigs, prowlike bosoms, shiny dresses.

As they made the left turn at the end of Bradford onto the southern tail of Provincelands Road, Coffin craned his neck to get a good look out the window. They passed the salt marsh and the breakwater, then swung into the traffic circle at the end of Commercial Street. Coffin took a deep breath. Kotowski's house glowed in the firelight, but it was not on fire—the big beachfront trophy house next door was.

The trophy house was a recent build—thrown up at the height of the Bush-era housing boom. Somehow the developer had gotten a variance from the zoning board and built a three-story structure that dwarfed the surrounding two-story houses, and came within a foot or two on each side of filling the entire lot. It had a flat roof, a rooftop deck complete with a heated swimming pool, its own boat dock, a billiard room, a screening room, and a solarium populated by a great many exotic orchids. It was meant to be impressive—an expression of unrestrained consumption—but now it was also very much on fire.

There were three police cruisers parked on Commercial Street with lights flashing, and both of Provincetown's functioning fire trucks were already hooked up to the nearest hydrant and dispensing heavy streams of water onto the fire—one onto the roof, the other into a broken downstairs window.

Coffin climbed out of the Town Car and stretched—his back was sore, and his arms ached a bit after his wrestling match with the Fiesta.

"We're out of here, Frankie," Rudy said. He was rolling a joint on the open glove box door. "Too many cops around. You know how it is."

"Thanks for the lift," Coffin said. "I owe you."

"In more ways than you know, Frankie."

"Rudy?"

"Shoot."

"When I go into work tomorrow, that bag of smack isn't going to be in the safe anymore, is it?"

"There's a bag of smack in the safe?"

"That's what I'm asking you."

"I don't know anything about any bags of smack, Frankie." He held up three fingers, put a hand over his heart. "Scout's honor."

"You were a Boy Scout?"

Rudy snorted. "Fuck, no. Do I look like the kind of guy who would've been into kneesocks and circle jerks as a kid?"

"Look, Rudy—" Coffin paused, scratched his ear. "I don't give a damn about the smack. I have a signed and notarized receipt that says I gave it into the custody of our town manager and our town attorney. Nobody can blame me if it goes missing."

"Good boy. Now you're catching on."

"But," Coffin said, "I worry about the safety of the person who may be driving around with that bag of smack in the trunk of his car right now. I know you've got your big friend here, and I'm sure he's very good at what he does. Just don't forget what happened to Branstool."

Rudy lit the joint with a chunky Zippo. The smell of lighter fluid and marijuana smoke drifted out of the car window. "Frankie, you know me, right?"

"Sure, Rudy."

"Then you know that with or without my business manager here, any smack-dealing, decapitating motherfuckers better watch out for *me*. They're on my turf out here, and if I want them they won't even see me coming." He snapped his big fingers. "Like a tiger in the jungle, Frankie."

Coffin yawned. "Okay," he said. "I tried."

"Yay for you."

"Rudy."

"Oh, for Christ's sake. There's more?"

"I don't want that shit ending up on the street out here. I want it off the Cape. *Entende?*"

Rudy took a deep hit from the joint, held the smoke, let it out. "Frankie," he said, shaking his big head, "you worry too much. You've got to relax yourself."

Though already quite large, the fire was not moving as quickly as the others had, and the firefighters and their equipment seemed to be working efficiently and well. Lola was there with her camera; Jeff Skillings and Pinsky were handling traffic. The crowd was large and boisterous: the trophy house had been a source of controversy even when it was under construction. Kotowski, especially, had made an issue of it: He'd filed complaints with the zoning board, called the building inspector at 4:00 A.M., picketed the property with homemade signs, shouted obscenities at the construction workers—all to no effect, except to reinforce his image around town as one of its last remaining crackpots. Kotowski stood at the edge of the crowd, grinning wildly in the firelight.

"Jesus, man, try not to look so happy," Coffin said. "People will think you had something to do with this."

"Your guy beat me to it. God, isn't it beautiful?"

It *was* beautiful, Coffin thought. Flames roared from the second-story windows; orange smoke rose in a vortex of sparks. The thing had been an eyesore—Coffin wasn't sorry to see it go.

"Burn, baby, burn," Kotowski said, as though he'd been listening to Coffin's thoughts.

For a second Coffin could almost imagine himself as Kotowski, living Kotowski's life—full of rage, painting his angry paintings, smoking a little opium on the back deck, paddling around in his kayak, nude except for his conical Vietnamese hat, haunting the rougher, darker corners of Provincetown late at night. Coffin shook his head: it seemed to work for Kotowski, but he was pretty sure it wouldn't work for him. He was going to be a father. And drive a minivan.

"I'm glad they saved the cat, though," Kotowski said.

"They saved a cat? Who?"

"The firemen—who else? The cat's over there," Kotowski pointed. "Those two bald guys are the owners."

Coffin walked over to the two bald men. They could have been twins, he thought: nearly identical in height and build—around 5' 9" and muscular—both with clean-shaven heads and the goatee-mustache combinations that pro baseball players all seemed to be wearing in the nineties. One of the men held a cat cradled in his arms like a baby. The cat was wrapped up in a towel, only its head and forepaws sticking out.

Coffin fished his shield out of his jacket pocket, showed it to the two men. "Detective Coffin," he said, "you're the owners?"

"We were," the man with the cat said.

"Sorry about your house," Coffin said.

"Are you? You're probably the only one, then. The rest of these people seem to be having a party."

Coffin looked at the crowd. The man with the cat was right: Someone had arrived with a thirty-six-pack of Coors Light, and now many of the onlookers were enjoying a cold beer. Coffin took a deep breath, let it out. "How's the cat?"

The man with the cat looked down at the furry bundle. "Ginky says hi," he said, waving the cat's black forepaw at Coffin. "He's a little freaked right now."

Ginky coughed. He was a Siamese. His blue eyes were round and manic, his ears were back, and his fur stuck out as though someone had jammed his tail into a light socket.

"Were you in the house when the fire started?"

"Justin was," said the man with the cat. "I went out to dinner at Al Dante's with a friend."

"So what happened?" Coffin said.

"I had the pan-seared lobster," the man with the cat said. "My friend Derek had the smoked duck. Total foodgasm."

Justin cleared his throat. "He means what happened *here*, Jason. When the house caught on fire."

Jason frowned. "God, I hate that tone of voice. You really think I'm stupid, don't you?"

"I don't think you're stupid. You just don't listen sometimes."

Jason shook his bald head. "Are you married, Detective?"

"No."

"Good for you. Stay that way."

"About the fire," Coffin said. "Justin, is it?"

"Yes. I was upstairs in the study, working on my memoir—"

"He calls it a memoir. It's mostly just gay porn," Jason said.

"It is not gay *porn*," Justin said. "It's a literary memoir with an erotic edge."

"That's what they all say, honey."

"Guys," Coffin said.

"He's mad because I ran out of the house without his cat."

Jason sniffled a bit. "No, no—you did what most people would have done. I certainly can't judge you for wanting to save your own skin."

Coffin took a deep breath. "So you were upstairs in the study."

"Yes. I had the fireplace on and a nice snifter of cognac and I was typing away on my iMac—"

"One-handed, probably," Jason said.

"I'm ignoring you right now," Justin said, putting his fingers in his ears. "And that's when I heard someone moving around down in the alley."

"About what time was this?" Coffin asked. He had his notebook out.

"I'm not sure—I was very absorbed in what I was doing. Around ten o'clock?"

"Absorbed *by* what you were doing," Jason said. "Not *in* what you were doing."

Justin rolled his eyes. "Oh for God's sake. Please, please, *please* shut the fuck up for just, like, two *minutes*."

"He's always hated Ginky," Jason said. He looked down at the cat. "Can you believe he didn't even *try* to save you? Can you *believe* it?"

Ginky growled a little, deep in his furry chest.

"Look," Justin said. "I'm not going to die for a fucking cat, okay? Especially one that poops in my shoes. If that makes me a bad person, then okay, *fine*." He threw up his hands—*I surrender*. "I'm a bad person."

"He only poops in your shoes because he knows you hate him."

"He poops in my shoes because he's fucking psychotic."

There was a murmur of excitement from the crowd. One of the two pumper trucks had stopped pumping; Walt Macy threw his hat on the ground in disgust. A tall firefighter opened a panel above the truck's rear bumper and began to tinker with the valves and switches inside it. Meanwhile, the fire seemed to be gathering itself like a lioness, about to charge its prey. Its roar grew louder as it sucked more oxygen into the house. A rush of smoke and sparks exploded from the upstairs windows as the fire found a new fuel source: some delicious couch or carpet, Coffin guessed; some wood sculpture, some antique four-poster bed.

"Gentlemen," Coffin said, "please." He turned to Justin. "When you heard someone in the alley, did you happen to look out the window?"

"You know, the weird part is that I *did* look out the window. Usually I wouldn't—a lot of drunk people use the alley to go out to the beach and pee—so why bother looking, right? But this time I did."

"So?"

"So, I looked out and there was a Tall Ship coming up from the beach, heading toward the street."

"Could you describe him?" Coffin opened his hands—a small shrug. "Her?"

"Not trying very hard. Like, sneakers and tube socks and some kind of kilt thing. Really bad wig—sort of red or purple, almost."

"Height? Build?"

Justin frowned. "You know, I could make a guess, but it wouldn't mean much. I just caught a glimpse. There wasn't much light."

"Okay. Then what happened?"

"Then maybe ten or fifteen minutes later I smelled smoke, just a whiff, you know? Then about five minutes after that I looked up and I thought holy *shit*. Smoke was coming up the stairs—a lot of it. Then the smoke alarms all went off—God, that sound just makes you in*sane*—and I grabbed my iMac and ran downstairs."

"You grabbed your *iMac?*" Jason sobbed, rocking the cat back and forth.

Justin turned on him. "Look, I was *scared*, okay? The fucking house was on fire and I was scared. I am sorry I did not try to save your goddamned shoe-pooping cat."

"So you ran downstairs. What did you see?"

"Fire. Smoke—lots of smoke, up around the ceiling. I got down on my hands and knees and crawled out the door."

"Where was the fire? What part of the house?"

"In the kitchen. First floor. It was like the wall was on fire."

"Which wall? Can you point to it?"

"The one by the alley—there. The fire was all around the window." He pointed to the east wall. There was a small condo village across the alley from the trophy house. Kotowski's house was to the west.

"Can you think of anything else that might be important?" Coffin said. "Any little detail we haven't talked about?"

"Just that I smelled lighter fluid before I smelled smoke."

"Lighter fluid?"

Justin nodded. "You know that smell—there's no mistaking it for anything else. I used to smoke, back in the day. Carried a Zippo for years. I got a pretty strong whiff of lighter fluid while I was writing, like it drifted up the stairs. I almost went down to check it out, but I didn't."

"He was too *absorbed*," Jason said.

"Jason, anything?" Coffin said.

"I think I'm in love with the fireman who saved Ginky," Jason said. "Did you know he gave him mouth-to-mouth?"

Justin shuddered. "Ew. Sardine breath," he said.

"One of the firemen gave mouth-to-mouth to a cat?" Coffin said.

"He most certainly did," Jason said. "That tall, lanky fellow over there." He waved in the direction of the new fire truck, where two firefighters were trying to restart the pumping mechanism. "Apparently they call him Stretch."

"Jesus. Of course they do," Justin said.

Coffin gave the two men his card. "Call me if you think of anything," he said. He scratched his ear—the night was cool but the late-season mosquitoes had rallied, rising up from the salt marsh in a fierce, whining cloud. "Before I forget—did you have a light on in the study, Justin?"

"Sure—my desk light."

"Would it have been visible from outside, do you think?"

Justin thought for a moment. "Definitely. The study's in the front corner, facing the street. You'd be able to see it from out here, for sure."

Coffin reached out to pet Ginky, but the cat hissed and bared his teeth. "Nice kitty," Coffin said, putting his hand back in his jacket pocket just as the broken pumper truck throbbed back into action, its limp, unattended hose suddenly stiffening and spurting wildly over the crowd. Stretch closed a valve and turned off the flow of water, and a team of firefighters grabbed the hose at its business end and started to lug it toward the house. Walt Macy spotted Coffin and waved him over.

"How's it going, Walt?"

Macy shook his head, picked his hat up off the ground, flicked a bug from the brim with his forefinger, and put the hat on his head. It was a navy blue ball cap with the letters PFD embroidered in gold above the bill. "What the fuck was I thinking," he said, "buying an Italian fire truck? Hell, I drove a Fiat in college. You'd think I'd know better."

"Looks like your boys are going in," Coffin said, as the hose-wielding team of firefighters advanced on the front door.

"We had the upper hand before our pumper went wonky," Macy said. "Now we're playing catch-up. We'll try to starve the fire at its base, but that means putting a lot of water on it in a hurry. Otherwise the whole structure's going to go—then it's down to keeping the neighbors from going up, too."

"Your boys are looking good tonight," Coffin said.

"Well, they've been getting plenty of practice," Macy said. "Honest to God, for a volunteer crew they're not bad—they're damned near fearless, I can tell you that. This is some dangerous shit we're dealing with—a lot of crews would stand back and let this fucker burn. Did you hear about Stretch, here, going in after the cat?"

"I did. Nice going, Stretch."

Stretch ducked his head shyly. "Thanks," he said. He shrugged. "Probably if I'd thought about it I wouldn't of gone in. It was pretty hot in there."

"I heard you gave him mouth-to-mouth."

Stretch nodded. He had deep, parallel scratches on his left cheek. "Yeah," he said. "By the time I got him out he wasn't breathing. I figured it was worth a shot."

"Good man," Coffin said, swatting at a mosquito that had bitten his neck. "What was it like—giving mouth-to-mouth to a cat?"

Stretch thought for a minute, then nodded his head. "Furry," he said.

Coffin laughed—a sharp little bark. He turned to Macy. "The owner said he went downstairs and the wall was on fire. That make sense to you?"

"Exterior wall?"

"Yep."

Macy frowned. "Could be electrical," he said. "I'm no fire investigator, but I've seen plenty of electrical fires that started inside the wall."

"The owner said he smelled lighter fluid, like you use in a Zippo."

"Well, then, that would imply arson. First one in an occupied structure, right?"

"I think so." Coffin yawned, smoothed his mustache. "Sorry," he said. "Haven't been getting much sleep."

"You and me both, my friend," Macy said.

The trio of firefighters were aiming a fat stream of water directly into the trophy house's open front door—the lead man, holding the nozzle, was down on one knee like a football player in pregame prayer. Gouts of steam poured from the windows, and a loud, continuous hissing complicated the roar of the flames with its sibilant overtone.

"Listen," Coffin said. "I don't mean to tell you your business— but are you sure you want to send those boys inside? Is it safe?"

"You worried about structure collapse?"

"I'm worried about all kinds of things."

"Collapse is probably not an issue here. I talked to the owners 'cause I thought I remembered when this thing was under construction. It's got a steel frame—it'd have to, or it'd never support the rooftop pool. They had some firm come in from off-Cape and weld it together."

The World Trade Center had a steel frame, Coffin thought. "Okay," he said. "If you're not worried, I'm not worried."

"Plus, hell—I'd like to win one. So far we're oh for three."

"So if it's not just a charred shell at the end of the night, that's a win?"

Macy pursed his lips, nodded. "That's about right," he said.

The clutch of firefighters had advanced as far as the front porch when Coffin noticed a strange, misty aura above the trophy house's flat roof, which appeared to be crimped and sagging. He was about to point it out to Macy when the house produced a rending shriek, like a torpedoed battleship breaking up as it sank beneath the waves. The firefighters dropped their hose and ran for the street.

"Holy shit," Macy said. "There she goes."

The roof crumpled slowly. The right side, where the pool was, inclined gradually toward the center of the house, while the left side drifted outward, steel screaming, welds and bolts popping in clusters, their rattling clangs as they failed like bursts of heavy machine-gun fire. The crowd whooped, ecstatic. Coffin could see the harborside edge of the pool as the roof slowly twisted and sank beneath its impossible weight—pool water escaping into the house, a little at first, then all at once a great tsunami roaring through the upper rooms and rushing down the broad interior staircase, the fire protesting with much hissing and steam (*fire is a cat,* thought Coffin), pool water inundating the second floor—Coffin could see a baby grand piano floating past the windows—water exploding down the stairs into the main entryway and out the front door, driving the onlookers cheering and screaming with fear and joy to the higher ground of Commercial Street. When the two-foot wall of water lost its momentum, it reversed itself and ran down the hill again, much of it streaming back into the smoking wreck of the house. The fire seemed to have gone out.

Macy took his hat off, scratched his bald head, put the hat back on. "Did that really happen," he said, "or am I having some kind of episode?"

"I'm not sure," Coffin said. "It's been a long day."

As the firefighters packed up their gear, Coffin leaned on the rear fender of the unmarked Crown Vic, smoking a cigarette he'd bummed from Pinsky. It tasted terrible. He felt guilty, but he didn't put it out.

"Well," Lola said, standing beside him. "That was exciting." She reached out, plucked the cigarette from Coffin's mouth, tossed it onto the pavement, and ground it out with the toe of her boot.

Coffin looked at her, looked at the crushed remains of his cigarette.

"Bad for you," Lola said. "Dad."

Coffin sighed. "What a night." He told her about Tony, and the Fiesta going over the cliff.

"Poor Tony," Lola said.

"Poor Tony? What about my car?"

"You hated that car."

"Then there was the ride home with Rudy and his accountant."

"Uh-oh. What happened?"

"I have a prediction for you."

"Do I want to hear it?"

"Tomorrow morning, someone will open the safe in the clerk's office and an item will be missing."

"A black leather gym bag containing a whole lot of smack?"

"Bingo."

"Some family you've got there."

Coffin laughed. "The Coffin jinx," he said. "It's not just about boats anymore."

"Should we turn him in?"

"To whom? I can guarantee you there's no evidence and no witnesses—if there were, no one would talk. That gym bag is long gone—he's buried it out in the beech forest or God knows where. He's been at this for years—he's good at it now." Coffin paused, scratched a mosquito bite on his bald spot. "Any sign of sweatshirt guy tonight?"

Lola shook her head. "Nope. He didn't turn up for this one. I looked and looked."

"He may have changed clothes," Coffin said. "The owner said he saw a guy in drag in the alley just before the fire started."

"Huh. What kind of drag? I mean, there's drag and then there's drag."

"Bad drag. Not really trying, he said." Coffin yawned, covered his mouth. "Jesus. I'm exhausted. Too many subplots."

Lola grinned. "I've been around so many fires, all of my clothes are full of smoke. My apartment smells like a freaking campfire." She held out her sleeve—she wore jeans and a leather jacket, her hair pulled back in the usual ponytail. "Here," she said. "Smell that."

Coffin sniffed. "I must smell like smoke, too," he said. "I've just been too tired to notice." He met Lola's eyes for a second, felt the tug of something like desire, though it wasn't desire, exactly. Lola was conventionally pretty—good jaw, straight nose, blue eyes—but what really got to you, he thought, was the way she carried herself, her complete physical confidence. He'd gone to the Thoroughbred races in upstate New York once; an old friend lived in Saratoga Springs. They'd had breakfast at the track, watched the horses work out. He'd been struck by their power, their dignity, and grace—there was something regal about them. Lola was like that, in a way—self-possessed, completely at home in her own skin.

"What are you grinning at?"

"I was marveling at your self-possession."

Lola laughed. "Because I wanted you to smell my sleeve?"

"Maybe so."

"Well, don't be fooled. It's just an act. Inside I'm all atwitter."

"Who isn't?" Coffin said. He opened the Crown Vic's passenger door, lowered himself into the seat. "Okay," he said. "I'm done. Take me home."

Coffin pulled the screen door open and stepped onto the porch. The swing was moving slightly in the breeze. He half expected to find Rudy and Loverboy camped out in his living room with lawn chairs and a cooler, but when he unlocked the door and stepped inside the house was empty and quiet. "Thank you, God," he said. The stuffed goat leered down at him from its place above the mantel. "What are *you* looking at?" Coffin said.

He climbed the stairs slowly—his back hurt a little; there was a faint ringing in his ears. He was dirty, he realized, and he smelled like sweat and wood smoke. He took a quick shower, brushed his teeth, and crawled into bed beside Jamie, trying not to wake her.

"Frank?" she said, still half asleep. "That you?"

"Yep. It's me."

"Okay. Good."

He kissed her on the forehead. "Go back to sleep."

"Sleep."

Coffin lay still, watching the purple darkness deepen and swirl. The bedroom sounded different now that most of the furniture was gone. Even the silence had changed—it was larger, more resonant.

He closed his eyes, and had just drifted off when Jamie said, "Frank?"

"Hmm?"

"You bring my malted?"

"No—sorry. Stuff happened."

Jamie reached out in the darkness, patted Coffin's arm. "'Sokay. Sleep time."

"Yeah," Coffin said. "Sleep time."

Chapter 19

The house was full of smoke. Alarms shrieked from the ceilings, the walls. Down the hall the baby was crying, a harsh, mechanical wail. Coffin ran to the baby's room—smoke filling the hallway, his throat burning—and reached into the crib. The seal baby was gone. Someone had taken the baby.

"Jamie?" he called. "I can't find the baby!" Panicked, he looked under the crib, under the rocking chair. The huge toy animals stared at him, baring their fangs. He waved at the smoke. His arms were so heavy, they could have been made of stone. He fell, crawled to the stairs on his hands and knees.

"Jamie! What did we do with the baby?"

The smoke alarms howled, the hallway tilted and swam. The seal baby lay at the top of the stairs, the fur on its round head wet and sleek, black eyes beseeching. He called out to Jamie again, but she was gone. He tried to pick up the baby, but it wriggled away. "Come back!" he called. "I'll save you! It's okay!"

The seal baby looked up at him, expression stoic and sad. It looked *familiar, Coffin thought, flames licking his bare feet. It looked like someone he knew.*

"Frank? Frank?" Jamie was shaking his arm.

"Huh?" Coffin said.

"You were yelling in your sleep."

Coffin ran a hand over his face, opened one eye. "Jesus," he said, sitting up, his voice a raspy croak. "My throat is killing me. What was I yelling?"

"Something about Morris, or Maurice," Jamie said. "You sound terrible. Are you coming down with something?"

"Maurice?" Coffin thought for a minute. "The seal baby," he said. He put a hand to his throat—it felt like he'd swallowed broken glass. "Weird. The seal baby turned into Maurice."

"You had your dream again? About the house being on fire?"

Coffin shook his head, trying to clear it. It felt heavy, solid, stupid. "Yeah, the baby keeps turning into a seal. Only this time, the seal baby was Maurice."

"Who's Maurice?"

Coffin rubbed his temples. "He's this kid—he worked at Yaya's, taking care of the seals. Remember? This summer?"

Jamie nodded. "The seals that somebody shot," she said. "So awful. You never found out who did it, right?"

Coffin shook his head. "Nope. There wasn't much to go on. Nobody even reported gunshots. It may have happened during the fireworks."

"Maybe we *should* leave," Jamie said. "Sometimes I think it's going bad here, you know? All these fires. Dead seals. Heads in lobster tanks."

"Sure," Coffin said. "I could be one of those old guys at Walmart who asks you if you need a cart. You know—a greeter." Coffin looked at the clock—it was 7:43 A.M. "Oh, shit—got to go."

Jamie put a hand on his chest. "Hold on there, wild man. You're not going anywhere. You're taking a day off."

Coffin shook his head. "I'd love to," he said. "Really, I would *so* love to take a day off. But there's kind of a lot going on. You know— fires. Heads."

"Call in. We have an appointment with my OB-GYN in Hyannis."

"Another ultrasound?"

"Yep. This is the one where they can probably tell the gender."

Coffin felt a small flicker in his chest. "Okay," he said. He swallowed, his throat on fire. "I'll try. I'm supposed to give a briefing this morning, but Lola can handle it."

Jamie clapped her hands. "Yay! I'll have you back before dark, I promise. It'll be great—we can go car shopping after the appointment."

"How about a Toyota Four Runner? Very masculine."

"The minivans have power sliding doors, Frank. Power sliding doors! Come on—get up. I made coffee."

Coffin closed his eyes—his head was throbbing. "I may be drinking tea for a few days. And I hate tea." The phone bleeped from its plastic stand on the floor.

"You should definitely not answer that," Jamie said.

Coffin gave her a look, picked up the phone, pressed TALK. "Coffin."

Jamie kissed his cheek. "I'll be in the shower."

"Frank?" It was Jeff Skillings. "Look, sorry to bother you at home but a couple of things have come up. You're not going to like either of them."

"Great."

"You sound terrible. You just wake up?"

"Yeah. I may be coming down with something."

"You should suck on those zinc things."

"I hate the zinc things. They're like sucking on a doorknob."

"Ha," Skillings said. "I guess they are kind of metallic tasting. So do you want the bad news, or the other bad news?"

Coffin coughed, then sneezed. "For fuck's sake," he said, reaching for a Kleenex.

"Seriously—zinc is what you need. And chicken soup."

"Thanks."

"Okay—first thing: the Truro police responded to a call about a car on fire out by Highland light last night. Ford Fiesta, mid-eighties, at the bottom of the cliff. They ran the VIN number this morning and it came back registered to you. They're treating it as a stolen vehicle. State police are involved."

Coffin closed his eyes. "Yeah," he said. "Long story. What's thing number two?"

"The town manager and the town attorney put a briefcase containing a large quantity of heroin in the Town Hall safe last night, and now it's gone."

"Gym bag."

"Sorry?"

"It was a gym bag, not a briefcase."

"If you say so. There's a special agent from the DEA here to pick it up—guy named Felcher. He drove down from Boston this A.M., and he's not happy."

"That's three things," Coffin said, blowing his nose.

"What? Oh, right. Three things."

"I'll be there in twenty minutes," Coffin said. He sneezed again and hung up.

The bathroom was warm, rich with steam. It was the only part of the house that had been refurbished since the 1950s—Coffin's father had done the work himself, in the long, cold winter of '76, just a few months before he'd disappeared from his fishing boat twenty miles offshore. There was a lot of avocado-green tile, and a big, green tub with a glass shower enclosure that was hard to keep clean. On the upside, Coffin thought, it was plenty big enough for two.

He dropped his boxer shorts, slid the door open, and climbed in. Jamie was shaving her left leg, her back to him, hair in a loose bun. She still didn't look pregnant from behind, Coffin thought; her ass was perfect. He put his hands on her hips.

"Careful," she said, straightening, leaning into him a bit. "I've got a razor."

He cupped her breasts. They were heavy, taut. "I know," he said. "It's mine."

Jamie turned her head, nuzzling into his cheek. "That's nice."

He pinched her nipples lightly, nibbled the rim of her ear, the base of his half-firm penis nestled against her tailbone. She dropped his razor; it clattered against the tub. She groaned, bent forward a little, pushing her backside against him. "Your turn, Frank," she said, reaching back with one hand to stroke him, cheek and shoulder on the tile wall. "Your turn."

Coffin sneezed, then sneezed again. "Ah, God," he said, eyes watering. "Sorry. Nothing says 'sexy' like a head cold."

Jamie turned, patted his chest, hugged him. "Poor baby," she said. She put a warm, wet palm on his forehead. "You're hot."

"Finally," Coffin said, trying not to cough. "She notices."

Special Agent Martin Felcher of the Drug Enforcement Agency was a little over six feet tall. He looked, Coffin thought, like a guy who enjoyed going to the gym. He was square-jawed, not quite thirty, unwrinkled except for a pair of deep grooves between his blond eyebrows. His eyes were stone gray, his hair close-cropped. Coffin had met a hundred guys just like him—he was pretty much your standard-issue fed.

"I have to tell you," Felcher said, "I'm finding this whole conversation a little surreal." He was sitting behind Coffin's desk, staring at Coffin over the tops of his steepled fingers.

Mancini was there, and Monica Gault, who sat in one of the leather guest chairs next to Coffin. The town attorney, Kirby Flint, stood near the wall, nervously fiddling with his tie.

"You shouldn't frown like that," Mancini said. He was half-sitting on the edge of Coffin's desk. He touched the bridge of his nose. "You're getting some lines right here."

Felcher frowned more deeply. "What you're telling me, in effect, is that you had a bag full of heroin in your safe, now it's gone, and you don't care. Would you say that was an accurate characterization?"

Coffin sneezed, took a Kleenex from his pocket and wiped his nose. "Look, Agent Felcher—"

"Special Agent Felcher."

"*Special* Agent Fe-fe—" Coffin paused, trying mightily not to sneeze. "*Helcher!*"

"Gesundheit," Mancini said.

"Thanks," Coffin said, blowing his nose. "We've had three major arson fires in the past five days. Two days ago, one of our officers found a human head in a tank full of lobsters. So yes, if we're going to be entirely accurate, it's fair to say I don't care very much. And it's not my safe."

"You don't care *very much*. I see. Would you care very much if I dropped trou right here and took a crap right in the middle of your desk? Because that's pretty much what you're doing to my investigation. We've had Dr. Branstool in our sights for months now."

"It's not my desk."

Felcher's face turned red. "Are you not the acting chief of police here in Provincetown?"

"I am."

"Are you not sworn to uphold the law?"

"I am."

"Then maybe you can explain to me how it is that *you don't care very much* that two million dollars' worth of heroin, by your own estimation, is missing from your safe."

"It's not his safe," Gault said. "It's the town's. Technically the heroin was in my custody."

"And mine," said Flint. "He has a receipt, if you'd like to see it."

"He has a receipt," Felcher said, leaning back in Coffin's desk chair. "He has a receipt. Isn't that special. I'm just wondering how that's going to go over in federal court when a judge orders the three of you into asset forfeiture as drug-trafficking suspects."

Coffin laughed, the image of the Fiesta bouncing over the cliff still fresh in his mind. "While you're at it," he said, "you can tell the judge why we went to the trouble of establishing a chain of custody and then stealing the heroin from ourselves, with a half-dozen police officers working down the hall."

Felcher scowled.

"He makes a good point," Mancini said, stroking his chin.

"Okay," Felcher said. "Fine. I'm operating on the assumption that this is an inside job. Let's assume the three of you are not suspects. Somebody knew it was in the safe, and somebody had the combination. How many people would have access to that combination, would you say?"

Gault shrugged. "I don't know," she said. "Dozens?"

Felcher's blond eyebrows went up. "Dozens? Are you serious?"

"The town has owned that safe since 1915," Gault said. "There's no record that the combination has ever been changed."

Felcher swallowed, his Adam's apple bobbing. "The combination has never been changed," he said. "Since 1915."

"Correct."

"I'm not sure anyone knows how to change it," Flint said. "We've never had a situation quite like this come up before, have we?"

"Not that I can think of," said Coffin.

Felcher swallowed again. A vein in his neck had begun to throb visibly. "If that many people had access to the safe, why not put it in your evidence cage?"

"Evidence box, you mean," Coffin said.

Felcher's eyes widened. "Excuse me?"

"It's not really a cage," Coffin said, blowing his nose. "It's more like a box."

"A box."

"A cardboard box."

Felcher tilted his head. "You keep evidence in a cardboard box."

"Exactamundo," Mancini said.

"As far as I know," Flint said, "this is the first time since Provincetown was incorporated that any evidence of any significance has gone missing."

Mancini grinned. "He's right—you should've put it in the box."

Felcher rubbed his eyelids with the thumb and index finger of his right hand. "I can't believe you fucking people," he said. "I've never seen anything like this."

"It's good for you," Mancini said. "How the other half lives."

Felcher leveled a gray-eyed stare at Coffin. "I'm going to conduct a full investigation," he said.

"Of course you are," Coffin said.

"I expect your cooperation."

"Gladly—in exchange for everything you know about Branstool's heroin operation."

"That's not information I'm authorized to share."

"Of course it's not." Coffin stood. "This meeting's over. You've got your troubles, we've got ours."

"Your fires are all over the news in Boston," Felcher said, smiling with one side of his mouth. "Heckuva job you-all are doing here."

"Arson isn't my best thing," Coffin said.

"Jesus," Mancini said. "I hope not."

After Felcher, Gault, and Flint were gone, Coffin called Lola at her desk on the second floor and asked her to join them.

Mancini stayed put. He sat slouched in the leather guest chair, legs stretched out and crossed at the ankles. He wore pressed jeans with gray socks, tassel loafers, and a black polo shirt, purple horsie logo over the right breast.

"You must really hate that Felcher guy," Coffin said, settling into his desk chair. It was still warm from Felcher's toned and muscular ass.

"It's not personal. Mostly I hate the DEA."

Coffin shrugged. "Feds are feds, pretty much."

"That's where you're wrong, Coffin. DEA has way too much power and no respect for jurisdiction. In the last thirty years they've made the drug situation in this country worse instead of better, and we have the highest incarceration rate in the world to show for it. It's like that headline in *The Onion*—'Drugs Win War on Drugs.' If it was up to me I'd disband the DEA and legalize pot, like, tomorrow. And I'm a freaking Republican."

"You sound like my Uncle Rudy."

Mancini scratched his head with a manicured finger. "Seen him lately?"

"Who's asking?"

"Call it idle curiosity."

"No. Not lately."

Mancini uncrossed his ankles, then crossed them again the other way. "Apparently there was some kind of incident in Truro last night."

"Oh?"

"Your car was involved. I'm surprised the state police haven't been by to see you."

Coffin shrugged. "Maybe they've got other things to do."

"That's it? That's all you've got to say?"

Coffin looked at Mancini from under his eyebrows. "You've met my cousin Tony."

Mancini nodded slowly. "He's the guy who walked out of the psych ward last night, right?"

"Yep."

"Where is he now?"

"At home, last I heard. But in the meantime . . ."

"Ah." Mancini brushed a speck of lint from his pants leg. "Nobody's hurt, then?"

"Nope."

Lola knocked—a light knuckle tap on the office door's frosted glass panel. Mancini stood, walked to the door, opened it. "That's some family you've got there, Coffin. You sure reproduction was such a good idea?"

Coffin grinned, then sneezed. "I tried to tell her," he said.

"Got some lab reports you might be interested in," Mancini said, when Lola had stepped into the office.

She was in uniform. She looked unnervingly fit and well rested.

"That was quick," Coffin said.

"The blood and tissue in the wood shop are Branstool's. Also, no hits for heroin in any of Branstool's hollow ducks."

"No surprises, then."

"Not for you, maybe. I figured he was bringing it into the country in those things."

"Then the whole wood shop would be a front?"

"Right."

Coffin shrugged. "Seems like a lot of trouble, when you're surrounded on three sides by water."

"So you're saying they just brought it in by boat."

"Probably. Boats are big. Lots of places to hide stuff on a boat."

"Then what's up with the ducks?"

"Distribution," Coffin said. "Outgoing. Put the smack in the ducks, glue them shut, FedEx them anywhere in the country. It's a pretty good cover."

"It's goofy," Mancini said, "but I guess it beats driving around with it in the trunk of your car."

"He wouldn't have been working alone," Coffin said. "Whoever his partners were wouldn't trust him that much."

"The big heroin distribution centers in New York in the seventies only hired women," Mancini said. "And they had to work naked. Kept employee theft to a minimum."

"Didn't look like street-level distribution was going on there," Coffin said. "You've been in Branstool's house, right?"

Mancini nodded. "The wood shop workbench produced hits for heroin, but there was no measuring equipment and no baggies."

"Whoever killed him could have taken that stuff," Lola said.

"True," Coffin said. "Let's you and I go see Dogfish this morning, see if he knows anything." He turned to Mancini. "Can you have your boys go through Branstool's credit card records? I'm looking for FedEx or UPS transactions. If I'm right, there'll be a lot of them."

Lola twirled her uniform hat on her finger. "Any toxicology reports for Branstool yet?"

"They're not ready," Mancini said. "Later today, according to the ME. Maybe you could call her, Coffin, and move things along."

Coffin smiled, then sneezed. "That was a long time ago," Coffin said.

Mancini turned to Lola. "Chief Coffin and the medical examiner used to be an item."

"I heard," Lola said.

"Ms. Block and I went out three or four times," Coffin said. "Years ago. I wasn't really her type."

"He had a pulse." Mancini smirked. "What are the odds Branstool was a junkie?"

"What are the odds of a massive overdose as the cause of death?" Coffin said.

"You think he was dead before they put him on the table saw?"

"Wishful thinking, maybe."

"If he wasn't, it would've taken a couple of guys, probably." Mancini stood up, straightened a pants leg. "I bid you adieu. I don't suppose there's anything new on your arsonist?"

"More escalation," Coffin said, "and a change in method."

"He set fire to the house from the outside, I get that. Not sure how that worked, but it's different."

Coffin smoothed his mustache. "He may have switched accelerants, too. He might be using lighter fluid now."

"I don't get how this is escalation. The church was a much bigger structure, right?"

"Yeah, but the church was unoccupied. The trophy house had lights on and people inside."

"Person," Lola said, "and a cat."

Mancini sucked his teeth. "That's problematic, all right. I'd be worried if I was you." He strode to the door, turned the knob. "Wish there was something I could do to help, but I'm running out of detectives. One's in the hospital—took a fall, apparently. The other one's taking a few personal days. You can have Pilchard if you want him."

"The guy in the brown suit?" Coffin said. "No thanks."

"Funny," Mancini said, stepping out into the hallway. "That's what everybody says."

"That was weird," Lola said, when Mancini was gone. "He was almost not a dick to you."

"Maybe he got lucky last night," Coffin said.

"Ew," Lola said. "I was really happy not having that image in my head."

Coffin stood. "Time to go see Dogfish."

"He's the guy who lives on the houseboat, right?"

Coffin made a face. "Thanks for reminding me," he said.

The Provincetown Police Department maintained an official police boat, awkwardly christened *PPD 2.* She was a twenty-seven-foot Boston Whaler, powered by two enormous Mercury outboards. Her predecessor, *PPD 1,* had been slammed into the wharf and partially sunk by Hurricane Charley, back in 1987.

The morning was still chilly and damp. MacMillan Pier jutted into the harbor like a long, concrete finger, pointing across the bay's gray chop to Branstool's house in Truro. Constellations of gulls orbited the fishing boats—shellfish draggers, mostly—that bobbed rusty and dispirited in their moorings. *PPD 2* was tethered to a large metal cleat about halfway out the west side of the pier, twin outboards rumbling.

"Mornin' Frank, Lola. Welcome aboard!" Teddy Goulet, the harbor cop, leaned in the wheelhouse, smoking a cigarette.

"Why is he always so fucking cheerful?" Coffin hissed.

"Not everybody hates boats as much as you, Frank," Lola said, climbing aboard with an easy grace that made Coffin's vision swim.

Coffin sneezed, then sneezed again. "Just fucking shoot me, would you?" he said, under his breath. He clambered into Goulet's boat as best he could, momentarily catching his pants leg on a small metal cleat that was bolted into the gunwale.

"You all right there, Frank?" Goulet said, peering at Coffin as Lola helped cast off. "You don't look so good."

"I have a cold," Coffin said.

"He hates boats," Lola said, looping the bowline neatly before dropping it onto the deck.

"Hates boats!" Teddy said, the engines burbling as he eased PPD 2 away from the pier. "Huh. I've loved being on the water my whole life. It's being ashore I ain't so crazy about."

Goulet hit the gas and headed out toward the breakwater, where Dogfish's ramshackle pontoon boat was anchored. Coffin swallowed hard and clung to the frame of the wheelhouse as *PPD 2*'s nose lifted a bit, and the bow cut a gray-green wake, unzipping the still harbor.

The houseboat was a crude affair, cobbled together from fifty-gallon drums and random bits of lumber Dogfish had salvaged or stolen from shipyards and construction sites. It was, Coffin thought, basically a platform floating on pontoons, with a small, leaky-looking shack more or less in the middle of its deck. The whole thing had been painted traffic-cone orange since the last time Coffin had paid a visit. The shack had no door—a tattered shower curtain fluttered in the door frame. Coffin stuck his head inside. "Knock knock," he said.

A bed and a ramshackle table were bolted to the floor. There was a small potbellied stove, with a stovepipe that pierced the ceiling. Two mismatched lawn chairs squatted near the table. Several large plastic jugs of water stood in a row against the wall. A small, pop-eyed bulldog stared at Coffin from the bed, next to what appeared to be a pile of laundry. The bulldog growled, bared its teeth. The pile of laundry stirred.

"Fuck, man," Dogfish said, sitting up. He was skinny and small. His eyes were bleary—it had been several days since he'd shaved. "A man's home is no longer his castle in this fucking state. The cops just walk right in."

"It's a commonwealth," Coffin said, "and the door was open."

"What happened to your collection?" Lola said. The last time she and Coffin had visited, the houseboat had been decorated with flotsam and jetsam found over years of walking the town beach at dawn: plastic baby dolls, driftwood, sea-glass—anything that floated or washed ashore. Now the houseboat was plain, except for the bright orange paint inside and out.

"It sank," Dogfish said. "*Dogfish I* is no more. This here is *Dogfish II*."

"*Dogfish I* sank?" Coffin said. "When?"

"About a year ago—she got run down in the fog by some yahoo driving a big ol' motor yacht. That's why the orange paint—I figure it'll enhance my visibility."

Coffin felt a little queasy. He folded himself into one of the lawn chairs. "Were you on board at the time?"

Dogfish shook his head. "Nope. Me and Pants here had rowed ashore in the skiff, to take care of a little business. When we got back there was nothing left but a lot of floating junk. We're only in about ten feet of water at low tide, so I salvaged a lot—but I haven't had the heart to redecorate. Losing *Dogfish I* was a serious blow to my morale. I've been self-medicating ever since."

"You've been self-medicating for fifteen years," Coffin said.

"Yeah, but now I've got a good reason."

"Your dog's name is Pants?" Lola said.

"Yeah," Dogfish said. "I rowed out here one night and there was some guy in the shanty, going through my stuff. Looking for my stash, probably. Pants jumps out of the skiff and latches onto the guy's crotch—damn near castrated him. I couldn't really call him Balls, so I went with Pants. Besides, he pants. Get it?"

Coffin looked at Lola. She raised an eyebrow. "Let's talk about smack," Coffin said.

"So you require my expertise," Dogfish said, standing up, digging in the pile of laundry for a pair of jeans. "What's in it for me?"

He was naked. He looked, Coffin thought, like a plucked chicken with a few crudely drawn tattoos. "How about," Coffin said, "we continue not to arrest you for dealing heroin?"

"What, that's it? No cash?"

"If you got busted again, how many offenses would that make?"

"Three."

"So," Lola said. "Fifteen to twenty? Sounds like a pretty good deal to me."

"Okay," Dogfish said. "Done."

"You drive a hard bargain," Coffin said. "What do you know about a guy named Branstool?"

Dogfish grinned. His teeth were snaggled, his gums receding. "I know he was over his head. Get it?"

Coffin looked at Lola again. "It doesn't really make sense," he said. "As a joke, I mean."

"Over his head how?" Lola said.

Dogfish pulled on a stained yellow T-shirt, knelt in front of the potbellied stove. "He was dealing with some very bad boys," Dogfish said, expertly laying a small fire. "And completely fucking up the local heroin economy in the process. I mean, I assume you've noticed that the whole town's *awash* in smack, right?"

Coffin nodded. "We're starting to catch on. We've had a couple of overdoses in the last few months, a few more possession charges than usual. Seems to be hitting the Eastern Europeans, mostly."

"Your guy was bringing in very high quality Afghani by the kilo," Dogfish said. "Red stamp, right?"

"Right," Lola said. "A red stamp with a mosque and Arabic writing."

"Most of it was going off-Cape," Dogfish said, striking a match. "But he was also skimming and distributing to a few local dealers. Not me, though."

"Why not you?" Coffin said.

Dogfish raised an eyebrow. " 'Cause I didn't want to get my fuckin' head cut off," he said. "Duh."

The fire crackled to life. Satisfied, Dogfish shut the little door in the stove's belly and filled a kettle with water from one of his plastic jugs. "Anybody for tea?" he said, holding up a chipped mug with a picture of Big Bird on one side.

"No, thanks," Coffin and Lola said, almost in unison.

"So who are we talking about here?" Coffin said. "I've heard everything from MS 13 to Ukrainians."

Dogfish snorted and put the kettle on the stove. "Ukrainians. Somebody's been messin' with you, man."

"Okay. Who, then?"

Dogfish stared at Coffin for a long minute, eyes narrowed, wary. "We never had this conversation, right?"

"Right."

"Okay." Dogfish sat on the edge of the bed, and Pants jumped into his lap. "This is a very unusual operation as I understand it. I don't know everything, though—all I got is bits and pieces."

"Fine."

"Okay, you know where heroin comes from, right?"

"Afghanistan?"

Dogfish closed his eyes, shook his head. "Well, of course, Afghanistan, originally. I mean before it gets here."

"Germany?"

"Okay—not bad. This stuff with the red stamps gets flown out of Afghanistan in bulk, hundreds of pounds at a time. It's partly a CIA thing—it's basically the deal we cut with the Afghani warlords to keep them from rejoining the Taliban and overthrowing the central government. They grow the poppies and process the heroin. It's a multibillion-dollar business at their end. The CIA offers protection and gets a cut. From there it gets a little murky."

"Who flies it out of the country?" Coffin said.

"Like I say, it's all very covert. You hear different things. Did you know there are as many private contractors operating in Afghanistan as American military, almost? There's over fifty thousand of them, and they've got a lot of the same equipment and training as the army and marines and whatnot, but basically no oversight, and almost complete legal immunity."

"My uncle's going to be jealous when he hears this," Coffin said.

"Look, don't take my word for it. It's all over the Internet," Dogfish said.

"He's actually pretty close," Lola said. "I'm not scared of much, but when I was in the service those guys scared the hell out of me. Mercenaries, is what they are. Hard-core hired killers."

"Great," Coffin said. "So the mercenaries fly it out?"

"Probably. Usually the route is Afghanistan—which is totally landlocked—to Turkey, over Turkmenistan and Azerbaijan and some other little shithole countries nobody ever heard of, because you can't fly through Iranian airspace or Pakistani airspace without starting frickin' World War Three. From Turkey it's flown or goes overland to Germany, Holland, or—old school—France. From there it's on a boat to the U.S., although it might switch boats a couple of times midocean. GPS makes that shit easy now."

"This is all fascinating," Coffin said, stomach lurching a bit as *Dogfish II* rocked gently on the harbor swell. "But could we cut to the chase?"

"You don't look so good," Dogfish said. "You okay?"

"He hates boats," Lola said.

"Huh," Dogfish said. "Is that, like, a phobia? Is there a name for that?"

"Thalassophobia is fear of the sea," Lola said. "I don't know if there's one just for boats."

Coffin looked at his watch, tapped the crystal, looked at Dogfish.

"Sorry. Okay, here's where it gets a little fuzzy, like I say. What I've heard is, Branstool was meeting his shipments right down on the beach below his house. Now, ordinarily you'd have a larger ship offshore and send a Zodiac or whatever in to make the drop. Pretty simple—the guy on the beach lights a signal at a specific time, and the guys in the Zodiac aim for it."

"How much would you drop at a given time?"

Dogfish scratched Pants behind the ears. Pants panted. "Depends," he said. "Maybe a couple kilos. Maybe a lot more."

"And money changes hands?"

"Maybe. Or it might all be set up beforehand—bank transfers, numbered accounts, the whole deal. Did you know Branstool? Before he got killed, I mean?"

"Yeah," Coffin said. "I knew him."

"So you know what a zero he was, right? I mean, most of the people you meet in this business are lowlifes, but at least they have some initiative, right? A little entrepreneurial spirit."

"But not Branstool?"

"No, man. Are you kidding? Dude was just a flunky—somebody's little paid clerk. The last fucking guy on the planet you'd think was distributing smack all over the country, that's for sure."

"You said 'ordinarily,'" Lola said. "Ordinarily there'd be a larger ship offshore, and a Zodiac would make the run to shore."

"Oh, right," Dogfish said. He dropped a teabag into a chipped blue mug and poured boiling water from the kettle. Then he sat down at the table and lit a cigarette. Pants jumped into his lap and stared up at him adoringly. "Yeah, well, that's the freaky part. This was a big money operation. What I've heard is that they flew the stuff in on a helicopter."

"So the mother ship would have to be big enough to land a chopper on," Coffin said.

"Right," Dogfish said, exhaling smoke from his nose. "A big motherfucker of a yacht, probably parked outside the territorial limit, where the Coasties can't get 'em. Small chopper—runs in low and fast. They've got all this stealth shit now that makes 'em pretty quiet. Make the drop in the dunes or on the beach—you don't even have to land, just throw the merchandise out the door and boom, you're gone. Nothing but a streak of light in the night sky."

Coffin nodded. "That would explain Tony's UFOs, maybe."

Dogfish pointed, cigarette between his fingers. "The UFOs!" he said. "Over Pilgrim Lake. I never thought of that." He laughed, a dry cackle. "All this time it was choppers full of smack."

"You've seen them?"

"No, but my buddy Leroy has. He thought he was losing his mind. Wait 'til I tell him." Pants had fallen asleep in Dogfish's lap, and was snoring loudly.

Lola pursed her lips. "You said Branstool was just a clerk. How did you know him?"

"He tried to recruit me, like I said. He didn't say so, but I knew he had to be skimming, and I wanted no part of it. The only way I survive in this town is to stay under the radar—strictly small-time. You know why they left his head in that tank, right?"

"It sure looked like a warning," Coffin said.

"Bingo," Dogfish said. "To every dealer on the Cape that was part of his network. I can tell you for a fact that the two guys he was working with here in town packed up and left the next day. Poof! Gone."

"So who's running the operation?" Coffin said. "Who killed Branstool?"

"Like I said, it's hazy. But I've got a theory—and you're not gonna like it."

Coffin sneezed. Pants woke up and growled.

Dogfish patted his head. "Good boy," he said. "Attaboy, Pants."

"Okay," Coffin said. "I won't like it. What's the theory?"

Dogfish lowered is voice. "It sounds completely fucking nuts," he said, "but we were talking about those contractors—the mercenaries? That's who I'd be looking at if I was you. They've got the equipment, the logistics, and the muscle. If things go to shit and somebody gets killed, they blame it on the Latin Kings or MS 13 or whatever. Or what was it you said? Bulgarians?"

"Ukrainians," Coffin said. "Posing as Chechens."

Dogfish cackled, a high falsetto laugh. Pants wagged his stumpy tail. "I love that, man. Ukrainians."

"So what did they need Branstool for?" Coffin said.

Dogfish rolled his eyes. "Cover. Somebody had to handle the distribution, but even more important, somebody had to launder the cash. You need a legitimate business to do that—but a nursing home will work in a pinch. It was a sweet operation, I gotta say. While it lasted."

Lola frowned, shook her head. "I just don't understand how a guy like Branstool could get mixed up with something like this. He was so—beige."

Dogfish tapped a fresh cigarette from his pack, lit it from the smoldering butt of the old one. "He was a customer for years," he said, squinting through blue smoke. "No joke. I sold to that guy since I first got into the business, almost. He had a nice little habit going, nothing unmanageable on his income. But then his wife left him and things changed. He started using a lot more—wanted me to give him credit. Then he stopped buying altogether and I figured he'd gone with another dealer, which was fine. Next thing I know, he wants *me* to deal for *him*."

"You think you know somebody," Coffin said.

Dogfish shook his head. "Nobody really knows anybody, man. We're all just these walking bags of meat and chemicals. What's to fucking know?"

"Okay," Coffin said, standing. "I guess that's it. Sergeant Winters, our friend Dogfish here is under arrest."

"Whoa whoa whoa!" Dogfish said, as Lola cuffed his hands behind his back. "What the fuck, dude?" Pants jumped from Dogfish's lap and growled.

"You're holding out," Coffin said. "Look at you—you're sweaty."

"I'm a heroin addict, man—I'm always sweaty."

"We had a deal," Coffin said. He patted Pants on the head. Pants drooled and wiggled his stump of a tail.

"Son of a *bitch*. You know I don't do well in jail. I got *needs*."

"Tell me about the Chechens," Coffin said.

"You're gonna get me fucking killed, Coffin," Dogfish said, shaking his skinny head. "Do you care, even a little? No, you do not."

"You've got ten seconds."

"*Okay*, Jesus. I've heard things, all right? Young guys—Russians is what I heard. I think they're out of Providence, or maybe New Bedford, but lately they've been trying to move in on the Cape. Lots of guns and tattoos. Extremely violent."

"Like what?" Coffin said.

"Like home invasion, rape your girlfriend, burn your house down violent. Ever seen *Scarface,* where they cut that guy up with the chain saw? Like that."

"Go on."

Dogfish grimaced. "Jesus. I'm dead. Just shoot me now."

Coffin turned to Lola. "Do you feel like shooting him?"

Lola shook her head. "Nah," she said. "Who'd take care of Pants?"

"Sorry," Coffin said. "I'm not carrying a gun."

Dogfish looked up at Coffin with something like pity in his eyes. "You're going to feel guilty about this, man. This is going to fucking haunt you."

"Keep talking."

"This is all hearsay, okay? I haven't met these guys myself, but people are talking. The one in charge is named Ygor—you know, like Dr. Frankenstein and shit. You don't want to fuck with him."

"No? How come?"

"Because he'll turn his buddy Vladi loose on your ass, that's how come. Mr. Chain Saw. I got no fucking idea how or if they're connected to Branstool, but nothing would surprise me. And that's all I know, I swear on my poor dead mother's grave."

"Russians?" Coffin said. "Are you sure?" He wagged an index finger and Lola unlocked the handcuffs.

Dogfish shrugged. "That's what I hear. They all sound like Boris and Natasha to me."

"Well," Lola said, after Teddy Goulet had dropped them off at the pier. "That was interesting."

Coffin's knees were wobbly. Goulet waved from the deck of *PPD 2*, but Coffin kept walking and didn't wave back. "That's a good word for it," he said, when the worst of the dizziness had passed.

"You okay there, Frank?" Lola said, peering at Coffin from under the brim of her uniform hat.

"Awesome, dude," Coffin said. He took a deep breath, then another.

"Good call on the Chechens."

Coffin shrugged. "The more Dogfish acts like something's farfetched or ridiculous, the more likely it is to be true."

"He has that in common with Mancini," Lola said. "But for different reasons."

They stood at the corner of Commercial and Standish streets, waiting to cross as a slow caravan of weekend traffic rolled slowly toward the west end, impeded here and there by small knots of pedestrians, a mix of Tall Ships and day-tripping tourists.

"Say what you want about Pinsky," Lola said, tilting her head at a pair of drag queens as they strode down the sidewalk in matching Daisy Duke outfits. "He's not afraid to follow his heart."

"If that's the applicable body part," Coffin said.

Lola grinned. "Good point," she said.

"Speaking of misty-eyed romantics," Coffin said, as they crossed the street, "how'd the meeting with the Realtor go?"

"Not great. She's worried we won't be able to get a loan."

"Bad credit?"

"Great credit—not enough income. She said we'd probably both have to take second jobs, and even then it might not be enough."

"That sucks," Coffin said. "Sorry."

"How about you? When's your furniture arriving?"

Coffin laughed. "I'm not sure. We have to order it first."

"Well, so—what're you getting? Where's it coming from?"

Coffin paused across the street from the Portuguese Bakery, his stomach growling. "I figured it was best not to ask," he said. "The nesting thing is fraught with danger, where the mate's concerned. I just do what I'm told."

Lola nodded. "Probably safer that way."

"You hungry?" Coffin said.

"Nope, had a big breakfast after the gym this morning."

"Hang on a second—I'll be right back."

Coffin stepped into the street and was nearly run down by a man on a moped. The man was dressed as a glittering, blue Lucifer, complete with large, batlike wings. He swerved, squeezed the brakes, tires squealing. He turned to glare at Coffin, baring enormous vampire fangs. "Almost got another soul," he said, before putting off toward the west end. "Your time will come, sinner!"

The bakery was crowded. A group of tall German tourists had taken all the seats, while others were milling around the glass display cases, pointing at the cakes and cookies, the croissants and breads, the turnovers, rolls, and scones. Malasadas—flat Portuguese donuts—fried in bubbling vats of oil in the front window. A half-dozen men in identical white sailor suits filed in behind Coffin, the smell of their mingled cologne competing with the scent of warm baked goods and coffee.

"Yo, Frankie," the counterman called, waving Coffin up to the front of the line. "What can I get you?"

"Just a couple of ham and cheese buns, Ernie," Coffin said. "And a large coffee."

"Excuse me," one of the Germans said, his consonants crisp with outrage. "Why is this man being served before us?"

Ernie scowled. He was about Coffin's age, but he kept his hair and mustache dyed jet-black. He wore white pants, a white T-shirt, a white apron, and a white paper hat. He had an anchor tattooed on his right bicep, with the name of a ship scrolled across it: S.S. *Charles S. Goodnight.*

"It's okay, Ernie," Coffin said. "I can wait my turn."

Ernie glared at the German. "Do you know who this man is?" he said, aiming a pair of pastry tongs at Coffin's heart.

"No," the German said. "I do not."

"This man is a goddamn hero," Ernie said. "This man puts his life on the line for the people of this town every goddamn day. Did you know that, Mr. Goddamn German tourist?"

The German blanched. "I did not know that," he said. "No."

Coffin shook his head. "Ernie, for Christ's sake." He turned to the German. "Sorry," he said. "We're Portuguese. We're very emotional people."

Ernie dropped four ham and cheese buns into a white paper bag and filled a large foam cup with coffee. "On the house, Frankie," he said. "How's your ma?"

"Still causing trouble, Ernie," Coffin said. "Still causing trouble."

"Atta girl," Ernie said. "You see her, you tell her Cousin Ernie said hello."

When Coffin had safely recrossed the street, Lola pointed at the grease-spotted bag. "I hope you're not actually planning to eat that," she said. "Whatever it is."

"Oh, hell yes," Coffin said, sipping his coffee. "You don't know what you're missing."

"Heart attack? Stroke? Early death?"

They passed the very fat man with the blue guitar who often sat on one of the wooden benches in front of Town Hall, and a man dressed as a scarecrow making surreal balloon animals, and the little shrine of flowers and votive candles on the spot where Miss Ellie had stood for years with her karaoke machine, singing "My Way" and "The Impossible Dream" in her warbly contralto. "There was about ten years when I worked out a lot," Coffin said. "Mid-twenties to mid-thirties. I was under a lot of stress, though, and I started having palpitations, so I went to see a cardiologist. He couldn't find anything wrong with my heart, but given the fact that I smoked, drank, and ate a lot of fast food he was kind of surprised that my resting heart rate was so low—about fifty beats per minute. I was spending a lot of time on the treadmill, I said—mostly to deal with the stress."

They climbed the broad stone steps in front of Town Hall. The painters were almost done with the exterior: it was a cool mint green with yellow trim. It looked, Coffin thought, more like an elaborate guesthouse than a government building.

"Okay, so?"

"So he asked me, 'Do you like working out on the treadmill?' And I said, 'No, not really.' And he said, 'That's funny, because I just read a study that says that you really can extend your life with exercise—by roughly the amount of time you spend exercising.'"

Coffin paused at the top of the stairs, slightly out of breath.

"Your face is kind of pink," Lola said.

Coffin looked at the grease-stained bag, then looked at Lola. "You are *such* a killjoy," he said.

Lola patted him on the back. "Somebody's got to watch out for you," she said. "You're a person of very little self-control."

Coffin thought of Jemma, her remarkable ass sliding into a tight pair of jeans. "It depends." He held up the bag. "What am I going to do with this?"

Lola took the bag, trotted down the stairs, handed the bag to a skinny, deeply sunburned man sitting on one of the wooden benches, then trotted back up. "Problem solved," she said.

"So you care about my health, but not his?" Coffin said.

"Ticky?" Lola said. "We're talking about a guy who huffs metallic paint under the Dick Dock. Whatever was in that bag is not the thing that's going to kill him."

Coffin held up his hands, palms out—*you win*. "You busy right now? Other than watching out for my cholesterol?"

Lola shrugged. "Other than arson and severed heads, I got nothing all day."

In the Crown Vic, headed out Route 6 toward Orleans, Lola squinted in the autumn glare, took her sunglasses from the pocket of her uniform shirt and put them on. "Who are we going to see, again? Maurice somebody?"

"Maurice from Yaya's, remember? The kid who took care of the seals."

"The seals? We're back on the seals again? I don't get it."

Coffin sighed, looked out the window. "You're going to think I'm crazy."

"Crazi*er*," Lola said.

They were passing through Eastham's narrow strip of clam shacks, tourist motels, gift shops, and gas stations. "I've been having these recurring dreams."

"Uh-oh," Lola said. "First Tony, now you. Genetics, or something in the water?"

Coffin grinned. "I know," he said. "It's stupid, right? We're going to show up at this kid's house and freak him out for nothing."

Lola shot him a look through her sunglasses. "So you dreamed about this Maurice guy?"

"Not at first. I've been having these dreams about fire. In the dream I'd wake up and there'd be smoke and flames everywhere. Jamie had had the baby already, and I had to save it. The baby was crying, so I'd run down the hall through all the fire and smoke and reach into the crib, and that's where the dream would end."

"Nothing too weird about that," Lola said, pursing her lips. "Pretty much your basic anxiety dream. Were you wearing any pants?"

Coffin laughed. "After a week or so it got a lot weirder. I'd reach into the crib and the baby would be a seal. The Seal Baby. I had to save the Seal Baby, and not let it die in the fire."

"Yep," Lola said. "That's definitely weird."

"And then last night the Seal Baby turned into Maurice. It looked at me, and it had Maurice's face."

"Dude. Paging Dr. Freud."

"Exactly. So then I started wondering if my subconscious hadn't made some kind of connection, you know?"

"Okay, like what?"

"Fuck if I know." Coffin shrugged. "He seemed like a nice young guy. No apparent motive. Early twenties. Not real bright. Lives with his mother . . ."

Lola turned and stared at him for a second, then fixed her gaze on the road again. "So he fits the profile, is what you're saying. Am I remembering right? Would he bit a bit less than medium height, thick through the chest and shoulders?"

Coffin nodded. "He would indeed."

Maurice Duval's mother lived in Orleans, her run-down cottage stuck in the middle of a strip of small businesses along the Cranberry Highway: Captain Elmer's Seafood on one side, JoMama's New York Bagels on the other. Her yard was scraggly and brown; a rusted rake lay on top of a loose pile of leaves. A dirt brown pickup truck was parked crookedly in the driveway: it looked to Coffin as though it had been painted with a brush, sometime around 1990. As Lola pulled up behind the truck, a black and white Orleans police cruiser slid silently up to the curb. The door swung open and a uniformed officer popped out: a square-jawed, barrel-chested young man who appeared to be about five feet tall.

"Bangs," the officer said, sticking out his hand. "You must be Chief Coffin."

Bangs's hand was small, almost like a child's. Coffin shook it. "This is Sergeant Winters. Thanks for meeting us."

"Thanks for calling ahead," Bangs said. "Chief likes it when our neighbors observe the standard protocol."

"Who doesn't?" Coffin said. "I'm the same way. Watch the back, would you, Bangs? And try to keep out of sight."

"That's why I'm here," Bangs said. He picked his way through the tufted, unmowed yard to the back of the house.

Coffin knocked lightly on the front door. Over time, he'd learned that the heavy cop knock almost never produced good results: People panicked, jumped out the windows, went to the bedroom to fetch their guns. Keep the uniforms out of sight and knock softly— that was almost always the way to go.

A woman answered the door. She was around Coffin's age, stocky, not very tall. Her hair looked slept in: It was cropped very short, dyed an odd, artificial auburn color. She wore a pale green bathrobe and bright red lipstick, freshly applied. Her eyes were bagged, the lids reptilian. She was smoking a cigarette. Coffin showed her his shield. "Mrs. Duval? May we come in and talk for a minute?"

The woman took a long drag from her cigarette, blew it out. "*Ms.* Duval. What's this about?" Her voice was gravelly. It made Coffin want to clear his throat.

"We'd like to talk to your son, ma'am. I understand he lives with you?"

"He's not here." There was a rustling commotion inside the house—just out of Coffin's line of sight.

"It's getting a little chilly out here, ma'am," Coffin said. The wind had picked up, and a light rain had begun to fall. "Could we come in for just a minute, please?"

"I don't have to let you in without a warrant," the woman said. "You got a warrant?"

Coffin held up his hands. "We're not here to search your house. We're not here to arrest anybody. I've just got a couple of questions to ask your son, and then we'll be on our way."

"I told you. He's not here. He don't live here anymore. I told him he had to help with rent and groceries or get out. I can't feed us both on what I make."

Lola took out a notebook and a pen. "Do you have his current address, ma'am?"

"He's stayin' with friends in Hyannis. I don't know the address. It's near the bus station."

"How about a phone number?"

"He's got a cell phone, but I think it got cut off."

Coffin heard a door close somewhere inside the house. "Who else is in the house with you right now, ma'am?" He resisted a powerful impulse to push *Ms.* Duval out of the way and chase down whoever was crouching in the dim interior rooms. He glanced at Lola: Her hands hung loose at her sides, but her jaw muscles were tensed.

"That's none of your business," the woman said, taking another drag from her cigarette. "Is there anything else? I'm in the middle of something important right now."

"That's your son's truck, isn't it?" Lola said, pointing at the listing hulk in the driveway. They'd run a records check on Maurice Duval before leaving the office, looking for outstanding warrants, arrest records, history of mental illness, firearms registration. The vehicle check was part of the routine. There hadn't been much: an outstanding speeding ticket, an old DUI. An '82 Ford pickup, formerly green but now a patchy, uneven brown.

"That piece of shit?" the woman said. "It ain't running. I told him to get it outta here, but he's too busy partying with his boys." She raised her eyebrows. They appeared to be tattooed on. "Is there anything else?"

"Does Maurice have a job? Maybe we can catch him at work."

"Yeah, he's got a part-time gig at Petzapawlooza in town. It's across the street from the CVS."

A man's voice called from inside the house. "Connie? Where the fuck didja go? I'm getting lonely in here."

Connie rolled her eyes, shook her head. "Look," she said to Coffin. "I don't mean to be rude, but this is a bad time. You want to leave me a card, I'll make sure to tell Maurice you're lookin' for him."

A man waddled down the hall in a sleeveless T-shirt and sagging boxer shorts. He was tall, with a big paunch and skinny, hairy legs. He had a black mustache, and was trying to ignite the butt of a green cigar with a Bic lighter. "Hey," he said. "It's that cop from Provincetown. Coffin."

Coffin nodded. "Mr. Stecopoulos. Nice seeing you again. We were just on our way over to Petzapawlooza to talk to your son."

Stecopoulos scowled at Connie. "You *told* him?"

Connie heaved an exasperated sigh. "No, dumb-ass—he *guessed*. *You* told him."

Stecopoulos puffed at the cigar, held it at arm's length, glared at it, tried to light it again with the sputtering Bic. "Well," he said, after a minute, "I guess the freaking cat's out of the bag."

The inside of Connie Duval's house was more orderly than the outside. The dishes were washed, the kitchen linoleum dingy but clean. The living-room carpet, the color of bread mold, had been recently vacuumed—the little parallel lines from the vacuum cleaner's wheels were still visible.

Coffin and Lola sat at the kitchen table, across from Connie and Stecopoulos. Bangs stood near the back door, warming his tiny hands on a cup of instant coffee. A pair of goldfish swam in a large bowl on the blue Formica counter.

"What can I tell you?" Stecopoulos said, looking down at the floor. "I lead a double life. My wife, if she found out? This would kill her."

"It's true," Connie said, tapping a fresh Virginia Slim from the pack. "She's not in good health. She's physically and emotionally very frail."

Coffin shrugged. "We can be discreet," he said. "Right, Bangs?"

"Righty-o," Bangs said. He sipped his coffee, made a face.

"But you want something in return, is that right?" Connie said. "Information. About Maurice?"

"It's about the seals, isn't it?" Stecopoulos said. He shook his head again. He'd put on a bathrobe, to Coffin's relief. It hadn't been easy, looking at his hairy shoulders.

Connie patted Stecopoulos's arm. "Donny loved those freakin' seals. He cried like a baby after they got shot. He came home and put his head in my lap and cried like a three-year-old, no fucking joke."

Stecopoulos crossed himself in the Greek Orthodox manner— three fingers, right-to-left across the chest. "Hand to God," he said, "Maurice had nothing to do with killing them. He's a good boy, he loved those seals—he had names for them, even. Clarabelle and Dawn and Sammy—I can't remember the other two. He didn't do it, I promise you."

"Okay," Coffin said. "How do you know that?"

"He was here with me," Connie said. "All night. We sat on the couch and watched TV 'til about eleven. Then he went to bed—he had to get to the restaurant early every morning."

Coffin looked at Stecopoulos. The goldfish hovered in their bowl, staring, faces enlarged by the curved glass wall. "Is that true?" he said.

Stecopoulos frowned, shook his head. "No," he said. "He was out that night. He had a girl in Eastham for a while—he was out with her."

"Then how do you know he didn't kill the seals?" Coffin said.

Stecopoulos looked down, then back up at Coffin. "Because I did it," he said. "I shot them."

"Oh, Jesus," Connie said, leaning back in her chair. "Smooth move, Adonis."

"Adonis?" Coffin said. "Really?"

Stecopoulos shrugged. "I was a cute baby," he said.

"Why would you kill your own seals, Mr. Stecopoulos?" Lola said.

"They were hurting the business," Connie said. "The food, the vet bills. And the animal rights whackos—people would say terrible things to Donny. The local PETA chapter organized a boycott, even. They were a burden, those seals."

Stecopoulos thought for a long minute. "That's part of it," he said at last. "I kept those seals a long time—their parents, too. I loved seeing them every day, swimming in their pool, playing, sunning themselves on the deck. They were a good draw for the business, at least until the last few years. But zoo stock or not, they're wild animals, you know? They'd sit by the fence at high tide, looking out at the harbor with their big, sad eyes. I'd look at them huddled up at the fence like that and it'd break my heart a little more every day. People think it's cruel, keeping seals. Maybe they're right."

"Why not just turn 'em loose?" Bangs said.

"They'd have starved," Stecopoulos said. "They never caught a fish in their lives. You can't just release a tame seal into the wild like that. They'd die a terrible death."

"What about aquariums or research centers?" Lola said.

"I tried Mystic, Woods Hole, the Franklin Park Zoo, New England Aquarium—they all said the same thing: budget cuts, recession, layoffs, yada yada. I must've called twenty places—no takers."

"So you just shot them," Lola said, hands flat on the table.

"He was impaired," Connie said. "He'd been drinking ouzo and listening to the soundtrack from *Zorba the Greek* over and over. It's enough to make anyone crazy."

"What about Maurice?" Coffin said. "Does he know you killed the seals?"

Stecopoulos scratched his chest through his T-shirt. "No. He looks up to me. I couldn't tell him a thing like that."

"Where is he now?"

Connie stared at Coffin for a second, then stubbed out her cigarette in a ceramic ashtray. "At work, like I said. He had a dog to groom."

"You still want to talk to him?" Stecopoulos said. "How come? I told you—I shot the seals, not him."

"It's regarding another matter," Coffin said.

Stecopoulos stared at Coffin, then at Lola, heavy brows knitted. "So I just confessed for no fucking reason?"

There was a long pause. Connie stood up, opened a cabinet, produced a bottle of Jim Beam and two glasses. "I need a drink," she said, pouring a hefty double. "Anybody join me?"

"Sure," Coffin said. "Why not?"

Connie poured him a double, too, and they clinked glasses. "Here's to the last thirty years of my life, fucking the dumbest motherfucker on the Cape," she said. "What d'ya think about that?" She downed her shot, poured another.

"Hey!" Stecopoulos said.

"Here's to love," Coffin said, raising his glass.

Stecopoulos nodded. "That's more like it," he said.

————

Petzapawlooza was wedged in between a garden store and a low-rent law firm, across the street from a large CVS drugstore, not far from the Super Stop & Shop and the Nauset Fish and Lobster Pool, an excellent seafood market that stayed open year-round.

There was only one car parked in front of Petzapawlooza: The shop windows held the usual assortment of caged birds and roly-poly puppies of dubious origin. A bell rang softly when Coffin and Lola stepped inside, but no one greeted them. The store smelled like hamsters. Bright fish swam in bubbling tanks. "Want a free lizard?" Coffin said, walking up to a large terrarium that held two green iguanas. "Now's your chance."

"I had a housemate once that had an iguana," Lola said. "All he did was hide behind the sofa. Somehow he got inside the walls and we never saw him again—we just heard him slithering around in there sometimes. His name was Walter."

Soothing Muzak drifted from hidden speakers. Neon-colored parakeets chirped and whistled in their cage. Faintly, Coffin could hear the buzzing of grooming shears coming from a back room. He put a finger to his lips, and he and Lola moved quietly, quickly, past the caged rabbits, the green python in its tank, the cat toys and dog collars, cat litter and dog food, until they stood just outside the swinging door that led to the back room. A sign on the door said EMPLOYEES ONLY. Lola pushed the door open silently with one hand, and Coffin stepped inside. A cocker spaniel stood patiently, muzzled, tethered to a grooming table, most of the fur sheared from the left side of its body. An electric grooming clipper lay buzzing on the concrete floor. The back door was open. A cool, damp breeze was blowing in. Maurice Duval was gone.

There was a flurry of shouts from the rear parking lot: a young, strident voice yelling, "Police! Get down!" and then, "Stand up, Duval!"

"Bangs!" Coffin said, running out to the parking lot, two steps behind Lola. "He got him!"

Bangs appeared from behind a rusty Dodge van, a young man in tow, head down, hands cuffed behind him. "Got your boy," Bangs said, grinning. "He came running out the back door just after you went in. We had a little foot pursuit, but I nabbed him."

The young man looked at Coffin, then at Lola. He was slender, fair-skinned. His black hair was long and straight. "That's not him," Coffin said.

"Oh, shit," Bangs said. "Seriously?"

Lola nodded. "Yep. Wrong guy."

"Okay," the young man said, shaking his head sadly. "Maybe you believe me now, ha?"

Coffin tilted his head. "You check his pockets?"

Bangs nodded. "No weapons, no drugs. Wallet, keys, iPhone." He handed the young man's phone to Coffin.

"Let's get the cuffs off him," Coffin said. "You got some ID, sir?"

Uncuffed, the young man took out his wallet, produced a driver's license. His name was Goran Milovanovic; he lived in Eastham. *Serbian,* Coffin thought.

"Why'd you run, Goran?" Coffin said.

"I don't want trouble," he said. "I see cops, I get the fuck out."

"Visa expired?" Coffin said.

Goran nodded.

"Where's Maurice?"

"He called, says he's sick. Asks if I can cover. I need the work—I say okay."

"How's your day been so far, Goran?"

"I don't understand."

"Would you say it's been a good day so far?" Coffin asked. "Or maybe not so great."

"I'm in dirty parking lot with three cops. I tore my pants. Not so good."

"I can make it a little worse," Coffin said. "Or I can make it a little better. Which would you prefer?"

Goran shrugged. "Better would be nice."

"You still have Maurice's number on your cell?"

Goran nodded. "Of course."

Coffin handed him the phone. "Call him. Tell him the boss gave everybody a nice bonus and his check is sitting here waiting for him. Tell him yours was three hundred bucks, but you think his is more."

"Okay, but he won't believe this."

"What would he believe?"

"Boss is pissed he's not here—he comes in right now or he's fired."

"Must be some boss," Coffin said, handing Goran his iPhone. "If he shows, we never saw you. No ICE."

"Terrible boss," Goran said, "but the animals, I like. They are very sad." He touched the iPhone's screen a few times, held the phone to his ear.

Coffin looked at Lola. They waited.

Goran's eyebrows went up. "Maurice," he said. "It's Goran. Pete comes to store and he's not happy. He says you got to come in. Yeah, man, I know. I'm just telling you what he said—you got to come in or he's letting you go." Goran paused, frowned, lowered the phone.

"Well?" Coffin said.

Goran pursed his lips, looked down at the rip in the knee of his jeans, nodded slowly. "He says Pete can go fuck himself. He says everybody can go fuck himself."

Coffin held out his hand. "Let me try."

Goran handed him the phone. Coffin touched REDIAL and waited. The phone rang once, then again. A voice said, "Hello?"

"Maurice," Coffin said. "What's up?"

There was a long pause. "Who is this?" Maurice said, finally.

"This is Frank Coffin, with the Provincetown police. Listen, Maurice—we need to talk. It's important."

There was another pause, then a burst of static. *Maurice must be in Provincetown,* Coffin thought. *The rest of the Cape has good reception.*

"Coffin," Maurice said, when the static had cleared. "Time's up." And then he hung up.

"What'd he say, Frank?" Lola said.

"Time's up," Coffin said, the hair on the back of his neck prickling. "Whatever that means. I think he's back in P'town—the reception was terrible."

"Sounds like P'town," Goran said. "Reception there always sucks."

"That's 'cause the closest tower's in Truro," Bangs said. "P'town won't let anybody build one."

Coffin handed Goran his iPhone, and a business card. "Thanks for your help, Goran. Call us if you hear anything from Maurice. Sorry about your pants."

"It's okay," Goran said, looking at the card, then down at his jeans. "I never liked these pants."

Maurice was wearing his mother's red wig, an old surf-green muu-muu, Converse sneakers. He'd parked his friend's Nissan just down the street from Coffin's place. It was a shabby little house—shingles curling with age, slight sag in the roofline—hardly worth burning. But it was the right distance from town center, he thought, and the neighboring houses were easily close enough that they, too, would be at risk. The fact that Coffin was a cop would mean that every fireman and cop in town would be there, trying to help. And that, he knew, meant that his last fire—the big fire he'd been planning all along—would be off to a roaring start before anyone could respond.

He opened the glove box. His plastic squeeze bottle of Ronsonol lighter fluid was still there, of course, and his long grill lighter with the flexible neck. He'd decided to switch from gasoline to lighter fluid after nearly incinerating himself at the church fire. Somehow the gas he'd poured in the sanctuary had ignited while he was still inside: a spark, maybe, or a pilot light. The resulting fireball had literally blown him out the door, singeing his eyebrows, leaving him dazed for a few moments, flat on his back in the oyster-shell parking lot. He'd been lucky—picked himself up, dusted himself off, melted out of sight down a dark side street, circling back twenty minutes later to watch it burn.

The lighter fluid was better, easier to control. It was too bad, he thought, that he was almost done. He was starting to enjoy his work. He was starting to get good at it.

Coffin's phone burst into a shrill fusillade of "La Cucaracha." He wrestled it from his jacket pocket, where it was stuffed along with his keys, a wad of Kleenex, and a plastic bottle of zinc soft chews. He looked at the screen: It read, HOME.

"Jamie?" Coffin said.

"Frank, where are you?"

"We're in the car. Heading back from Orleans. We had a close call with a Serbian dog groomer."

There was a rush of white noise. "What?"

"Sorry. It's been a weird day."

"It just got weirder, Frank. The nursing home called."

"Uh-oh."

"Your mom's had a stroke, Frank. About an hour ago, they said. I'm really sorry."

"How bad is she?" Coffin said.

"She's conscious, but right now she can't talk, and can't move her left side."

Coffin said nothing for a long moment. Lola glanced at him, glanced back at the road.

"Frank?" Jamie said. "You okay?"

"Yeah," Coffin said. "Yeah. I'm okay."

"The nurse said you might want to come see her," Jamie said. "You know. Soon."

Coffin nodded. "Okay. We'll be there in a few minutes. I'll have Lola drop me off."

"Bad news?" Lola said, when Coffin had stuffed his phone back into his pocket.

Coffin leaned back. The Crown Vic was just cresting the hill at High Head, the view opening up dramatically: the silver mirror of Pilgrim Lake on the right; North Truro, Provincetown Harbor, and the curve of waterfront on the left. "Yeah. My mother had a stroke. About an hour ago."

"Oh, Frank," Lola said. She reached over, put a hand on his shoulder. "How is she?"

Coffin shook his head. "Not good. The nurse said I'd better hurry and come in."

Lola turned on the flashers and stepped on the gas. The Crown Vic surged forward, the g-force pressing Coffin back in his seat. The Days cottages whipped by, thin, blue slices of harbor flashing between them. He watched the speedometer rise: by the time they passed the first Provincetown exit at Snail Road they were doing 110. They reached the Conwell Street exit a few seconds later, and Lola whipped the Crown Vic around a dump truck, roared through the red light, passed two Tall Ships on bicycles, and took the left onto Conwell at just under 70. Four seconds later she took a hard, sliding right onto the crushed oyster-shell surface of Cemetery Road. There was a quick blur of gravestones, and by the time Coffin could take a breath and let it out they'd pulled up in front of Valley View, trailed by a rolling cloud of dust.

"Holy shit," Coffin said, gripping the armrest, heart pounding. "Where'd you learn to drive like that?"

Lola shrugged. "The army," she said. "It was part of the MP training."

Coffin climbed out of the passenger seat. "Put the department on alert. I'm pretty sure Maurice is in town, and he sounded like a man with a plan. We want to talk to every short, stocky guy in Provincetown who's wearing a red wig."

"Any other week, that'd only be three or four guys," Lola said.

Coffin straightened, took a deep breath, let it out. "This is going to suck," he said.

Lola leaned over, looked up at him through the open passenger door, blue eyes bright in the Crown Vic's dim interior. "We take care of the family, Frank," she said.

Coffin nodded. "Yep," he said. "That's what we do."

Coffin's mother was gaunt and pale. The left side of her face was locked in a snarling grimace; the right side seemed composed, at rest. Her right eye tracked Coffin as he walked into the room and sat down by her bedside; the left eye stared straight ahead. Kimberly, the fat nurse, was making some notes on a chart. A portable heart monitor beeped from its tall stand. An IV bag hung from another stand, behind the head of the bed. The two prongs of a slim oxygen hose were fitted into Coffin's mother's nostrils. Her right eyebrow arched; her right eye stared at Coffin, glinting. She gripped a ballpoint pen in the claw of her right hand—a pad of Post-it notes lay on her lap.

"We're not taking heroic measures, per your mother's orders when she was admitted," the nurse said. "We're giving her oxygen and saline, as you can see, and we may start her on IV blood thinners to try to prevent a recurrence once we've determined whether the stroke was the result of a clot or a hemorrhage. Otherwise we're just letting her rest, poor thing."

"How is she?" Coffin said. "I heard about the paralysis."

"Well, yes, the initial paralysis is quite severe. We don't know the full effects yet—she seems alert, and she's been writing us notes, as you can see."

Coffin's mother had stuck a Post-it note onto the edge of a rolling tray at her bedside. The note was written in a spidery, barely legible hand. It said, *Fuck off.* Coffin's mother pointed at the note with her pen, then pointed at the nurse, then pointed back at the note, her good eye glinting ferociously.

"Maybe she wants you to leave," Coffin said.

"Gee," said the nurse. "You think?"

When the nurse was gone, Coffin patted his mother's good hand. "I came as fast as I could, Ma," he said.

His mother nodded, picked up the pad of Post-its. She wrote slowly, laboriously. She peeled the Post-it from the pad and stuck it to Coffin's sleeve. *Kill me*, it said.

Coffin closed his eyes, opened them again. "Ma, you know I can't do that. This is awful, what's happened to you—but I can't kill you."

His mother stared at him for a long, unblinking ten seconds, then scribbled another Post-it, writing more quickly this time. She peeled it off the pad, stuck it to his shirtfront. *Pussy*, it said.

On his way out, Coffin stopped by Branstool's office. It was empty—the furniture was gone, the carpet appeared to have been freshly shampooed. He passed the nurse's station on the way to the front door. He dug his phone out of his pocket, about to call Lola.

A beeping alarm sounded behind him, coming from his mother's hallway. Two aides appeared from the dining room and walked swiftly toward the noise. The nurse at the station turned and trotted after them. Coffin followed them down the hallway at a half-run. By the time he got to his mother's room, it was over. Her face looked frozen—head thrown back, mouth wide-open, eyes already starting to haze. The aides and nurses stood around her bed. One of the aides turned off the heart monitor, and the alarm stopped its shrieking. The ballpoint pen lay on the floor. Coffin felt a wave of dizziness; his peripheral vision narrowed. One of the nurses was holding his mother's hand.

Chapter 20

Coffin walked home through the graveyard, the last bright leaves drifting down around him, into the silver-green grass. He passed the Coffin family plot: his father's gravestone, his brother's, his grandfather's and great-grandfather's. His father had been lost at sea, his brother was MIA in Vietnam and was presumed dead. Now his mother was gone. They were all gone.

The sunset was putting on its usual light show, the sky streaked in lurid shades of magenta and gold. Ten feet away, a crow perched on an alabaster headstone. It stared at Coffin with a bright, malicious eye.

"Ma?" Coffin said. "That you?"

The crow tilted its head and made a low chuckling sound. Coffin could see its black tongue moving inside its beak. Then it hopped from the gravestone and flew over his head, wings beating, pushing its feathered weight into the wind.

"Happy trails, Ma," Coffin said, watching the crow dwindle and disappear over the treetops. "Happy trails."

Coffin paused outside his house. There was a new Toyota minivan parked at the curb. It was tomato red, and very shiny. Its grille curved upward in a cartoonish smile. Coffin sighed. "Jesus Christ," he said. "It's a *happy* minivan."

Jamie sprawled in a lawn chair in the empty living room, her little bookshelf stereo on the floor. She was listening to Etta James sing "Li'l Red Rooster"—an acoustic arrangement that always made the hair on Coffin's arms stand on end. The goat stared down from the mantel, left eye catching the slanted light through the window.

Jamie stood, hugged him. "I'm so sorry, Frank," she said.

Coffin shook his head. "I know it doesn't make sense, but it was . . . sudden. She was sick for so long, but then she was just gone."

Jamie patted his back, kissed his cheek. She was warm and round. She felt good. "It makes total sense. You can absolutely get that someone is sick, that sooner or later they're going to die, but that doesn't really prepare you for when it finally happens. It's still a shock."

"She was there, and then she was gone," Coffin said. "I sat with her for a long time—she was conscious, seemed to know what was going on, sort of. Then she dozed off, so I figured I should check in at work. I didn't even make it to the front door."

Jamie held him tight. Pregnant, her skin smelled faintly of bread. She looked up at Coffin, her wide-set eyes a little misty. "Now I feel bad about getting rid of her furniture," she said.

"Don't," Coffin said. "She wasn't in those chairs—she turned into a crow."

"A crow?"

He told her about the crow he'd seen in the graveyard. "It had this *look* in its eye," Coffin said. "And it almost said something. You know how crows sound like they're talking sometimes?"

"A crow. She could have done a lot worse." Jamie squeezed Coffin again, kissed his cheek. "How are you, Frank? Can I get you a drink?"

"I'm tired," Coffin said, following her into the kitchen. "And sad. You would have really liked her, before the Alzheimer's."

Jamie opened the liquor cabinet, revealing its array of bottles, looked at Coffin over her shoulder, eyebrow raised.

"Maybe one of each," Coffin said.

"Don't go overboard," Jamie said. "I'm going to give you a healthy, life-affirming blow job as soon as you've had a chance to relax a little. I owe you."

"Great!" Coffin said. "But you don't owe me."

"Oh, yes I do," Jamie said. "Check this out." She handed Coffin a four-inch square of slick paper. It had a dark background with a truncated cone of light in the middle, Jamie's name and the date along the top in computer type. Lying at the bottom of the light cone was the outline of a baby—its head disproportionally large, its arms and legs slightly blurred, one hand clear and exact, cupped below the chin. The umbilical coiled from its belly like the cord from an electric guitar to an amplifier. The baby was looking out at Coffin, as though it could hear the ultrasound wand passing back and forth over Jamie's belly. The spinal column, ribs, and skull glowed in sharp relief against the dark background—the baby grinned out at Coffin, all cheekbones and eye sockets.

"Yah!" Coffin said, laying the printout on the counter. "Ghost baby!"

"I know, right?" Jamie said, dropping ice into a rocks glass. "Is that not the creepiest thing ever? But it's *our* ghost baby, Frank. And for that you get a blow job. Maybe two. Maker's Mark, Stoli, or Walker Red?"

"Maker's," Coffin said. He tapped the printout. "Am I seeing what I think I'm seeing?"

Jamie glugged three fingers of bourbon into the glass, handed it to Coffin. "Yep. If you think you're seeing girl parts."

"Whoa," Coffin said. "Ghost baby is a girl."

"We should be thinking about names," Jamie said.

"How about Spooketta?"

"How about Sarah, after your mother?"

"Almost the same thing," Coffin said.

"Come on," Jamie said. "It's the great circle of life! The old pass on, the new generation takes their place. That's totally what's going on here, Frank."

Coffin took a long sip of bourbon, then another. "I'm not such a fan of those strict old Yankee names," he said. "There's a lot of them in my family—Sarah, Abigail, Elizabeth, Hannah—they sound like straight-backed chairs. How about Lucinda?"

"As in Lucinda Williams?"

"Sure. Or maybe Etta. Etta James Coffin. It's got a nice ring to it."

Jamie looked at him, gray eyes slightly narrowed. "Here, or upstairs?"

"Sorry?"

"Do you want it here, or upstairs on the bed? I'm happy either way, but I'm not sure how long I can kneel on this hard floor in my present condition."

"Upstairs," Coffin said. "Definitely."

Rudy and Loverboy arrived at the Herring Cove parking lot early—to scout, Rudy said. He knew the location like the back of his hand—the long, narrow lot, closed to automobile traffic at its far end where the dunes took over, the only entrance a narrow opening that turned hard left, past a park service booth where summer tourists could purchase a day pass for parking, and then out to a larger lot, and then the Province Lands Road, that ran through the dunes and scrub pines, connecting Herring Cove with Race Point to the west, and the end of Commercial Street to the east. It was as good a place as any, Rudy figured, to sell almost three million dollars' worth of smack back to the people it belonged to.

As usual for October, the few scattered sunset watchers had gotten back in their cars and split the moment the sun had disappeared into the bay. There were a couple of parked Winnebagos (one containing four people, the other five), and a couple of bonfires (National Seashore permit required) maybe a hundred yards apart, about as distant from each other as it was possible to get without being too far from the comforts of the RV—a bathroom, a few cold beers in the fridge. Rudy had observed both groups for twenty minutes or so through a pair of binoculars as he and Loverboy pretended to watch the sunset: The group at the east end of the lot was comprised of two overweight, late middle-aged couples. The men were trying to surf cast, hoping, Rudy guessed, to get lucky and land a late-running bluefish. The women were drinking beer, smoking cigarettes, and laughing at the men. The group at the west end was comprised of a somewhat younger couple—in their forties, as opposed to their sixties—and three skinny, sulky teenaged girls. No Chechens.

Rudy checked his watch—about twenty minutes to nine. "They'll get here early," he said. "They'll want to check it out before they expose themselves. Make sure there's no cops. Make sure it's not a setup."

"Just like us," Loverboy said, drumming his fingers slowly on the Town Car's steering wheel.

"Exactly. Except these Chechen motherfuckers have no intention of just doing the deal and going home with their smack. You can bet your Tongan ass they're planning to leave here with the smack *and* the money."

"Just like us."

"Exactly. But we wouldn't cut a guy's head off with a table saw, even for two million bucks."

Loverboy pursed his lips, nodded. "True," he said. "We take the high road."

"Of course we do," Rudy said. "It goes without saying."

"Company," Loverboy said. A car was making the turn at the mouth of the lot. At first Rudy could only see the headlights—they were bright, and seemed to be on high beam. The car moved slowly. After a minute or so, when the headlights were no longer pointing directly at them, Rudy could see that it was an SUV; a big Cadillac Escalade, fully pimped with underlighting and fancy rims. Even at a range of seventy yards or so, Rudy could hear the bass thumping out of the Escalade's subwoofers.

"Two thousand and five called," Loverboy said. "It wants its automotive aesthetic back."

"Why not just hire a fucking marching band?" Rudy said. "People got no discretion."

Loverboy had parked near the middle of the lot—roughly halfway between the two RVs. The Escalade swung in beside them. Its headlights went dark, and the music stopped. Then all four doors swung open at once, and four skinny young men jumped out. They all appeared to be in their late teens or early twenties. They all had pistols jammed into the waistbands of their jeans.

"Here we go," Rudy said, touching the butt of the Glock 21 in his coat pocket. The two men climbed out of the Town Car.

"Yo," said the first Chechen. He had tattoos up and down both arms. He stuck out a hand—Cyrillic lettering tattooed across his knuckles—and Rudy shook it.

"I am Ygor," the Chechen said.

"Where's Dr. Frankenstein?" Rudy said.

Ygor nodded, lit a cigarette. "You said you were coming alone, homes."

Rudy shrugged. "So did you. Call it a misunderstanding."

The second Chechen pulled up his pants, which had been dragged dangerously low by the weight of his gun. He pointed at Loverboy with his first two fingers, thumb extended. "Where'd you get the fucking Wookiee, man?"

Loverboy made a low rumbling sound in his chest: a lion annoyed by a fly.

Rudy sighed. "You don't want to call him that. He doesn't like it."

A third Chechen, taller and even skinnier than the rest, smacked the second Chechen's skinny chest with the back of his hand. "Vladi," he said. "For fuck's sake. Show some respect. Is business."

"You gents got the cash?" Rudy said. "Let's get this done."

"What's with fucking family hour?" Vladi said, pointing his two fingers at the bonfires. "We said we should meet in secluded location. You call this secluded?"

"I call it insurance," Rudy said. "After what happened to Branstool, I thought, why take unnecessary chances?"

"That was Vladi," Ygor said. "He gets little bit excited sometimes."

"That beige-wearing motherfucker was ripping us off," Vladi said. "Are you ripping us off, old man?"

"Look," Rudy said. "We're out of earshot. We're in the shadows. What's the problem?"

"No problem," Ygor said. He pushed a button on his key fob and the Escalade's lift gate opened with a faint hydraulic whoosh. He reached inside and pulled out a large aluminum briefcase.

"Here is money," he said. "One million dollars finder's fee. Let's see the jones."

Rudy reached into the Town Car's backseat and pulled out the gym bag. "It's all here," he said. "Five kilos."

"Five kilos?" Ygor said. He had a tattoo of a black widow spider on his neck. "You said six."

"You said a million two," Rudy said. "You say potato, I say potahto."

"Potahto?" Vladi said, squinting like Gary Cooper about to go for his gun. "What the fuck is potahto?"

"It's a song," Loverboy said. "Gershwin. 'Let's Call the Whole Thing Off.' It's very famous."

Vladi scowled. "Potahto. That's some fucked-up shit. Who is this Gershwin? Some kind of faggot?"

Loverboy growled. A deep rumbling. A temblor.

"A million for five keys," Ygor said. He took a meditative drag on his cigarette, let the smoke leak from his nose. "Okay. Deal. You open yours, I'll open mine. Count of three."

"Fine," Rudy said.

"One," Ygor said. "Two—"

Vladi pulled his gun out of his pants and pointed it at Loverboy. It was a big nickel-plated Colt semiauto. He held it sideways, like a movie gangsta. "Don't be giving me no fish-eye, Sasquatch," he said.

"Oh, shit," Rudy said. "Here we go."

"Three!" Ygor said, throwing open the briefcase.

Something hit Coffin lightly in the chest. His eyes fluttered halfway open, but after a few seconds he decided he'd dreamed it and closed them again. A few seconds later, whatever it was hit him again—this time on the shoulder. It was Jamie—she was lying with her back to him. She reached back and whacked him a third time, perilously close to his groin.

"Fire," she said.

"What?"

"*Fire.*"

Coffin opened his eyes, sat up. It was dark. He smelled smoke. "Jamie," he said. "You need to wake up."

"Hmm?"

"You need to wake up. You're right—there's smoke."

Coffin climbed out of bed—the mattress and box spring still on the floor—reached for his pants, pulled them on. The bedroom door was open; he flipped on the light. The hallway was filling with smoke. "Jamie," he said. "You need to get up. The house is on fire."

Then the smoke alarms went off—first in the living room, then a second or two later at the top of the stairs. The shrieking was deafening. Coffin covered his ears.

Jamie sat up, eyes wide. "Holy shit," she said. "The house is on fire!"

The Glock was in the old man's hand so quickly that Ygor thought for a moment it had simply appeared there—a magic pistol, suddenly pointed at his left eye. He grinned, raised his hands slowly, knowing the two Americans were outnumbered, knowing his boys were fast and brutal.

Still, it was hard to think clearly when someone was pointing a gun at your eye, hard to look away from the bore of the old man's pistol, which, he had to admit, was impressively large. But something violent was happening just past the edge of his peripheral vision, so he turned. The Wookiee had crossed the two meters of parking lot between himself and Vladi with such speed that he might as well have flown, Ygor thought. Vladi wheeled, but before he could bring his pistol around and pull the trigger the Wookiee slapped the gun loose with one enormous hand and punched him in the face with the other. There was a splattering crunch, and Ygor was showered with blood and broken teeth. The thoroughly unconscious Vladi toppled backward into Dmitri. Dmitri, howling with rage and encumbered by the limp weight of Vladi's body, yanked at his pistol, which had gotten tangled in his jockey shorts.

"Careful," the old man said. "You're gonna shoot your—"

Dmitri's gun went off with a flat, muffled crack. Dmitri shrieked and crumpled onto the asphalt.

"—dick off," the old man said.

That left Aleks, who, like his compatriots, was actually Ukranian and not Chechen at all. Had he been Chechen, Ygor thought, on the claustrophobic ride into Provincetown inside the old man's trunk, he might have had the wherewithal to move three or four steps to his left, putting the Escalade between himself and the enraged Wookiee, who had picked up Vladi by the ankles and was swinging him in a long arc like a human baseball bat. Instead, foolishly, Aleks stood his ground, drew his pistol, released the safety and somehow squeezed off a shot just before Vladi's head, moving at Louisville Slugger speed, struck him squarely on the ear, knocking him over the Escalade's hood and onto the beach, where he lay twitching. The sound, Ygor decided, after he'd had a few days in jail to think about it, was something like the dull *clonk* of two coconuts being slammed together, but wetter.

"Home run," Loverboy said.

"Son of a bitch," Rudy said. "Are you hit?"

"Me?" Loverboy said. "Nope."

"Could have sworn I heard that bullet hitting meat. Maybe I'm hallucinating."

"Wouldn't be the first time."

"Or the last."

"I think is Vladi," Ygor said. "He's bleeding from chest wound, looks like."

Vladi lay facedown on the asphalt. His breathing was ragged. Loverboy turned him over on his back, pulled his blood-soaked shirt open. There was a large, messy exit wound just below his sternum. "Talk about bad luck," Loverboy said.

"He is dead?" Ygor said.

"No," Loverboy said. "Not yet."

"Well," Rudy said, "this was exciting, but I think we'd best be on our way." He tilted his head toward the nearest bonfire, where the four fat people were frantically trying to dial 911 on their cell phones.

"Good luck getting a signal out here," said Loverboy.

Ygor nodded. "Can you hear me?" he said. "No—I can't. I'm in P'town."

"When I was a kid," the old man said, "they told us we'd all have rocket cars by now. Instead all we got were these fucking cell phones."

He closed the silver briefcase—which was indeed full of hundred-dollar bills, if not exactly a million dollars' worth—and threw it and the gym bag into the backseat of the Town Car. Then he popped the trunk and told Ygor to climb in. "We'll leave your boys out here for the cops to clean up," he said. "You get to go to jail instead of the hospital. Lucky you."

"And when I tell police about all that heroin?" Ygor said, curled awkwardly in the bottom of the trunk.

"Heroin?" the old man said, slamming the lid. "What heroin?"

"Fucking Christ," Jamie said, rummaging in the rumpled bedclothes. "Where the hell are my underwear?"

Coffin threw open the west window, which was directly above the screen porch and was the obvious escape route in case of fire. "Holy shit," Coffin said, looking out. The screen porch was fully engulfed: flames snapped and roared just under its roof, licking three or four feet into the night sky. A gust of wind drove a shower of sparks at Coffin's face. He slammed the window shut. He looked out of the south window, which faced the street, but it seemed like a long way down—maybe a twelve-foot drop onto the narrow sidewalk—with nothing to break their fall.

"I can't find my fucking underwear!" Jamie shouted. She was wearing a short, hot pink nightgown, trimmed in purple lace. "I'm not jumping out a damn window with no drawers on."

"Forget your underwear," Coffin said. He grabbed her hand. "Come on, we'll go out through the baby's room. We can drop down onto the shed roof from there."

The hallway was filling with smoke—it boiled near the ceiling, and Coffin knew it might be a matter of seconds before the combustible gases in the rugs, the curtains, and the wall paint ignited, before the whole house flashed over and incinerated them in the intense heat. "What about downstairs?" Jamie shouted, smoke alarms howling. "What about the kitchen door?"

"No way," Coffin said, pulling her down the hallway. "Too hot down there."

The baby's room was at the end of the hallway, the farthest part of the house from the screen porch. Coffin flung the door open, pulled Jamie in, then shut the door behind her. There wasn't a lot of smoke. The big stuffed animals he'd bought—giant bunny, giant zebra, giant giraffe—goggled from their spot next to the window. Coffin grabbed the giraffe and laid it down in front of the door, trying to keep smoke from seeping in through the crack. The baby furniture hadn't arrived yet—there was no crib, no rocker, no changing table.

"Frank," Jamie called, struggling with the window. "This fucker's stuck."

"Hang on," Coffin said. "We'll break it if we have to." He strained, wrenched the window open—it had been humid, the sash was swollen—and kicked the screen out onto the lawn. He looked down: his father had built a small garden shed onto the side of the house, filled it with a lawn mower, rakes, hoses, gardening tools, most of which had gone unused. It was about five feet high, and directly below the window—an asymmetrical stroke of luck. Had his father thought of it as a fire escape, built below the window of the room his sons had shared?

The shed's corrugated steel roof sloped away from the house at a reasonably gentle angle. The drop from the windowsill was about seven feet—a lot less, Coffin thought, if you lowered yourself from the windowsill feet first, and then let go. Then it was only a foot or two.

"I'll go first," Coffin said. "Then I'll help you get down."

"Frank," Jamie said, the howling of the smoke alarms muffled a bit by the door. "What about the animals?"

"What?"

Her eyes were wide. Even in the dark room, Coffin could see a single, glistening tear trailing down the side of her nose. "The stuffed animals. We can't just let them burn. You bought them for our daughter."

"Jamie—"

She looked at him, blinked, shook her head as if to clear it. "Right," she said. "Fuck the animals. Out you go."

Coffin climbed out awkwardly, scraping his back on the open sash, elbows propped, gripping the windowsill with both hands, scrabbling down the cedar shingles with his bare feet, then letting himself slide a bit, arms straightening.

"How'm I doing?" he said, hanging straight down, cheek pressed against rough shingles. He couldn't turn his head enough to look down.

Jamie peered out of the window above him. "Good. Looks like you just have to drop maybe three feet. But Frank?"

"Yeah," Coffin said. His arms ached.

"I don't know if I can do what you're doing."

"Come on," Coffin said. "You're a yoga instructor—pound for pound you've got way more upper body strength than I do." He took a deep breath, let it out. He could hear sirens coming, not far away now. "Okay, I'm letting go."

"Careful—" Jamie said, but Coffin had already dropped to the roof of the shed. He landed hard, left ankle twisting on the uneven surface, knees scraped on the shingles, right hand sliced by something—a stray nail head, maybe—on the way down.

"Ow," he said.

"Are you okay?"

"Yeah," Coffin said. "Come on—your turn."

"Maybe I should wait for the firemen," Jamie said. "Sounds like they're almost here."

Coffin could hear the fire roaring: a big, burning lung, sucking oxygen. The fire trucks were almost there—they'd slowed to negotiate the tight corner of Alden Street and Cemetery Road, only a block away. He pictured the fire and rescue boys trying to save Jamie, the ladder tipping over, the house collapsing on top of the whole crew in a burning shower of cinders.

"Better not wait," he said. "Just sit your butt on the windowsill, let your legs hang out, and then slide down onto my shoulders. It's only about two feet."

"Okay," Jamie said, coughing. "It *is* getting pretty smoky. Here I come." She swung a long leg out of the window, then her head and upper body emerged, then the other leg.

"Are you sure you can hold me? I'm pretty fat."

"You're not fat. You're round. It's different."

Coffin stood with his hands braced against the side of the house, knees bent slightly (the left one was probably bleeding, he thought), looking up at Jamie. Her nightgown had ridden up around her hips.

"Nice view," he said. His nose was running; he wiped it on the back of his wrist.

"Shut *up*," Jamie said. "Are you ready?"

"Yep," Coffin said. "Slow and easy now. Just slide down, one leg on each shoulder."

Jamie slid, landing solidly on Coffin's shoulders, right hand propped against the shingled wall of the house, left arm wrapped around Coffin's head. "You got me?" she said. Coffin's hearing was muffled by Jamie's thighs, but he still heard a low *whomp*, like the sound of a charcoal grill being lit after it's been doused with starter fluid. He guessed that the upstairs hallway had flashed over.

A fire truck rattled up to the curb, siren wailing. Four firefighters piled out and started shouting instructions at each other. Somebody turned on a spotlight: it searched the windows of Coffin's house briefly before falling on the shed.

"Whoa," one of the firemen said. "Check it out."

Coffin staggered a half-step back as he took Jamie's weight, hands gripping her thighs, her round belly pressed against his forehead, the dark, fragrant ruff of her pubic hair in his face.

"Frank?" a voice said. It was Walt Macy. "That you?"

Coffin sank to one knee, set Jamie down on her feet, untangled himself while Jamie adjusted the hem of her nightgown. "Yeah, Walt," Coffin said, straightening up. "It's me."

"You all right? Everyone get out okay?"

"Everyone's fine," Coffin said. "How about a ladder, and a blanket for the lady?"

"Right-o," Macy said, signaling one of the firemen. He watched the fire for a second, big mustache bristling. "You're lucky you got out of there. That's a hell of a fire."

"It's like your dream," Jamie said, when they were standing barefoot next to the fancy Italian pumper, Jamie wrapped in a blanket, Coffin wearing a borrowed sweatshirt. The sweatshirt was huge, size XXXL: the pointy-hat Patriots logo swooped across its chest.

"Yeah, but without the Seal Baby," Coffin said. "Thank God."

"The Seal Baby is Maurice," Lola said. She'd arrived in the Crown Vic a minute or two after the first fire truck, siren on and lights flashing. Tony was there—cleaned up and in uniform. At least half of the fire and rescue squad had turned out: Coffin's torn hand had been hugely bandaged, his scraped knee disinfected three times over.

Jamie put her arm around his shoulder. "Your poor old mom," she said. "There goes her house."

The fire crackled and danced in the upstairs windows. Coffin felt strangely elated. "There go our clothes," he said.

Jamie sighed. "Yeah, I'm losing a lot of great shoes. And my favorite jeans. And that peridot necklace you gave me."

Coffin turned to Lola. "Where's Skillings and Pinsky?" he said. "Something up?"

"Some kind of big fight out at Herring Cove," Lola said. "Injuries. Shots fired. We've got a meat wagon on the way to Hyannis, one bullet wound, one probable DOA. The state police are working the scene."

"Jesus," Coffin said. "Busy night."

Lola's shoulder radio sputtered, and then Marge the dispatcher said something Coffin couldn't make out.

"Son of a bitch," Lola said, heading for the Crown Vic. The radios in the fire trucks and rescue vehicles had all crackled to life at the same time.

"What?" Coffin called after Lola. "What is it?"

"Fire at the Crown and Anchor," Lola said, one foot inside the car. "Big one. All available units."

"Let's go," Coffin said.

"Frank, for Christ's sake," Lola said. "You don't have any *shoes* on. Your pregnant girlfriend's wearing a *blanket*." She climbed in, started the Crown Vic's big engine. "Your mother died and your house burned down in the same damn day. What, you're gonna go catch a bad guy now?"

Coffin held up a finger: *one second.* He turned, kissed Jamie on the cheek. "You okay?" he said.

"I'm sad about those damned stuffed animals," Jamie said, sniffling a bit. "But yeah, I'm okay."

"Who can you stay with tonight?"

"I'll call Corinne—she'll want to hear the whole story. Jesus, Frank—are you sure?"

"Yeah. Yeah, I'm sure." He kissed Jamie again, this time on the mouth, and then climbed into the Crown Vic.

The Crown and Anchor was, emphatically, on fire. The flames appeared to have spread quickly through the west wing, and now they were leaping inside the second- and third-story windows. A rambling, hundred-year-old wooden structure, the Crown was laid out in a big L shape on two sides of a paved courtyard: the east wing ran across the back of the property, parallel with town beach; the west wing stretched roughly a hundred feet from Commercial Street to the rear of the property. The complex housed numerous guest rooms, a restaurant, three bars—including the Vault, Kotoswki's favorite leather bar, and the Paramount, home to Provincetown's popular and long-running drag show. The Paramount was also the venue for the climactic event of Fantasia Fair—the Fall Fashion Extravaganza.

Lola and Coffin were the first police officers on the scene. Lola parked the Crown Vic, flashers throwing their wobbling light against the storefronts. She moved quickly to clear the courtyard of spectators—mostly Tall Ships, there for the fashion show—driving them back across the street, out of harm's way in case the Crown's tall façade collapsed.

"Were you-all inside when the fire started?" Coffin asked them.

They nodded, wigs bobbing. "It was terrifying," said a short, stout person in lavender taffeta. "We barely got out. The smoke! We could hear the fire crackling upstairs!"

A tall, slender person who appeared to be wearing nothing but a blond Lady Godiva wig, a flesh-toned G-string, and very high heels said, "I'm, like, oh my *God,* we're all going to be trapped like rats!"

"Is anyone still inside?" Coffin asked them.

The Tall Ships furrowed their plucked brows, pursed their painted lips, shook their wigged heads. "No," the tallest Tall Ship said. She was about 6' 4", Coffin guessed, and wore a maroon evening gown. "I don't think so. We were pretty much the last ones out."

"Story of my life," said the short, stout Tall Ship.

"What did he say?" said a Tall Ship who must have been seventy-five or so, a sparkly tiara slightly askew on her long, black wig.

"He wants to know if anyone's still inside."

"I think there might be," the older Tall Ship said. "It was the damnedest thing."

"What was the damnedest thing?" Coffin said.

"We're all running like mad, all us girls, trying to get out the doors over here." She waved an evening-gloved hand toward the Paramount's main doors—they swung outward onto the courtyard, and were usually left open in warm weather. "The alarms are going off—it's crazy. But I see one girl going the other way—back toward the back of the building."

"Kind of a stocky person, wearing an auburn wig?"

"That's right! Hell of a thing. Running right back into a burning building!"

Two Provincetown fire trucks came howling down Alden Street and slowed for the hard right onto Commercial. That meant there was only one old pumper, PFD 3, at Coffin's place: Walt Macy had evidently decided that the house was a lost cause. The single pumper was staying behind to keep the rest of the neighborhood from burning down.

"So, are you a cop, or what?" the tallest Tall Ship asked.

"Yep," Coffin said, walking toward the Crown and Anchor's open front doors. "You want to trade?"

"If you're a cop," the tallest Tall Ship said, dropping his falsetto, "where are your freakin' *shoes?*"

"Frank!" Lola called, stepping away from the large crowd of gawkers that was already forming on the sidewalk. "Frank—what the hell are you doing?"

"He's in there," Coffin said. "Maurice is still inside." He sneezed, then sneezed again.

"You're not going into a fucking burning building, Frank," Lola said. "You're exhausted, you're sick, you're not thinking straight, and you're barefoot."

"We could have died," Coffin said. "Jamie could have died."

Lola pointed to the Crown's third-floor windows. "Look up there, Frank. Look at how intense those flames are. Anybody that's still inside had better get out quick, or they're toast. If Maurice is still in there, he won't last long."

"The east wing doesn't look as hot," Coffin said. "He could be hiding in there. Or trying to make sure it goes up, too."

Lola put a hand on his arm, gripping his bicep. She was shockingly strong. "Frank," she said. "I know you're upset—I would be, too. But let's play it smart, okay? Skillings and Tony will be here any minute. We'll watch the exits, and grab him when he squirts out. If he doesn't come out, he dies in the fire."

"What if he already got out?" Coffin said.

"Then there's no fucking point in going in after him, is there?"

And then Maurice appeared in the Crown's main doorway, coughing, eyes streaming, green muumuu smeared with ash, his strange purplish wig scorched and askew. He wiped his eyes on his sleeve, spotted Lola and Coffin, and disappeared back inside the burning building.

"Dude," Rudy said, sliding his cell phone into his jacket pocket. "I'm just saying that was *not* the fucking plan. Not even close."

"He shouldn't have said that about Gershwin," Loverboy said. The Town Car's steering wheel looked like a toy in his hands.

Rudy lit a joint with his Zippo, held the smoke, coughed a little, let it out. "I was always more of a Cole Porter fan myself."

"Cole Porter was a great songwriter. Gershwin was a genius."

They said nothing for a while, the Town Car accelerating hard on Route 6, headed toward Truro. Rudy sat back in his seat, looking out the window.

"Nothing but sand, scrub pines, and salt water," he said, after a minute. "No wonder the fucking Pilgrims left."

"Whoa," Loverboy said when they'd cleared the dunes, the bay and its view of Provincetown opening up on their right. "Big fire. Looks like town center."

Rudy stared. "Looks like it might be the Crown and Anchor."

"Bummer," Loverboy said.

Rudy shrugged. "It's the only way they'll ever get the semen off the walls."

"So Felcher's unhappy?" Loverboy said, after a minute.

"Fuck him," Rudy said. "There's lots of people who'd be glad to pay a fair price for this smack. Doesn't have to be Felcher."

"You can't blame him. He was expecting a big bust and five free kilos of jones. Now the local cops got his bust and he's got to buy the jones from us."

"Fuck him. What's he gonna do?"

"Seize our assets. Throw us in jail."

Rudy grinned. "Did you know that Special Agent Felcher coaches ninth grade girls' volleyball in his free time?"

"And?"

"And he's got lousy impulse control."

"If there's no video, it didn't happen."

"There's video."

Loverboy smiled, his huge, perfect teeth gleaming in the dashboard lights. "What a pleasure," he said, "working with someone who understands the basic principles of business."

"You've got to fuck them before they fuck you," Rudy said. He took another deep hit from the joint, pinched it out between his thumb and forefinger, and stashed the roach in his shirt pocket. "That's right out of Machiavelli, baby."

"Come back here, you little weasel," Lola hissed, running at top speed through the Crown's open doors. Coffin tried to keep up, but he stepped on a shard of broken glass in the courtyard and had to stop for a second to pick it out of the sole of his foot.

"Son of a bitch," he said, pausing in the doorway. The smoke was thick. He could hear the fire roaring upstairs, over the shrieking din of a dozen smoke alarms.

"Lola!" Coffin shouted. He couldn't see much: The emergency exit lighting was on, but shrouded in smoke. "Where are you?"

"He went up the back stairs," Lola shouted back—she was maybe twenty feet ahead, the sound of her voice retreating into smoke and drifting ash.

Coffin followed, running as best he could. His cut foot squished on the rug at every step. He found the stairs—he could hear Lola's footsteps pounding up them, not too far ahead.

"He's headed for the deck!" Lola yelled. "I just saw him."

Upstairs, the heat was intense. Coffin could feel the flames at his back—the fire gnawing the west wing like some great, hungry animal. More than anything, he wanted to get out. Coughing, he ran down a smoke-thick hallway, toward an emergency exit light. He pushed the door open and felt the shock of the chill night air; he took a deep, gasping breath. A broad wooden deck ran across the rear of the building, facing the harbor. Lola and Maurice had disappeared.

"Frank!" Lola called. She was ten feet below him, crouched on the beach, at the edge of a crowd of onlookers. It took Coffin a second to realize that she'd just jumped from the deck. She gathered herself, started running, service weapon in hand.

The onlookers turned, watched the pursuit. Lola pointed. "There he goes! Freeze, Maurice!"

Coffin saw Maurice sprinting across the dark beach toward Cabral's wharf, a dilapidated wooden dock that warped into the harbor: arthritic, leaning, long abandoned. The tide was out; there were lots of places to hide among the tilted forest of pilings. "Shoot him!" Coffin yelled.

Lola steadied her pistol with both hands and squeezed off a shot, the Glock's flat report just audible over the roar of the fire. Maurice yelled but kept running, disappearing into the deep shadows under the wharf.

"Shit," Coffin said. He swung himself over the railing, then dropped onto the beach, making sure to bend his knees. He landed on all fours, bare feet digging into the soft sand. "Ow," he said.

A gaggle of partially dressed drag queens stood on the beach in their lingerie: bustiers and garter belts, feather boas, stockings, and padded bras. They were wrapped in bathrobes, in various stages of makeup, some with wigs, some without. They were crying.

"Did *he* set the fire?" one of them said, pointing after Maurice. "That *person?*"

"Yeah," Coffin said, limping as fast as he could after Lola and Maurice.

"He burned up all of our clothes," the drag queen cried. "Our beautiful *outfits!*"

"He tried to *kill* you," Coffin called, without turning to look over his shoulder.

"Same thing!" the drag queen shouted.

Lola had reached the wharf. She was crouched in the shadows of two thick pilings. As Coffin approached, his cut foot stinging like mad, she put a finger to her lips.

"He's still in there," she whispered, over the crackling roar of the burning hotel complex, a hundred yards away. "He hasn't come out the other side."

"You start at the top and work your way down," Coffin said. "I'll take the water end and work my way up."

Lola nodded. "If you see him, try to flush him my way," she said.

Coffin sniffed. His sinuses were brittle; everything smelled like smoke. But there was another smell—chemical, sharp. He put a hand on Lola's arm. "You smell that?"

Lola looked at him, eyes deep-set in the shadows. "Lighter fluid," she said.

A few drops of something cold dribbled on Coffin's neck. He touched his fingers to it, sniffed them: *lighter fluid.* He looked up, and there was Maurice, lying on the warped planks three feet above them, long plastic grill lighter in one hand. Before Lola could raise her Glock the lighter scritched and a long tongue of flame squirted out, catching the hood of Coffin's sweatshirt.

"Jesus, Frank!" Lola said. "You're fucking on fire!" She peeled her jacket off and threw it over Coffin's head, beating it with her hands, killing the flames. Coffin tore the jacket off—*pain, smell of burnt skin, burnt hair*—fumbling with his bandaged hand, then the still-smoking sweatshirt, dragging it over his head at the same moment Maurice jumped onto Lola's shoulders, driving her face-first into the sand.

"Mother*fucker!*" Lola yelled, Maurice on top of her, knees pinning her arms, the Glock trapped under her body, Maurice with the squeeze bottle of lighter fluid in his hand, wildly spritzing her hair, her uniform shirt, his muumuu.

"Oh, God—" Lola yelled, bucking, kicking in the sand. "Frank!"

Coffin dove—jaw colliding with Maurice's shoulder, teeth rattling, bare arms locked now around Maurice's arms, around his torso, feet driving, Maurice scrambling backward (*scritch* went the lighter), surprisingly strong. Maurice screamed and Coffin looked down—blue flames flickered up from the green muumuu, around Coffin's arm, around Coffin's face, singeing his mustache, his eyebrows. He let go, flung himself down in the sand. For a long second Maurice stared at his burning muumuu, wide-eyed, confused, the flames growing and spreading up his belly and chest, the length of his arm, the nearly empty bottle of lighter fluid in his hand igniting with a flash, liquid fire spewing everywhere. Maurice howled and ran down the beach, blazing like a lit match.

"Put it out!" he shrieked, panicked, running back toward the huge Crown and Anchor fire, flames rising around his face, in his hair. "Put it out!"

Gasping, gagging, Lola snatched her jacket up from the sand and chased after him, threw the jacket over the burning muumuu, shoved Maurice into the cold water of the harbor, dragged him deeper, pushed his head under once, then again. She pulled him out, a hard fist cocked back, but then she saw that most of his hair was gone, his eyebrows were gone, and charred, red welts were rising from his neck and face and scalp. There was no more fight left in him.

"Ah, Jesus," Maurice said, breathing fast, staring blindly into the orange sky. "I'm all burned up."

And then Tony arrived, lumbering across the beach from the Crown at a half-run, gear belt clanking. "Need a hand?" he said.

Chapter 21

The burn center at Massachusetts General Hospital was one of the best in the world. The hallways were hushed and sparkling clean; the patient rooms were state of the art, the staff were kind, empathetic, and thoroughly professional. Coffin couldn't wait to get out of there. Maurice lay in his hospital bed, so swathed in bandages he could have passed for a mummy on Halloween. Mancini sat in a vinyl guest chair. Maurice's state-appointed lawyer sat in another. Coffin and Lola stood by the door. A nurse stood by the head of Maurice's bed. A Boston uniformed cop stood guard in the brightly lit hallway.

"Okay," the lawyer said. "You're saying that if my client will plead guilty to three counts of burning a dwelling—that's the Coffin house, the West End house, and the Crown and Anchor—for a maximum of ten years each, *and* plead guilty to the shed fire, the condo fire, and the church fire for a maximum of five years each, the state will drop the attempted homicide charges. That's the deal?"

"That's the deal," Mancini said. He was wearing a charcoal

gray, pin-striped suit that made him look like an investment banker.

Maurice was shaking his head. "Not the condo fire," he said, through his bandages. "I told you, I didn't do that one." It was hard to understand him. His lips had been badly burned, and according to the nurse it hurt him to talk.

"Did you try to kill Detective Coffin?" Mancini said.

Maurice stared out of the holes in his bandages, but said nothing.

"Then shut the fuck up," Mancini said. "If we go to trial I'll do everything I can to see you do the max on every charge—that's ninety years even without the attempted homicides."

"Let's say forty-five," the lawyer said. "Up for parole in thirty."

"Thirty years," Maurice said. "Fucking hell."

Mancini glowered. "You're lucky. I should throw away the fucking key."

"Can I ask a question?" Coffin said. His neck and right forearm were bandaged. A big patch of hair on the back of his head had been singed down to the scalp; half of his mustache was gone.

Mancini shrugged. "I think you're entitled."

"I still don't get why you did it, Maurice. The church, the Crown, my house. I don't get it."

"The seals," Maurice said. "Because they killed the seals."

"The *seals?*" Coffin sat for a minute, smoothing what was left of his mustache. "I don't understand."

"Nobody *did* anything," Maurice said. "Nobody was *punished*. You didn't *do* anything."

"So you took it on yourself?"

Maurice nodded. "The seals never hurt anybody. They were innocent creatures, and those fucking drag queens killed them. That's why I burned the Crown."

"And the church?"

"I wanted people to be scared. I wanted to punish them."

"Your father killed the seals, Maurice."

Maurice stared at him, dark eyes glittering through the holes in his bandages. "My father?" he said, after a long silence. "*Donny* killed the seals?"

"That's right," Coffin said. "Donny. He confessed a few hours before you set my house on fire. He said they were ruining the business."

There was another long silence. "Jesus Christ," Maurice said at last. "You're fucking *kidding* me."

Provincetown's jail was a primitive, two-cell affair that mostly housed drunks and perpetrators of domestic violence. Like most jails, it smelled of Lysol with lingering undertones of mold, vomit, body odor, and shit. Ygor had a cell to himself, but that would change later in the day when he was transported down to the county correctional facility in Buzzard's Bay. Ygor sat on his bunk in an orange prison jumpsuit and slippers. He had a large and very colorful black eye. Coffin sat on a plastic visitor's chair outside the cell. Lola stood nearby, back to the wall.

Coffin leaned forward. "So a *Wookiee* attacked you and your friends? That's your story?"

"He was huge person, like Wookiee only clean-shaven," Ygor said. "Huge and very fast. There was old man with him, too."

"And this happened why?"

Ygor shrugged. "There was dispute over musical composer. Some people have no sense of humor."

"And then they brought you here, the Wookiee and the old man? And next thing you remember is waking up in this jail cell?"

Ygor nodded. "That's right. I don't know why I am here. I'm completely innocent."

"What about the six grams of heroin in your pocket at the time Officer Pinsky found you unconscious on the front steps?"

"They must have put it in my pocket. I don't use heroin."

"What about the stolen Escalade out at Herring Cove, where we found your friends?"

"I didn't steal it. That was Dmitri."

"Tell me about Branstool, Ygor. Who cut off his head?"

Ygor's unswollen eye was cool and gray, his face deadpan. "My friend Vladi confessed to me that he did it. I wasn't there."

"Vladi's the one that died out at Herring Cove?"

"That's right. Vladi had very hot temper. I tell him, Vladi, it's going to get you in trouble, but he doesn't listen."

"Where's the rest of Branstool, Ygor?"

Ygor shrugged again. "Like I said, I wasn't there. If I would guess, is probably in ocean. Food for crabs. Food for fishes."

Billy's was packed—Coffin had never seen it so crowded, though he realized that his perception was colored a bit by the fact that Rudy and Loverboy were sitting at the bar, taking up as much physical and psychic space as four or five normal-sized people. Gemma was there, too, standing at Rudy's elbow, wearing black leather pants that appeared to have been applied with a spray-gun, and a black ruffled blouse open almost down to her navel. It was the quiet week between Fantasia Fair and Halloween, so most of the police force were there, too, except for the two on-duty officers. Lola and Kate were picking out songs on the jukebox: Amy Winehouse's "Me and Mr. Jones" followed by the Stones' "Wild Horses." Pinsky and the impossibly glamorous LaWonda, resplendent in an electric blue, sequined minidress and five-inch platform heels, stood near the bar, sipping cosmopolitans. Skillings and his partner Don, who was a vice president at Fishermen's Bank, stood with them, drinking the good eighteen-year-old Talisker, a rousing single malt from the Island of Skye. Doris and Tony sat in a booth—Tony seemed to have returned mostly to his old self: his uniform was sloppy, his left shoe untied. He guzzled a tall draft beer against his doctor's orders, while stealing occasional glances up at the wavering picture on the TV screen. Walt Macy was there, too, and five or six of the fire and rescue crew, big men and women bellied up to the bar. Ernie from the Portuguese bakery was drinking a gin and tonic, and chatting up Roz from the Fish Palace. A brace of old people in wheelchairs had gotten a ride over from Valley View in the nursing home van; they sat looking flushed and happy, drinking short draft beers and shots of Jagermeister. Six or seven of Yelena's incredibly good-looking friends had also come—Captain Nickerson swung on his little swing, head cocked, one bright eye staring at the cluster of Eastern European girls, who were drinking shots of pepper vodka and slamming their empty glasses down on the bar. "Show us your tits!" Captain Nickerson shrieked, but this time, out of respect, they didn't. Yelena and Squid were both hustling to keep up: Even Kotowski was pretending to work, pouring the occasional shot, opening a beer here and there, lit cigarette dangling from his lower lip. Coffin's mother was there, too—or some part of her, Coffin thought: The part that hadn't turned into a crow—her ashes inside an ornate brass urn that sat squarely in the middle of the bar.

There had been many toasts: to Coffin's mother, mostly, but also to the men and women of the Provincetown Fire Department, who had performed heroically given their fraught relationship with their equipment, and despite not actually having put out any of the fires.

The Crown fire had been enormous: an eight-alarmer, with fire trucks and crews coming from as far away as Sandwich, lined up half the narrow length of Commercial Street, unable to get close enough to help. The crowd of spectators had grown large and bois-terous: The startled Tall Ships and the weeping drag queens had been joined by a contingent of drunks from the Old Colony Tap, and another group of drinkers from the Captain Alden. People from all over town and then Truro and the rest of the outer Cape had showed up to watch the old hotel burn: sparks and embers swirled and stormed overhead. Sheets of burning roofing had drifted up to High Pole Hill and started small brush fires there, which had mostly been put out by residents. The entire Crown and An-chor complex had ultimately burned to the ground, as had a small indoor shopping mall next door that contained three gift shops, a tattoo parlor, a taco stand, and a spiritual reader's practice. It had looked for a time as though the rest of the waterfront might go, too—the wind was stiff and burning embers were sailing every-where. But then the rain had begun: a hard, drenching rain that fell through the night and late into the morning, finally putting the fire out.

Coffin's house had been a total loss, too. Only the chimney had been left standing. The stuffed goat's head that hung above the mantel was scorched, but otherwise more or less intact. Coffin and Jamie were staying in Lola's condo until the insurance check for the house came through; Lola and Kate were living together in Kate's little rental house on Allerton Street.

There were toasts to Coffin and Lola, too, for finally catching the arsonist—the burn on Coffin's neck was still bandaged, though not quite as ostentatiously as it had been a couple of days before.

Coffin sat at the bar, Jamie beside him, a long arm draped around his shoulders. "Well, Frank," she said, "Satisfaction" thumping from the jukebox, the buzz of conversation all around them, "you're a hero. Again."

Coffin shook his head. "I'm not a hero. I never would've figured out that it was Maurice if it wasn't for the Seal Baby. And he burned down half the town before we got him. Not our best work."

"I'm not talking about *that*," Jamie said. "I'm talking about the way you saved me and your unborn daughter from a burning building. That's some mighty sexy stuff right there, Detective."

"Chief."

"Acting chief."

Coffin grinned. "You're a lot more athletic than I am—you could have climbed out of that window without any help from me."

"But I didn't have to, Frank—that's the point." She kissed him on the cheek. "You saved me."

Kotowski slouched down to their end of the bar, Newcastle Ale in hand. "So what's this I hear about a dream?" he said.

"Here we go," Coffin said.

"Frank was having a recurring dream about a fire in our house, and a baby that turned into a seal, and then the last time he had the dream the Seal Baby looked like Maurice."

"So then we went looking for Maurice, and it turned out he was the arsonist," Coffin said.

"Whoa," Kotowski said. He looked at Coffin with something like respect. "You are a fucking freak of nature, Coffin," he said. "I'm impressed. Too bad you didn't catch him before he burned down half the town."

"Quibbler," Coffin said, sipping his scotch.

Kotowski belched softly, thumped his chest with a loose fist. "We've got firemen who can't put out a fire and cops who can't catch a criminal. What's next—garbage men who take your trash and throw it all over your lawn? What are we paying you public employees for, anyway?"

"The firefighters are volunteers," Coffin said. "We're not paying them anything. And they *were* pretty damned heroic—you should have seen them at the church fire—completely fearless. And don't forget Ginky the cat."

"So what's your excuse?"

"I blame the police artist," he said. "Strangely, his cubist sketch of the suspect failed to produce any leads."

Kotowski laughed, drained his beer, opened another. "I'm going to miss your ma," he said. "She was a real pistol."

"That she was," Coffin said. "I'll miss her, too."

"She's in the next life now," Jamie said. "I wonder what *that's* like."

"Feathers," Coffin said. "Wind. Roadkill."

"Frank thinks she came back as a crow," Jamie said.

Kotowski frowned. "Jesus, Coffin—if I didn't know better I'd think you'd gotten all spiritual on us. Next you'll be telling us about your freaking yoga practice."

Jamie cleared her throat, raised a hand. "Ahem! Yoga instructor."

"I know *that*," Kotowski said. "I'm talking about *him*. If he goes all New Age yoga-crunchy on me—no offense—I won't be able to tolerate him anymore. Who the hell am I going to *drink* with?"

"Don't worry," Coffin said. "It'll pass."

"It'd better," Kotowski said. He took a long slug from his beer.

"I'm going to let you two gentlemen hash this out," Jamie said, patting Coffin on his unburned shoulder. She stood, round and radiant, golden late-afternoon light slanting in through the big front windows, illuminating her hair. She kissed Coffin on the cheek again, then navigated slowly through the crowded bar toward Lola and Kate, who were leaning on the jukebox, heads together.

"Christ on a cracker," Kotowski said, watching her. "She's like some freaking fertility goddess. How'd a toad like you ever land such a gorgeous female?"

Coffin shook his head. "Life is full of mysteries."

"So when's the baby due?" Kotowski said.

"February fifteenth. Give or take."

"What are you going to do about a house? You can't move in with me, you know—no squalling brats at Chez Kotowski, thank you very much."

Coffin shrugged. "I don't know. We'll buy something, I guess. We'll get some money from the insurance company, and Jamie's got some family money. I haven't had time to really think about it."

"So you're staying here? I *knew* it. Your kid's going to grow up to be some moody, ironic hipster, you know. And that's best-case scenario."

"If it was up to me, I'd probably buy a place in Wellfleet, or maybe Eastham. But Jamie likes it here." Coffin shrugged. "What can I say? I'm not in charge."

"Oh my God," Kotowski said. "You are *such* a pussy."

Acknowledgments

My sincerest thanks to the many readers who've gotten in touch, one way or another, to tell me they enjoy these books. Thanks also to Marty Wood and Karen Havholm (an URCA grant is a wonderful thing), to Peggy Govan and John Pollitz at McIntyre Library, to Brent Halverson for the great simile, and to all of my friends and colleagues who've said supportive things about these books. Thanks to Brady Foust for asking me every Friday for two years if the book was done yet. Yes, Brady—it's done. Much gratitude to Maria and Kelley, as always. Thanks to Polly Burnell, Stephen Desroches, Jimmy McNulty, Jen Rumpza, and all the other wonderful P'town folks who took the time to talk fire and/or UFOs with me. Enduring affection and thanks to Roger Skillings, simply one of the best people on the planet. As always, big-time love and devotion to my wife, Allyson, who lets me take time away from the life of our busy household to write things (next year, it's your turn).

And, a special note of acknowledgment and thanks to my friend and researcher, Ian Jacoby, for compiling and distilling much of the factual information necessary for the completion of this book. Without him, no one in *Fire Season* would have given mouth-to-mouth to Ginky, the Siamese cat. Ian's work was funded by a Faculty-Student Collaborative Research Grant through UWEC's excellent Office of Research and Sponsored Programs.